"So you have come through the gate of light as have the other cattle of this world."

The astonishment on Andrew's face made the Tugar roar with delight. "Yes, we of the Horde know of the light, the gate that opens to bring us new races of cattle to feast upon. Some have tried to resist us; their bones filled our feasting pits."

Suddenly the Tugar's arm swung out. Andrew tried to duck under the blow, but it caught him on his left shoulder and he tumbled to the ground. The sharp crack of a carbine echoed out, and the Tugar staggered back. As Andrew came to his feet, there was a moment of silence. Then the Tugar's now bloody hand shot out, pointing at the rifleman.

"Kill me that cattle!" the Namer roared.

"Regiment take aim!" Andrew shouted and five hundred men snapped their rifles down on the Tugar forces. . . .

RALLY CRY

William R. Forstchen

A ROC BOOK

ROC
Published by the Penguin Group
Penguin Books USA Inc., 375 Hudson Street,
New York, New York 10014, U.S.A.
Penguin Books Ltd, 27 Wrights Lane,
London W8 5TZ, England
Penguin Books Australia Ltd, Ringwood,
Victoria, Australia
Penguin Books Canada Ltd, 10 Alcorn Avenue,
Toronto, Ontario, Canada M4V 3B2
Penguin Books (N.Z.) Ltd, 182–190 Wairau Road,
Auckland 10, New Zealand

Penguin Books Ltd, Registered Offices:
Harmondsworth, Middlesex, England

Published by Roc, an imprint of Dutton Signet,
a division of Penguin Books USA Inc.

First Printing, May, 1990
12 11 10 9 8 7 6 5 4

REGISTERED TRADEMARK—MARCA REGISTRADA

Printed in the United States of America

ACKNOWLEDGMENTS

A special thanks to Mr. John Keane, great-grandnephew of Andrew Lawrence Keane, and president of the 35th Maine Historical Society, who first shared with me the interesting story of that famed regiment's history over a decade ago. Through his tireless help I was able to contact a number of descendants of members of the regiment and examine a wide variety of documents related to its illustrious history, which helped so much in the creation of this story.

For the interested traveler, a monument to the 35th is located in the small hamlet of Keane, Maine, a short drive down coast from Freeport, Maine. It's a simple affair, so typical of Maine. A bronze plaque bears the names of the six hundred and thirteen men who set voyage on that fateful trip, and above the plaque the statue of a Union soldier looks out to sea.

Good luck finding it!

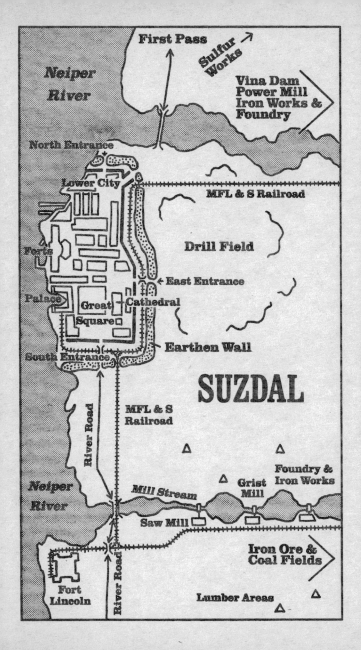

BOOK I

Chapter 1

January 2, 1865
City Point, Virginia (major supply and shipment center supporting the Union Army besieging Petersburg and Richmond)

The thunder of artillery rumbled across the storm-lashed midnight sky. Turning in his saddle, Andrew Lawrence Keane looked back, as if the distant flashes were a siren song, whispering for him to return into the caldron of flame.

"Not our fight anymore, colonel."

"It feels strange to be leaving it, Hans," Andrew said softly, and even as he spoke he continued to look back, watching as the silhouette of Petersburg was revealed by the bursting shells.

"Strange to be leaving, is it? Damn glad, I am," Hans snapped. "We've been in the trenches before that damn rebel city for the last six months. It'll be good to stretch our legs and see something else for a while, even if it does mean we've got to take one of them damn boats to get there."

Pulling out a plug of tobacco, Hans bit off an end, and then offered a chew to his colonel.

Andrew smiled and waved his hand, declining the offer. For two years Hans had been offering him a chew and for two years he'd always turned him down. Shifting his gaze away from the gunfire, Andrew looked down at his sergeant major. The man's face was dark, like weathered canvas, and careworn and thin, wreathed in a beard flecked with streaks of gray. The lines about his eyes were deeply engraved from the years out on the prairie, watching across its shimmering heat and snow-covered vastness. The scar on his cheek from the Comanche arrow was a souvenir of twenty-one years' service in the army. It wasn't the only scar, and as the sergeant continued to walk by Andrew's side, a slight limp was noticeable, a gift from a reb sniper before Cold Harbor.

Looking down at his friend, Andrew remembered the first time the offer for a chew had been made, and a smile lit his features, even though the memory still embarrassed him.

Antietam was their first fight together. He had been a green and frightened lieutenant, and Sergeant Major Hans Schuder was the only veteran with the newly recruited 35th Maine. With five thousand men of the first corps, they had crossed the forty-acre cornfield, trampling down the ripened stalks on that September morning in '62. Forever afterward one simply had to say "the Cornfield" and any veteran of either the Union or Confederate side knew what it meant. In crossing that field, they stepped through the gate to hell.

The rebs had hit them from three sides. One moment all had been quiet; he could even remember the cries of the startled birds above them as they left the field and crashed into the woods beyond. In a moment the silence of that morning was washed away in fire and smoke, and the roaring scream of ten thousand rebs smashed into them.

He had stood transfixed, terrified, his company captain screaming out commands to him. An instant later the captain lay spread-eagled upon the ground, his unseeing eyes staring up at Andrew, a puddle of blood and brains beneath him.

All he could think of was getting behind the nearest tree, so another such bullet would not find him as well. Dammit, his terrified mind had screamed out, you're a professor of history! What in hell are you doing here?

And then that soft, gravelly voice had whispered to him.

"Son, would you care for a chew?"

Old Hans was standing beside him, offering a plug of tobacco. He barely came to Andrew's shoulder, his five-and-a-half-foot frame contrasting to Andrew's slender, almost fragile six feet and several inches of height. At that moment Andrew still remembered Hans as if he were a giant towering above him, cold gray eyes staring into his.

"Lieutenant, the regiment's shot to hell and pulling back. I think you'd better help lead the boys out of here." He spoke as if advising a lad momentarily confused by the rules of a strange new game.

And in that moment Andrew started on the path of becoming a soldier, for what else could he do, with those eyes upon him.

That evening Colonel Estes had come to Andrew and promoted him to captain for displaying such cool-headed courage on the field. The men of his company had patted him on the back, calling him a stout fellow who knew how to lead. He knew that before the battle Estes had had his doubts, and openly mumbled about having a bespectacled, bookish college teacher in his command. But that night Andrew knew that at last he'd been accepted.

The curious thing about it, Andrew thought, was that he could not remember what he had done. All he could recall was how, throughout the day, Hans had stood by him, just standing, watching, and occasionally offering advice.

"Son, I saw you," Hans said to him that evening, "I saw you and knew you'd be a soldier, once you learned how. You'll do well in this war, if you don't get kilt first."

That was the last time Hans had ever called him "son." From then on it was Captain Andrew Lawrence Keane, and Hans spoke the words with pride, as if he had somehow molded them.

After Fredricksburg it was Major Keane, and Hans, who knew all the workings of the army, patiently tutored him, with a thousand anecdotes and tales, on how to be an officer who could lead.

And then there was Gettysburg.

On the afternoon of the first day they stood under a hot July sun. The smell of crushed hay rose from beneath their feet as they waited for the storm approaching from the west.

It was as if an ocean of butternut and gray were sweeping toward them, twenty thousand rebs pouring down off Mc-Pherson's Ridge, a chorus of fifty cannons heralding their approach.

It was there that Andrew truly felt the strange, thrilling joy of it all. Red flash blossoms of death crashed about them, while the long thin line of blue waited like a stone wall to break the approaching wave.

The reb gunners quickly found their range, and the regiment was bracketed by a dozen thunderclap bursts. In that fraction of a moment Colonel Estes no longer existed and Andrew stood alone, in command of the 35th.

The line wavered, for all the men had seen their beloved colonel fall.

But this time there was no need for Hans to whisper to him. Unsheathing his sword, Andrew stepped before the ranks and, turning, faced what was now his regiment.

"Hell's gonna freeze over before they take this hill," he roared, and his men shouted back their defiance to the enemy.

The storm broke upon them and they held, trading volley for volley at fifty paces.

All through that hot afternoon of hell they stood, the heavy double line melting beneath the sun and flame into a thin ragged knot of men who would not run. His heart had swelled to bursting and tears of pride would blind him as he paced the volley line, shouting encouragement, stopping occasionally to pick up a fallen musket and fire, while Hans strode beside him, never saying a word.

There was, however, that one numbing moment when he turned to Hans to somehow find consolation. Going down to the left of the regiment, to check on whether the 80th New York were still holding their flank, he stopped for a moment with Company A.

His younger brother, Johnnie, had joined the regiment but the week before. He wanted to send the boy to a safe job in the rear, but pride had prevented him from showing favorites.

That damn foolish pride.

John, what was left of him, was lying as if asleep beneath the shade of an ancient maple tree.

Andrew gazed upon the fragile broken body, and then to Hans. But the old sergeant was silent, grim-faced, as if telling him that now was not the time to mourn. Kneeling down, Andrew kissed his only brother, and then rose blindly, to return to the fight.

In the end the division finally gave way, and within minutes the entire army was streaming back to the safety of the hills on the other side of Gettysburg.

But his regiment did not run. Knowing someone would have to slow the reb advance in order to buy time, Andrew understood his duty—if need be, to sacrifice his command.

Step by step they gave ground slowly, firing a volley, retreating a dozen paces, and firing again. The rebs lapped over around the flanks, but could not press on till this final barrier was removed. But the 35th refused to break.

Pulling back to the edge of town, they blocked the streets,

and the time was bought. Two-thirds of his men were gone, paying the price for a precious fifteen minutes that might decide who would finally win.

Raising his sword, Andrew started to shout the command to pull back to Cemetery Hill, and then the blinding lash of fire swept over him. The last thing he could ever recall of Gettysburg was the falling away into a great gentle darkness, which he thought was the coming of death.

As if from a great distance a voice called, and Andrew stirred from his reverie.

"Did you say something, sergeant?"

"Just asked if your wound troubled you, sir," Hans said, looking at him with concern.

"No, not at all, Hans, not at all," and as he spoke he realized that he had been absently rubbing the stump of his left arm with his right hand.

Hans watched him for a moment, like a mother gazing upon her injured child. He grumbled as if to himself, and spat out a stream of tobacco juice. They rode on in silence until finally they crested a low hill, where the military depot and anchorage of City Point lay spread out before them.

"There's the boat, sir," and Hans pointed down the road to where a single transport rested, tied off to the dock.

"Never did like those damn things," Hans growled. "When I came over here in '44 thought I was like to die."

As he spoke of the memory the German accent returned.

Andrew always thought it a bit of a paradox. Here Hans had deserted the Prussian army to escape the brutality, and the first thing he did when reaching the States was enlist to go fight on the plains.

"35th Maine!" a voice shouted from out of the shadows. "Is this the 35th?"

"Over here," Hans snapped, and a portly man came lumbering up from the dock.

"You're late—we've already missed the damn tide!"

Hans bristled at the man's tone.

"And who the hell are you?" the sergeant snapped.

The dark shadowy form looked at the sergeant and without comment turned away.

"Where the hell is this Keane fellow?"

Andrew held out his hand to stop Hans.

"I'm the one you're looking for," Andrew said softly,

bringing his horse up till it brushed against the rotund man, forcing him to step back a pace.

"And whom do I have the honor of addressing?" he continued slowly, in a tone that Hans knew was deceptive, since Andrew usually became almost deferentially quiet before he exploded.

"Ship's Captain Tobias Cromwell of the transport *Ogunquit.* Damn it all, colonel, you were supposed to be here yesterday morning. The rest of the fleet sailed yesterday afternoon. Everyone else is aboard and waiting for your command, so we can get the hell out of here!"

"We were delayed," Andrew replied, still holding his temper in check. "Seems the rebs had a little farewell entertainment planned and my brigadier needed to hold us in reserve till the party was over."

"Damn poor planning, I say," Tobias snapped. "Now get those men of yours aboard so we can get out of here. I don't like it one damn bit that my ship is the last one to sail. And remember this, colonel—aboard my ship you and your men answer to me."

Without waiting for a response the captain turned and stormed away toward the dock, shouting imprecations at any who stood in his way.

"Well, I'll be damned," Hans growled softly.

"Let's hope not," and dismounting, Andrew ordered Hans to see to the boarding of the men.

"Well, I'll be damned. . . ." The thought whispered through him. It'd been a vague premonition that had hung over him ever since Gettysburg.

Three nightmare months he had spent in the hospital, his shattered arm gone, tortured by fear-tossed dreams that fate was now toying with him, sweeping him on a tide he could no longer swim against. The nights were filled with the screams of dying men, filled with the haunted eyes of boys who had seen too much, and the mute faces of the dead looking at him from the shadows of a distant land. But worst of all was the one dream that still brought him up screaming and thrashing in the sweat-soaked sheets.

For three months he had healed, at least outwardly. In spite of his premonition of fear, his pulse quickened at the thought of returning to the madness. With his wound, and the Congressional Medal of Honor that Lincoln had pinned to his pillow, he could have gone back to Maine in honored retirement. Instead he had rushed back to the front, as if racing to a lover's embrace.

He loved the fury and the pageantry, the power war pumped into his veins even as it tried to kill him. When the thunder boiled over in the distance, and the popcorn rattle of musketry called from up the road, his heart would again race madly, and he would be filled with a fierce, all-consuming joy once more. It somehow transported him, sweeping him up and causing him to forget himself, his former life, and the memories of the woman who had wounded his soul.

How could he return to the quiet of Bowdoin College, now that he had tasted of the blood-filled chalice?

So he had returned to command the 35th. It was now a shattered regiment, yet a regiment of men who somehow felt a perverse pride for the killing he had done to them.

It was a regiment that he led through the Wilderness, and finally into the scorching trenches before Petersburg. And all the time the nightmare voice had whispered to him that they were all damned. That the fighting would go on until finally they were all dead. Dead by his shouted commands, until only he alone would be left, blood-dripping sword in hand.

And, God help him, somehow he loved it so. For here, thin and bespectacled, a slender, frail slip of a man with a body near shattered, he felt himself truly alive.

Through the rain-swept shadows his boys, boys of eighteen and twenty years with the eyes of old men, passed before him and filed aboard the ship that would take them to yet another battlefield somewhere down on the North Carolina coast. To a battlefield yet unnamed where he would be forced to feed more boys like John into the furnace. Boys whom he had come to love. Their dark smiling faces, forever changing to be replaced by new faces, yet always the same, looking to him and him alone, for he was, after all, the hero of Gettysburg.

Reining his mount off to the side of the road, he sat in silence and watched his men march past, boarding the ship to whatever destiny the fates had laid out before them.

"Say, Hawthorne, there's the ship."

Vincent Hawthorne raised his eyes from the back of the man in front of him and saw the shadow of his commander and the ship awaiting them.

"Wonder how many of us bloody Keane will kill this time."

"Come on, Hinsen, he ain't that bad," Vincent replied.

"All officers are bastards," Jim Hinsen snarled. "Look what he did to us at Gettysburg, and in the Wilderness for that matter—plugged us right in the middle of the fight, the bastard did."

"Shut up, you little cuss, you damn whining cur!" Sergeant Barry snapped in his high staccato voice, coming up beside them. "You two weren't even there! You're nothing but fresh fish, damned draftees and bounty boys, so don't say 'us' when you speak of this regiment, until you've seen the elephant and earned the right."

"I didn't say anything against him," Vincent replied softly.

"Well, I'd better not hear it," Barry responded, "and if I were you I'd stay away from Hinsen here."

Without another word Barry pushed forward to help guide the men onto the ship.

"Bastards, they're all bastards," Hinsen mumbled, his voice barely heard.

Shamed, Vincent didn't respond. It was true that he was a fresh fish, joining the regiment only within the last month. But how could he explain that as a Quaker, he had joined only after a long moral fight within as to the evil of killing versus the need to end slavery? And besides that, he could not help that he was only seventeen and had had to commit the sin of lying about his age in order to get in.

He stole a sidelong glance at Hinsen, who was still cursing beneath his breath. He shut out the curses, and silently thanked God that at least the twenty-mile march was over, and he had survived it without the shame of collapsing from the exhaustion that in the last mile he thought would come near to killing him.

"Some of them don't sound too happy."

Andrew nodded as Emil Weiss, the regimental surgeon, came to stand by Andrew's side. Andrew looked down at the bald pate of the doctor, barely able to see the ruddy face, wreathed in a flowing white beard, that was usually lit up from a little too much medicinal brandy.

Andrew swung down off his mount. He handed the horse over to a staff orderly, who took Mercury off for loading.

"If they weren't complaining I'd start to worry," Andrew

said philosophically. "I'm just glad Hans didn't hear that little exchange Barry got into or there would have been hell to pay."

"Mother Hans, clucking over his killer chicks," Weiss chuckled.

"All your medical supplies in order?" Andrew asked.

"Never enough," Weiss grumbled. "Dammit, son, never enough bandages, and that tincture of lime, can never seem to get an adequate supply."

Weiss had joined the regiment shortly before Gettysburg, a fact which Andrew was forever thankful for. In spite of what the other surgeons said about the 35th's "crazy Jew doctor," Andrew and the men swore by him, a rare thing in an army served more often than not by half-trained country physicians and butchers.

Weiss had studied in Budapest and talked incessantly about an unknown doctor named Simmelweiss who had figured out something called antisepsis back in the late '40s. Andrew had listened to some of the debates Emil had, his fellow surgeons calling laudable pus a good thing, and saying infection was simply a fact of wounds. Emil would always wind up roaring that they were medieval butchers, and infection could be stopped by boiling the instruments and bandages along with hand-washing between operations with tincture of lime.

Whatever it was the doctor knew and used, the men of the 35th were found to have nearly twice the chance of surviving a wound as men from the other regiments.

Andrew again touched the stump of his arm and felt he could claim loyalty to Weiss from very personal experience. Since Gettysburg he didn't even bother to correct Weiss for calling him "son." After all, the man was twice his age, and for that matter every man in the regiment, including the much-feared Hans, was addressed that way by Weiss, even when the old doctor was in one of his typical bad tempers.

"The last of the men are aboard, sir," Hans reported, strolling up to join the two officers who stood by the edge of the dock.

"How are the piles, sergeant major?" Weiss asked, as if inquiring about the gravest of injuries.

Hans deftly shot a stream of tobacco juice that barely missed the old surgeon.

"Perhaps our good colonel here should order you in for surgery—I could clear them up for you in a jiffy."

"With all due respect—like hell, sir," Hans grumbled.

For the first time in days Andrew threw back his head and laughed at the embarrassed discomfort of his sergeant and friend.

"Well, gentlemen, shall we get aboard? I think it'd be best not to keep our good captain waiting."

Not looking forward to what he knew would be life with an unpleasant ship's captain, Andrew strode up the plank, following the last of his men. Besides that, there was the other problem as well, for like Hans he suffered violently from seasickness, and the thought of it made him shudder.

"Colonel Keane?"

A young naval officer stood upon the deck of the steamer waiting for him.

Andrew nodded in reply as the sailor saluted.

"I'm Mr. Bullfinch, sir. Captain Cromwell awaits you and his officers in the ship's wardroom. I believe, sir, the rest of your officers are already there."

"Well, gentlemen, we must not keep the captain waiting," Andrew said evenly, and they followed the young ensign aft.

"Ah, so the good colonel has at last deigned to join us," Cromwell growled as Bullfinch led the three into the narrow confines of the officers' mess.

Andrew looked about the room. His company officers were all present, but his second in command, the regimental quartermaster, and the rest of his headquarters staff were not there.

"Your staff have already left with General Terry."

Andrew recognized the remaining men of the 44th New York Light Artillery and nodded a greeting to Major O'Donald, their burly red-bearded commander, who with mock severity raised a glass of wine in his direction.

"Into their cups already," Weiss whispered.

The reputation of the 44th was well known. Recruited from the Five Points district of New York, they were considered some of the hardest drinkers and brawlers in the army. Their only saving grace was that no matter how hard they brawled among themselves and with anyone who wandered near them, they were ten times harder on the rebs.

"I'm going to make this short. I still have to see to the rest of our delayed loading," Cromwell said, looking accusingly at Andrew, who stared back evenly at this man who seemed to be going out of his way to make an enemy.

"Aboard this ship, I rule and you follow. Your men are to stay out of our way. Any problems between your men and mine, I handle it."

"The 35th takes care of their own," Andrew said softly.

"Aye, lad, and the same for the 44th," said O'Donald.

Tobias looked from one commander to the other.

"Regulations state—"

"I know the regulations, captain," Andrew said, his voice pitched so low that those in the far corner of the room could barely hear him. "But I will not surrender authority of my command over to you. I acknowledge your right to run this ship. I would not consider interfering, but likewise I shall not accept your interfering in my command. If there is a problem between your people and mine we shall both look into it according to military law."

"Like I already said," O'Donald retorted, coming around the table to stand by Andrew's side.

Tobias looked from one to the other, aware of the barely suppressed grins from the other infantry and artillery officers, who, unlike Tobias, knew what could happen if their respective commanders were aroused.

Tobias started to speak and then fell silent.

"If there is a problem," he finally replied, "then it'll be your responsibility, for I plan to put your statements into my report."

"By all means do so," Andrew stated. "We must, of course, follow the proper procedures. As I likewise shall do."

There was an icy silence that held for what seemed like hours but in fact was only a matter of seconds.

"Well, we understand each other then," Tobias replied, suddenly changing to a display of bluff comradely spirit.

"Before sailing, General Terry left you written orders which I believe you are already aware of."

Andrew merely nodded.

"There's a nurse from the Christian Sanitation Commission aboard this ship. She missed her transport, which left earlier," and as he spoke he gave an obvious grimace of disdain. "I don't like women aboard this ship—it's nothing but trouble. I've quartered her in my cabin, where a guard has been posted. I think we're in agreement that her quarters are strictly off-limits to both enlisted and commissioned personnel.''

"I am sure we can trust that all here will observe the necessary proprieties," Andrew replied sharply, "as I am sure your men will as well."

Tobias stared at Andrew coldly.

"We sail within the hour then," Tobias continued. "Weather being good, we should make the passage down the James River and into the Chesapeake before tomorrow evening. Out into the Atlantic it'll be another twenty-four hours to our rendezvous point off Beaufort, North Carolina, and from there we proceed to our station off Fort Fisher.

"As you know, the men of the 24th Corps are already trained in amphibious operations and will take the beach and piers where your people will be unloaded. From there on you're no more concern of mine."

"A situation I'm sure we are all looking forward to," O'Donald replied.

"Yes, I am sure of that," Tobias replied icily.

Without another word Tobias turned and left the wardroom, his officers falling in behind him.

"Well, lads," O'Donald laughed as the door slammed shut, "I'd say it's time for another round," and with a roar of approval his officers and some of Andrew's people gathered around the towering red-headed artilleryman.

Going to the far corner of the room, Andrew pulled off his rubber poncho and stretched out on a narrow sofa. Leaning back, he was soon lost to sleep, in spite of the uproar around him.

There was a blinding flash of light, another, and then yet another. But strangely there was no report as the white puffs of bursting rounds exploded around him.

Clouds of smoke swirled past, obscuring everything, blanketing him like a fog rolling in from sea. There was a shadow in the fog which gradually took form.

"Johnnie!" he cried, rushing through the white mist.

"Andrew, I'm afraid," and his brother came up to him, his eyes wide with fear, arms outstretched like a small boy looking for comfort.

Andrew couldn't reply. Reaching out, he took his brother's hand and started walking back in the direction John had

come from. Through his hand (strange, it was his left hand)
he could feel John trembling.

The sulfurous smoke parted, and there before him was a
blood-covered field, filled with a carpet of dead that stretched
to the far horizon, blue- and butternut-clad bodies mingled
together for as far as the eye could see.

"Andrew, I'm afraid," his brother whispered.

"I know, boy. I know."

"Make me go home to Ma," and now the voice was that
of a little boy.

He could feel himself shaking, the field strangely out of
focus as he came around behind his brother, placing both
hands on John's shoulders.

He pushed the boy forward.

As if he were sliding down an icy slope, Johnnie slipped
into the bloody field, even as he desperately tried to kick
back away.

"Andrew!"

The blue uniform started to peel off his body, and as it
did the flesh melted away, like ice disappearing beneath a
July sun.

And then he turned to look back, but now it was only a
skeleton, and, merciful God, it was a skeleton that still had
eyes.

"Andrew, I want to go home!" the fleshless skull screamed,
and then he fell away, his bones falling apart to mingle with
the thousands of bloated bodies that now as one turned, and
with ten thousand eyes gazed upon him.

"Johnnie!"

"It's all right, it's all right."

"Johnnie, for God's sake! Johnnie!" Andrew sat bolt
upright, the room now coming back into focus.

"John," he whispered, as gentle hands reached about
him, rocking him slowly.

"It's all right, colonel."

Colonel. Someone was with him, a woman. In an instant
he felt the rigid control return, and looking straight ahead
he stood up and the arms about him drew away.

"Just a bad dream, that's all," she whispered.

He turned and looked back down at the woman. Her
eyes, dark-green eyes, were locked on him. She seemed to
be about his age, in her late twenties or early thirties, with
pale skin and high cheekbones. Her hair was drawn up

under the bonnet of a Sanitation Commission nurse, but a thin strand hung down over her forehead, revealing a pleasing reddish-blond tint.

She stood up beside him, coming just to his shoulder.

"I was walking the deck and I thought I heard someone in here, so I came in and found you," she whispered, almost apologetically.

"It was nothing," Andrew said in a quiet, distant voice.

"Of course," and she reached out and patted his hand in a friendly fashion. "Don't be embarrassed, colonel. I've been a nurse since the beginning of this war. I understand."

There was a moment of awkward silence.

For the first time he noticed the room was empty, except for the two of them.

"Where is everybody?"

"Oh, things ended here several hours ago. I heard your doctor telling everyone to leave you alone, that you needed your sleep. It's just another hour to dawn."

Andrew rubbed the sleep from his eyes, and with his right hand tugged his jacket to try to get out some of the wrinkles.

"I'd better get to work," Andrew said woodenly. "I shouldn't have slept like that without checking my men first. Anyhow, it's time for morning roll."

"Let the men sleep a bit longer, Colonel Keane. This is their first night out of the trenches in months."

Andrew looked again at her and smiled. She had made her comment gently enough, but there was a slight note of command to it as well.

He wanted to say something back as a retort, but her smile completely disarmed him.

"All right, then, for your sake, Miss . . ."

"Kathleen O'Reilly," and she extended her hand, "and I already know that I have the honor of addressing Colonel Andrew Keane of the 35th."

Rather at a loss, Andrew awkwardly took her hand and then quickly let go.

"Well, now that we've been introduced," she continued, "shall we take a walk upon the deck? I know if my old supervisor were here, she would not consider this proper for us to be unchaperoned and alone in a room."

"I think, Miss O'Reilly, you can take care of yourself quite well."

"I most certainly can, colonel," and he noticed a slight edge to her voice.

Picking up his poncho and helping Kathleen with her wrap, Andrew led the way out onto the main deck. The sky was dark and threatening, with intermittent spits of rain and sleet lashing across the deck. Andrew took a deep breath, the chilled air clearing his head.

"Actually, it's kind of lovely," he said softly. "Reminds me of home back in Brunswick, Maine."

She was silent, leaning over the railing and watching the dark edge of the riverbank slip past.

"And where are you from, Miss O'Reilly?"

"Boston. I can remember a night like this—walking home from church . . ." *With Jason,* she continued to herself.

Suddenly curious, Andrew leaned against the railing beside her.

"A happy memory, I take it."

"Once," she replied softly. She dropped her head to hide her eyes.

"Care to talk about it?"

"No more than you do about John."

There was no rebuke in her voice, only an infinite sadness.

For long silent minutes they stood together, watching the lights along the shore drift by.

"We were engaged," she said softly. "He was killed at First Bull Run."

"I'm so sorry."

"Yes, and so am I," she replied evenly. "So that's how I became a nurse instead of a wife, my good colonel. And your John?"

"My younger brother," and he fell silent again and finally broke it with a single word.

"Gettysburg."

"So we both have our sorrow from this war," she stated in nearly a whisper. "Any other brothers?"

"No."

"So at least you will not have that pain again. And believe me, colonel, I shall never bear the pain of losing a loved one again, at least that much I have learned."

She looked up at him, and in the first faint light of dawn he could see the hard set to her features.

"I'd best be going now, colonel. I do have my duties to attend to. Good morning to you, sir."

"And to you," Andrew replied softly, extending his hand to hers.

Barely touching his hand in response, she nodded primly and, turning, walked back toward the stern of the ship.

Alone, Andrew continued to lean against the rail, watching the white wake of the ship plowing out as it slowly made its way down the river, cautiously running between the channel markers.

The rain started to lash down harder, cutting into him with icy needles. Having lived along the coast of Maine his entire life, he felt he knew something of the weather, and a chilly feeling inside told him that before the day was out there'd most likely be a real blow rolling up from the south. He could only hope their damn headstrong captain would be smart enough to anchor in the shelter of Norfolk and wait it out, schedule or no schedule.

Chapter 2

January 6, 1865
Four hundred miles southwest of Bermuda

For the first time in three days, Andrew realized, the seasickness had left him. He paused for a moment in wonder; was there nothing left in him to get sick with, or was it the simple stark terror of what was happening?

Tobias, insisting that the growing storm would not interfere with his schedule, had passed out of the Chesapeake and on into the Atlantic, even as the wind gust picked up to thirty knots. From there it had simply gotten worse, and by the end of the day they were racing before a southwesterly gale of near-hurricane proportions. The boilers had long since been damped down, and now they were running barepoled before the wind.

Hanging on to a railing next to the wheel, Andrew watched as Tobias struggled to keep them afloat.

"Here comes another!" came the cry from the stern lookout.

Wide-eyed, Tobias turned to look aft.

"Merciful God!" he cried.

Andrew followed his gaze. It seemed as if a mountain of water was rushing toward them. A wave towered thirty or more feet above the deck.

"A couple of points to starboard!" Tobias roared.

Mesmerized, Andrew watched as the mountain rushed down upon them and the stern rose up at a terrifying angle. Looking forward, he felt that somehow the ship could never recover, that it would simply be driven like an arrow straight to the bottom.

The wall of water crashed over them, and desperately he clung to the rope which kept him lashed to the mizzenmast. The ship yawed violently, broaching into the wind. As the wave passed over them, he saw both wheelmen had been swept off their feet, one of them lying unconscious with an ugly gash to the head, the wheel spinning madly above them.

Tobias and several sailors leaped to the wheel, desperate to bring the ship back around.

"Here comes another!"

Rising off the starboard beam, Andrew saw another wave towering above them.

"Pull, goddammit, pull!" Tobias roared.

Ever so slowly the ship started to respond, but Andrew could see that they would not come about in time. For the first time in years he found himself praying. The premonition that had held for him and the regiment, that they were damned, was most likely true after all, even if the end did not come on a battlefield.

The wave was directly above him, its top cresting in a wild explosion of foam. The mountain crashed down.

He thought surely the rope about his waist would cut him in two. For one wild moment it appeared as if the ship was rolling completely over. His lungs felt afire as they were pushed beyond the bursting point. But still he hung on, not yet ready to give in and take the breath of liquid death.

The wave passed, and Andrew, gasping for air, popped to the surface. They had foundered, the vessel now resting on its portside railing. Helpless at the end of the rope, he looked about, cursing that his fate was in the hands of a captain who had killed them all for the sake of his foolish pride.

"Damn you!" Andrew roared. "Damn you, you've killed us all!"

Tobias looked over at Andrew, wide-eyed with fear, unable to respond.

Tobias's gaze suddenly shifted, and with an inarticulate cry he raised his hand and pointed.

Andrew turned to look and saw that yet another mountain was rushing toward them, this one even higher than the last, the final strike to finish their doom.

But there was something else. Ahead of the wave a blinding maelstrom of light that appeared almost liquid in form was spreading out atop the wave like a shimmering cloud of white-hot heat.

The cloud swirled and boiled, coiling in upon itself, then bursting out to twice its size. It coiled in for a moment, then doubled yet again.

"What in the name of heaven—?" Andrew whispered, awestruck by the apparition. The intensity of the light was now so dazzling that he held up his hand to shield his eyes from the glare.

There seemed to be an unearthly calm, as if all sound, all wind and rain, were being drained off and they were now lost in a vacuum.

But still the wave continued to rise behind it, and then, to Andrew's amazement and terror, the wave simply disappeared as if it had fallen off the edge of the world. Where a million tons of water had been but seconds before, now there was nothing but a gaping hole, filled by the strange pulsing light.

Suddenly the light started to coil in yet again, then in a blinding explosion it burst back out, washing over the ship.

The deck gave way beneath Andrew's feet, and there was nothing but the falling, a falling away into the core of light as if they were being cast down from the highest summit.

There was no wind, no sound, only the falling and the pulsebeat of the light about them. As his thoughts slipped away, he could only wonder if this was death after all.

He awoke to the glare of the sun in his eyes. Groaning from the bruises that covered his body, Andrew sat up and looked around.

Were they dead? Was this the afterworld? Or had they somehow survived? He came to his feet, and from the way the protest of bruised muscles coursed to his brain, he somehow felt he must be alive after all.

But how? Was the light a dream, the falling a wild hallucination? All he could recall was that endless falling, the light pulsing and flaring. He struggled with the memory. He seemed to recall awakening at some point, and still they were falling in silence, the light about them shaped like a funnel, spiraling downward and dragging the ship with it.

Improbable, he thought. The wave must have knocked him unconscious and somehow that damned captain had managed to save them after all.

The deck of the ship was a shambles. All three masts were down, with rigging, spars, and canvas littering the deck from stem to stern. In more than one place Andrew could see a lifeless form tangled in the wreckage. He'd have to get the men moving to start cleaning this up and disposing of the dead.

But where were they? He raised his eyes. They were aground, the shore a scant fifty yards away. The sandy beach before them quickly gave way to brush and low trees, and beyond he could see a series of low-lying hills.

Fumbling with his one hand, he managed to untie the rope about his waist.

It was hot, nearly summerlike, and he could feel the beads of sweat coursing down his back, trapped by the still-damp wool of his salt-encrusted uniform jacket.

Rubbing the back of his neck, which felt sunburned, he turned and saw a dull red orb already halfway up the sky. It didn't look quite right, he thought, somehow bigger. Not thinking any more of it, he turned away.

They were alive, but where? Had they run all the way to Bermuda, or were they now wrecked somewhere along the coast? It had to be somewhere in the south. It could never be this warm in the north at this time of year.

Could it be the Carolinas? But no, he remembered that the hills didn't come this close to the sea. Perhaps he was mistaken, but best not to take any chances—they'd have to assume they were in rebel territory till it was proved different.

"Colonel, you all right?"

Hans popped his head up from an open hatchway, and for the first time in memory, Andrew could see that his old sergeant had a look of total bewilderment on his face.

"All right, Hans. Yourself?"

"Damned if I know, sir," and the sergeant pulled himself

up onto the deck. "I thought we'd gone under, and then there was this light. For a moment there I thought, Hans, old boy, it's the light of heaven and those damned stupid angels have made a mistake. And the next thing I know I wake up still alive."

"What's it like below?" Andrew asked.

"Six hundred men puking their guts out. Ain't very pleasant, sir. Couple of the boys got killed from the battering, a number of broken limbs, and everyone with bruises. They're just starting to come to now."

"Well, go below and start getting them up on deck. There's work to be done."

"Right sir," and the sergeant disappeared back down the ladder.

"So you finally decided to get up."

Andrew groaned. He knew he shouldn't think it, but he found himself wishing that Tobias had been swept overboard.

"Where the hell are we?" Andrew asked, turning to face the captain, who was strolling down the deck toward him.

"South Carolina, I reckon. I'll shoot an angle on the sun and soon have it figured out."

"How did we get here?" Andrew asked, unable to hide his bewilderment.

Tobias hesitated for only a second.

"Good piloting, that's all," he replied, but Andrew could sense the doubt in his voice.

"And that strange light?"

"St. Elmo's fire, but I reckon a landlubber like you never heard of it."

"That wasn't St. Elmo's, Captain Tobias. It knocked all of us out and we woke up here, and I daresay you can't explain it any more than I can."

Tobias looked at him, trying to keep up the front, then turned away with a mumbled curse.

"We've been hulled. I'm going below to check the damage. I suggest we get started straightening this ship out, and I expect your men to help where need be."

Without waiting for a response, Tobias headed for the nearest hatchway and disappeared below.

Within minutes the deck was aswarm with men staggering up from below, most of them looking rather the worse for wear. As quickly as they came up, the various company commanders tried to sort them out and run a roll. Spotting

Kathleen coming out from the captain's cabin, he hurried to her side.

"You all right, Miss O'Reilly?"

She looked up at him and smiled bleakly.

"Long as I live I'll never set foot on a ship again." The two of them laughed softly.

"Sergeant Schuder told me there've been some casualties. I'd deeply appreciate it if you would find Dr. Weiss and give him your assistance."

He continued to look at her closely, not wanting to admit that he had been concerned for her.

"Colonel, sir!"

Andrew looked up to a private standing atop the ship's railing and pointing off to shore. He came up to his side and looked at the boy, trying to remember his name. The boy was nothing more than a mere slip of a lad, standing several inches below five and a half feet in height. His red hair, freckled face, and cheerful open expression gave him an innocent, almost childlike look. Andrew fished for his name, wondering how this lad had ever gotten past the recruiting sergeant. Then again, army recruiters were simply interested in warm bodies, nothing more. Suddenly the name came back to him.

"What is it, Hawthorne?"

Vincent looked at him for a moment, swelling a little with the fact that the colonel knew his name. That was another thing learned from Hans—always know their names, even though too often the knowing in the end would cause pain.

The boy was silent, still looking at him.

"Go on, son. What is it?"

"Oh, yes, sir. Sir, look over there, near that cut in the dunes a couple of hundred yards up the beach. Seems like a cavalryman."

Andrew shaded his eyes and looked to where the boy was pointing.

Damn big horse. Looked to be a Clydesdale.

"Strange thing, colonel—it seems he's carrying a lance or spear."

Andrew looked around for Tobias, hoping he could get a spyglass, but the captain had yet to reappear.

"Son, do you know where my quarters are?"

"I think so, sir."

"Well, run quick—there's a single chest there. My name's

on the top. Inside you'll find my field glasses. My sword's there as well. Now fetch them quick, lad."

"Yes sir!"

Obviously impressed with the responsibility given to him, Vincent jumped off the railing and raced below.

Andrew leaned over, still shading his eyes, and tried to get a better look at the lone horseman.

"Stay where you are, dammit," Andrew whispered. "Just don't move."

"Got something, colonel?"

Andrew turned to see Pat O'Donald coming up to join him.

He pointed to where the lone cavalryman sat, half concealed.

"How'd your men take the storm?" Andrew ventured, while waiting for Vincent to return.

"It's not the man, it's the horses," O'Donald said sadly. "We brought along enough for two guns and a caisson—the rest went on another ship. Most of them will have to be destroyed, or are already dead. I checked your horse, sir—he made it through all right."

The tearful remorse in the major's voice was rather a strange paradox coming from a man with his reputation.

"Your field glasses, sir," Hawthorne cried, near breathless as he raced up to Andrew's side.

Andrew brought them up and focused.

"Well, that is the damnedest," he whispered softly.

If this was reb cavalry, then they sure as hell were scraping the bottom. The man wore a beard that came near to his waist, with long shaggy hair curling down past his shoulders, and which, even more curious, was topped by what appeared to be a conical iron helmet. His dirty white tunic, which looked as if it had a high clerical collar to it, was buttoned off to one side.

The man didn't even have boots; his lower legs were covered with rags, wrapped cross-hatched with strips of leather. And Hawthorne was right—the man was indeed carrying a spear.

In front of Petersburg he saw deserters coming in almost daily, but at least they still were carrying guns and had a semblance of a uniform.

Andrew handed the field glasses to O'Donald, who started to laugh.

"Faith and upon my soul! So there is the vaunted reb cavalry."

As if realizing he was being watched, the lone horseman turned his horse about, and kicking it into a trot he disappeared from view.

"Old men and children in the trenches, and now cavalry carrying spears on draft horses. Won't those poor sots ever give up?"

Still laughing, he handed the field glasses back.

"He might look comical, major, but this could prove serious."

"And how so?"

"Those low hills there. Whatever it was you were laughing at could be going to get help right now. If they have a single section of artillery handy, all they need do is position themselves up there and shell us into surrender."

O'Donald fell silent and turned to look back down the deck.

"Too much of a cant here to deploy my guns to respond."

"Exactly," Andrew replied. "We'd better get my men ashore immediately and dig in. Get your men moving and bring those Napoleon field pieces of yours topside. That lifeboat there should be enough to ferry them ashore."

Andrew looked back to where Vincent still stood.

"Son, you'd better help me on with that sword," he said softly.

"Colonel, with the captain's compliments he wants you back aboard ship."

"Damn it all, what now?" Andrew turned on the messenger and saw that it was Bullfinch, the young ensign who had first led him aboard ship.

"I'm sorry, sir, but the captain did not confide that in me," the boy said meekly.

"All right. Just give me a minute."

Andrew quickly surveyed the ground around him. One thing could certainly be said for the men of his regiment—six months of siege work in front of Petersburg had taught them how to dig. A triangular outworks forming a perimeter a hundred yards across at the base was already laid out in the dark loamy soil. It was already several feet deep on the two sides facing inland. O'Donald's men were finished with the first gun emplacement, commanding the apex of the line, and were now turning their attention to flanking position. One twelve-pound Napoleon had already been ferried out and emplaced. Looking back to the ship, he could see that the second weapon was being lowered over the side.

It must have been one hell of a wave that pushed them this far in, Andrew thought, as he looked at the damaged hull resting in less than ten feet of water. Even as a nonsailor Andrew had realized another curious fact about the place they had come to rest: there was no tide.

And there was the question of the sun. His timepiece was useless after the soaking the storm had given it, but somehow the day had seemed awfully damn short. Besides that, from the ship's compass the shoreline ran due east to west, and he could recall no such coastline south of New York.

"Keep the boys at it, Hans," Andrew shouted, and following the ensign, he waded into the near-tropical warmth of the ocean and accepted the helping hands of two sailors aboard the ship's launch. Seconds later they were alongside the *Ogunquit,* and with the help of a sling, Andrew was deposited back on deck.

There was a look of anxiety on Tobias's face, something that Andrew actually found to be pleasing.

"What is it, captain?" Andrew asked coolly.

"Colonel, can you climb the rigging?" And so saying he pointed up to where the shrouds to the mainmast still clung to the shattered maintop, thirty feet above the deck.

"Lead the way."

This was something he would never have worried about once, but since the loss of his arm, Andrew found the prospect somewhat frightening—though he'd never admit it in front of this man.

Tobias scrambled up ahead of Andrew, almost as if taunting him. But all thought of insult died as he finally reached the shattered platform.

"One of my men spotted the first contingent. I thought you should take a look."

Fumbling for his field glasses, Andrew looked off to the distant horizon.

Through a gap in the hills it seemed as if an ocean of men were swarming toward them.

"There must be thousands of them," Tobias whispered.

At the head of the column rode a contingent of several hundred horsemen, followed by what appeared to be an undisciplined horde, which, after clearing the gap, spilled out in every direction.

"My glass has more power than your field glasses," Tobias offered.

It took a moment for Andrew to brace himself and focus the awkward telescope. He trained it upon the head of the column, and a gasp of amazement escaped him.

It looked like an army out of a distant dream. At the head of the column rode half a dozen men carrying square banners mounted upon crosspoles. The lead banner portrayed crossed swords of red on a white background, looking vaguely like a Confederate battle standard; the next was of a horseman with a double-bladed ax above him. The others had the appearance of stylized icons, being the portraits of men in what Andrew felt was a near-Byzantine style.

The horsemen, most looking like the scout they had seen earlier on the beach, carried spears. Some had shields slung over their shoulders, and most of them were wearing conical helmets, festooned here and there with fluttering ribbons. A number of horsemen in the column looked as if they were wearing rough plate armor. The heavily armored warriors rode in a tightly clustered group around a portly, bearded man in gold-embossed armor, who rode beneath the horse-and-ax standard.

Andrew swung the glass around to the swarms of infantry. They looked like true medieval levies armed with an insane assortment of spears, swords, clubs, and pitchforks.

Andrew looked over to Tobias, who wordlessly returned his gaze.

"Captain—just where in God's earth are we?" Andrew whispered.

". . . I don't know," Tobias finally admitted.

"Well, dammit, man, you'd better figure it out, because we sure as hell haven't landed in South Carolina!"

Andrew started back down from the maintop and jumped to the deck, Tobias following him.

"Get Dr. Weiss up here!" Andrew shouted, heading for the rail.

"What are you going to do, colonel?" Tobias asked.

Andrew turned on the captain, but found himself completely at a loss for words.

"Can you get this ship afloat again?" he finally asked.

"Where's the tide?" Tobias asked in a whisper, drawing closer. "If we had beached at low tide there might have been a chance—but where's the bloody tide? And besides, there's a hole down belowdecks big enough to ride a horse through."

"Then figure something out, because we sure as hell don't want to stay here!"

"Wherever here is," Emil retorted, coming up to join Andrew.

Together the two went into the lifeboat. Before it had even reached shore, Andrew leaped out, Emil puffing to keep up.

"What is it, colonel?"

"I want you to see what's coming," Andrew said. "Tell me if it looks like anything you've ever seen."

He already had a strange suspicion, but immediately pushed the thought aside; it was simply too absurd.

Racing ahead, all dignity forgotten for the moment, Andrew rushed to the entryway of the fortified position.

"Hans! Sound assembly!" Andrew roared.

The clarion notes of the bugle and the long roll of the drum sounded. With the first note, Andrew felt a shiver run down his back. Suddenly the racing panic in his heart stilled; a crystal clarity of vision came over him.

The encampment exploded into action. Men raced to pull on their jackets, snatch up muskets, and sling on cartridge boxes.

Following the lead of the infantry, O'Donald called for the two pieces already ashore to be wheeled into their emplacement. Then he led his command to fall in by the men of the 35th.

Within seconds the old ritual, which they had acted out hundreds of times before, was played out: the ranks forming, muskets being grounded, the men dressing the line. Then when all were in place each company snapped to attention, their company commanders turning and coming to attention when all was in order.

A hush spread across the field, and in the silence, they all heard for the first time a distant sound which every veteran knew: the sound of an army advancing in their direction.

Andrew surveyed the line of five hundred men who were his, and the eighty men of O'Donald's command behind them. Every other time, it had been easy enough to explain what they were about to face; orders from above would tell him where the rebs were, and whether he was to hold or attack. There'd be a couple of comments about the honor of the regiment and the pride of being from Maine, and then they would move in.

But this was different. Heaven help them all, what could he say? He paused, trying to collect his thoughts. The men started to look uneasily at each other, while in the distance the rumble of the approaching host grew louder and louder.

There was no brigadier above him now, nor regiments falling in to either flank. This time he was alone, just as at Gettysburg, and the decision was his.

"Uncase the colors!" Andrew roared.

A stir went down the line as the standard-bearers lowered their staffs. Men to either side rushed out to pull off the flag casings. In the faint afternoon breeze the blue flag of Maine snapped out. It was followed seconds later by the shot-torn national standard; emblazoned upon its stripes in gold lettering were the names of a dozen hard-fought actions which the regiment had survived with honor.

The men looked to each other, some eagerly, others pale with nervousness; uncasing the colors usually meant action was in front of them.

"Look to those colors, boys!" Andrew shouted, and as one each man's gaze turned to the standards they had followed across countless fields of action.

Andrew knew it was a rhetorical flourish, but he had to start somewhere, and for the men of his regiment—of any regiment— the shot-torn flags were symbols of pride and honor.

"There is a lot I cannot explain to you now," Andrew continued. "You'll see things you might not believe or understand at first. All I ask is that you obey my commands. Just trust me, lads, as you have on every field of action. Follow my orders, and I'll see all of us through this."

He fell silent. This wasn't the typical flag, Maine, and the Union speech. He sensed their uneasiness, but there wasn't time to explain further.

"Companies C through F, deploy to the east wall. H through K, to the west wall. I want A and B, with the colors, in reserve in the center. Major O'Donald! To me, please! Now fall into position, boys!"

The encampment became a wild explosion of movement as the formation broke and men ran to their positions.

"What is it, colonel?" Pat said, coming up to join him.

"Look, Pat, I can't explain the situation now—I still don't understand it myself. We'll just have to wait and see. Let's go up to your emplacement and watch the show."

The two commanders, trying to appear outwardly calm, strode across the encampment area. They reached the battery where O'Donald's twelve-pound brass Napoleons were deployed.

"They're getting closer," Pat whispered. "God, it sounds like thousands of them."

"There are."

"Here they come!" came a shout from an excited private down the line.

A lone horseman, bearing the crossed-sword standard, crested the hill a half mile away. Within seconds he seemed to be engulfed in a human tide as thousands of infantry poured over the hill around him. Farther to the left, the advancing column of horsemen appeared.

"Worst damn reb infantry I've ever seen," O'Donald sniffed. "No lines at all—must be local militia."

O'Donald turned to his men.

"Load case shot, four-second fuse!"

"Wait on that," Andrew said softly.

O'Donald turned back to Andrew.

"Now look, colonel, darling—my boys here know their business."

"Pat," Andrew said evenly, "I am the senior officer on the field. Trust my judgment on this. You'll see for yourself once they get closer."

Andrew forced the slightest of smiles, not wishing to appear an autocratic commander. The artilleryman paused for a brief moment, and then called for his men to hold.

"Colonel, if they're militia, we can break them up real quick before they get into musket range."

"They don't have muskets," Andrew said quietly.

"What?"

"Just watch."

The host continued to swarm forward, the cavalry keeping pace with the infantry. Gradually, out of the swarming mass, individual forms started to take shape.

"What in the devil are they?" Pat gasped.

"Damned if I know," Andrew said, still trying to smile.

A loud murmur started to break out in the ranks, men crying out in confusion at the sight before them.

"You're the history professor," Emil said, coming up to join the two commanders, "so please help me retain my sanity and tell me what they are."

"I was hoping you would know," Andrew replied. "We couldn't have been blown all the way to Arabia, and they look European, not black or eastern."

"Well, what they're carrying looks straight out of the Middle Ages to me," Emil replied. "Damn it all, look at those weapons and armor! Those things are museum pieces!"

"I know, doctor," Andrew murmured, "I know."

Just what in hell was he facing? He still couldn't figure it out. For all the world he felt as if he were facing a host straight out of the tenth or eleventh century.

"Over there on the crest of the hill! Are my eyes deceiving me?" Pat exclaimed.

Several teams of horses came into view.

Andrew found himself breaking out into a nervous laugh.

"It's their artillery, Pat. Catapults—they're bringing up catapults."

The three officers looked at each other in dumbfounded amazement.

"I guess whoever they are, they mean business," Emil replied.

"He's right, colonel. That isn't any friendly town council coming out to greet us."

Andrew merely nodded, watching as the host continued to deploy. There was no real order to it. From out of the cavalry column half a dozen horsemen broke away and started to canter across the field in front of the peasant mob. Distant shouts echoed up, and, still several hundred yards out, the enemy army came to a halt.

A loud chant suddenly went up, drifting on the late-afternoon breeze.

From out of a high-wheeled cart traveling with the cavalry there appeared several men, dressed in long flowing robes of gold and silver. Each carried a smoldering pot on the end of a length of chain. Swinging the pots over their heads, they started to walk down the length of the line. As one, the thousands of men fell to their knees.

"They're blessing themselves," Pat whispered, and even as he spoke he made the sign of the cross, most of the men in his command following suit.

Raising his field glasses, O'Donald scanned the line.

"Looks like they're doing it backward, though," he mumbled as if to himself.

"We'd better do something, colonel, darling," Pat said,

looking over to Andrew, "for as sure as I'm damned to hell, I think those beggars will charge once the blessing gets done."

"All right, then," Andrew said softly. "Load solid shot and set to maximum elevation."

"Why, that will put it clear over the hill."

"Just do as I say, but have that canister ready in case I'm wrong."

Without waiting for a response, Andrew turned and strode back to the center of the encampment.

"35th Maine, fix bayonets!"

The old sound that was the prelude to battle rattled out as five hundred bayonets were snapped out of their scabbards and locked into place.

"Companies C through K, prime and load!"

Hundreds of rammers were now pulled. Charges were bitten open, and powder and shot slammed in.

"Companies A and B, load blank charges only and deploy behind the artillery!"

Nervously the men looked to their commander, wondering what he was planning.

"C through K, you will fire only on my command! I want all weapons at shoulder arms. I'll personally shoot any man that levels a rifle before my command!"

The regiment was silent, almost numbed by the bizarre spectacle before them.

Andrew faced the double rank of the two companies that moved up behind the field pieces.

"I don't think they understand who we are," he said evenly. "If we can give them a good scare without bloodshed, we might be able to talk later. It'll be up to them, so when I give the command, aim high, and fire off a damned good volley. Then we'll see what happens."

"One of them coming up, sir," Hans said, now standing beside Andrew, which he always did when there was the scent of battle in the air.

A lone horseman carrying the crossed-sword standard started to gallop toward their line.

"Hans, just cock that carbine of yours and keep an eye on him."

Andrew climbed atop the gun emplacement and slid down the other side. The horseman drew closer. This was like something straight out of a Sir Walter Scott novel, he thought, complete to the armored knight coming to demand submission. But the man approaching him looked more like a ragged beggar than a knight. His armor was nothing more than a dozen heavy plates stitched onto a leather tunic. A sword was belted about his waist, and the heavy lance he carried glinted wickedly in the reddish light of the sun.

Andrew spared a quick glance again to the sun. What was wrong with that thing? It looked much too big. He focused his attention back to the rider, who reined in a dozen paces away.

The rider stood in his stirrups and scanned the encampment. Then he called to Andrew:

"K kakomu boyaru vy podchinyaetes?" (What boyar do you serve?)

Confused, Andrew could only shake his head.

"Nemedlenno mne otvechayte! Boyary Ivor-i-Boros trebuyut bashey nemedlennoy sdachi." (Answer me at once! Boyars Ivor and Boros demand your immediate surrender!)

Andrew extended his right hand outward.

"I am Colonel Keane of the 35th Maine Volunteers, of the United States Army."

The rider reined his horse back several paces.

"Vy yazychnik, vy ne govorite po hashemv yazyku. Zavaytes!" (You are heathen—you do not speak our tongue. Surrender now!)

In the man's tone Andrew heard a note of fear. There was something strangely familiar about the language and the uniform. Everything was like an object barely discernible in a deep and shifting pool.

Suddenly he recognized a word from the man's speech. Somehow he had to reach this man.

"O'Donald, get out here!"

The men saw the towering redheaded Irishman clambering out of the gun emplacement, and reined his horse back several more paces.

"You said you saw them making the sign of the cross?"

"That I did, colonel."

"Then do likewise."

A look of solemn concentration came over O'Donald, and raising his right hand he made the sign of the Catholic faith.

"Vy nad nami nasheetivayes!" (You mock us!) the horseman roared. Leaning forward, he spat on the ground, and

swinging his horse about, he galloped back toward the waiting host.

"I think we'd better get inside!" O'Donald roared, and grabbing hold of Andrew by the shoulder, he drew him back into the lines.

"You made a mistake!" Emil shouted, trying to be heard above the roaring host.

"How?"

"Tell you later!" And shaking his head he went back to the medical tent.

Andrew wanted to hurl a curse at him, but there was no time for it now. Suddenly he realized what the mistake was, and silently cursed himself for it.

"Here they come, colonel," Hans shouted.

Andrew turned.

By the thousands the infantry started to swarm forward, the cavalry breaking into a canter and swinging wide toward the beach.

"When I tell you, Pat!" Andrew shouted. "Companies A and B, present!"

A hundred rifles came to the shoulder, aiming high into the air.

Andrew looked toward the host. They were less than two hundred yards away. Just a few seconds more and . . .

"Fire!"

A sheet of flame and smoke snapped out, the thundering volley echoing across the field.

The wild advance slowed, nearly halting.

"Now, Pat! Let's scare the devil out of 'em!"

Shouldering the gunner aside, O'Donald grabbed the lanyard and pulled.

The Napoleon cannon leaped back, belching a tongue of fire and billowing smoke. The thundercap report echoed out across the field.

The thick smoke cloud hung above them, so Andrew scrambled up the embankment for a better view. Cheering started to break out from the Union soldiers deployed down the line. A gentle breeze stirred across the field, lifting the curtain of smoke.

By the thousands the peasant host were streaming to the rear, many in their panic throwing aside their pitchforks, clubs, and spears. It was a total and complete rout!

Grinning, Andrew looked down at O'Donald.

"Told you it'd work!"

"Ayè, a grand sight it is!" O'Donald laughed.

Andrew let the men cheer themselves hoarse, as he strode down the line, complimenting them on their steadfastness. Even better than a victory was a victory won with no bloodshed on either side.

"Well, let's leave the next move up to them," Andrew said philosophically, walking back to the artillery emplacement.

"I think they have already decided their next move," Hans said coldly. He pointed off toward the left flank. The three wagons with the catapults atop them were being pushed forward. The rest of the peasant host had finally stopped running at the crest of the hills a half mile away, where they waited.

Fascinated, Andrew watched as the firing arm of the first catapult was cranked back. The arm snapped up, the crack of the weapon echoing across the field. Seconds later the other two machines discharged as well. Large stones soared upward, tumbling end over end until they seemed to hover nearly motionless in the sky.

It was like watching the mortar shells back in the trenches, Andrew thought, and he could see that all three rounds were going off to his left.

The three projectiles reached the apex of their flight and, tumbling end over end, smashed into the *Ogunquit*.

Dammit, they were going to smash up the ship!

"All right, Pat," Andrew said dejectedly. "Looks like they won't stay scared. Take their artillery out."

"What I've been waiting to hear!" Pat shouted. "Load solid shot!"

His gunners set to with a will, ramming home the cartridges and twelve-pound balls, while the gun-layers swung the two artillery pieces around.

Pat stepped behind each of the two pieces, sighting down the barrels and giving quick commands to raise or lower, and to move the weapon to one side or the other.

"Fire on my command!" he roared. "Number one, fire!"

The gun seemed to literally leap into the air, kicking back several paces.

"Number two, fire!"

The shots screamed downrange. One struck the cart holding the first catapult, splitting it right down the middle, and the weapon flipped off the back. The second machine suddenly collapsed on itself in an explosion of splinters and coiling rope.

There was a moment of stunned silence, pierced only by a distant shriek of agony. All resolve vanished, and the entire host melted away in a wild stampede of terror.

"Well, that should be the last of them," O'Donald pronounced proudly, patting the hot barrel of his gun.

"I don't think so," Andrew replied grimly, as he turned and walked away.

Just who the hell are these people? he wondered. Though reluctant to admit it, he did recognize one word the envoy had spoken, and that had aroused in him a terrible, impossible suspicion.

The man had said "Boyar." And he realized that Emil had noticed O'Donald's mistake, that to these people the big Irishman had made the sign of the cross backward. Could he somehow be in medieval Russia?

He turned and looked back. Where were they, and just who in hell were these people?

"Patriarch Rasnar, I did not ask for a religious interpretation. I want answers, not doctrine! Could this be like the Primary Chronicles? Yet more men coming from the tunnel of light?"

With a snort of disgust, Boyar Ivor came to his feet, kicking the coals of the fire so that a shower of sparks rose heavenward. Turning away with an angry curse, he stormed off into the darkness.

"But this is a religious matter—it has nothing to do with the Chronicles," Rasnar roared, his flowing robe of gold and silver embroidery swirling out about him as he followed after his boyar.

Boyar Ivor turned to face the man. How he hated him. For fourteen years, since the death of his father, he had been locked in a never-ending struggle of power with this so-called holy man. Rasnar's thin ascetic face, wrapped in a bushy black beard that matched his dark-circled eyes, drew closer.

His father had stripped the church of its temporal powers, but the balance was a precarious one, for the rule of steel was constantly offset by Rasnar's manipulation by fear of destruction and damnation. Yet each needed the other to maintain control over the peasants. Steel and fear to keep them in line for when the dread from the west came again.

He knew his knights and landholders were watching this confrontation, and in the fine balance of power between the boyars and the church, he could not lose, on even the most minor of points.

"How else can you explain them?" Rasnar whispered darkly. "This is not as we came from the blessed land. They have appeared to us with the weapons of Dabog. You smelled the smoke—it was the smoke of the fire that torments the fallen. They have been sent by Dabog, the evil one, to destroy us, unless we destroy them first."

Ivor could hear the mumbling of his knights. They were still terrified by what had happened. He knew Rasnar sensed it as well, and would press on that. If he conceded, and did not find another answer, Rasnar's priests could use it to their advantage, perhaps even turning the knights against the boyars, blaming them for what had happened.

Already one of his spies reported hearing several priests say that the blue devils had been sent to punish the rulers for having seized the power of choosing and taxing from the church.

"So what do you propose?" Ivor whispered, so that none would hear his question.

"The proper prayers must be read, the men must be blessed, and you must send forward with the rising of Perm's light at dawn."

"They'll be slaughtered. And besides, why should I send them forward?"

"The church has no power to do such a thing. Remember, it was you boyars who took that away from its rightful control," Rasnar replied sharply. "And once destroyed," Rasnar added smoothly, "their devilish devices must be taken by the church for safekeeping."

Ivor gave a snort of disdain.

"Oh, so it is all that simple. And what do you propose then to do with these devices, which you have now openly called unholy?"

"Why, destroy them, of course," Rasnar replied sanctimoniously.

Ivor threw his head back and laughed.

"Do you hear that?" he roared so his knights would hear. "The church will take the devices and destroy them. Of course, I should fully trust you in this, your holiness?"

Rasnar did not reply, his gaze fixed darkly on his hated rival.

"But you are forgetting one thing," Rasnar whispered,

putting his hand on Ivor's shoulder and leading him farther into the darkness.

"And that is what, your holiness?" Ivor asked, still grinning.

"The Tugars."

Ivor whirled about and faced the priest.

"What of the Tugars?" Even he found it difficult to control the fear in his voice.

"I am trying to save you from yourself and your grasping designs," Rasnar whispered. "I saw your face when the thunder weapons fired. You were afraid, yet already your thoughts were turning. You imagined what such things could do against Boros of Novrod, or Ivan of Vazima. You wish to take these things and use them in your own mad dream for control of all the Rus."

Ivor was silent as the priest repeated what he had been thinking.

"You could succeed with these things," Rasnar whispered, "but what then of the Tugars? What will they say when they come and see what you have done? The last time a single boyar united the Rus without their permission, they broke his body and sent him to the pit. What will they say with you having these devices?"

"I would give them to the Qar Qarth as a sign of my loyalty," Ivor replied nervously.

Now it was Rasnar's turn to grin as he shook his head.

"The Tugars appointed boyar and church to rule together," Rasnar said quickly, "and I will not allow you to seize their devices and will denounce you to the Qar Qarth as having plotted against their rule. What is to stop you from using such things to throw down my church?"

"You bastard," Ivor hissed. "I will not allow you to seize such things and use them against me."

"Remember as well," Rasnar continued, ignoring the insult, "if we do not eliminate these demons, the Tugars will find them and we might be blamed."

"How?" Ivor asked nervously.

"Because if they can do what they did to us, and if they are still here, perhaps they will try it on the Tugars as well. And we both know who the Tugars will blame."

Ivor's eyes grew wide with fear.

Rasnar saw that he had hit the right point.

"Kill them now, lord boyar, turn the weapons over to the church for safekeeping," Rasnar whispered.

"But the Tugars are still four winters away," Ivor replied, trying to temporize.

"Yet is it not said the ears of the Tugars encompass the world?" Rasnar replied softly.

Rasnar smiled and put his hand on Ivor's shoulder in a conciliatory gesture.

Ivor, known as Weak Eyes, squinted and looked toward the encampment of the strangers, which appeared as hazy blotches of firelight on the other side of the field. Who were these men? Were they demons after all? Could they be a threat to the balance between his Suzdalians and the Tugars?

But what power? he thought. First I could unite all the Rus under my banner and then without any havens and rival boyars for him to rush to I could bring down Rasnar and place my puppet in his place. Surely the Tugars would not object to that. And besides, the Tugars are four winters away, but the Novrodians are only a day's march to the east.

If he destroyed them now, there would be the struggle for the weapons, for surely Rasnar would strike fear into everyone's heart with his shoutings from the pulpit of the cathedral. If he let them live and used them, there would be a problem as well, but they could be used, and mastered. Perhaps they could even be turned against the church, making it appear as if they were demons who had simply gotten out of control. When the time finally came, they could then be disposed of. Thinking about something as terrifying as the Tugars required too much effort, and he pushed the thought of them away.

Ivor looked back at Rasnar and grinned. Brushing aside Rasnar's hand, Ivor started back to the campfire, where his arms men waited expectantly. Damn fools, he thought. In spite of today's display, they were most likely still eager to charge the blue warriors yet again.

He had to act quickly, for most likely word had already reached Novrod of this strange occurrence. It was not wise to leave his city for too long with his mounted border watchers.

Returning to the flickering circle of light, Ivor settled down on his camp stool and looked about at the nervous stares that greeted him.

"Send for that damned bard of mine," Ivor snapped.

Grabbing hold of a wooden mug, Ivor leaned over and scooped out a tankard of stale beer from the small barrel by his side. Draining the drink off, he scooped out another round and looked up to see the peasant he had sent for.

"Where in the name of Kesus have you been?" he roared.

The rotund peasant looked at him wide-eyed.

"Composing a new ballad in honor of my lord," he said nervously.

"Kalencka, I know damned well you were hiding. I saw you not with my household when we advanced. I grant you the scraps of my feasting table, and dammit, I expect payment of loyalty in return," Ivor roared.

"But my lord, I needed a vantage point to observe your heroic actions so I could record them later in the Chronicles."

Ivor looked at the man with a jaundiced eye.

Damned peasants, they were all alike. Lying, murderous scum, loud to complain, first to run away, and always ready to blame their betters for every ill. There were times he thought he or the Tugars should simply murder the entire lot so he wouldn't have to put up with their stench.

"You seem to be able to talk your way out of anything," Ivor replied coldly, "so I've decided you can be of some use to me rather than stealing from my table for nothing but badly worded verse in reply."

"Whatever you wish, my lord," Kalencka replied, bowing low so that his right hand swept the ground.

"Go to the camp of the blue ones."

Kalencka looked up at Boyar Ivor, his eyes growing wide with fear.

"But my lord," he said softly, "I am a ballad maker, a chronicler, not a warrior."

"That is why you are to go," Ivor retorted, the tone in his voice making it clear that any argument could have the most unpleasant results.

Ivor looked around at his men and then to Rasnar.

"There is no rush in these things," he said evenly. "First let us see who they are. Perhaps we can learn their secrets as well and then use such things against them."

Without a word, Rasnar turned away and stormed off into the darkness. Ivor followed him with his gaze. There would be trouble over this. Perhaps he could lure him out of the cathedral and across the square to the palace for a very special meal if things got too difficult. Even as the thought crossed his mind he decided that until this thing was settled it would be best to receive the holy bread from a hand other than the patriarch's.

Ivor looked back at Kalencka, who was still before him, his nasty peasant eyes staring at him.

"Get out of my sight," Ivor roared. "Go to their camp now. Tell them they are on my land and I demand an explanation. When you have mastered something of their language I want their leader brought to my presence for a meeting. I want information from you as well, and don't return until you've found something of interest for me. I am leaving my half brother Mikhail in command here and will take my border riders back to the city." As he spoke he pointed to a towering bearlike warrior standing to one side of the fire.

Ivor smiled and looked over at his brother. If something did go wrong, he thought craftily, Mikhail could take the burden. Besides, Rasnar would most likely return to Suzdal tonight, and it would not be wise to leave him alone in the city. More than one boyar had left his town only to return days later to find the gates locked to him.

"Now get out of my sight and do something, you stinking scum," Ivor roared.

Bowing repeatedly, Kalencka retreated from the wrath of his lord. Once out of the circle he finally straightened up and looked about.

"Well, this is the mouse leaping into the mouth of the fox," Kalencka mumbled to himself, "and the wolf stands by to watch his two meals dance."

Kalencka looked over toward the blue warriors' camp. He couldn't simply walk up to them in the dark. If they were demons it wouldn't matter, but if they were men, they might think he was trying to sneak up.

Taking a torch from one of the guards that surrounded Ivor's camp, he started out alone across the open field, hoping that the flickering light would dispel any suspicions.

From over in the blue warrior camp he heard a rising chorus of shouts. Perhaps they were preparing to attack. But there was no getting around it now. He knew one of Ivor's guards would be following at a distance to put an arrow through him if he turned back. The wolf was definitely at his back, so it was to the fox then.

But even a mouse can talk, he thought to himself, so that the wolf and the fox will not see him but only each other.

Try as he could, Vincent Hawthorne could not stop himself from shaking. Hinsen wasn't helping the matter at all.

In his sheltered life growing up in a Quaker community, Vincent had never met a man like Hinsen.

His world had been one of farm work, meeting for worship, and the Oak Grove School of Vassalboro. Even a trip to Waterville, six miles away, was something usually only done with his mother or father, who openly stated that the mill town was a place of sin which should be seen only when absolutely necessary. His life had in no way prepared him for his first day in the army.

He had heard dozens of new words, put together in all sorts of combinations that he had never imagined before. For the first time in his life he had witnessed cardplaying, dice-throwing, and the drinking of intoxicating liquids, and, to his stunned dismay, had actually seen soiled doves, which the men called hookers, after the hard-fighting General Hooker, who, legend had it, traveled with such ladies of the evening in his camp.

The steady stream of obscenities from Hinsen he had learned to ignore, but to now hear the man desperately praying out loud was totally unexpected and thus unnerving.

Yet he could understand. He looked off to what he assumed must be east and touched the Bible in his breast pocket.

There were two moons in the sky.

As darkness fell the stars had come out, and that had been bad enough, for nothing in the heavens was right. The gentle splash of what should have been the Milky Way was now a brilliant shimmering band shaped like a wheel, which filled half the sky with such a glow that it was almost possible to read his Bible from the light.

When the stars first came out, Sergeant Barry had come along and said they must be south of the equator. Vincent heard a couple of former sailors over in Company B scoff at that, but he clung to what Barry had said.

And then the moon had appeared. But it was too small, far too small, and did not look right at all. To the left of it another moon appeared scant minutes later, and now all about him was in an uproar.

Some like Hinsen were openly on their knees, praying at the top of their lungs. Others, some of whom he knew to be battle-hardened veterans, were weeping, calling for home or loved ones, while here and there a voice was shouting for Colonel Keane to get them out and take them home.

Vincent looked over to the beached ship, and though he had come to dispel the man, he was glad that Captain Cromwell was still aboard, for more than one man was blaming the situation on him, and calling for a lynching.

There was nothing to be done, Vincent realized. If Keane knew the answer, he would be out and around telling them, but over in officer country he saw the colonel and the other officers talking, raising their heads to look about the encampment, and then in bewilderment to the twin moons that were moving rapidly into the sky.

"Thou shall not be afraid of the terror by night," Vincent whispered, touching his Bible. He turned back toward the circle of fires around the camp.

Shocked, he cocked his rifle and brought it up. There was a light moving toward him. In all the confusion no one had noticed it, and it was coming straight at him.

"Sergeant of the guard!"

His voice could be barely heard above the confusion.

"Sergeant of the guard!" Vincent looked over his shoulder, desperate for some help, but all around him was confusion.

The light was drawing closer.

By the starlight he could see a lone man bearing a torch, standing rigidly before him, not twenty yards away.

"Sergeant Barry!" Vincent cried.

Still no response. He had to do something. He was supposed to be on sentry duty, and Barry had roared at him more than once about staying exactly where he was put. He just couldn't run back to one of the officers; they might think he was running away.

He had to do something.

Taking a deep breath, he clambered up over the breastworks. Lowering his rifle to the advance position, he started out across the field toward the solitary figure.

Could he shoot this man? Vincent wondered. Since the start of the war he had wrestled with that. To kill was the greatest sin, the elders had taught him. But to him the enslavement of fellow men was just as heinous. For that reason he had finally resolved to run away and join the army, hoping nevertheless that in the confusion of a battle he would never see a reb that he would be forced to aim at.

But as far as he could tell, these men weren't rebs. What now? Even as he advanced he decided that come what may he would not shoot, but nevertheless, as if in spite of himself, he kept his gun cocked and pointed.

Gradually the silhouette took on features. The man was short and rotund. He was dressed in a simple pullover shirt that fell to his knees and had a wide flowing black beard that cascaded down nearly to his waist.

Vincent stopped, his leveled bayonet pointed squarely at the man's oversized stomach.

"Identify yourself, friend or foe," Vincent squeaked out.

The man before him started to break into a grin, and held his two arms out to either side, still smiling.

"Go on, tell me who you are," Vincent whispered.

Ever so slowly the man thumped his chest with his right hand.

"Kalencka."

Vincent let the point of his bayonet drop. How could he stick this man? The fellow was grinning at him.

"Who the hell is out there?"

"It's me, Sergeant Barry!"

"Damn you, soldier, who the hell is me!"

"Private Hawthorne. I've got one of them out here."

"Well, goddammit, private, bring the prisoner in!"

"You heard him," Vincent said softly. "You've got to come in with me," and motioning with his rifle he indicated that the stranger should lead the way.

"Kalencka."

"I guess that's his name," Emil said softly.

Andrew nodded and sat down on his camp chair. Exhausted, he tried to focus his attention. It seemed that all discipline in the regiment was near to breaking. He could hear Schuder roaring out commands, but still there was the shouting. Damn it all, he was terrified himself. There could only be one explanation to all of this, but his mind recoiled at the enormity of it all.

Somehow they were no longer on earth. What other explanation was possible at this point? But each time he tried to come to grips with the thought, he felt as if he wanted to crawl away, fall asleep, and pray that when he awoke he would either be dead from the storm or somehow back in the world he knew and could understand.

The crack of a carbine snapped his thoughts back. The camp fell silent.

"All right, you ignorant, whining, lazy bastards!" Schuder roared. "You're nothing but fresh fish, the whole damned lot of you. And I thought the 35th had men in it. You're crying like green boys being led to see the elephant. Now goddammit, act like men, or so help me I'll thrash the next man who so much as peeps, mit god I'll do it!"

Andrew held his breath. The sergeant major was the most feared man in the regiment, and he could only hope the fear of Schuder would be greater than the unknown that confronted them.

There were a couple of low murmurs.

"I heard you, Fredricks, you little milksop, you whinny coward."

There was a loud snap and a grunt of pain, and Andrew winced. He hoped his officers all had the good sense not to be looking; otherwise there'd be hell to pay for Schuder.

"All right then, you bastards, we understand each other. Now back to your posts."

Seconds later the tent flap opened and Schuder strode in and saluted.

"The camp is back in order, sir."

"I could hear that, Hans," Andrew said, suddenly realizing that Hans's little display had braced him back up as well.

"All right, then." Andrew turned his attention back to the man who called himself Kalencka.

"Kalencka is your name?"

The man nodded and tapped himself on the chest. Smiling, he stepped forward and touched Andrew, his eyebrows raised in an exaggerated quizzical manner.

"Keane."

Kalencka looked at him and smiled.

"Cane."

"Close enough," Andrew laughed.

"Doctor, what do you think?"

"It's too uncanny, son," Weiss replied. "Some years ago I went to Lodz to visit my uncle and his family."

"In Russia, isn't it?" Hans asked.

Kalencka turned to face Hans.

"Rus!"

Emil looked at Kalencka and nodded eagerly.

"Da, Rus!"

Kal grinned at him.

"Da, Rus," and with a broad sweep of his arms he turned around.

"Suzdal, Rus," Kalencka said.

"Da, da." Standing up, Emil reached into his haversack and pulled out a bottle, uncorked it, and held it out.

"Vodka," Emil said.

Kalencka grinned broadly, even as he gingerly took the bottle and peered at it cautiously. Understanding, Emil took it back, put the bottle to his lips, and took a healthy slug. Smiling, he offered it back, and the peasant followed suit, took a couple of gulps, and a quizzical expression formed on his face as Emil took the bottle back.

"Gin," Emil said, pointing to the bottle, "and not your rotgut variety either."

"Major darling, I've been feeling a bit of a chill meself," O'Donald said hopefully.

"We all need a shot or two," Andrew said, and with a look of remorse, Emil gazed fondly at the bottle and handed it over to the artilleryman.

"Gin," Kalencka said with a broad grin.

Grabbing the bottle back from O'Donald, while it was still at the major's lips, Emil passed it back to Kalencka.

"Don't ask me to explain how," Emil said softly. "As I was saying, when I went to Lodz some years back I saw thousands of peasants dressed almost like this one. And damn my eyes, Andrew, this man's speaking Russian or something awful close to it."

"And you can speak it too?" Andrew asked hopefully.

"A couple of words, that's all. Enough to talk my way past the goyim."

"The what?"

Emil shook his head and grinned. "Ah, you Americans. Never mind."

Emil looked up at Kalencka, who was starting to get a little bleary-eyed.

"Kal, gin."

"Da, da. Gin."

"Well, colonel, I guess we'd better start the language lessons."

Kal looked about at the men and smiled. These were the best damned spirits he'd ever had, and for the first time in his life he thanked Ivor Weak Eyes. Perhaps these foxes weren't so bad after all.

Chapter 3

"Beautiful morning, isn't it, son?"

Andrew turned to see Emil emerging from the shadows.

"Quiet. It's just so peaceful and quiet," Andrew replied. He looked about and smiled softly. In the trenches this was always his favorite time. It'd still be dark enough so you could climb out, stretch your legs, and just listen to the gentle quiet before dawn. At those moments it'd seemed as if the war were a million miles away.

"Maybe it's the same right now on another world," Emil replied evenly.

"Just where in heaven are we?" Andrew asked.

The doctor smiled sadly and shook his head, while looking up to the sky.

"I don't know how or why," he replied, his voice carrying a slight sense of awe. "But I think wherever our war is, it's somewhere out there. We're not on earth, that's for certain. The sky alone proves that."

"But those people," Andrew started, pointing to the camp-fires that shimmered in a glowing arc around them.

"God alone knows the answer, colonel. But we've had that Kal with us for three days now. The language is Russian, or a form of it at least. You know that and so do I."

"Seems like something out of the tenth, maybe eleventh century, I'd venture," Andrew said, as if to himself. "But how, dammit? How? From what little I've been able to learn from Kal, he talks about a Primary Chronicle that tells of his people crossing here in a river of light. Now, I remember that the Primary Chronicle is a history of the early Russians. But we aren't in Russia. The sky and that strange red sun prove that. So tell me, Emil, where are we?"

Emil reached up and laid his hand on Andrew's shoulder.

"That is not your concern, if I might be so bold," Emil said sharply.

"And what does that mean?" Andrew replied, feeling somewhat irritated by the doctor's tone.

"Andrew, you're pondering an impossible. Chances are we'll never know the how of it, or the why. Even if we did, chances are we still couldn't change it. Your job now is to lead. To find a way for us to survive on this world. If an answer ever comes, we'll cross that then. But we can't stay here surrounded forever. For the time being we must find a place to live."

Emil stopped for a moment, and with a smile reached into his tunic and pulled out a flask and offered it.

Without comment Andrew uncorked it and took a long pull.

"Somehow we've got to make an accommodation with those people out there. You no longer command a regiment—you're the general in charge, and a diplomat now as well."

"So you're telling me to stop worrying and do my job, is that it?" Andrew said coldly.

"Just that you historian types want to know all the answers," Emil responded with a chuckle.

Andrew turned away for a moment. He knew the old doctor was right. For three days the regiment had been here, dug in and terrified. And the terror had been in him as well. Only iron discipline had kept him going, following the mechanical routines of running a regiment. In the evening he sat with Kal, trying to master the language. But when he was alone the cold terror would start to creep in.

Just what was he going to do?

"Worry about keeping us alive," Emil said softly as if reading his thoughts. "Let me spend my time figuring out the hows and whys of it all."

Andrew turned back to the doctor and smiled.

"Where the hell is that Hans? Time for the men to get up. After roll, let's you and me sit down with Kal," and capping the bottle he tossed it back to the doctor.

"Boyar, I Keane see your boyar."

At least that's what Kal thought he heard. Cursed strange how they tried to speak the mother tongue. He looked at Andrew and smiled.

"You Cane, see Ivor, talk friendship. I go back to Ivor and talk peace for you," Kal ventured back in English.

Andrew smiled and nodded in an exaggerated manner. Kal could not help but chuckle inwardly. In three days he'd learned far more of their language than he was willing to let on. Of all the Suzdalians, in fact of all the Rus, he alone could communicate with them. Ivor would really need him now.

For years he'd lived at the edge of Ivor's table, making up bad verse for the scraps of comfort offered to him. And more than once he'd feared that Ivor might think him just a little too smart for a peasant and have him garroted. It'd been a dangerous game he played, all with one final hope. That when the Tugars came, he and his family would be exempt from the sacrifice, as were the rest of the nobility.

Continue to play dumb, he thought. Just play dumb and learn quietly from these bluecoats. Already he'd seen enough to leave him filled with terror. One of the young bluecoats, the one called Vincent, had shown him how his metal rod could kill an enemy many paces away. Ivor in his fear might try to destroy them and take the metal rods. But if that happened, Kal realized, he'd be out of a job as translator. No, peace would be essential, for him to serve as the go-between and thus secure himself in Ivor's court.

He looked about the tent and smiled his best stupid grin.

"Da, da, yes, friend, bluecoats and Rus, good. Kal talk peace for Rus, for bluecoats."

"Well then, let's get started," Andrew announced, and standing up he beckoned for Kal to follow.

"Kal, take this," Emil said, extending his hand.

Kal took the strange object which he had seen on the faces of Cane, Emil, and a number of other bluecoats.

"For Ivor," Emil said.

"He called the man Weak Eyes," Emil said, looking over at Andrew. "I've got a couple of extra pairs of glasses. Most likely nothing near what the man needs, but it might sway him a bit."

Emil took the glasses from Kal's hands and showed him how to put them on. Kal gasped with amazement, peering around curiously, and then took them off.

"Make Ivor's eyes better," Emil said. "Gift from Cane and me."

The peasant looked at the glasses in awe and nodded.

Stepping out into the reddish light of the noonday sun,

the three walked toward the battlement walls. Three days had made the position impregnable, Kal could easily see that. The triangular fort was ringed by an earthen wall, as high as a man could reach, with an eight-foot-deep ditch in front. Even now the men were still working, building platforms for the monstrous metal tubes, one for each corner, and the fourth now mounted on an earthen mound in the center of the camp. Even if these men did not have the smoke killers, they'd be near impossible to destroy, Kal thought, looking about the encampment.

For above even their weapons Kal could not help but notice how the boyar Cane so easily controlled his men. There was something strange here. Cane would chat with even the youngest, like Vincent, who behaved as if he were a noble. But with merely a soft-spoken word from Cane, all would rush to form their strange lines, standing as straight as their metal tubes.

Another word spoken and five hundred knives would flash out and be attached to the tubes. Another word and all the tubes would be pointed a certain way. Here was a strange power, Kal realized, but a power that strangely did not come from the lash, as he had always assumed power must.

This was not as the world should be. Peasants are to be driven by the lash and fear. Nobles defer to the boyar, but among themselves fight and brawl for prestige and position. And the priests—there were no priests here. No gold robes that all but the boyar must bow to as they spoke the words of submission to Perm, his son Kesus, and the sacrifice of the Tugars.

Still pondering these questions, Kal struggled up to the top of the parapet, Keane at his side.

"Kal."

Kal turned to look back to the colonel.

In Andrew's hand was a small metal flask, which he offered to the peasant.

"Boyar Ivor?" Kal asked.

"Nyet. For Kal," Andrew said, smiling.

Cheerfully the peasant took the flask, and with a wink tucked it into his tunic. With a sweeping gesture, he bent over, his right hand touching the ground. Straightening back up, he slid down the embankment and started back to the Suzdalian camp.

He looked back once more to the one armed boyar in the blue coat. He could not help but like the man.

"Father, the guards report that Kalencka has just come through the south gate. Mikhail has come back with him as well."

Ivor stood up, and tossing a half-eaten pheasant aside he wiped his greasy hands on the front of his tunic.

"It's about time that idiot showed up," and he slapped his son on the shoulder.

"Andrei, that peasant better have their secrets, and some sort of an agreement," Ivor growled.

"Perhaps they could be of some service after all," Andrei ventured.

"If we know their magic, why keep them?"

Ivor didn't venture anything beyond that, even to his son. The threat of the church was only all too real. The church was supposedly neutral in the eternal bickerings between the dozen kingdoms of Rus. Already he was starting to regret his confrontation of the other night. Push the patriarch Rasnar too far and the church might weigh in on the side of his rivals, declaring him heretic. Most likely some of the boyars would not turn on him because of the church and it would still leave him with many of his own landholders feeling nervous. Rasnar had been strangely quiet since their return, and that was cause enough for worry right there.

Walking over to the narrow window of his feasting room, Ivor looked across the great square to the cathedral of the Blessed Light of Perm. Most likely that bastard was looking over here at him, pondering the same questions, he thought darkly.

This problem with the bluecoats had to be settled. He could already sense they were near impossible to destroy, and that was part of the reason Rasnar was pushing him on to try it. Many of his warriors, knights, and peasant levies would die in the attempt, leaving him the weaker. As the most powerful of the boyars, he would suffer, leaving him vulnerable against the others, and still there would be no guarantee that he would know their secrets.

There was the other problem as well. Thousands of peasants and many of his nobility were still out there, watching the bluecoat camp, leaving his marches with Novrod the weaker. And finally there was the simple question of his prestige. If he did not come out of this looking as if he had won, more than one noble would be willing to ally with Rasnar in a bid for power.

Picking up a half-filled tankard, he drained off the contents, then, leaning back, emitted a long sonorous belch.

"Ah, that's better, damn me. Now let's hear what this peasant has to say. Bring him to me."

Kalencka was ushered into the room, with Mikhail at his side.

"Oh mighty Ivor, I come back with important news," Kalencka said, bowing low.

"Have you learned their magic, then?" Ivor ventured.

"That I have done, most noble one," Kalencka replied.

"And?"

"It is a magic they alone can wield," the peasant replied, keeping his features in a grim countenance. "They have a secret powder that they only can use. If anyone else dares to touch it, he is burned, if he has not permission."

Ivor pulled on his beard.

"But they are in awe of your power as well, my lord Ivor," Kalencka continued, looking straight at his lord with unblinking eyes. "They wish an alliance under your power, to serve you in return for the right to live here and acknowledge you as their boyar."

Kal still held Ivor with his gaze.

"Perhaps we could lull them and then surprise and annihilate them," Mikhail ventured.

"A laudable plan, my worthy noble," Kal said evenly, "but there is still the powder."

Mikhail looked at Kalencka darkly.

"It is a good plan," Ivor said out loud, wishing to show his warlike spirit.

"A good plan, of course," Kal agreed, "but, my lord Ivor, they could add to your power against the Novrodians. Already they've indicated a desire to help you in such matters."

"Will they do this?" Ivor asked.

"Of course, my lord. But it'll take some time, my lord. They are weak from their great journey and desire first to build homes for themselves, and then they will serve."

"Weak, eh?" Ivor mumbled.

"But even weak they still have the magic powder."

Ivor turned away. Damn it all, this required too much thinking. Why couldn't these blue devils simply be armed like other men? Then he could charge in with lance and ax, smash some heads, and give his nobles a good time. Instead there'd have to be thinking done on this one, and Ivor dreaded the prospect.

"Tell their boyar to come to Suzdal to meet with me. In the city he will be more awed by my power." And perhaps I can take him prisoner alone, Ivor thought, a smile lighting his features.

"My lord, their boyar, Cane, has already expressed that desire, but said he wishes to bring the guards that his honor demands."

"Oh, all right then, damn him," Ivor replied.

"As a token of their friendship their healer sent this present," and approaching Ivor, Kal reached into his tunic and pulled out the pair of glasses.

Ivor took the spectacles and gazed at them with open curiosity.

"What devilry is this?" Ivor whispered.

"Their leader, Cane, and the healer both wear them. It confirms power on the user, and gives strength to one's eyes."

Ivor looked darkly at Kal. It was Rasnar who had placed upon him the name Weak Eyes, and though bad eyesight afflicted many, Ivor was highly sensitive about the matter, feeling it was a sign that he was not as noble and manly as others.

"May I?" Kal asked, taking the spectacles from Ivor's hands and extending the ear pieces. Nervously he held the glasses and slipped them onto Ivor's face.

The boyar stepped back with a startled cry. He looked about the room, peering first at Kal and then to the tapestries on the wall.

A grin of delight crossed his usually grumpy features, and he rushed to the window to look out over the square.

Gasping, he looked back at Mikhail.

"It is magic!" Ivor shouted. "Rasnar with all his healing prayers could never do this. I can see everything!"

Excitedly, Ivor looked back at Kal.

"Such things are dangerous," Mikhail growled darkly.

Ivor turned to his half brother and gave a snort of disdain.

"And you have the weak eyes too, as did our father," Ivor chortled sarcastically. "But I no longer do."

"May I gaze through them?" Mikhail asked, his curiosity gaining the upper hand.

"No! Such things are only for a boyar," Ivor replied triumphantly.

Mikhail said nothing, but Kal could see that his boyar had made a mistake. Ivor could show a fair degree of cunning when need be, Kal thought, but when it came to Mikhail he did not fully realize just how much his bastard half brother held him in secret contempt. The peasant remained silent, not wishing to draw notice by even daring a glance in Mikhail's direction.

Ivor's display of joy lasted for some minutes, until finally the rotund boyar settled back into his audience chair.

"Extend my thanks to this Cane when you go back to his camp," Ivor said. "And look about you sharply to see what other such gifts they might give unto me."

"Of course I am already doing what you command," Kal replied. "But to learn all such things and to serve you best, may I offer a humble suggestion?"

"Go on—what is it?"

"It would be best for you if this humble servant, in the service of the lord, be allowed to live permanently among the bluecoats. Then I could watch them for you throughout the day and night. It was I who first suggested the gift of the glass objects wishing to help my lord. My presence there will mean you will have a loyal spy, who might be able to bring other such things as well, and perhaps learn the secret of their powder.

"I am nothing but a stupid ignorant peasant, so they will trust me more readily. Far better I perhaps than one of your nobles or household who would perhaps arouse their suspicion."

He heard a sharp intake of breath from Mikhail, who stepped forward to speak.

"It is I who should do this instead," Mikhail said rapidly. "This stench-dripping fool is too ignorant for such a task. Better a noble of breeding and intelligence, my brother."

Ivor looked from one to the other and smiled softly.

"The idiot is right," Ivor said evenly. "One who looks as stupid as he will not arouse their mistrust. I therefore decree that only he alone shall be allowed to learn their speech for now."

And besides, Ivor thought, he is my man, and would not dare to use such knowledge against me.

Kal breathed an inner sigh of relief.

"Their language—is it difficult?" Andrei asked curiously.

"Most difficult indeed," Kalencka replied, rolling his eyes. "A speech not fit for the tongue of any noble Rus."

"Then learn it yourself, damn you," Ivor retorted, "and learn it well."

"Only to serve my lord," Kalencka replied, bowing low.

"You answer only to me," Ivor replied. "If I hear that you are within a hundred paces of Rasnar at any time I will have you flayed alive, and your daughter and wife held for the coming of the Tugars."

Kal could not hide his trembling at the threat, and Ivor chuckled darkly.

What frightened him even more, though, was the look of open hatred Mikhail gave to him. He had guessed right on that one, sensing the noble's plan when he had insisted personally on riding with him back to the city, pumping him for information all the way.

"A good plan, yes, a good plan," Ivor mumbled, looking curiously at his brother and then back to the trembling peasant.

"And mark this well," Ivor said darkly. "Say but one word of the Tugars to them and I'll not kill you on the spot but will save you and your family instead for their festival of the moon passing."

"Never would I do such a thing," Kal whispered.

"Let it be known to all others as well," Ivor said sharply, looking to his speaker of decrees who stood in the corner. "Let it be known by all that whoever attempts to tell the bluecoats of the Tugars will be saved for the festival as well."

Ivor leaned back in his chair. Perhaps Rasnar was right about how the Tugars would feel regarding these bluecoats. He could use them for more miracles like the glasses he held in his hands, but in the end they would go to the pits, thus granting exemptions to others that would beg him for such things when the time came.

"Bring their Cane before me tomorrow morning," Ivor growled. "Now leave me."

And standing up he put the glasses back on and strode from the room, peering about and gasping with amazement.

As Kal withdrew, still bowing, he spared a quick glance to Mikhail, who was looking straight at him.

Do not growl at the wolf so loud that he might hear, Kal thought nervously, for he will never forget the challenge.

"All right then, boys, look sharp now, the colonel's expecting you to act like the soldiers you are. You men of Companies A and B have been selected for this honor—now live up to it."

Vincent tried to push his narrow chest out even farther as Sergeant Schuder stopped in front of him, gazed for a moment, and then with a snort of disgust continued down the line.

Vincent breathed a sigh of relief. For some reason the colonel no longer terrified him—in many ways he looked on his one-armed commander as a father—but Schuder was more like the old schoolmaster at Oak Grove, ready to explode with Old Testament wrath at the slightest provocation.

From the corner of his eye Vincent saw Keane approaching, with Dr. Weiss riding alongside and Major O'Donald and Kal walking in front of them.

Keane reined his mount up in front of the company and looked the ranks over.

"All right then, lads," Keane said softly, as if addressing a group of friends about to embark on an afternoon stroll.

"Kal here," and he pointed to the peasant standing beside him, "indicates we can make a peaceful arrangement with these people. I'm trusting all of you to do your duty. I want those people out there to see the type of soldiers we are. But one mistake and it could go badly for the lot of us. I expect this to go smoothly, and it's important we don't show the slightest trace of fear. So look and act like soldiers, no matter what you see. If things should turn ugly, you are to fire only on my command, or Sergeant Schuder's. Any questions?"

"Colonel, just where in hell are we?" Vincent could tell by the defiant tone that it was Hinsen.

Keane reined his mount around and came up to stand directly in front of Hinsen. With a cold look, the colonel stared down at the private.

"That is what we are going to find out, private," he said sharply. "Let me worry about that. You're new to this regiment, private, so I'll let it pass this time. But the veterans among you know that the 35th has always seen its way through, no matter what was put in front of us.

"Now, are there any other questions?"

The men were silent.

"All right, then. Major O'Donald is senior in command until I return." As he spoke he looked over to where Captain Cromwell and his crew stood. Vincent instantly sensed that there was some conflict brewing there, the way the two men looked at each other.

"Sergeant Major Schuder, get the men moving."

Hans stalked down the length of the line, sparing a cold glance for Hinsen, to the head of the column.

"Uncase the colors," Schuder roared, in his best parade-ground voice.

The staffs were lowered for a moment and then raised up again, revealing the shot-torn national standard, and alongside it the dark-blue flag of Maine, snapping in the morning breeze, the blue turned almost lavender by the reddish light of the sun.

"Company, right face! Forward, march!"

As one the hundred soldiers turned and started for the sally port. Andrew galloped down the length of the line, to fall in the lead, while a single caisson and field piece clattered into position at the end of the column.

"Sergeant Dunlevy, if there's trouble," O'Donald roared, "give 'em a whiff of double canister," and the artillerymen shouted lustily as they passed before their commander.

The tiny column passed through the sally port, and over a wooden bridge spanning the moat.

Vincent looked around nervously at the open field ahead. Thousands of peasants stood upon the far hills, while ranging out to either side came several hundred horsemen. Schuder had already told them that if there was trouble, they'd simply form a square and fight their way back. But they were only a hundred strong, with a single field piece, while whatever it was they were facing numbered in the thousands. He knew that somehow the colonel was putting on a show of bravado, but it didn't do anything to make him feel any less nervous.

"Musicians, give us a song. 'Marching Through Georgia.' "

The single drummer rolled a flourish, and the fifer started the tune.

"All right, you men, sing, damn you," Hans shouted. "At the top of your lungs now."

"Ring the old bugle, boys, we'll sing another song."

Vincent fell into the step of the tune, a new favorite with the troops, even though it was about Billy Sherman's boys, and the column's step fell into a rhythmic swing.

"Hurrah, hurrah, we bring the jubilee—hurrah, hurrah, the flag that makes men free."

The tiny column crossed the open field of waist-high grass, and cresting the top of the hill, they stepped out onto a rutted road that wove along the side of the ridge.

For Vincent the view beyond was breathtaking, and filled him with a deep longing for home and the woods of Maine. The valley before him was covered with towering stands of birch, mingled with what looked like spruce, stately white pines, and an occasional maple. From the vantage point of the crest, Vincent looked back out toward the sea, and to the west he could see distant hills beyond. The middle of the valley before him was cut by a broad meandering river that curved and wove through the valley, emptying into the freshwater sea a dozen or so miles farther up the shore.

The column pushed on, "Marching Through Georgia" being replaced by "The Girl I Left Behind Me," and then for good measure "The Battle Hymn of the Republic."

The men sang with a will, as much to brace up their own courage as to impress the horsemen around them.

As the minutes passed and the trail turned down toward the river, the open fields gave way to stands of towering timber.

The march was soon into its second hour without a break, and the sweat coursed down Vincent's back. But the colonel would not call a halt, as if to show the watching columns weaving along on either side the toughness of his men.

A lush open field opened up on the left, spreading down from the road to the broad muddy river swirling by. To their right a tumbling stream cascaded down from the hills, and at a rickety wooden bridge over the narrow waterway Keane finally called a ten-minute halt in ranks.

Taking off his hat, Vincent looked around, admiring the view. It was a lovely peaceful spot, with cattle grazing in the field, herded by wide-eyed peasants who stood motionless, staring at the strange procession.

The stream passed by with a merry, soothing sound of

dancing lightness, its waters reflecting the curious reddish light of the sun, twinkling and sparkling like liquid rubies.

The brief rest passed all too quickly, and the column pushed on, leaving the tranquil spot behind. The road continued northward, past yet more open fields and stands of heavy timber. A village appeared on the road ahead, and marching through, Vincent was appalled by the disgusting squalor of the place, so unlike the neat, whitewashed villages of Maine. Filthy barefoot children stood in the doorways of the log huts; women who he felt might be only twenty-five or thirty, but looking as if they were fifty, stood silent at their passage.

A single large structure of logs, two stories high and covered with ornate carvings, dominated the rude square in the center of the town, and from its windows a number of women dressed in colorful robes watched as the column passed.

"The local grandee," Bill Webster said. Vincent looked over at the nearly bald private, whom Vincent found to be an intelligent pleasant fellow.

"Everyone in squalor except for the nobles," Vincent replied coldly.

"My pop's a banker," Webster replied, "but he did it on his own, same way I plan to. It don't look like that applies around here."

Vincent was silent, not wishing to pass judgment, but as they left the village behind, he could not help but feel uncomfortable with what he had seen.

The road continued on, until straight ahead the woods rose up in what appeared to be a solid wall of massive pines, the road through them the slenderest of ribbons. A number of horsemen galloped ahead, cutting in front of the column.

"If there's gonna be trouble," Schuder shouted out, "this is as good a place as any. So look lively, boys."

The horsemen, who had kept their distance at the start, had seemed to take nerve. While most held back, here and there a mounted warrior pressed down to within a dozen yards of the column, expression openly hostile. Occasional shouts, which were obviously threats, were hurled in their direction, but with Schuder constantly pacing and repacing the length of the line, no one dared to respond.

From the corner of his eye, Vincent saw one warrior, far

bigger than the rest, who kept arguing with the men about him, and then looking back to the column.

His mount alone was enough to give Vincent the shakes. The horse was bigger than a Clydesdale, and with each toss of its head, it revealed twin rows of yellowed teeth that seemed designed for nothing more than biting somebody's arm off.

The warrior was a huge barrel-chested man with a glistening blue-black beard that spilled over his chain-mail shirt and reached nearly to his waist. As if he knew Vincent was watching him, the warrior raised up his right arm and waved a double-headed ax in the young Quaker's direction.

Vincent quickly looked away, and there was a round of hoarse laughter. The axman started to angle his mount in toward the column.

The woods closed in on either side, and through the trees Vincent could see the man tailing him not half a dozen paces off. He knew there was going to be trouble, as sure as if he were back home and turning the corner he had suddenly spied the Pellegrino brothers waiting to beat on "the Quaker sissy."

The woods opened back out again, revealing the river off to their left. Ahead, just to the side of the road, Vincent could see a knot of horsemen, looking toward the black-bearded warrior who galloped up to join them.

Vincent watched the group warily as he marched past, and it felt as if all of them were gazing in his direction and talking darkly. The lone horseman broke away and trotted straight toward Vincent.

The horseman reined up, brushing his mount against the frightened private, forcing him to step back. A gruff laugh erupted from the other horsemen, who started to trot down toward their comrade. Suddenly it seemed as if dozens of mounted riders were streaming out of the treeline to join the knot of men moving toward the column.

Vincent pushed grimly forward, trying to conceal his trembling.

"Ty Ostanovis pered vashim nachal' stvom." (You there, stop for your betters,) the axman roared, cutting his horse directly in front of Vincent, who came to a stop and looked up at the towering form above him. Behind him the rest of the column cluttered to a halt.

"Care for a little hunting?" a gruff voice called.

For the first time since he joined the regiment, Vincent was glad to see Sergeant Schuder, who pushed to the front of the crowd. The horseman remained immovable, looking down at the men with disdain. Vincent could see that Keane, the color bearers, and the musicians had come to a halt. Keane sat motionless, Dr. Weiss by his side, neither one bothering to turn around and watch, as if such a display were beneath their dignity.

With a dramatic flourish, Schuder cocked his Sharps carbine and scanned the sky with such a determined expression that the bearded axman paused and looked up to the sky.

Several raucous crows passed overhead, cawing loudly. In one fluid motion Schuder snapped the weapon to his shoulder. The gun exploded.

End over end, a broken body tumbled from the sky to land on the side of the road, a dozen yards away. The black-bearded warrior gave a shout of terror, his horse rearing up wildly. For a second Vincent thought that both rider and mount would tumble over onto him. The warrior swung his mount around and galloped back to his comrades.

Schuder eyed him meditatively as he cocked his piece and slid in another round.

"Prettiest shot I ever made," Schuder mumbled, after spitting a stream of tobacco juice toward the discomforted warrior.

"All right, damn you, close up," Schuder roared. "We ain't got all day."

Kal came up to stand by Schuder's side.

"Mikhail your enemy," Kal whispered.

"Yeah, well, any time he wants," Schuder retorted, and fixing Mikhail with his gaze, he spat another stream of juice. Turning, he started back up the road.

"Thanks, sergeant," Vincent said as Schuder passed him.

Schuder turned and gazed at the private for a moment.

"You did well, lad," Schuder mumbled, and then, double-timing, he ran ahead to report to Keane, who throughout the affair had not once bothered to look back.

The horsemen gave the column a wide berth, but still continued to ride parallel. Vincent could not help but shoot a quick glance toward Mikhail, who glowered back darkly.

Vincent swallowed hard, and bracing his shoulders he doggedly marched on, joining in as Schuder called for another round of "Marching Through Georgia."

The trail continued to weave its way around low tree-clad hills and gloomy dales thick with the scent of pine, to rise up to pass through an open field that was covered shoulder-high with sunflowers in full bloom.

After yet another bend, the road curved sharply down again toward the river, running along the edge of a sharp ridge. Keane reined his mount in and paused.

Vincent breathed a sigh of relief. They'd been marching hard, and the sweat-soaked wool trousers of his uniform were chafing his legs raw. Perhaps Keane would give them a brief halt again.

The colonel urged his horse forward after a moment, and wearily Vincent stepped forward, but after a dozen paces he saw why the colonel had stopped.

It was something straight out of a fairy tale, and in spite of the discipline the men could not help but voice their amazement.

Kal, falling back through the ranks, pointed forward.

"Suzdal. Suzdal!"

The wooden walls of the city rested on a series of hills reaching down to the very edge of the river in a great arc that finally swung back up over the hills and away from view.

Great log structures three and four stories high crowded in one upon the other in what appeared to be a mad jumble. As the tiny column drew closer, Vincent could not help but exclaim over the wood carvings adorning all the buildings and walls.

Dragons carved out of entire logs and painted with every color of the rainbow twisted and swirled atop the battlements, wrestling with giant bears ten feet tall. Dwarflike creatures seemed to have popped out of the ground like toadstools, their wooden eyes gazing unblinkingly at the tiny column of blue. Other carved creatures like giant totems now lined the road, and Vincent had to suppress a shudder of fear. They stood eight to ten feet high. They appeared to be great hairy creatures, with open leering mouths and fangs that to Vincent's eyes almost seemed to be dripping with blood.

He noticed Kal gazing at the men closely, a sudden look of worry on his face. Something was bothering Kal. He managed to catch the man's gaze. The peasant, noticing him, broke into a smile and came up alongside.

"Suzdal beautiful," Vincent remarked, grinning broadly.

"Da, da, beautiful, yes," Kal responded eagerly.

Vincent looked at the man closely. The others might think him a dumb peasant, but Vincent sensed there was an intelligence to this man that no one had yet to pick up on.

A pealing of bells echoed out across the countryside, the most beautiful sound Vincent had ever heard. This was not the monotone tolling of the single bell in the Methodist church tower back in East Vassalboro. The bells here seemed to cover every note across several octaves, so that it seemed as if a virtual symphony filled the air.

As they approached the main gate of the city the barrier was thrown back, and before him Vincent saw a broad avenue that led into a square. The streets were lined with thousands, all of them silent.

As they crossed under the rounded stone gate, Vincent felt a moment of fear at the sight of the thousands waiting for them. But he quickly saw that his fear was a counterpoint to the fear of those awaiting him. The citizens of Suzdal, though eager to see the strangers, drew back at the approach of the column. Many lowered their gaze, raising their hands in symbols to ward off the evil eye. The column pushed forward into the broad open square several hundred yards across. Vincent looked with amazement at the single stone structure that dominated the center of the city. It was obviously a church of some sort, for the walls facing the square were covered with iconlike paintings that soared fifty feet or more up to the very eaves. To the left of the main door was a towering figure that appeared ghostlike, wrapped in black robes.

Vincent pointed at the figure and looked at Kal.

"Perm. Father God."

To the right of the door was another figure, this one in white with a golden beard. To Vincent's amazement a cross was behind the man.

"Jesus?" Vincent asked tentatively.

"Da, da, Kesus."

Surprised, Vincent looked around to his comrades, who had noticed the massive icon as well.

"Well, I'll be damned," Hinsen ventured, and the others looked at him with disdain. Somehow maybe they were on earth after all, Vincent thought hopefully.

To either side of the two were dark figures, looking

almost demonlike in visage, with long hairy bodies, pointed ears, slanted eyes, and sharp glistening teeth. They immediately reminded Vincent of the wooden statues lining the road. Gathered about their feet, smaller figures of men and women stood about them with heads lowered.

"And those?" Vincent asked tentatively.

Kal seemed to hesitate for a moment.

"What are they?" Vincent asked, somewhat more insistently.

Kal shook his head and then turned away.

What were they? Vincent wondered. He could see that the rotund peasant was fearful to speak further on the subject.

Could they be demons? Whatever they were, the images upon the church wall gazed upon them with lust-filled eyes, and he could see a fear in Kal as well at the mere sight of them.

The column crossed the open square. Several knights had pulled in front of Keane and were beckoning him to follow. A massive log structure faced the cathedral from the other side of the square, more ornately carved than any building Vincent had seen so far. A portly man wearing a flowing robe of burgundy came out of the building to stand atop the flight of wooden stairs. To his amazement, Vincent saw that the man was wearing glasses. The low murmur of the crowd in the square dropped away to a whisper, and by the thousands the Suzdalians bowed low, brushing the ground with their extended right hands.

"Company, halt!"

Schuder stepped out from the ranks.

"Company, attenshun! Present arms!"

Vincent snapped to attention and brought his weapon to the present.

The square was silent. Keane swung down from his mount, Dr. Weiss following his lead. Dusting himself off, Keane looked back at the ranks.

"Sergeant Schuder, detail twelve men with Sergeant Barry to go in with me. Unlimber the Napoleon and the rest to form square about it, at parade rest. You're in charge out here, Schuder. Handle any problem as you see fit."

Schuder looked at the men. "First three ranks, fall in behind the colonel, the rest form open square. Now step lively, men."

Vincent realized that he had been detailed to go forward.

"Shoulder arms," Sergeant Barry snapped, and with Vincent in the lead the twelve men stepped forward to come up behind Keane.

Without looking back, the colonel mounted the steps, his men falling in behind. Reaching the top of the steps, Keane drew up before Ivor, snapped to attention, and saluted.

"Colonel Keane of the 35th Maine," he said evenly, which Kal quickly translated.

Ivor looked at him appraisingly, putting on a show of bravado for the thousands in the square. With a snort of disdain he turned about and strode into the building. Sergeant Barry growled softly at the slight to their commander, but a quick look back from the colonel stilled any comment.

Following their commander, the escort marched into the broad dark halls.

Flanking either side of the entryway were two more images like the ones painted on the church wall.

Just what were they? Vincent wondered, for the mere sight of them gave him an uneasy feeling of dread.

Muzta, Qar Qarth of the Tugar horde, rode quietly through the night. This was the time he always loved the most, the gentle settling of the darkness, the march of the day completed. From seventy thousand yurts came the murmuring of his people, the laughter of the children, the voices of his warriors, the singsong chants of the shamans and legend speakers who wove the tales and memories of the Tugar people. Yet as he looked out across the horde he could also sense their fear.

Campfires were springing up, flickering flames to cast back the shadows dotting the steppe from horizon to horizon. Gaining a low crest, he paused for a moment, speaking softly to Bura, his old cherished mount. The horse snickered in reply. Bura had been given to him upon the day he was proclaimed Qar Qarth, King of Kings, ruler of all the clans of the Tugar realm.

"How long has it been, old friend?" he whispered softly.

Over a circling, at least. Curious with the thought, he let his mind drift backward. It was before the cattle city of Constan that his first father had passed. Constan was now four seasons passed yet again.

A hot place, Constan. The cattle there had gained in wealth, sailing their white vessels across the landlocked sea.

It was there as well he had fought his last battle, against the Merki horde, sending them reeling back, leaving the great northern steppes to the Tugar horde.

Now that had been a fight. Three days and nights, the great northern clan of two hundred thousand warriors, to face the half million of the south. Twenty blood clans against fifty, and he, Muzta, leading the final charge, with the great Qubata praising him afterward for his valor.

How they had slain before the inland sea, until the waters ran red with blood. What joy he had felt, the greatest moment of his life. His father dying as only a Tugar should die, leading his host in the great charge.

And since then? He had given his people a complete turning, a total circling of the world, in peace. They had ridden the great northern steppe completely around the world, and none had dared to poach upon their path.

"A quiet evening, is it not, my Qarth?"

Muzta turned and barked a soft laugh of greeting.

"Qubata, old comrade, don't tell me it is already time."

Qubata, first of all the generals of the Tugar horde, edged his mount up alongside his lord and bowed low in the saddle, an action which still caused embarrassment for Muzta.

He could remember sitting upon Qubata's knee, the warrior singing to him the chant of Hugala, how the legendary warrior had been first to ride about the world, proving that the great northern steppe was one.

Even then he was the first of the generals of the clan. But he was Qar Qarth, and so the ritual must be observed. To do otherwise meant death for the offender, for such was the law of the people.

Qubata remained silent, turning his head upward to observe the glowing splendor of the Great Wheel.

"The kuraltai awaits, my lord," Qubata whispered softly.

"Let them wait awhile longer," Muzta replied evenly.

"It is not good, my lord," Qubata prodded. "Tula is again speaking, and there are those who listen."

"I'll remember their names," Muzta replied, looking at his general with a cold smile. "I am still the Qarth."

"And Tula's clan is the strongest in our confederation, my lord."

"I know, curse him, I know."

He found himself half wishing that the Merki horde would return. That at least would divert them from this crisis and allow his people to vent their fear upon a common foe. That was an enemy to be understood, almost loved in a way. Sword could be matched against sword. Of the harvesting of cattle there was no joy for the warrior, only the taking of food. The enemy he faced now was beyond that type of understanding, and it filled him with a quiet dread.

He could not hide out here, for in his heart he knew that was what he was doing. Cursing softly, he kicked Bura into a gallop and started back for the heart of the camp.

As he passed through the encampment of his elite guard, shouts of warning ranged before him announcing the approach of the Qar Qarth. He crested a low hill, and the great yurt came into view. A hundred paces across, its barrel-thick center pole reached to the height of ten; from atop it the horsetail standard fluttered fitfully with the evening breeze. Bringing Bura up to the edge of the platform, Muzta leaped from his mount, and striding past the ceremonial fires of cleansing, he entered into where the clan heads awaited him.

"So, Tula," he said coldly, "I leave to think upon what was said and you fall back into your old position."

The assembly fell quiet. Muzta gazed about the room, fixing each in turn with his gaze. There was no reply.

"It is the right of the clan leaders to speak what is in their heart, my Qarth. Though you are appointed above us, still the Tugar people are free to speak."

Tula came to his feet, stretching his towering ten-foot frame. Rubbing the shaggy growth of coarse brown hair on his arms, he strode to the center of the tent to face Muzta.

The room was silent, expectant. Only a member of the golden clan could be the Qar Qarth, and thus Muzta's position could not be challenged. But it was the right of a clan leader to leave the Tugar horde if he so desired. Such an event could only mean one thing—a bitter civil war, for control of the northern steppe.

"And what is it that you wish to say?" Muzta said coldly.

"The snows of winter have passed, and we have come near to starving. You have decreed that the feeding must be of the old form—only those who spawned may be taken, and those of high birth are to be spared, except at the moon festivals.

"We starve, my Qarth, because of that."

"You think only of your belly for today," Muzta growled.

"If we did otherwise there would be no feeding when we had ridden about the world once again, for the cattle would be gone. We must leave the breeding stock to replenish the fields."

"But if there are no Tugars left because they starve, then what is the purpose? I say let us harvest all the cattle—let us worry about what we eat in the future when the future comes."

Muzta turned away with a snort of disdain.

"He is right, my Qarth." It was Suba, leader of the Merkat clan.

Muzta looked back over his shoulder. So you have turned too, he thought quietly.

"Before we always followed the dictates of our forefathers, who spread the cattle that came to us throughout the world," Suba said softly, rising up to stand by Tula. "We harvested the cattle that had spawned, and those who were not of prime stock. When we rode about the world and returned there would be another generation of food. But that was before the spotted sickness struck the cattle.

"For all we know, the spotted sickness might slay them all. It is a pestilence of fear, my lord. Since first we saw it at Constan, it has swept into a fire, slaying the cattle by the tens of thousands. And since they die, my lord, we starve."

"So slaughter them all, eat now, and then starve later, is that it?" Muzta barked.

"At least then we'll have a chance. We can worry about finding more cattle when we ride back this way again, or sweep into Merki lands and take their cattle."

"And if I say no?" Muzta said coldly.

The room was silent. If there was to be a breaking of the clan it would be now. He already had his plan, had formed it days ago, but he wanted to see what Tula and any of his followers would do.

"Do you want war, then?" Muzta said coldly, fixing each in turn with his gaze.

It was a delicate balance, and he spared a quick glance to Qubata, and could see the concern in the old warrior's eyes.

"If our confederation should break," Qubata said quietly, "know that word shall fly to the Merki horde. For remember what Jemugta, father of Muzta, taught us. If we are but single reeds, scattered to the winds, we shall each be broken, but together we are strength," and as he spoke he

pointed to the ceremonial bundle of reeds tied by Jemugta's
own hands and lashed to the center post.

"A starving bundle," Tula growled.

"But hear first what it is my lord wishes before you vote,"
Qubata interjected. And walking to the far side of the tent,
he pulled open the sacred scroll, the great map first forged
by Hugala.

"We are here, encamped east of Mempus," Qubata stated.
"Normally we pass at our leisure to where the cattle of
Ninva await us. It is the wish of Muzta that we not stop
there for the winter. Rather we shall march quickly, sparing
not our mounts, sweeping up to Maya by the end of the
season. From the western kingdom of the Maya we move
the following spring to their eastern realm of Tultac and
then winter the following year here."

And he stabbed at the map with his finger.

"The realm of the Rus."

"But that is four seasons' march in two," Tula retorted.

"Exactly," Qubata replied.

"Our old ones, our young, cannot make that," Suba
protested.

"They will have to. Perhaps in doing that we can outrace
this spotted sickness and feed to our fill once it is left
behind."

"And it will also place us two seasons' march ahead of the
Merki to the south," Muzta said softly, his features alighting
with a smile as he moved to Qubata's side. "If needs be we
can dip southward and grab something extra for our larders."

A number of chieftains smiled at that part of the plan.

The room was silent. He was asking for two tough seasons
ahead, four years' ride compressed into two. But if it suc-
ceeded they could feed, and yet still preserve the cattle of
the northern steppe for when next they rode through here
again in twenty seasons.

Muzta looked back at Tula, a smile still lighting his features. His rival was silent. So the trap had worked. He had
lured out a clan leader whom he had suspected of wishing to
break the confederation, and the information that Suba was
behind him was of even greater value. Jemugta had taught
him well how to ferret out possible challenges to the golden
clan of the Tugars.

"Is there even a need for a vote now?" Qubata said
evenly.

The old general watched the interplay. No one could refuse the plan, but he could see the silent rage in Tula and Suba as well. They would need to be watched.

A murmur of approval swept through the tent praising the wisdom of the Qar Qarth, and as Tula returned to his seat, those about him edged away.

Muzta smiled softly.

"Then let us feast!"

From out of the corner Alem, the soothsayer and chooser of cattle, rose up on spindly legs. The old Tugar went to the entry of the tent, which was swept open.

Smiling Alem led two cattle in chains into the tent.

"For the approval of my lords," Alem said softly. There were barks of delight from the assembly. These were prime cattle, not yet of breeding age and obviously of the highest caste.

"Their livers shall be baked in wine sauce," Alem announced. "Crust had already been rolled for the kidney pies, and as a special treat we shall cook their brains inside their skulls."

Alem looked back at his trembling meal and poked them tentatively with his long sharp finger.

The two clung to each other, terror in their eyes.

Muzta surveyed them with disdain.

"Drain their blood well—I want some soup with my meal," Muzta said softly.

Alem with a gleam in his eyes beckoned for the guards to drag the two humans out to the slaughter pit.

At least we shall eat well for tonight, Muzta thought to himself.

Munching absently on the cracked marrow from a cattle bone, he considered the Rus people in their wooden cities and felt a thrill of anticipation. He was partial to their meat, far better than the cattle they would pass by in reaching there. They seemed to have a finer grain to their flesh. With a smile he settled down upon his throne as servants brought in cuts of roasted cattle limbs for an opening snack while the high piercing shrieks of the main course, about to be slaughtered, rent the air.

Chapter 4

Attempting to suppress a yawn, Andrew looked about the room. It had been a night without sleep, compounded now by a hangover that made his temples feel as if they were about to explode.

He had expected that there would be a simple straightforward meeting with Ivor, an agreement struck, and then a return back to the encampment. That was mistake number one.

A grand feast had to be presented first. The meal had not been all that bad—most anything was better than the food at the regimental mess—but it had dragged on for hours, so that he felt as if he were being subjected to an endurance test.

The meal had started with baked fish and eels, then progressed to cuts of pork, roast mutton, and what looked like pheasant. But that was only for starters. With great pageantry and fanfare an entire roasted bear was paraded into the feasting hall, still wrapped in its fur, its grimacing head mounted atop the carcass on a silver pole. That had been a hard one to take, for he had always felt a soft spot for bears, and though raised in the woods of Maine had never found it in his heart to hunt for bear or any other creature.

There had been an underlying level of tension throughout, the fifty-odd nobles about the table eyeing him with outright suspicion, while Kal with his limited ability attempted to explain what was being said.

But the second mistake had been their vodka. Drink after drink was raised, which Kal insisted he must reply to as well, or the nobles would not think him a man.

Somehow he wished he could have put Schuder in his place. The old sergeant would have drunk all of them under

81

the table. He was finally reduced to simply sipping as each toast was raised, and the nobles openly chuckled at his distress.

Emil, however, had pulled it all off in grand style, matching them glass for glass, finally raising a number of toasts himself until the assembly had collapsed into drunken squalor.

Now if only the good doctor could give him a miracle cure for this damned hangover, he thought glumly as he stood up and stretched.

Emil at least could sleep, and he looked across to his friend sprawled out on the cot opposite him. But the luxury of sleep was something he would not allow himself. All of this could still be a trap. He had insisted that Schuder and the men be moved into the courtyard outside his window, where throughout the night the men had stood at arms, half of them asleep, the other half awake. For himself he had sat things out till dawn, revolver in hand.

It could be possible that Ivor was waiting for a lowering of his guard. But even more than Ivor it was the black-bearded warrior Mikhail and the one Kal said was the priest Rasnar, who had briefly appeared at the feast, that worried him the most. Perhaps he could work out something with the boyar, but there were other pieces on the board as well that would have to be played against if they were going to survive here.

A low groan echoed out from under the pile of blankets in the corner.

"My hand to God, I'll never drink again."

A sallow face appeared, bloodshot eyes blinking in what appeared to be a vain attempt at focusing.

"Where the hell are we?" Emil gasped, swinging his legs from the pallet. With a moan he tried to stand up, and then collapsed again, cradling his head in his hands.

"Where are we?" Andrew laughed, shaking his head. "Damned if I know."

"Oh yes, that," Emil replied. He smacked his lips, giving a grimace of disgust at the foul taste in his mouth. Groaning, he made a second attempt at standing, barely succeeding.

Emil fumbled around for his glasses, put them on, and looked about the room.

"If these people aren't descendants of medieval Russians, then I'm a blind man," Emil said, speaking as if every word emitted were a source of pain. "Look at that city out there," and he pointed out the window to the splendor of Suzdal now awash with the golden light of dawn.

Groaning, Emil walked over to the window, and Andrew stood up to join him.

"When I traveled in Russia to visit my family I saw places like this. And that damned drinking ritual, that's Russian, believe me. One good thing, though—wherever we are it's not the Russia of earth. Just curious, I drew a star of David for Kal, and didn't get the slightest response. So my people aren't here, and thus that good old Russian pastime of pogroms isn't one of their hobbies.

"Before I did that I'd been thinking a wild one that somehow we've crossed time, but that's definitely not the case."

"It's not earth," Andrew replied, "yet these people here seem to be from earth. So we still have a mystery."

The two friends paused for a moment, turning their attention to the view out the window. The palace was situated on the highest hill of the city, so all of Suzdal was stretched out before them. All the structures, except for the limestone churches, were built of logs. But these were not the rough cabins Andrew was used to seeing in the backwoods of Maine. Most of the buildings were three, even four or five stories in height. The entire city seemed to be a wood carver's fantasy, the creative talents of the people let loose in elaborate carvings that adorned even the most modest of structures.

Dragons appeared to be leaping from rooftops, angels looked heavenward, bears cavorted, cornices were intertwinings of warriors in battle, and dwarfs stood as guards before doorways. The buildings were not just the dark color of aged wood, but instead were painted with swirling displays of flowers, trees, geometric patterns, and symbols of various trades, all in a riot of color to make a rainbow look dull by comparison.

Already the streets were aswarm with early risers. Merchants were pulling back the shutters to their shops, some of them already crying out with singsong voices, beckoning for customers to examine their wares. A wreath of smoke hung over the city from thousands of cooking fires, and the savory scent of cooking drifted on the morning breeze.

The air hummed with the voices of tradesmen, shoppers, and laughing children. From the church came the distant sound of a rich and wonderful plainchant, heavy with basses and offset by the high notes of tenors, all of which was counterpointed by the pealing of the multitoned church bells that seemed to give the air a crystalline lightness.

Down by the river the wharves were bustling with activity. The ships lining the shore and dotting the river were a pure delight to the historian in Andrew. They looked like clinker-built long boats straight out of the Viking age. The vessels were somewhat heavier and beamier than the graceful long boats of old, with high sweeping bows and sternposts, the sides of which were adorned with red and blue paint, drawn yet again in the delightful patterns so prevalent in the city. Many of the vessels were adorned with dragon heads, and he could not help but smile at the sight of them, remembering his childhood fantasies of Viking explorers sailing through the misty seas of Maine.

"Quite a trade system they have, for that many vessels," Andrew said softly. "Must be a number of cities on this river and out across the sea where we wrecked."

"I heard several mentions of a place called Novrod," Emil replied.

"Novrod," Andrew said softly, and his features brightened. "Damn me, Novgorod! It was a major trade city of early medieval Russia. One of their most famous princes, Alexander Nevsky, ruled that city during the Mongol invasion."

Emil's advice from earlier came back to him. Let others worry about where they were now, even though the curiosity of it all was at times near overwhelming.

"Sergeant Schuder, everything in order?" Andrew asked, leaning out of the window.

Turning from the task of chewing out a private, Schuder strolled over and saluted.

"Still quiet, sir, but some of the men are grumbling because they aren't allowed to eat the food here and are stuck with hardtack and salt pork."

"Can't be helped," Emil replied, loud enough so that the men could hear. "Until we're sure of these people, a little poisoning could eliminate us rather easily."

And besides, Emil thought to himself, grimacing with the memory of last night's meal, the way they serve their food was enough to turn his stomach. He'd given up kosher when he'd come to America, but that was the least of his worries now. The wooden troughs the meals were served in were caked with an accumulation of grease that nauseated him. Sanitary conditions around here were positively medieval, just like the rest of the city, and they could get poisoned anyhow, even if it was unintentional. The hypochondriac in him was already exploring inwardly, wondering when the first effects of that bear meat would hit.

As he looked at the city he shuddered inwardly. He could see people drawing water from the river, even as sailors emptied slop buckets over the sides of their vessels not a dozen feet away. The place had a fetid smell of unwashed bodies, raw sewage, and filth that had most likely been accumulating for generations. Even as he looked across the square he saw a rat scurry out from an alleyway, followed an instant later by several ragged children waving sticks.

An upper window opened on a building across from the palace and a cascade of liquid poured out, its nature all too obvious. He could barely suppress a retch at the sight of it.

Many of the people he watched passing by seemed ill-nourished, with pasty complexions, the poorer folk dressed in little more than rags. The mere contemplation of trying to help solve all the problems of sanitation, nourishment, and health left him feeling helpless. Undoubtedly their surgeons still cut and slashed on victims tied to the table, probing with filthy hands and gore-encrusted instruments. They'd most likely hang him for even trying to suggest any change, for undoubtedly any new ideas would be regarded as witchcraft.

"It looks strangely beautiful," Andrew whispered, looking back at Emil.

Before the doctor could reply, a knock on the door interrupted them. Andrew nodded to the doctor, who went over and unbolted the latch.

It was Kal.

"Sleep well, yes?" the peasant asked, stepping into the room with a bright cheery smile.

Andrew nodded in reply. Kal looked closely at Emil, and his broad peasant features crinkled up, his eyes showing the merriment that a drinker feels at the sight of a hungover comrade.

With exaggerated gestures Kal placed his hands to his temples and groaned.

"Shut the hell up," Emil snapped, turning away.

Kal stepped back through the door, beckoned, and then reentered the room. Behind him a young girl of sixteen or seventeen stepped into the room carrying a tray laden with cups and a steaming pot-of tea. She was dressed in a simple peasant dress of white, embroidered around the high collar and hem with blue thread. The dress was bound tightly at the waist, showing off a slim girlish figure. Her strawberry-blond hair peeked out from under a plain white scarf. Smiling nervously, she stepped into the room, her eyes the same pale blue as Kal's, her high cheekbones, full lips, and smiling features so identical to Kal's that Andrew realized immediately that it was the translator's daughter.

Smiling, Andrew gave a bow of acknowledgment that caused the girl to blush and lower her eyes.

Andrew pointed to Kal, still smiling, and then to the young girl.

"Daughter?"

"Da, uh, yes, Cane. Daughter, Tanya."

Emil stepped forward and bowed formally as well, to Kal's evident delight and Tanya's confused embarrassment. Coming back up, his face contorted in a grimace, he groaned and rubbed his temples.

With a conspiratorial wink Kal patted Emil on the shoulder. Reaching into his tunic, he pulled out a ceramic flask, uncorked it, and poured some of the contents into one of the cups of tea.

"Hair of the dog, is it?" Emil said, taking the cup. Sipping the scalding hot drink, Emil mumbled to himself and then quickly drained off the cup.

Kal watched him expectantly. Suddenly the doctor's features started to lighten.

"Well, I'll be damned," Emil exclaimed. "There was a touch of the juice in that, to be sure, but there was something else as well, and by heavens it's cleared the cobwebs away."

Andrew tried a cup, and to his amazement the slightly minty drink worked the same effect, and within minutes he felt refreshed.

"Look better," Kal said, still grinning, "See Ivor, talk peace now."

"Let's get this over with," Andrew replied. "We've been away from the regiment too long already. I want to get back today—otherwise Pat might bring all the boys up here thundering for our release."

Buckling on his sword, with Kal's help, Andrew went over to the window.

"Sergeant Schuder, we're going in for the meeting now."

"Be careful, sir," Hans said, lowering his voice. "If it starts to look like trouble, just fire off a shot, and the boys and I will be in after you."

"We'll be all right, Hans."

This was a different type of combat, and he could see that Hans was uneasy about it, wishing to be alongside his colonel, carbine ready, rather than standing outside worrying.

"Nothing but a little bluff work now, Hans. The weapons have them half scared already. Just relax and I'll be out shortly."

"Take care, colonel," Hans said, and to Andrew's surprise the sergeant reached up and patted him lightly on the arm.

Andrew could not help but smile at this momentary break with formality, something he had not seen since Hans found him in the hospital at Gettysburg and the old soldier had burst into tears at the sight of him.

"All right, Kal, let's get this over with."

He bowed again to Tanya, and as he did so he could not help but notice the beauty of the girl, and the proud look of her father that Andrew had shown such formality to one of his class.

"They're in there meeting with him right now," Mikhail said coldly, the disgust in his voice obvious.

"Ah, my son, so that disturbs you."

"It is an evil," Mikhail replied, looking straight into the prelate's eyes.

"But of course," and as he spoke Rasnar beckoned to his personal secretary to pour some tea.

"Well done, Casmar," Rasnar said, waving for the priest to withdraw.

"It is good to know that there are loyal members to the holy church such as yourself, Mikhail," and as he spoke he made a sign of blessing over the bearlike warrior and beckoned for him to take a seat.

"It is good you came and talked to me over these last several days," Rasnar continued smoothly, sitting down beside Mikhail. "I can see why you are distressed by this foolish decision of your brother to make a peaceful agreement with the blue devils."

"There are others who feel as I," Mikhail growled. "My brother is a madman. Even if the devils are humans, they are foreigners, and thus suspect. They even make the holy sign of blessing backward and thus mock you and our holy church, yet still Ivor will deal with them."

"Abomination," Rasnar replied smoothly.

"Since Ivor received that demonic gift to cure his weak eyes he has been bewitched by them."

"Perhaps he has been driven mad by the gift," Rasnar said softly.

Rasnar fixed the warrior with his gaze. Of course, he knew that each of them was playing a game with the other. As an illegitimate brother to Ivor, Mikhail had no direct hope to the throne of the arch boyar—as long as his brother lived, that is. And of course the appearances in his chambers over the last several days were an open bid for support.

"You realize," Rasnar said quietly, "that I have often wished that things had been somewhat different."

"And how is that?" Mikhail asked cautiously.

"Just that I have always wished that your father had brought your mother to the altar rather than Ivor's," the prelate said evenly.

"My brother should be the bastard," Mikhail growled darkly. "That fat damned weak-eyed fool. I should be the boyar of Suzdal, dammit—I should be the one!" As he spoke he pounded the table with his fists.

"Exactly as I've often thought and wished," Rasnar replied.

And of course you would be far more pliable, the priest thought, still smiling in an understanding way.

"You know, of course," Rasnar said, "that holy church would view a change with the utmost understanding and would speak well of it from the pulpit. If the bluecoat leader should fall, I daresay his fellow demons would quickly be defeated, then their weapons would be properly stored away in the hands of the church where they rightfully belong."

Mikhail looked darkly at Rasnar.

"But the church would be willing to give several such devices to its most loyal servants," Rasnar added dryly, and Mikhail smiled.

"It is time for my morning prayers," and the tone of his

voice was one of dismissal. "But know, my friend, that your loyalty to holy church will bring you blessings."

With a bow Mikhail turned and started for the door.

"I will remember your name in my mass this morning, but act quickly, my friend, for such a chance to have their leader away from protection might not come again," Rasnar said, and the warrior turned, looking back at the prelate with a crafty smile.

The door closed, Rasnar could not help but chuckle. So the brother was willing to knife brother over this issue. He had none of the guile of Ivor. Most likely his pride had been wounded by the encounter on the road and the incident over the glasses, and now it could only be salvaged through destruction. He had planted the suggestion of Mikhail being the translator, but that damned peasant had ruined that idea as well. Mikhail never was one to understand diplomacy; he could well imagine what he and his confederates were planning to do at this very moment.

The father of Mikhail and Ivor had led the boyars revolt against the church power, stripping its direct right to the tithe of the peasants and declaring that the boyar of Suzdal was the supreme ruler of the church.

It was time to wrestle that control back, and perhaps the bluecoats could be the catalyst. Mikhail would be most pliable indeed, and when there was no longer a need an accident could be arranged and then the church would rule and nobles would answer, as it had once been.

"Casmar!"

The door opened and the young priest entered, bowing low.

"Order up a mount and courier. I might have orders to go out to the prelates of the other cities within the hour."

"I want them to swear full allegiance to me alone," Ivor said evenly, "to serve as my guard in time of war, to enforce my rules in time of peace. Tell them that."

Kal turned away from his lord and looked across at Andrew.

"Ivor says, peace between you and him. You help him and he help you in return."

Andrew nodded sagely, putting on a display of profound thinking. In spite of the rifles and artillery he knew the Suzdalians had the advantage. If need be they could simply starve them out, or just swarm over them, using their thousands of peasants in wave attacks. They needed time to repair the ship and gain their bearings. If at a later date things got too uncomfortable, they could always pack up and leave for some other place. He had to come to some sort of an agreement, even if it meant serving this nobleman for now.

"It sounds as if it might be acceptable, but there must be guarantees."

Kal looked back at Ivor.

"He begs to accept."

Ivor grunted an assertion.

Andrew leaned over to Emil, and regardless of the issue of politeness he started to whisper.

"Do you somehow sense this Kal isn't quite translating straight?"

"Son, he's had only six days to learn what he has—don't push the man."

"Still," Andrew said, "I think that peasant is smarter than the entire lot of them, maybe sharper than all of us as well. I wouldn't be surprised if for every word he acknowledges knowing he's picked up ten on the side."

"What is it that those two are whispering about?" Ivor asked, looking at his two guests with a jaundiced eye.

"My lord wishes to know if you will accept his offer as stated," Kal said, looking back at Andrew.

Andrew sat silent, fixing Ivor with his gaze.

"We shall want our own land, on the river, between the sea and this city. If we wish to leave, we must be free to do so."

Kal listened carefully to what was being said. He thought he understood correctly the part about the land. How was he going to get past this one? So far he'd played it off successfully, letting each side hear what he wanted, speaking in a gray area and making each think that the other was eager for an understanding.

But the land issue would be tough. No one demanded land of a boyar, it was given. He knew as well that the bluecoats wished to stay together and to live alone while Ivor wanted them separated and scattered.

Kal looked over at Ivor.

"They are eager to be your vassals."

He hoped that Ivor would make some concession for that.

"Then tell them that they will be broken into small groups and assigned to serve under my border watchers."

Kal gulped, for there was no way he could get around this arrangement.

In the background, Kal heard a muffled shout, and the unmistakable sound of steel striking steel.

Ivor, ever the warrior, reacted in an instant. Kicking back from the table, he swung out his two-handed sword and raced for the door.

Barely had he reached it when the low rounded portal smashed in on its hinges. Kal, knowing what was coming, dived under the table and scurried for the far corner of the room.

Dance with the wolves and get bitten if the music stops, he thought ruefully.

"Mikhail, you bastard!" Ivor roared.

Ivor fought desperately to hold the door but gave back before the crush. As Mikhail cleared the doorway, swinging his two-handed ax low, other warriors piled in after him.

There was a thunderous explosion. Startled, Kal looked up to see Andrew holding a short metal tube, with smoke powering out.

There was a moment of stunned silence as all turned to face Andrew. The man next to Mikhail crumpled to the ground, blood pouring from his mouth.

"Those who die killing demons go to paradise," Mikhail roared.

With a wild shout his cohorts poured into the room after him.

"Ivor, to me!" Andrew shouted. The boyar, still trading blows with his brother, looked back to the bluecoat. Realizing that he was about to be surrounded by men pressing in to either side, Ivor broke off and rushed back to the far corner of the room, where Andrew and Emil stood back to back.

There was another roar, and another, and two more warriors were pitched to the ground, the one next to Mikhail spraying those about him with a shower of blood and brains.

"Emil, take the gun!" And tossing the revolver to the doctor, Andrew unsheathed his blade and pressed up to Ivor's side. A warrior, nerving himself, rushed in on Andrew, battle-ax raised high. Turning, Andrew jumped aside, and with raised point drove his weapons into his opponent's throat. The pistol barked again, knocking another man over.

"Two rounds! Hold them!" Andrew shouted.

"For what, damn it?" Emil cried, and the pistol barked again, bowling over a man coming straight at him with lowered spear.

Screaming with rage, Ivor cut at his brother, who warily kept to the side of the room, putting Emil between himself and his attacker.

The pistol exploded again, bowling over a man who had leaped atop the table with a crossbow. The weapon snapped off as he pitched over, driving the dart into the ceiling.

"Goddammit!" Emil roared, hurling the now empty revolver at the next warrior approaching him. The warrior went down, a chair shattering across his back. Kal stood up, holding the broken back of the chair, and reached down and scooped up the empty revolver.

Closing his eyes, he squeezed the trigger as another warrior closed in. The weapon clicked on an empty chamber, but the warrior it was pointed at stopped dead in his tracks anyhow, his face pale with fear.

"The magic is gone!" Mikhail shouted. "Finish them!"

There was a moment of silence as if both sides were somehow taking measure of the other. Warily, another warrior closed in on Andrew, who, not waiting for the attack, leaped forward, catching the man in the face, driving his blade through bone and muscle. His victim fell back, screaming.

Suddenly there was an echo of gunfire from out in the hallway.

"Hans, in here!" Andrew roared.

A volley of musketry tore down the hallway. There was a wild explosion of action as the warriors still pressing into the room turned to face their new foe.

"Present, fire!" Another volley echoed out, and the attackers, with wild shouts of panic, broke and poured out of the room. Mikhail, shouting with rage, made one last blow toward Ivor and, turning, fled from the room, Ivor storming after him.

Andrew, running after the boyar, slammed him up against the wall.

"My men will shoot you!" Andrew screamed.

Ivor, his face contorted with rage, started to turn on Andrew, but Kal rushed forward, shouting an explanation.

"Colonel!"

"In here, Hans."

Pointing his carbine at chest level, Hans pushed his way into the room. When he saw Andrew a slight smile crossed his lips.

"A little fun in here, I see," he said grimly, poking one of the bodies with the toe of his boot.

Hans stuck his head back out the door.

"Well done, boys. Let the others chase the dogs down." He came back into the room.

Andrew patted the sergeant on the shoulder.

"Saw about thirty of these heathens stroll into the palace looking rather grim, so I thought it'd be best for me and some of the boys to kind of follow behind just to make sure everything was all right," Hans said softly, looking about the smoke-filled room.

The palace was now in an uproar as Ivor's guards, rousing themselves at last, came pouring into the corridor.

Kal came up to stand by Andrew's side. Nervously he extended the pistol, handle first.

Smiling, Andrew took the weapon and holstered it, and then looked over to Ivor. Andrew could not help but notice the shocked look in Ivor's eyes at the sight of Kal holding the weapon.

"Kal."

"Yes, Cane."

"Tell your Ivor we want land, and a place to live, or we'll take our services elsewhere," Andrew said quietly.

"And Kal, make sure you translate correctly," he added, smiling.

The peasant forced a weak smile and turning to Ivor started to speak rapidly.

"From the looks of things," Andrew said evenly, looking back over to Emil, "he's going to need us as much as we need him."

Chapter 5

"Here it comes, colonel!"

Smiling at Private Hawthorne's excitement, Andrew stepped out of his cabin and started down toward the river, keeping a stately pace, his new orderly, barely able to contain his schoolboy enthusiasm, walking beside him. He could feel the excitement of the moment as well, but dignity demanded that he show an outward calm. As he walked through the encampment he felt a quiet sense of pride at all that had been accomplished.

It had been four weeks since the fateful meeting with Ivor. Mikhail, in his attempt to kill Ivor, if anything guaranteed the existence of the regiment, for at least the time being. Andrew had left the palace with a grant of land, which they might choose, along with a steady supply of food, in return for protection against Mikhail, who had fled to Novrod, where Boyar Boros had offered him protection.

With O'Donald and Emil they had picked their site out with care. Emil had insisted that a fresh stream, emitting from a spring, was essential for their water. O'Donald wanted a clear field of fire for the artillery, Tobias a deep anchorage for the *Ogunquit*. Then there was the question of wood supply for the cabins, and firewood. They had to be close enough to Suzdal for trade, but far enough away so that if Ivor plotted a move against them there'd be enough warning.

It had taken several long hard days of riding back and forth across the countryside to pick the site, which in the end was the place where they had paused for a rest on that first march toward the city. Andrew looked about him and smiled inwardly. He had selected well.

Fort Lincoln, as they had named their new home, was positioned on a low bluff looking out over the Neiper River. They had laid out a square perimeter a hundred and fifty yards on a side. The men, who had practiced such work for survival before Petersburg, had set to the digging with a will. A ditch fifteen feet across and eight feet deep had been excavated the length of the perimeter, the earth piled up to form a parapet topped with sentry posts. Firing platforms for the infantry, which were flanked on the four corners by massive salients for artillery, were set so that all approaches could be swept by a deadly hail of fire.

Singling out the men who had been lumberjacks back in Maine, he had sent them into the high stands of pines to start harvesting the thousands of logs needed for the town, while the rest of the men started in with the digging.

Once the fortification was completed the men had turned their attention to living quarters, using the stacks of logs that had been snaked down from the woods above the new town. Company streets were laid out in the standard checkerboard pattern. As if looking for a sense of home in a foreign land the men insisted that there be a town square, a request which Andrew readily agreed to.

The Presbyterians in the company had already erected a small log church on the north side of the square, while the Methodists under Captain Bob Fletcher of Company B were already talking of building a sawmill so they could build a proper clapboard church on some ground staked out to the south of the square.

Andrew had designated the east side of the square as the living area for officers, staff, Kal and his family, and Miss O'Reilly and for the infirmary. Her cabin had been one of the first to go up, and the men of Fletcher's company, who had volunteered to build it, had lavished the simple structure with loving detail, managing to somehow trade for some panes of glass so she could have a real window. Kal's wife, Ludmilla, was soon a regular guest there, and curtains had been added to the window, with a plot of transplanted flowers lining the snake rail fence the men had put up around her new home.

Across the square on the west side, volunteers were already laying out the foundation for a regular town meeting hall, to go up alongside the planned armory, their efforts yet another attempt to recreate home in this strange and distant land.

Almost all the soldiers' cabins had been finished, and homey touches were starting to crop up. Street signs had come first, with all the old traditional names—Maple, Oak, Church, and Main. The martial names were there as well, Grant, Sherman, Antietam, and for the main north-south thoroughfare the honored name of Gettysburg, where the regiment had known its finest hour.

In the free time Andrew granted after a day of labor on fortifications, cutting lumber, and the myriad of tasks needed to settle in, the men had started to show their creative skills.

Several had turned their attention to woodcarving, as if inspired by the Suzdalians' exotic carvings. American eagles were popular as adornments over the doors of the small soldiers' huts, as were carvings of women, ships, and even a map of Maine.

Nearly every day a delegation of men came to Andrew looking for his approval for a project. To his delight, Jacobsen and Gates, both from Company C, had come to him only that morning. Jacobsen pointed out that he knew how to make paper, while Gates suggested that he might be able to carve out a set of type and thus start a newspaper. Andrew readily gave both of them permission to try their hand at it and exempted them from all duties except the daily drill.

Outside Fort Lincoln, another town had started to spring up as well. Unlike the encampment, this was a haphazard affair that Andrew was coming to realize was the typical approach of the Suzdalians.

Merchants had quickly set up shops, first under nothing more than tattered awnings, which over the weeks were converted into rough-hewn cabins. Now there were several hundred living in the informal village, their shops and homes lining the path which had been cut up to the main road to Suzdal.

Fortunately for the regiment, the rate of exchange was excellent. Most of the men had some coins on them, or greenbacks, which the Suzdalians honored with enthusiasm, if for no other reason than their value as ornaments and curiosities coming from the hands of the men who were now known as Yankees.

Gold and silver were already part of the Suzdalian economy, and a man lucky enough to have a handful of silver dollars or a gold twenty-dollar piece was considered to be fabulously wealthy. Beyond money, most anything the men owned was highly sought after. An issue of *Harper's Illustrated Weekly* had almost triggered a riot when a private had pulled it out of his haversack and offered it in trade for a bearskin. With that revelation the men had taken of late to cutting out pictures and even the newsprint for trade.

Andrew had been forced almost immediately to issue the strictest of orders against any trade involving powder, bullets, even the percussion caps for the muskets, which the Suzdalians looked upon with superstitious wonder.

The issue of powder had really worried him, since several merchants had appeared one night, offering significant sums in gold for nothing but a single cartridge. Fortunately they had approached Sergeant Barry, who had spurned the offer and reported the incident. Knowing that the mystery of powder was important to their survival, he had paraded the entire regiment immediately and placed down a law that any man caught in such a trade would receive six months in the yet-to-be-constructed guardhouse for such an action.

Fortunately the men had taken the warning to heart, knowing it was in their best interest. But as an additional precaution all men were to turn in their loose rounds and were issued two ten-round sealed packages for immediate use, which were to be checked daily by their company officers.

He had attempted to place injunctions against another form of trade as well, especially after seeing a woman sauntering outside the north gate wearing an infantryman's kepi hat.

Emil had dragged the entire regiment out on parade that night and given them a bone-chilling lecture about what might be caught, spiced with dire warnings about the ultimate effects. Andrew knew that it was useless. Several men in the regiment were down with a social disease and still under treatment with mercury by Emil. He had called them in for a special talk and made it quite clear that if a single Suzdalian contracted anything he'd have them whipped about the camp and would consider turning them over to Ivor for justice. The threat was empty in that respect, but the last thing they needed was to start an epidemic which could be traced directly back to the regiment in short order.

Emil had already been in a boil about that and disease in general, so horrified was he by the medieval conditions of the Suzdalians. Nothing had happned yet, and he could only hope that Emil's precautions would spare them.

The water coming down from the hill and running near

the north wall was crystalline pure. At Emil's insistent demands the Suzdalians who had set up camp outside the gate were forbidden to wash in the stream, and only to draw water where the rest of the regiment drew theirs.

Emil had run around frantic in the first couple of weeks, personally overseeing the location of the regimental sinks, shouting about proper sanitation, inspecting the men for lice, and demanding weekly baths in the Neiper River. The men bore his orders with good-natured grumbling, having realized after two years' experience that somehow this physician's requirements had spared them the dreadful disease rate of the rest of the Union Army.

So far the men had been as healthy as any regiment could expect to be. One man had died, injured when a falling tree had backlashed, crushing him to the ground.

He was the first to rest on what they now called Cemetery Hill, and Andrew had noticed the impact it had on the Suzdalians to see that a Yankee could bleed and die the same way they could. It seemed that after his death the Suzdalians who came to gaze at the camp were not so filled with superstitious fear.

A high-pitched shriek rent the air and roused Andrew from his thoughts. Falling in with the other soldiers rushing by, he climbed the riverside parapet and looked out over the flowing Neiper.

From around the bend in the river the *Ogunquit* was now in view. The ship moved briskly against the current, smoke pouring from its single stack.

Hundreds of Suzdalians lined the riverbank shouting with wonder at the sight of a ship moving against the current, without oars, its masts bare-poled.

Kal, wide-eyed with wonder, came up to Emil.

"How do you do this?" he exclaimed.

"Ah, it's not magic, my friend, just a machine, like the other machines I told you about."

"You Yankees and your machines," Kal mumbled in awe.

A jet of steam escaped from the ship, and a second later the sound of the high-pitched whistle echoed past the camp yet again.

"Go ahead, my lads, give 'em a salute!" O'Donald roared, and in response to his command one of the Napoleons on the encampment wall kicked back with a thunderous roar that mingled with the triumphant shouts of the men from the 35th.

"Tobias will be insufferable now," Emil said, coming up to Andrew's side.

Tobias had argued vehemently in favor of locating the camp right where the ship had come to rest, but even he was finally forced to admit that the site Andrew had selected for their encampment was far more hospitable than the wind-swept dunes that had been their first landfall in this new world.

Anything that could be moved had first been stripped from the vessel. Tons of equipment for the North Carolina campaign had been stored belowdecks, and as the ship's manifest had been brought ashore Andrew found himself breathing an inner sigh of relief.

There were rations enough for six months, along with half a million rounds of rifle ammunition and two thousand rounds for the field pieces. There were thousands of yards of rope, hundreds of uniforms and shoes, lamps, coal oil, tents, shovels, picks, axes, medicine, including ether, and the myriad personal effects of six hundred men and one woman.

With all the burden removed, cables had been run to shore, the ship had finally been keeled over, and the gaping hole near the bow repaired.

Next came the hard part, refloating the ship. Cables were run out through the bow and anchored firmly in deeper water. First the men had tried to pull her off by hooking the cables to the capstan, but even with sixty men on the bar the ship refused to budge.

Finally it had turned into a massive engineering project under Tobias's direction. Pilings were sunk a hundred yards forward of the ship. Once a secure foundation was laid, a massive vertical windlass was secured on shore.

On the appointed day, nearly the entire regiment turned out. Several cables were run out from the ship to the heavy blocks attached to the pilings and then back to shore. Straining at the bars, joined by the half-dozen surviving mounts and a dozen horses loaned by Ivor, the men had set to. For several long minutes the hundreds of men had strained at the bars, cursing and swearing as the ship seemed glued to the sandbar. Then with an audible slurping groan the vessel popped free, sending the entire regiment sprawling to the ground even as they cheered lustily.

It had taken several days to reload the vessel from shore, and then finally after weeks of silence the boilers of the *Ogunquit* were fired up, while hundreds of Suzdalians had stood in awed silence to watch yet another miracle of the Yankees.

"Of course, he's going to want to go gallivanting all over now that the ship's working," Emil said, leaning against the parapet.

"Fine with me," Andrew said evenly. "Perhaps it'll keep that man busy for a while. Still thinks he can find a way back home, I bet."

And shaking his head, Andrew started down to the dock, Emil, Hans, and Kal in tow.

The *Ogunquit* was coming down hard and fast, the pilot showing his exultation by repeated blasts on the whistle.

Coming abreast of the fort, Tobias swung the transport in toward shore so that it appeared at first as if he would slam straight into the rough dock that had been laid out into the river.

At what appeared to be the very last second the bow of the vessel came about, and the anchor chains rattled free with a roar. Ever so easily the *Ogunquit* swung about into the current, coming to rest alongside the dock.

"Hans, I think the boys deserve a celebration," Andrew said, smiling.

"Just 'cause that sailor got his ship back, sir?"

"In part, but you're forgetting the date as well."

Curious, Hans looked over at Andrew.

"Namesake of the fort," he said with a smile. "Today's our President's birthday."

With glass raised, Houston, the youngest officer in the regiment, came to his feet.

"Ladies and gentlemen, a toast." As one the company came to their feet. "To the President of the United States, Abraham Lincoln, on this his fifty-sixth birthday. May he have good health, a long life, and four more years with a nation at peace."

"Abraham Lincoln," and the glasses were drained while the single fifer played "Hail to the Chief."

Smiling, Andrew nodded for the glasses to be refilled. It was no longer the traditional brandy, what little that was left was being held in reserve by Emil. But Kal had managed to procure a small barrel of vodka of the most potent variety for the occasion.

"Ladies and gentlemen, the Union. Wherever it is, may it endure forever."

There was a moment of silence, for such a toast could only invoke painful memories of home.

"The Union," and quietly the glasses were drained.

The mess settled back in their rough-hewn chairs.

"Gentlemen, I might regret this," O'Donald said evenly, and reaching into his haversack he produced a small box and opened it.

There was a gasp of delight from around the table.

"Havana cigars, the finest, and maybe the last for this blessed group. Pass 'em around and enjoy them while you can. I've been a Republican since I stepped foot off the boat in '56, and Lincoln's my man, God bless 'im."

There was a shout of approval for O'Donald's sacrifice. Tobacco was so scarce that men were offering up to ten dollars in gold for a single plug. Even with a war on, there had always been trading across the picket lines back home, but tobacco seemed to be unknown here. The pangs of withdrawal affected nearly every man in the ranks.

Leaning back, Andrew pulled out a match. He knew it was a waste of a good lucifer, but he went ahead anyhow and struck a light off his chair and soon had the tip of the cigar glowing a bright cherry red.

With a merry glance, Andrew watched Kal and his wife and daughter out of the corner of his eye. The Suzdalian had seen the men smoke before and had seen matches as well, but for his wife and daughter it was obviously a first.

"Try one, Kal," Andrew said, offering the box to his translator.

"Thank you, colonel." Trying not to show any trepidation, the peasant took a cigar out of the box, and imitating the other men he sniffed it first, the action drawing a round of smiles from the assembly. Biting off one end, he put the cigar in his mouth and, leaning over a candle, puffed the cigar into life. The room was silent.

Smiling, he pulled happily and inhaled. The coughing explosion that followed elicited a gale of laughter, which

Kal took good-naturedly, while his wife looked at him wide-eyed, as if her husband had suddenly gone mad.

With watery eyes, Kal drained off a glass of vodka, and though he gamely kept the cigar alight, the puffs were with little enthusiasm.

"How do you Yankees find pleasure in this?" Kal finally asked, still gasping and looking slightly green for his effort.

"I wonder myself at times," Emil retorted. "Always had my suspicion the filthy habit can kill you."

"You people are such a mystery," Kal said, pulling the cigar out of his mouth and looking at it meditatively, imitating the manner that Andrew used when smoking his pipe.

"And how's that?" Andrew ventured.

"This thing you call the Union, for one. I'm curious. Your Private Hawthorne's told me about Boyar Lincoln. But a boyar he sounds not like at all. A boyar that frees slaves, and a country where free men fight to do the freeing of those chained to the soil?"

"The Union we fought for is our country," Andrew replied, and he looked around the table at his men. "Every man and woman here volunteered to fight to save that country. We believe that all men are created equal."

Slightly incredulous, Kal looked at the colonel, and putting the cigar back in his mouth, he puffed contemplatively.

"As I learn more of your language, and the thoughts it expresses, the more I am confused."

"How so?"

"Why should men of noble birth fight to free those who are born to work the soil and woods?"

"Because it is what our country stands for. In America we have no nobles."

"But Boyar Lincoln who you drink to?"

Andrew laughed softly, shaking his head. He'd heard Lincoln called many things. During the worst days of the war, before Gettysburg, even he had cursed Lincoln for the fool commanders appointed to lead the Army of the Potomac. But it was a soldier's right to curse his leaders, and he imagined that even Lincoln would understand that. But Lincoln as a boyar was a first.

"Lincoln is not a boyar, not even a noble. He came of the peasants the same as you and I. The home he was born in was the same as the cabin I and my men now live in. He is one of us, Kal. In America there are no nobles, no boyars, no peasants, only free men, all of them equal. There were some in our country who thought otherwise, and in the end we had to fight them to end the evil of slavery."

Leaning back in his chair, Emil cleared his throat, and immediately Andrew realized the mistake he had made. Relations with Ivor were still tense. Neither side had yet to figure out what accommodations were to be made between the two societies. In his heart he knew it would most likely come to a head sooner or later. He preferred later. Given enough time they could at least get organized, and if needs be search out some land to claim their own, beyond the control of Ivor, or the other boyars and find refuge there. Or even better perhaps find a way back home.

But what he had just said was revolutionary for the Suzdalians. He found it strange that a society could exist with absolutely no concept of personal freedom and equality. As a historian he knew the genesis of American freedom was born out of the social order of England. He knew as well that the brutal autocracy of Russia had been created as a means of surviving under the Mongol yoke.

The thought of that started his mind to thinking. For two hundred years the Russians had lived under the threat of total annihilation if they dared to defy their conquerors. The nobles had maintained order for their eastern masters and thus guaranteed life both for themselves and for the peasants. While England was planting the first seeds of representative government, Russia had, and of necessity, been ruled by the lash.

The thoughts started to merge together, but he suppressed the temptation to ask, and instead shifted back to a more immediate concern.

"What I've just said—is this for your lord Ivor's information, or for your own knowledge?" Andrew asked.

Kal merely smiled.

"And what do you think my lord Ivor would say of this idea you speak of—this Union and boyars who are of the people and not the nobility?"

Still trying to smile, Andrew could only shake his head.

"I don't think he'd like it," Andrew said evenly, looking straight into Kal's eyes. Hell, he could just imagine it. The huge boyar would undoubtedly explode in a wild torrent of curses, in the same way he had when they had met only the day before and Andrew asked for an increase in the allocation of food. That had only been placated when he had promised the nobleman a ride aboard the *Ogunquit,* which was scheduled for tomorrow.

"I think you are right," Kal replied, chuckling as if they were now sharing a joke.

Andrew breathed an inner sigh of relief. Somehow he trusted this man, and felt that the peasant had thrown in with him.

"You know something, Kal?" Emil said, leaning over the table. "We're all amazed at how fast you've learned our language—your translations have helped us tremendously—but I've had the feeling that you don't quite translate everything that's said when we meet with Ivor."

Kal showed the most innocent grin possible.

"Just whose side are you on?" Andrew asked, still smiling.

"Why, the people's side," Kal said evenly, and the assembly laughed good-naturedly at the response.

"You'll be a politician yet," O'Donald cried.

"Is that good, this politician thing?" Kal replied.

"Depends on who you speak to," Emil said evenly, patting Kal on the shoulder.

Andrew watched the man closely, the earlier temptation to ask the question coming back again. He felt that his man was at ease.

"Tell me, Kal," Andrew ventured in an offhand manner. "Those statues we've seen, and the painting on the wall of the church. Just what are those creatures, anyhow?"

For a mere second Kal's features froze, and turning, he looked back at Andrew.

"What statues?" he asked quietly.

"The ones lining the road. Those horrible-looking things nearly twice the height of a man. It's like they're all covered with hair, and what teeth on them!"

"Just old gods," Kal said quickly. "Hell creatures destroyed by Perm and Kesus."

"Strange I see them nearly everywhere," Andrew continued. "I heard a mother say something to a child the other day. I think she called them Tugars."

It was the look in the mother's eyes that had unnerved him. The child had pointed, obviously asking a question, she had said the word "Tugar," and then with obvious fear had quickly turned the child away.

But it was not Kal who reacted. As he said the word, Tugar, Tanya and Ludmilla both looked at him with a start.

Obviously flustered, Kal fumbled for a response.

"They are nothing," he said quickly. "I believe it is time that I go."

Standing, he turned to Andrew and gave the traditional bow, right hand extended so that the fingertips swept the ground as he bent over. Ludmilla and Tanya did likewise.

Rising from the table, Andrew followed them to the door. Putting his arm around Kal's shoulder, he stepped outside into the starry night.

"Did I upset you by asking of the Tugars?" Andrew asked.

With frightened eyes, Kal looked up at the colonel.

"Before no one, but especially Ivor or Rasnar, say that word. It is dangerous."

"But if they are only banished old gods, like our devil back home, why should you be afraid?"

"This is different," Kal said. "It will not go well if they know that you are aware of such things."

Andrew could see the fear in Kal's eyes, and nodding an agreement he patted the man on the shoulder.

"Tomorrow, then, we shall take Ivor for his ride on the boat?"

Kal merely nodded, and taking the hand of his daughter and his wife, started down the village green to the cabin which Andrew had arranged for them.

Andrew returned to the officers' mess, and he could see that the men were waiting for him.

"So what the hell is this Tugar business?" Tobias growled from the other end of the table.

"Damned if I know," Andrew said, settling back into his chair.

"Scared the bejeebers out of the man," O'Donald replied, drawing on his cigar.

"And the girl as well," Kathleen ventured.

"Well, I think we should ask this Ivor and find out," Tobias announced.

"No!"

Startled, the assembly fell quiet. Something about his earlier musings and the reaction of Kal was connecting half a thought. What it was Andrew wasn't sure. But he knew it would be dangerous to ask any questions now.

"I'm ordering all of you to forget this conversation. If I hear you or anyone else in this camp say the word 'Tugar,' I'll haul you up on charges. There's something dangerous about asking, Kal told me that, and I believe him."

"Peasant superstition," Tobias growled. "And besides, what damn charges will you press, colonel, sir? I have a right to freedom of speech."

"You can say what you want, captain, as long as it does not contradict my orders," Andrew said slowly, "but I am in command of this unit until such time as we ever find a way home. And I am ordering every man here never to make reference to these Tugar creatures."

With a snort of disgust, Tobias leaned back in his chair. Andrew waited for a response, but the captain was silent, eyeing him with contempt.

"Now there is other business to attend to. The encampment is basically completed, and the ship has been freed. Therefore, starting tomorrow, I'm granting leave, starting with one company a day, so the men can go into the city."

"You think that wise, Andrew?" Emil asked.

"Why?"

"That place is a pestilence waiting to happen. I don't like the idea of the men going in there. Won't surprise me if there's plague or some such thing just waiting to happen."

Andrew could well understand the argument. He had wrestled with it as well. He wished he could just keep the men within the stockade, limiting contact until such time as they had their bearings and were ready to move on. But they were men. Morale was slipping badly. In the first weeks, mere survival and the building of the camp had kept them busy. But Hans had been keeping tabs, and morale was starting to take a serious shift.

Most were still badly frightened by the experience. Nearly a quarter of the command were married men, and from their ranks had been coming the loudest complaints for a desire to return home. He had to let the men out, to see this new world, to form friendships with the people and to just let off some steam. He could only hope that Emil could keep things under control if something did break out.

"I'm sorry, Emil, I've weighed the risk and it's one we'll have to take. The boys are tough. Just lecture them firmly about the water, and the disease. No one's to go near their churches, and by heavens I'll have any man drunk up for a bucking and gagging on the village green."

"Who goes first, colonel darling?" O'Donald asked expectantly.

"Take half your battery," Andrew said. "We'll have a gun aboard ship fire a salute when we take Ivor back to the city tomorrow. Then they're free for the day. Company A can go with us as well. Captain," and he looked back at Tobias, "you can order your men as you see fit."

Tobias merely nodded a reply.

"And the ladies?"

Andrew turned in his seat to Kathleen.

"Well, ah, you see . . ."

"Colonel Keane," Kathleen said evenly, "I can take care of myself, thank you, and have no intention of staying prisoner in this camp."

"Mutiny," Emil mumbled, a smile lighting his features.

Flustered, Andrew searched for a reply, finally realizing that Kathleen's features were creased by the slightest of a bemused smile at the consternation of the usually self-assured officer before her.

"If you would allow me to be your escort tomorrow I would be honored," Andrew said quietly.

"I will consider it," Kathleen replied.

"Well, ah," and Andrew nervously cleared his throat, and lapsed into silence, a habit all his friends knew about when in the presence of a woman, and secretively they smiled at each other.

Andrew looked over at Emil, who was sitting beside Kathleen. The doctor left him dangling for long seconds. Finally Hans took pity and, clearing his throat, leaned over toward Andrew.

"If I might remind the colonel," he said evenly, "there is some business we must attend to."

"Yes, of course, sergeant," Andrew said with a sigh of relief, turning away from Kathleen's penetrating gaze. "Thank you for reminding me."

Regaining his composure, he looked down the table to his company and staff officers, who had sat with smiling patience during the exchange.

"Other business then, gentlemen. Let's start with Mr. Houston's idea."

"My boys want to get started on that sawmill, sir," Tracy

Houston, the diminutive captain of Company D, said, speaking from the other end of the table. Houston was only nineteen, looking even younger thanks to a shock of unruly blond hair and a cloud of freckles that covered his face. But his features were a stark contradiction to a hardened officer who had won a commission in the field for gallantry during the Wilderness campaign.

"Start them tomorrow right after the ceremony with Ivor. You've got the site?"

"A good one, sir. About a quarter mile east of the encampment. There's a good head of water coming through a narrow gorge, so the dam won't take much work. My man Ferguson is a wonder—he's already laid out the site and figures he can have an overshot wheel with a fifteen-foot drop working inside of a month if the whole company pitches in on it. Privates Ivey and Olsen helped build a mill dam back in Vassalboro. The main problem is that we'll need a forge with some good iron to turn out a blade."

Andrew looked over at O'Donald. Every battery in the army had at least one blacksmith assigned to it who could handle the shoeing of the horses and repairs to the equipment.

"Dunlevy's the man," O'Donald stated. "Now if he could build that forge next to the dam and get some power off it for a bellows, why, you'll have the finest blade in this bloody country inside a month. We need a good smithy works here."

"Agreed, then. I'll get Ferguson to work on a gear system to give power to a forge and sawmill, but it'll mean a bigger wheel, most likely. I'll get one of the boys to figure out what's needed."

"What about power for a grain mill?" Fletcher, the plug-shaped commander of G Company, asked.

"Why's that?" Andrew asked.

"They don't have anything like it here," Fletcher replied. "These poor sods are still doing it by hand. Figure if we put up a grain mill, it'll be business for us, so we ain't relying so much on that boyar fellow for a handout. One of my boys already found a good quarry site, on the other side of the river, for mill stones. Figures he could carve out a good set in a couple of weeks."

Smiling, Andrew leaned back in his chair. He'd been worried about what to keep his men occupied with, but in the worrying he'd forgotten about their character. They were Mainers, and any man of sense knew that when it came to Yankee traders a Mainer could skin a man from Massachusetts or Connecticut coming and going.

Andrew looked over at Ferguson.

"It's your site."

Houston tugged at his thin scanty whiskers for a moment, eyeing Fletcher with suspicion.

"Give me the men of your company to help build our dam first—do that and we'll give you the first boards for yours, plus a couple of squads to help build your dam. You'll get wood as well—that is after the Methodist committee gets theirs for the church. Anyhow, that gorge could support half a dozen mills and dams at the very least."

"Will you throw in Ferguson to help lay out the grain mill?"

"Hold on here," Andrew said chuckling. "What is this?"

"Just a little business dealing, that's all."

For a moment Andrew was ready to object. They were all the same regiment, but instantly he realized that if anything these ventures and the concept of company projects were just the tonic they needed.

"All right then, gentlemen. Trading for labor between companies while on regiment time is all right, but only for approved projects for the good of the regiment. If any profits are made selling services to the locals, half will go to the company which started and is running the affair to spend as they see fit, the rest goes to the regimental coffers."

The various commanders nodded their agreement.

"Speaking of ironworks . . ." Mina, commander of E Company, began.

"Go on, then."

"Has anyone given a thought to where we are going to get iron for blades and horseshoes and other such things?"

"And I suppose you have the answer," Andrew replied.

"Just so happens I do," Mina said proudly. "Several of my boys worked the zinc mines up on the edge of the White Mountains. I studied a bit of metallurgy myself at the state university. The boys and I have been wandering about, and we've found a likely site for some ore, about four miles farther up the mill stream. We'll need to cut a trail up there, but it could be producing a good supply of ore. All we'll need is a wheel powering a furnace and a kiln to bake the stuff down, and we'll be hauling iron out of there inside three months."

"And I suppose you'd like your company to get started on this."

"With the colonel's permission, of course."

"But of course," Andrew said, smiling. They'd need iron, and, heaven knew, an endless variety of other things as well.

"While we're at it, why not locate Dunlevy's foundry next to the kiln?" Mina said quickly. "We'll get a regular ironworking shop going, straight from the kiln and into a full-size works."

"A number of my boys would be happy to get into that," O'Donald interjected. "It'll keep 'em out of trouble. I think I can dig up some leatherworkers to turn out some good sets of bellows for the works."

Andrew sat back smiling and nodded his agreement, and the various officers started to talk excitedly among themselves.

"Anything else for right now?" Andrew asked, extending his hand for silence. The officers who had not presented projects looked rather crestfallen, feeling as if their pride had been cut for not coming up with such obvious ventures. Andrew could see the competition was now on. And here he had been worried about morale. Within a week he could expect every company to be venturing into some activity or another.

"All right then, gentlemen. A good evening to you then. Don't let the party end on my account—it's just that I have a long day with Ivor tomorrow."

Standing, he left the table. Emil followed him with his gaze, knowing that most likely the real reason was the headache from Andrew's old wound. But if the man wouldn't come to him there was nothing he could do.

Stepping back out into the fresh evening air, Andrew took a deep breath, the light chill helping to clear his head a bit. The pain had set in earlier in the day, and as usual he had borne it in silence. There was no use complaining anyhow. It was just an old reminder, and absently he rubbed his temples as he walked down the company street. Taps would soon sound, and already the men were settling in for the evening.

The chill was refreshing, a reminder of home. Kal had said there was a winter here with snow, and that harvest time would be upon them in another month. Funny—back home another month would show spring in Virginia. Perhaps the last spring for the war.

The war. How was it going? Strange, something that had

been a part of his every waking moment for nearly three years was now an infinite distance away. Gaining the parapet, he climbed up to an empty picket box and looked out over the river, which shimmered silver in the starlight. Overhead the Wheel, as the men had taken to calling the vast spiral above them, shone in all its glory, filling near the entire sky in a swirl of light.

"Think it's up there someplace?"

"Ah, Kathleen," Andrew said softly, extending his hand to help her up the wooden steps.

"A beautiful night, colonel."

"Please, just 'Andrew' is fine when we're alone."

"All right then, Andrew," she replied softly. "Tell me, do you think home is somewhere up there?" As she spoke she looked heavenward.

For a moment he looked at her with a sidelong glance. The starlight played across her features, giving her a soft radiant glow. He felt a tightening in his throat at the sight of her like this. For weeks he'd been so overwhelmed with business that the thought of her presence barely crossed his mind. This evening was the first time he'd truly noticed her again, and the memory of their first conversation had come back. And now she was alone beside him.

"Would you care to venture an opinion, Andrew?"

"I wish I could," Andrew replied awkwardly. "We had a telescope at the college. Dr. Vassar would invite me up on occasion and we'd look at the heavens. He believed the stars had worlds around them, perhaps the same as our own. But as to where home is . . ." He trailed off into silence.

"Well, I'd like to think that somewhere up there is home," Kathleen replied, her voice almost a whisper. "Maybe that star right over there," and she pointed vaguely to one of the arms of the wheel.

"And perhaps Vassar is looking here right now," Andrew said softly. "Perhaps looking and wondering what is happening here."

Kathleen looked at him and smiled.

"What empires are being dreamed tonight, beyond the starry heavens?" Andrew whispered.

"A touch of the poet in you, colonel. You surprise me—I thought you more the cold military type."

Andrew looked over at her and smiled, shrugging his shoulders in a self-deprecating manner.

"Just a line I once penned back in my student days."

Kathleen smiled softly and reached out to touch his arm.

"Would you escort me back to my cottage?"

"But of course," and leading the way, Andrew helped her down the steps.

As they started back up the avenue, the sound of taps echoed over the encampment, and the two stopped for a moment and listened.

"Such a sad sound," Kathleen whispered as the last note drifted away with the breeze.

"Why do you think that?"

"Just strange that the army should play it to lull the men to sleep, and when they bury them as well," she replied, as they continued on their way.

"Fitting, perhaps. It always makes me think of Gettysburg. I remember the night before the battle hearing it played for the first time, as we settled down to sleep. And then for weeks after, while I was in the hospital, I heard it played over and over as the boys who died were buried up on the hill outside town. But it's a comfort somehow. It speaks of rest at the end of day, and at the end of the strife, both for a day, and finally for a life."

"Such a melancholy turn to our conversation," Kathleen replied. "Or is it that our war has just marked you and me far too much, and haunts us with its presence?"

"But maybe it isn't our war anymore."

"You mean you think we'll never get back home."

Andrew looked over at her and smiled his thin sad smile.

"Would that upset you so much, Miss Kathleen O'Reilly?"

"No, I don't think it would," she said evenly. "After all, my fiancé is gone."

Andrew looked over at her.

"We were engaged shortly before the war. He left for the army in '61, a three-month enlistment," she said softly. "He promised to be back, saying the war would be over before the summer was out and then we'd be married."

"And he never came back," Andrew whispered.

Kathleen nodded and turned away.

Andrew reached out his hand, resting it lightly on her shoulder.

"Oh, I'm all right," she said, looking back and forcing a smile.

"And is that why you became a nurse, because of him?"

"I had to do something, and it seemed somehow fitting. Funny, I often wondered what I'd do when the fighting stopped, for it was a way of losing myself. Now maybe I'll never have to face that question. Perhaps this fate of ours has decided it for me."

Andrew could not help but smile. So she was more like him than he'd thought. The war, which in its horror repulsed him, had at the same time woven a spell about him. A grand undertaking of which he was a part had come at last to sweep him into its tide and carry him away. Try as he could, he had not been able to imagine returning to Bowdoin after the war, to a life as nothing more than a professor of history in a small college town. He had felt the strange grandeur of becoming lost in a vast undertaking, a knowing that he was a part of something beyond himself.

Could she understand that? he wondered.

Reaching the town square, he walked with her to the door of her cabin.

"I lost myself in it, Andrew, and I learned as well that never again would I ever risk the pain of seeing yet another love walk out the door with a promise of return. I've learned that at least," she said, a sad gentle smile lighting her features.

She turned away from him and opened the door. To his own surprise he reached out and took her hand so that she turned back to face him.

"Kathleen, I understand all of that. Perhaps someday I'll tell you of my reasons, my fear, as well. But for right now I would enjoy the honor of your allowing me to escort you into the city tomorrow." His voice tightened up with nervousness.

The slightest of smiles crossed her features.

"I would be honored, Colonel Keane, but I hope you understand what I've told you, and that you'll respect my feelings."

Andrew nodded lamely, his hand dropping away from hers.

With a quick curtsy she turned and stepped into her cabin.

For a long moment Andrew stood outside her door, feeling like a foolish schoolboy. Turning, he started back for his cabin, not even noticing that his headache had disappeared.

"Regiment, present arms!"

As one the men of the 35th snapped muskets to the present position, the dark blue of the state flag snapping in the wind and dipping in salute, while the national colors stayed upright.

Swinging his mount out, Andrew positioned himself in the middle of the open gate. Drawing his sword, he brought the weapon to the salute position while controlling Mercury with his knees.

Proceeded by the sun-and-crossed-swords standard of Suzdal and the bear-head emblem of the house of Ivor, the column of knights came through the gate, with Ivor at the lead. Sheathing his sword, Andrew swung his mount around, coming up to ride by Ivor's side.

Riding next to the massive Clydesdale-like horse, Andrew felt as if he were accompanying a giant. Ivor perched atop his huge mount, looked about with a regal bearing through Emil's spectacles, which were perched upon the end of his round bulbous nose. Andrew watched his companion closely. He had learned already that Ivor was not the type to keep his emotions well hidden. He could see Ivor's surprise at the accomplishments of the last four weeks. Fort Lincoln was well laid out, with spacious streets, the village green as a drill field, surrounded by earthwork fortifications that were truly intimidating.

Somehow Ivor presented a somewhat incongruous appearance, the plate-mail armor, pointed steel helmet, and shield and spear offset by the nineteenth-century technology of glasses, and the *carte de visite* of Lincoln, presented by Andrew, which Ivor had attached to his shield as if it were a talisman.

"Your health is good?" Ivor asked in Rus.

Not wishing to reveal any knowledge yet of the language, Andrew looked to Kal, who, balanced precariously on Emil's mare, was now riding alongside Andrew.

He knew Kal was aware that Andrew had gained some command of the language—after all, it was Kal and now Tanya who were teaching him. But the peasant revealed nothing and rendered the necessary translation.

"Ask his lordship if he is ready for the boat ride," Andrew asked.

Ivor forced a smile.

"Da, da," but Andrew could see his nervousness, for undoubtedly among the people who had watched the dock-ing yesterday had been some who had gone straight to Ivor with reports. Turning slightly, Andrew noticed that Rasnar was with the company, and from what little he had gained of politics so far, he knew that the priest was most likely a sworn enemy.

As the column passed down Gettysburg Street, the various companies fell in behind the small procession, and with drums rolling the regiment marched smartly on its way. There was a long flourish and roll, and the regiment broke into an old favorite, a slightly obscene version of "Dixie" that made Andrew wince. Of course, Ivor and his companions wouldn't know the words, but it was something he'd give Hans a chewing-out for later.

Approaching the dock, they passed O'Donald's command, three of the field pieces unlimbered in action front along the road, the gunners standing to their position. Pulling out his sword again, Andrew managed a salute, which Pat returned with his usual dramatic flourish, his massive red mutton-chops and walrus mustache drawing more than one envious look from the knights.

Unable to contain himself, Ivor looked back over his shoulder, surveying the cannons and the regiment marching behind him. From the look on his face it was obvious that he was deeply impressed by the precision and discipline of the troops.

Going out the west gate, the procession reached the dock and ramp that led to the deck of the *Ogunquit*. The vessel was decked out with all its signal flags upon the bare poles of the masts, so that it appeared ready for a festival. Tobias was there, the thirty men of his command turned out in their best dress blues, all of them obviously proud to have their ship back.

Again Andrew was forced to draw sword while mounted, and snapped a salute to the captain, who for once gave a sharp reply. Andrew could not help but notice how the diminutive captain was puffed up because his transport vessel was now the center of all this attention.

Dismounting, Ivor and his companions stood around nervously, all except for Rasnar, who stood to one side, flanked by a single priest, eyeing all that he saw with suspicious disdain.

O'Donald and the half of his command set for a day in town came forward, and after a brief explanation through

Kal they finally convinced the knights to relinquish their bridles so that the horses could be led up the ramp and tied on deck.

Once the animals were secured, Tobias came up to Ivor, saluted, and invited him to come aboard.

"My people tell me your ship moves without sails," the boyar said, looking to Kal and Andrew, his anxiety finally showing in spite of the front he had to maintain for those around him.

"Through demon craft," Rasnar growled sharply.

"If such were true, then your presence on the deck would drive the demons away," Andrew replied, looking straight into Rasnar's eyes, "and thus it would not move."

Kal, obviously uncomfortable with the exchange, sounded nervous as he translated.

Rasnar, caught by Andrew's offer, fell silent, staring at Andrew with open hatred.

"My men worship Kesus as well, for is it not true that both your people and mine come from the same place, where Kesus was God?"

"Yet you speak not of Perm," Rasnar ventured, "Father God of all."

"Another name but the same God."

"Kneel and beg the forgiveness of Perm," Rasnar barked, "then perhaps I shall know better what you are."

"In my belief I do not kneel to God," Andrew said quietly, "for that is not my way." And besides, it would mean my acknowledgment of you in front of the others, he realized.

"I and my men would consider it a good act if your holiness would bless the ship," Andrew finally replied, shifting the subject away from the confrontation. "Thus if your suspicions of demons is true, they will flee at once, before the presence of one as holy as you. If demons drive the ship against wind and current, it will not move, and thus you will be proved right and I will then kneel before you for forgiveness."

Rasnar stood silent for a moment, and finally with a muffled comment that Andrew suspected was a curse, the priest pushed his way past the knights who had been watching the harsh exchange of words.

Raising his staff, the priest in a soft voice muttered a prayer, finishing with a wave of his staff in the sign of the cross.

Andrew quickly looked over to O'Donald and his mostly Catholic command. But the men had already been briefed and did not make their sign of the cross when the blessing was finished.

"Captain Tobias, have we your permission to board?" Andrew asked.

Tobias, obviously enjoying the fact that Andrew was now on his territory, merely nodded, and then, broadening to a smile, touched Ivor on the shoulder and invited him to climb the ramp.

Falling in behind Ivor and Tobias, Andrew and Kal mounted the deck. After that prayer he could only hope that Tobias's boilers were in good working order; otherwise there'd be hell to pay with Rasnar.

After the knights came the men of Company A, obviously delighted with their first prospect for a day's pass. Behind them came O'Donald's men, who were shouting back to their forlorn companions about the pleasures that awaited them.

Mounting the quarterdeck, Tobias stepped into the pilot house with Ivor at his side. With a dramatic flourish, Tobias pulled down hard on the whistle, and a high-pitched shriek echoed down the valley.

With shouts of dismay the knights standing on the quarterdeck looked wildly about. Some fell to their knees blessing themselves, while others drew swords, ready for battle against whatever terror was being unleashed upon them. Even Rasnar blanched at the sound, which quickly turned to rage at the bemused looks of the foreigners.

There was a long moment of tension, as Kal ran through a quick round of translations to calm their fears. After several moments, Ivor was finally convinced to pull the rope himself. Another round of shouts greeted his action when he pulled the rope down, and instantly released it as if he had touched a venomous snake. Smiling understandingly, Andrew gestured for him to try again. There was another tentative whistle. Then, nerving himself, the boyar pulled down hard. Craftily Ivor watched his knights' look of terror.

Finally the boyar broke into a rolling gale of laughter and like a schoolchild given permission to raise a racket repeatedly sounded the whistle.

"I want one!" Ivor shouted. "I want scream maker for my palace!"

"It'll take a couple of days," Andrew replied, thinking quickly who in the ranks could fashion a small boiler and steam whistle, "but we would be honored for you to have such a gift."

Ivor was all smiles with this promise.

"Colonel, sir."

Andrew turned to see Hawthorne standing by the quarterdeck railing.

"What is it, son?"

Hawthorne stepped forward, pulling his knapsack off from his shoulders. Opening it up, he brought out a small wooden clock, carved by hand.

"Sir, I thought with your permission I could give this to Boyar Ivor as a token of friendship from myself and the enlisted men."

Andrew could not help but smile at the boy's earnestness.

"Does it keep time well?" Andrew asked.

Smiling, Vincent pulled out a small pendulum, attached it beneath the clock, and set it to ticking.

"There's only an hour hand, sir—it made the gearing a lot simpler. I set it to the time on this world, which seems to be twenty-three hours long. But it'll do."

"Well done, lad," and Andrew patted the young Quaker on the shoulder. Kal quickly translated the conversation and following Hawthorne's lead explained the workings of the clock.

Opening up the back panel, Vincent showed Ivor the gears working inside, and the boyar cried aloud with wonder at this new toy, which he accepted with evident delight.

Ivor cuffed Vincent playfully on the shoulder, sending him reeling back, and the knights laughed gruffly at the sight.

"If we could get started?" Tobias finally asked, interrupting the conversation, and with a nod of agreement from Andrew, the ship's captain called for a casting away of lines.

Tobias signaled below to the boiler room, and dark puffs of smoke belched from the smokestack and the lines were cast off. A vibration ran through the vessel, and then ever so slowly, and then with increasing speed, the *Ogunquit* started on its way.

Forward the leadsmen called out the sounds, keeping a sharp watch for sandbars and snags as the *Ogunquit* swung out into midstream and then pointed its bow upstream. It was soon making a good ten knots.

Ivor, Rasnar, and the knights stood in stunned silence for several minutes, while Tobias, with Kal's help, worked quickly to explain the nature of what was happening. Finally Tobias simply pointed to a hatchway, and the party went below, Andrew bringing up the rear.

The engine deck was hot, the thunderous pounding of the twin reciprocating cylinders working their steady rhythm.

Tobias tried to explain the workings of the steam engine, pointing to the spinning driveshaft leading aft to the single screw, but it was obvious that this device was completely beyond the assembly. Andrew noticed, though, that the priest standing behind Rasnar, whom he heard addressed as Casmar, seemed filled with an enrapted awe of the thundering heat-shimmering device.

The priest, as if sensing that he was being watched, turned and looked at Andrew. A friendly smile lit his features, which Andrew returned.

Shaking their heads, the party went topside, with Rasnar whispering darkly to several of the knights, who obviously were listening rather intently to what was being said. Andrew and the priest fell in at the end of the group. Casmar pointed to the machine.

"Wonderful," he whispered, looking about nervously as if checking to see if Rasnar had noticed him. And then, lifting the hem of his robes, he went up the ladder.

Returning to the deck, Andrew saw Kathleen and O'Donald deep in conversation, and they beckoned for him to come over.

"So what do they think of the old demon kissing machine?" O'Donald asked merrily.

"Just don't call it that," Andrew said, trying to sound reproachful. "Rasnar might hear you."

"Ah, him. I know the type—most likely thinks our language is demon speech and wouldn't soil his tongue or mind to learn it, now would you, fellow?" And as Pat spoke he looked straight at the prelate, all the time smiling his biggest grin, which showed the blank spot where two front teeth had been knocked out in some now forgotten barroom brawl.

Coldly Rasnar walked past the group and up to the bow of the ship to stand with several knights who had obviously decided to stay near a holy man in this time of supernatural peril.

Ivor and the rest of his knights, however, wandered about the deck, looking at every fixture, pulling on the cables, hefting the belaying pins, and gathering around the single field piece, mounted on chocks amidships.

Word of the voyage had obviously spread about the kingdom. Down from the hills flanking the river came an unending stream of peasants and horse-mounted landholders, their shouts of wonder and dismay echoing across the flowing brown waters of the Neiper as the ship steamed past.

Seeing that he had an audience, Ivor went back to the quarterdeck and ordered his banner to be shown, at the sight of which the crowds lining the river bowed, sweeping the group with their right hands.

He stepped into the pilothouse, repeatedly pulled on the whistle, and then stepped back out again. Taking his standard, Ivor waved it to and fro so that all ashore knew that their lord had control of the scream maker.

Bemused, Andrew settled against the railing and watched as the dark muddy waters of the Neiper flowed by. The landscape was in many ways so like home. Dark heavy pines hugged the shore, giving way to pastures and fields of wheat already ripened and ready for harvest.

The difference, though, was in the farms. There were no homesteads here, the well-ordered holdings of hardworking Mainers that he was so used to. Instead the homes of the peasants were clustered together in small villages, the buildings rough-cut log cabins, adorned with the usual Suzdalian carvings. Each village surrounded a more massive log cabin, sometimes two, even three stories in height, the obvious mansion of the landholder, flanked in turn by a small stone or wooden chapel topped by the lightning bolt of Perm pointing up to the heavens.

"You know, Andrew, it reminds me somehow of the South."

Andrew turned to see Kathleen leaning against the rail, shading her eyes to the morning glare and looking out over the water.

"Strange—the land looks a lot like Maine to me."

"Oh, the land, I think it reminds me more of Indiana, right on the edge of the prairie. I went there once with my father, when he worked for the railroad. Kal told me that only a day's ride west and south of here the terrain opens out into open lands that go on forever.

"But I was thinking more about the farms," Kathleen continued. "Back home every man owned his own plot, no matter how miserable, and usually the pride showed. Here it's like the plantations, one man living in luxury and the rest in grinding poverty."

The thought troubled him. As the boat edged in close to shore, preparing to round the next bend, he saw how most of the peasants were barefoot, or simply had rags tied about their feet, which were laced up with leather thongs. Their clothing was nothing more than a simple oversized shirt that came down to the knees and was held at the waist by a strand of rope. All the men were bearded, the few old men sometimes having beards that reached nearly to the waist. The women were similarly dressed, occasionally offsetting their features with a brightly colored kerchief to cover their hair, while the younger girls would use a bright strip of cloth as a belt, to tighten their loose shifts about their waist.

All of them stood fascinated, shouting with terror as Ivor continued to pull the whistle.

Cries of "Yankee, Yankee," echoed from the shore as the boat drifted past, and Andrew waved good-naturedly, the more daring waving back timidly in response.

As they rounded a bend in the river a shout of delight came up from the men on the deck, and Andrew could hear Kathleen's gasp as the city of Suzdal came into view, its golden church domes shimmering in the reddish light of the early-morning sun.

"Why, it looks like something out of a fairy tale," she cried delightedly, and Andrew found that he could only agree. Though he had now been to the city a half-dozen times it still filled him with wonder, this city so unlike anything he had ever beheld before.

Passing the southside parapets, the *Ogunquit* raced down the length of the city, the wooden walls looking out over the river lined with thousands of spectators whose shouts nearly drowned out the ever-continuing blasts on the whistle. From battlement walls brightly colored pennants snapped in the wind, matching the bunting of the *Ogunquit*, giving to the event a holiday air.

For Andrew it seemed especially pleasant this morning, since a rising breeze out of the west was blowing the city's stench in the other direction.

Dozens of wharfs lined the quay, and Tobias steered the

Ogunquit toward the longest, which projected fifty yards or more out into the river.

Ropes snaked out and were quickly secured to the massive pilings, and with a rattling crash the anchor dropped free for added insurance. The crew below damped down the boilers and a heavy vent of steam lashed out, sending the Suzdalians on the dock racing backward, while for good measure Ivor continued to give repeated blasts to the whistle.

"I'll be glad when he's finished with that thing," Kathleen mumbled. "Almost drove me mad," and Andrew smiled in agreement.

"I'm required to be his guest for a feast," Andrew said. "Rather than wait for our visit to the rest of the city, would you care to join me?"

Kathleen looked at Andrew and smiled sadly.

"Are you merely asking me to be your escort for a state function, or is there more to it, Colonel Keane?"

Taken aback by her directness, Andrew hesitated. He found himself fascinated by the sad gentle smile lighting her features, and the way the reddish light of the sun tinted her soft wavy hair. There was a tightening to his throat at the sight of her, but in a moment his normal rigidity returned, for he could see the barrier she was again putting up about herself.

"Either way that you wish it," he finally replied.

Next to them the gangplank rattled down, and Ivor strolled down it first, waving to the crowd with a dramatic flourish, to the cries of admiration from his people for his obvious bravery at having ridden upon a Yankee machine.

"Best be going," Andrew said nervously, extending his hand to her. She hesitated for a moment, looking into his eyes as if searching for something.

"Don't get too close to me, Andrew," she whispered. "I can't allow that ever to happen." She took his hand, and together they walked down the gangplank and on into the city.

Chapter 6

"Just fascinating," Kathleen exclaimed as they turned another corner and found themselves in a narrow street lined with shops devoted to leatherwork. The cries of the merchants dropped to a curious murmur at the sight of two Yankees approaching. Andrew was starting to realize that his having only one arm was a source of some mystical wonder to them. Several women had come up to him, touched his empty sleeve, and then bowed low, making a blessing sign.

But even more curious for the crowd was the woman by his side, her hoop-skirted dress drawing an unending stream of excited comments. Kathleen had shown a gentle understanding, repeatedly stopping so that curious women could touch the crinoline dress and exclaim over the fabric. Andrew could not help but laugh when one old woman, bent with age, had come up, her curiosity so strong that she had actually lifted the hem of Kathy's dress, pointing and shouting excitedly at the arrangement beneath. The nurse had turned scarlet at the display, as half a dozen women were immediately on their knees, looking under the dress, talking eagerly to each other. Andrew finally had to drag Kathleen out of the circle of women which had gathered around, the old crone and her friends following them for several blocks obviously intent on getting another look. Finally Andrew was forced to offer a copper penny to bribe the woman and her friends into leaving.

The day drifted into midafternoon, and the mere thought that it would soon be over tugged hard at Andrew. The feast at Ivor's palace had started to turn into yet another raucous affair. But fortunately he had an excuse to leave, explaining that he desired to show Miss O'Reilly the sights of the town.

For that matter his own curiosity had been aching as well, for in all his previous visits he had come straight to the palace, taken care of the necessary negotiations, and immediately ridden back to the encampment. For the first time since their arrival in this strange world he felt he was truly having a day off to explore, and to experience the company of a woman as well, something unknown to him since the start of the war.

There had never been time for such a thing before—at least, that had been his excuse before the war. In the company of women he had always found himself tongue-tied. Too self-conscious about his lanky frame, towering height, and decidedly bookish appearance, Andrew had found it near impossible to make such acquaintances. Well-intentioned friends had of course tried to help with introductions, but somehow they had never seemed to develop.

There had only been one woman of importance—Mary. It was the year before the war. Their courtship had been brief but passionate, with an engagement and promise of marriage in the spring of '61. He had believed in her more than anything else in the world, her every word never doubted, her promises of what would happen when they were married a thrill beyond imagining.

Only weeks before the wedding there came a night when he had planned to work on lessons, but unable to stop thinking about her, he had set off instead for a surprise visit to her home. He knew Mary's parents were away, but they trusted him and would not object to his being in the house with her alone. The front door was ajar, and with the mischievous intent of startling her he stepped in.

There came a sound from her bedroom, an all too unmistakable sound, gentle cries that until that moment he dreamed would only be shared with him alone. Though filled with loathing for stepping into that room, still he had to know— and then wished he had never done so, for the sight of her in bed with another still haunted him.

Three years later, in the spring of '64, a colonel from another regiment told him that their division commander had stated, "That book-learning professor from the 35th has ice in his veins and fire in his soul for a damn good fight. Damn me, I think he knows nothing of fear, and pain doesn't scare him."

Andrew smiled inwardly at the memory of that. Perhaps

after all it was Mary who had made him such a good soldier, for he could be icy cold with nerve, and yet have a passion to turn to destruction when need be. He had come to learn that a happy man does not rush into a war—it was only the youth filled with naiveté and those who had already been hurt beyond caring and wished to somehow escape their sad empty lives that joined with eager intent.

"Why do you look so sad, Andrew?"

"Oh, nothing, Kathleen, nothing at all," he said quietly, trying not to look at her. Could she be touching him after all? he wondered. Could he ever trust another woman after what had happened? In his heart he doubted if he ever would.

"Just look at the beauty of this," she exclaimed, going over and picking up a finely wrought box for jewelry, its lid glowing with enamelwork portraying a warrior bowing to a lady dressed in shimmering robes of blue.

Andrew looked at the merchant and smiled, pointing to the box.

"Andrew, don't."

"Please—a little keepsake for giving me such a lovely day."

"I couldn't," she said shyly.

"But it's already been done."

Andrew reached into his pocket and pulled out a silver dollar and flipped it to the merchant, not bothering to haggle.

Excited with such an offer, the merchant bowed back, and reaching beneath the table pulled out a gorgeous scarf of red embroidered with silver thread, indicating that it was a gift for the lady in return.

The merchant then pointed to the box and the figure upon it.

"Ilya Murometz," he said.

"Ilya Murometz?" Andrew replied excitedly.

Smiling, the merchant nodded as he took the box and scarf to wrap up.

"That's a name from old Russian folk legends," Andrew exclaimed, looking at Kathleen. "I remember reading about him in a collection of folk tales. A fabulous character, one of my favorites. So that proves it even more so. These people are medieval Russians, transplanted here the same way we were."

"But how?"

"That's the mystery we've still got to figure out."

The merchant held out the gaily wrapped package to Kathleen, who, smiling, took it, while behind him his entire family and staff of craftsmen bowed low at the honor of the visit, and the incredible sum in silver paid for their work.

"I think you paid too much," Kathleen whispered. "A couple of copper coins would have done just as well."

"I made a friend there. By evening this whole street will know of the purchase and think better of us for it."

"And charge outrageous prices the next time we come shopping here."

"I think of diplomacy, you think of shopping."

"Call it being a practical single girl living on her own."

They continued down the street, followed as usual by a curious crowd, so that Andrew felt as if he had an entourage. As they turned the next corner, two men from Company A strolled by, one of them with a woman, obviously of dubious morals, clinging to his arm. Instantly the men snapped to attention and saluted. Andrew looked at the young soldier with the girl; he nervously turned a deep shade of scarlet at the sight of Kathleen observing him thus.

"Enjoying the town?" Andrew asked.

"Yes sir," the two chorused.

"Well then, carry on, and stay out of trouble. Remember the boat leaves before dusk."

Without another word, Andrew strolled on, feeling slightly embarrassed for Kathleen. But he was surprised to hear her chuckle.

"I was tempted to ask the youngster if his mother would approve of his company, but I thought it'd be simply too cruel."

A bit shocked, Andrew looked over at her and was about to reply when a shout echoed down the street.

"Colonel Keane!"

Looking up, Andrew saw Hawthorne running toward him. Out of breath, the boy stopped and saluted.

"There's trouble, sir. Major O'Donald and some of his boys got into a tavern brawl. A couple of our boys got busted up pretty bad, but one of theirs is dead, sir."

"Damn!"

"It's looking ugly, sir. The boys have barricaded themselves in the tavern. It's just down the street from the palace on the main square. There's a regular mob growing outside. Soon as I heard what happened, I came looking for you, sir."

"Good work," Andrew replied. "A couple of the boys just went up the street. Tell them to catch up with me—I'm going back to take care of this. Rouse up anyone else you see and send them packing to me. Now move!"

Andrew grabbed hold of Kathleen's hand and at the run started back into the center of town. Within several blocks he started to hear the angry murmur of the crowd, until finally turning a corner into the square he was confronted by the sight of several hundred Suzdalians milling about.

"You stay here," Andrew commanded, looking at Kathleen.

"I'm going with you," she said defiantly. "Some of O'Donald's boys are hurt."

"I'm not taking you into that crowd."

"Stop being such a gentleman, Andrew Keane. Now let's go."

Andrew could not help but smile. Nearly a dozen men of Company A came filtering over to him from the edge of the square along with a group of O'Donald's command, obviously drunk and cast out from some other tavern in town.

"I want no shooting," Andrew snapped. "You artillerymen, keep those pistols holstered, and by God if one of you speaks a word I'll bust all of you straight into a month in the brig. Now let's go."

Near running to keep up, Kathleen followed Andrew across the square. She now saw him transformed, cold, determined, and yet somehow relishing the prospect of this challenge.

At the group's approach, the crowd gave back sullenly.

Even from the outside of the building Andrew could see that the tavern was a wreck. The heavy wooden door was torn right off its hinges, lying in the street. Stepping into the gloomy interior, he saw O'Donald and half a dozen of his men standing in a cluster in the corner of the room. O'Donald had his sword out, and all the men stood with pistols drawn. Ivor and a dozen armed guards stood in the middle of the room, the rest of the tavern packed behind them with angry onlookers.

"All right, what the hell is going on here?" Andrew snapped sharply, stepping between the two groups.

As one, near every man in the tavern started shouting at once.

"Goddammit, everyone shut the hell up!" Andrew roared. His command seemed to need no translation, and the room fell silent.

Andrew looked at Kal, who nervously stood by Ivor's side.

"Kal, tell me what happened."

"Keane. There was a fight. A man of Suzdal is dead," and he pointed to the bar, where a corpse was laid out, the side of his head bashed in, with blood still oozing slowly from his shattered nose and his ears.

"He smashed up James," O'Donald growled. "That man started it."

"Later, O'Donald," Andrew snapped, not bothering to look back at the major.

Kal pointed to half a dozen Suzdalians standing at the bar, one of them holding an obviously broken arm. A member of the group gestured toward O'Donald's men and started shouting.

"He claims O'Donald and his companions started a fight for no reason," Kal stated. "The Yankee lying on the floor then hit Boris, the dead man, with a broken chair leg."

Ivor and the assembly growled darkly as the man spoke.

Andrew looked back at O'Donald.

"Well, what's your side?" he asked, a note of disgust edging his voice.

"It's a lie, colonel darling. We was having a nice sociable drink. I even stood those blackguards a round, I did. Then one of them tried to pick Jamie boy's pocket, and that after we'd stood 'em a drink! So Jamie punched him one. A beautiful blow it was, right to the jaw. Then that Boris fellow was on him with a knife. Well, we all set to, trying to pull that thieving bastard back. Jamie got stuck, but by the saints he still had the strength to pick up a chair leg and send that devil sprawling. Well, we cleaned them out of here, and before you could shake a stick this mob starts to form outside crying for blood."

Dammit, Andrew thought darkly. O'Donald was a regular lightning rod for trouble. He knew the major most likely wouldn't try to lie to him, but his reputation for trouble had been known in the division long before they had embarked.

"Well, it's a hell of a mess now," Andrew snarled, and

walking over to their side he knelt down by James. Kathleen was working feverishly on him, trying to stanch the blood flowing from an ugly knife wound in his side. A froth of blood gurgled from the man's lips.

"How is he?"

Kathleen looked up at him.

"They punctured his lung. I can't tell how bad the bleeding is inside. We've got to get him back to Dr. Weiss."

"All right, make a stretcher from one of those busted tables. Let's get him out of here."

Ivor started shouting darkly at Kal.

"Ivor says that a man of Suzdal died by your men. The man who did it must die now!"

Andrew turned and looked straight at Ivor. He had to handle this one carefully. Seeing a back room, he pointed to it. Ivor and Kal following, the three went into the room and closed the door.

Andrew turned to Ivor and extended his hand in a gesture of exasperation.

"Seems like your people started it," Andrew said, going at once to the attack.

"Not as I see it," Ivor snapped.

"Come now. You saw those men. They're gutter sweepings. I know a band of cutthroats when I see them. One of your people tried to rob one of mine, then mine was knifed while defending himself. I should be seeking damages from you."

"Never!" Ivor roared. "I want your man for justice and blood money for the poor victim's family."

"I will not leave my man here," Andrew said coldly. "He needs our doctor now if there's any chance for him to live."

"I'll agree to this," Andrew continued. "If he lives my man will stand trial. Since this is your kingdom but involves one of my soldiers, we'll have two judges, you and me."

"I stand as sole judge for Suzdal," Ivor said darkly. "You will whisk your man back to your fortress and hide him there."

"That would be madness on my part," Andrew replied quickly. "I want your friendship, not your animosity. I acknowledge you as lord of Suzdal, and I am your guard and vassal. But my people are different from yours and I am responsible for them."

"And blood money?"

"I will pay that now," Andrew said, "since your man is dead. If mine should die, though, then the balance is even, for they killed each other, and the matter is settled."

"Ridiculous!" Ivor snapped. "He must face my justice right now!"

Andrew was silent, staring into Ivor's eyes. The boyar did not give this time. Andrew knew the man was in a corner; the crowd outside wanted blood for blood. If Ivor should back down, word would fly that the Yankees had more power than their own boyar. In a way Andrew could almost feel sorry for him. But if he gave his men over to Suzdalian justice and a precedent was set, there could be no end to legal entanglements, his command subject to execution on the most arbitrary of laws. The sight upon his last visit of several rotting corpses hanging from the south wall had made him aware of that. It was something he could never permit happening to his own men.

"Will you agree if I promise this?" Andrew said, trying to find an out. "My man shall be taken back tonight for treatment. I will stay here as a hostage, guaranteeing that as soon as he is well enough to be moved, he will be returned to your palace. There a trial shall be held, but we must judge this together."

Wide-eyed Kal could not help but let his admiration show. It was unheard-of for a noble to offer himself as hostage for a peasant. In such affairs a noble would not even care about what happened to one of his people, and more than likely would spear the man on the spot, just to get the argument out of the way so as not to disturb an evening of drinking.

"I do not like this," Ivor growled, trying to hide his amazement at Andrew's offer.

"That is all I can offer," Andrew said evenly, trying to not let his desperation show. He wasn't one for suicidal gestures, but he would be damned if he would allow one of his command to be dragged out, executed, and then impaled on the city wall.

"There is no other way," Ivor said darkly. "I cannot let my people think that you have such influence over me. There is enough trouble with Rasnar as is—he will seize that and use it against me. Perhaps this fight came from his own hand. I have risked too much by having you here already."

Andrew looked at Ivor in shock. He had never expected such candor.

"Then we are stuck, my friend," Andrew said evenly.

A loud shout suddenly echoed from the next room, and before the three could even react the door burst open. A disheveled warrior, sweat streaming from his face, bowed at the sight of Ivor and started speaking, his voice near cracking with excitement.

Bellowing a wild curse, Ivor stormed out of the room.

"What's happening?" Andrew cried, looking at Kal.

"It's the Novrodians! They're raiding a village north of the city!"

Ivor came storming back into the room and looked at Andrew.

"You are my liege man. One of my villages is under attack!"

Both of the men looked at each other with what almost appeared to be relief, for the impasse of the moment could be forgotten.

"How far away?" Andrew asked.

"It's up the river, an hourglass ride away, and a brief ride inland. You can almost see it from here."

"Hawthorne! O'Donald!"

The young private appeared in the doorway, the towering artilleryman barging in behind him.

"Vincent, run quick now, back to the *Ogunquit*, and tell Tobias to get his boilers up at once. O'Donald, leave two men to get James to the palace, grab the rest of your boys, head for the boat, and fire off a blank round. That should bring the rest of our people running. Now move it!"

Andrew looked back to Ivor.

"Get as many of your foot soldiers to my boat as you can, as quickly as possible. We'll go up the river and hit them. The rest of your force can go overland by horse. We'll land north of the village and move in, while you'll move in from the south." Startled, he realized that he had not bothered with Kal but had spoken in Russian.

Ivor suddenly smiled at him, his suspicions confirmed.

He cuffed Andrew on the right shoulder and stormed out of the room, roaring and cursing for his men to follow.

Andrew stepped back into the now-empty tavern. Kathleen was still bent over James, who was moaning weakly, and came to her feet as Andrew approached.

"Fortunate you have a little war to divert everyone's attention from this," she said.

He could not admit to her that it was indeed fortunate.

"Stay with James and help him any way you can."

"We need Dr. Weiss," she replied coldly.

"It can't be helped now—there are more pressing needs."

"There are always more pressing needs than a man's life, isn't that right, Colonel Keane? An innocent man gets knifed by these barbarians, but you rush off to help them anyhow."

"I'm sorry, Kathleen," and he extended his hand to her.

She turned sharply away and knelt back down by the wounded soldier.

Without another word Andrew left the tavern. Racing to the dockside, he did not even notice the two pennants that suddenly broke out from atop the highest spire of the cathedral.

"Drop anchor!"

Within seconds the landing boats rattled down and the men started to swarm over the side. The Napoleon field piece, swinging from the end of a winch, was already poised. Working feverishly, the sailors swung the gun out and eased it down to the lifeboat, where planks had already been laid across the gunnels.

Andrew grabbed hold of a sling and was lowered over the side, into a boat already packed with ten men of Tobias's command, who, armed with muskets, had been converted into marines.

Moments later they were on shore. Company A leaped from their boats and with practiced skill spread out into an open skirmish line, while with much heaving and cursing, O'Donald's men lifted the one-ton artillery piece off the boat and pulled it up on the beach. The boats were pushed off and headed back to the *Ogunquit* to pick up Ivor's troops.

"The village is just on the other side of that ridge, a verst or so away. That trail through the woods leads straight to it," Kal said, pointing to a series of low-lying hills that marched down from the east.

It was obvious to all that something was happening on the other side of the ridge, for the sky was blanketed by a dark roiling cloud of smoke from the burning town.

Andrew took another look at the rough map Kal had sketched for him. Ivor and his knights would be galloping out from the city, coming up the road toward the village. He hoped the Novrodians would be looking in that direction, never expecting a flank attack from the direction of the river. With a little luck they'd hit them hard, driving them back before dark. Chances were it was nothing but a raid anyhow, but it'd be a good opportunity for the residents of another city to see his men in action, and to solidify his position with the Suzdalians as well.

"All right, let's move out!"

Spread in open skirmish line, the fifty men of A Company started into the forest, while O'Donald's men and the converted marines grabbed hold of the traces for the artillery piece and started to pull the Napoleon up the trail. Behind them the first of Ivor's men were now landing, and moved up behind the advance.

Running forward, Andrew reached the front of the skirmish line. The men were grim, silent, back again to the old game they had learned in Virginia of hunting other men. Instinctively they moved from tree to tree, pausing for a moment, and then with a low rush sprinting ahead another ten yards. They weren't facing men armed with rifles, but an arrow could kill just as easily.

A hundred yards was gained, then another hundred. As Andrew kept pace with the line, he saw the trail before him straighten out and the crest of the hill a quarter mile away. So close were they now that the crackling roar of the burning village could be plainly heard, with smoke billowing up on the other side of the crest. He paused and leaned against the trunk of a gnarled oak.

A flutter of breeze snapped past him. It took a moment for what had happened to register. Turning, he looked—the arrow buried in the tree next to him was still vibrating.

"Everybody down!" Andrew roared.

Several things seemed to occur at once, as if in slow motion. A soldier standing in the middle of the trail started to spin around, an arrow quivering in his chest, his eyes looking beseechingly at Andrew. Rifles rattled off to either side, and above the noise the clear clarion call of a horn sounded.

The woods exploded into action. Dozens of warriors seemed to spring up from the ground. Swords drawn, they rushed forward, screaming fierce battle cries.

Andrew felt the hair on the nape of his neck stand out. They were coming on like Confederate infantry, shouting what sounded like the dreaded rebel yell.

Mark your target, mark your target, he kept chanting to himself as he drew careful aim at an ax-wielding beserker. The man went down, shrieking hoarsely.

Another target loomed up on his right. He snapped off a round; the man kept coming, but the second round sent him to the ground.

Turning, Andrew stepped back from the hard-pressed skirmish line and looked about.

It was a trap—they'd walked straight into a goddam trap. Memories of the woods of Antietam washed over him. From the right he could see they'd already been flanked. Forward it looked like hundreds of warriors were closing in.

Clear your thoughts, he told himself. You're not a fresh fish anymore, dammit.

A warrior broke clear through the skirmish line rushing straight at Andrew, sword raised high.

He drew careful aim, dropping the man so close that he had to jump aside as the corpse rolled past.

"Company A, pull back! Pull back to the artillery!"

Blue-clad forms came running out of the battle smoke, and the enemy host roared with delight.

Turning, Andrew started to run down the trail. A soldier beside him stumbled over, an arrow sticking out of his back.

Andrew whirled around, aimed, and dropped the archer. Holstering his gun, he grabbed the boy, dragging him to his feet.

"You've got to run, boy!" Andrew screamed. "Run, dammit!"

Half-dragging, half-pushing the wounded soldier, Andrew turned the bend in the trail. Fifty yards ahead the single field piece was already poised, the gunners ramming a cartridge home. O'Donald and a dozen of his men were running up the trail, pistols drawn.

The roaring charge from the right flank grew louder. Suddenly there was a wild clashing of steel as Ivor's foot soldiers waded into the fight, plugging the hole.

One of O'Donald's men grabbed the wounded soldier from Andrew. Turning, Andrew looked about. The charging host were coming on relentlessly, his boys pulling back in for the trail.

"Back to the gun!" Andrew roared.

His men streamed past as O'Donald's men spread out across the trail. With pistols leveled they delivered six sharp volleys, stemming the attack for the moment and buying precious moments of time.

Andrew stayed with them, knowing that Captain Mina would rally the defense.

"All right, lads, let's run for it!" O'Donald yelled. As one the men turned and started to run, leaving two of their companions dead on the trail.

At the sight of their fleeing, the Novrodians sprang forward with wild shouts. It seemed as if hundreds of them were pouring into the attack.

O'Donald, filled with the fierce joy of combat, turned, produced another pistol from his belt, and snapped off several more rounds, roaring with delight as three more men went down.

Reaching the gun, the group rallied. Andrew looked about quickly. His men were forming up in a V formation to either flank of the gun, rapidly reloading, as Mina grabbed and pushed bodies to create a double volley line, the obviously terrified sailors filling in the gaps, while Ivor's foot soldiers formed a shield wall to either flank. Turning the bend in the trail, the enemy host slowed at the sight of the gun, while through the woods to either side the charge started to press in.

"Hold fire on the gun," Andrew shouted. "Let 'em get close. Company A first rank present! Fire!"

A sharp volley snapped out.

"Reload. Second rank fire!"

Within seconds the woods filled with smoke as volley after volley snapped out, the men drawing their courage back from the old familiar routine.

Ahead the enemy host seemed to be building up for the rush, while on the left archers were gaining position and started to pour in a deadly fire.

Suddenly a single form leaped forward from the mob ahead. It was obviously a priest, his golden robes swirling madly as he shouted and roared, his staff on high. With a wild cry he started forward. In an instant the floodgates opened and the host swept forward.

"Stand clear!" O'Donald roared.

The Napoleon leaped backward, the thunderclap explosion tearing through the woods. Sickened, Andrew turned away as the double load of canister slashed into the enemy ranks. The attack forward had simply disappeared.

There was a moment of silence, as both sides paused to gaze at the carnage. Half a hundred bodies were piled up before the gun. In three years of war, Andrew had never seen such destruction from a single round.

Several of the sailors turned from the ranks, retching at the sight. The rest of the men stood silent. Singly, and then as one, the Novrodians broke and started back up the hill.

"They've learned never to charge guns," O'Donald said coldly.

"Load solid shot—let's give 'em a chaser."

The gun leaped again. The round crashed into the woods, snapping down several trees.

"All right, keep the ranks close," Andrew shouted. "Forward, at the double. O'Donald, hold here, get ready in case we're pushed back again. Somebody give me a pistol."

One of the artillerymen tossed him a loaded revolver, and leading the way, Andrew started up the trail. Trying not to look too closely, he stepped past the bodies. Turning the bend in the trail, he saw a small band of the enemy starting to regroup.

"Volley fire forward," Andrew shouted.

Rifles snapped to position, and a sheet of flame lashed out. Cartridges were torn, steel ramrods slammed fresh rounds home, and weapons were brought back up.

"All right, forward again at the walk!"

With leveled bayonets the company spread out to either side of the trail. Arrows snicked past, and with a grunt of pain another man went down by Andrew's feet. Another bolt shot past, slashing into Andrew's empty sleeve, so that it dangled loosely by his side.

For the first time he realized that he was being singled out as a target, but the realization only gave him a grim determination to drive the enemy back.

Another volley was fired, a twenty-yard advance, and then another volley.

They gained the end of the woods and saw the burning village before them aswarm with several hundred men pulling back, rushing to their horses, which were picketed in a small clearing at the other end of town. Many of them were already mounted, waving their weapons and shouting defiantly.

A high clarion call sounded off to the right. Stepping out into the clearing, Andrew could see Ivor and his men charging out of the woods a quarter mile away, Novrodians fleeing before them.

By the time Ivor was within hailing distance the last of the attackers had already disappeared off toward the east.

"Captain Mina," Andrew said grimly, "take roll, and get our dead and wounded back to the ship."

Andrew stepped out of the woods and started toward Ivor. A wave of light-headed giddiness swept over him, and his knees felt loose and rubbery. For a moment he thought he might vomit, and he had to struggle for control. It was always the same after a fight, the exhilaration giving way to shock at what he had done with such cold joy only moments before. His memory flashed to the bodies swept to the ground as if from the blow of a giant. At least the rebs knew what artillery could do. This felt more like murder than anything else, and he was sickened at the thought.

But it was a trap. That was already obvious. They'd been waiting for him.

Ivor reined his mount in, while signaling for the rest of his command to sweep forward in pursuit of the enemy.

Kal—where was Kal? Andrew wondered, suddenly worried. The peasant had been aboard the boat and landed, and he had not seen him since. But as if by magic the peasant appeared out of the smoking woods to stand by his side.

"Just where the hell were you?" Andrew asked.

"Where else, when nobles fight?" Kal replied honestly, "Hiding."

"Maybe you're even smarter than I thought," Andrew replied, seeing nothing but common sense in the response.

"So you had a good fight," Ivor shouted, reining up by Andrew's side.

"Could call it that," Andrew said laconically. "Would you care to see?"

Turning, he pointed back down the trail, and together the three started back.

Rounding the bend in the trail, Ivor drew his mount up short. Wide-eyed, he looked at the carnage. Dismounting, he stepped gingerly around the bodies, looking first at the ground, and then at the torn and shattered trees to either side of the path.

Turning, he looked Andrew straight in the eye.

"I'm glad after all I decided not to fight you," he said quietly.

"So am I," Andrew replied in Russian.

Ivor walked over to the body of the priest and kicked it over. The face was half gone. With a curse, Ivor spat on the corpse.

"Halna, priest of Novrod. So the church is now against me in the open."

"And someone knew we were in town today, and planned this attack to lure us out, and perhaps defeat me," Andrew replied.

"Who else but Rasnar?" Ivor said darkly. "I know my brother Mikhail fled to Novrod, so that is the plot."

"So what are you going to do?" Andrew asked.

"Nothing."

"Nothing, and leave that snake in the middle of your city?"

"He is the arch prelate of all the people of Rus," Ivor replied sharply. "Move directly against him and not only will I face Novrod, but Vazima, Kev, Zagdors, all the cities of Rus. My father wrested temporal power from his father. Because of that I have the support of the nobles of all the cities. They would not support a move to depose me, for it would threaten their position. But not even I would dare to face him directly in this. So I will act as if this were nothing but yet another raid, as we all engage in to keep our neighbors off balance from time to time."

"Madness," Andrew said grimly.

"When you know more of my world, you'll not say that," Ivor said, a sharp tone of admonishment in his voice. "Your men harvested many heads for my wall. My prestige in this little fight will grow, and others will think twice before crossing me. You've caused trouble for me, Keane, but you have your uses as well."

Ivor walked back over to his mount and swung his bulky frame back into the saddle.

"I shall see you back at the city—we'll feast tonight. And yes, our argument of earlier is settled. Your man died just before I left, so now there is no problem between us. Now the people will like you again."

Astounded, Andrew watched as the boyar galloped back up the hill.

Andrew turned and looked at Kal.

"He's mad."

"We are all nothing but part of his game," Kal whispered.

"All know that in the end the struggle between the lords and the church will soon be decided. Peasants fear nobles, peasants fear priests as well—whoever wins their argument, it will stay the same for us. As for you and yours, when wolf is done fighting wolf, the victor will devour the new fox."

John Mina and his command came down the trail, carrying half a dozen bodies.

"What's the bill, John?" Andrew asked.

"Not good, sir. Ten men dead, thirteen wounded, but they should pull through all right. Four men were killed when we first got hit, and their bodies were stripped, so they've got muskets and ammunition now."

"Dammit."

So that was the most likely cause of it as well, Andrew realized. Get some guns and figure out how to use them.

"There's something else, though," Mina continued.

"Go on."

"Two men missing, sir. No one saw them go down. I think they've been captured."

"Who are they?"

"Brian Sadler was one of them, sir."

"And the other one?"

"Hawthorne, sir."

Chapter 7

Terrified, Hawthorne tried not to watch, but driven by some horrible compulsion he couldn't turn away.

The previous night, he'd been slung over the back of a horse like a sack of grain and, tied and blindfolded, carried back to Novrod.

Each breath now felt like fire, and he wondered if some ribs might have been cracked. But for the moment that was the least of his worries.

"Make gun work!"

What was before him seemed straight out of a medieval nightmare. Private Sadler was strapped to a chair, his head encased in a metal cap, with screws over each temple.

"Make gun work!" the priest roared.

"You can kiss my hairy ass!" Sadler screamed.

Smiling, the priest took hold of the screws and turned them another half twist. Sadler arched up in the chair, screaming with pain, and then collapsed.

Sobbing, Hawthorne tried to tear himself free from the ropes that held him to the wall. The priest looked over at him, chuckled softly, and then went back to work.

"Make gun work!"

Sadler spat in the priest's face.

The screws were turned again. Hysterical shrieks rent the air, joined by the begging pleas of Hawthorne to stop the madness.

The priest came up to Vincent and held the musket up before him.

"You make work, I stop."

God in heaven, how could this be happening? Hawthorne wondered. He could stop Sadler's anguish, but then another machine of killing would be in the hands of these men.

"Don't do it!" Sadler sobbed. "They'll use it against our men."

The priest turned back to Sadler. Advancing, he prepared to turn the screws yet again. This time, however, a priest who had stood in the shadows stepped before Sadler and started to argue with the torturer.

The man kept pointing to Sadler and shaking his head. It was obvious to Vincent that the man was worried that Sadler would die if the screws were turned any tighter. Blood was pouring from Sadler's nose, and it appeared as if his eyes were about to burst from their sockets.

Finally the torturer smiled as if in agreement to a suggestion. The screws were loosened, and shuddering Sadler sank down in the chair.

The torturer left the cell. A moment later the door opened again, and Hawthorne's eyes grew wide with terror.

The priest came back into the room carrying a wire basket nearly six feet in length and a foot in diameter.

Inside, a dark-green snake coiled and slithered, hissing menacingly. As it opened its mouth, twin fangs glistened evilly in the torchlight.

"Not that!" Sadler shrieked. "God in heaven, not that! I can't take it!"

Two assistants came into the room and dragged a high table over to Brian, while the master torturer opened one end of the basket and placed it on the table. Untying Sadler's right arm, the two assistants started to push the limb toward the opening.

"God, God save me!" Sadler screamed.

"Stop it!" Hawthorne cried. "I'll show you—just stop it!"

The priest looked over to Hawthorne and smiled, gesturing for Sadler to be spared.

Hawthorne was cut down from the wall, and the priest tossed the musket into his hands.

"Make fire and smoke," he ordered.

Trembling, Hawthorne rested the butt of the Springfield rifle on the floor and motioned for the cartridge and cap box to be brought over.

As he finished, the torturer came up to stand by his side with drawn dagger ready to strike.

Cautiously, Vincent brought the weapon to his shoulder, pointed to the iron-barred window, and squeezed.

Badly frightened, all in the room jumped back.

Vincent handed the weapon back to the priest. Gingerly the man took the weapon. Sniffing the barrel, he exclaimed at the sulfurous smell and gazed darkly at the trembling youth.

Taking the cartridge box, he pulled out a paper-wrapped round, and following Vincent's directions, tore the round open, poured the powder down the barrel, pushed the bullet in, and then rammed the charge home. Cocking the piece, he placed a percussion cap on the nipple.

Hawthorne pointed to the trigger, and gestured to indicate how the weapon should be held.

The priest brought the weapon to his shoulder and pointed it straight at Hawthorne's face.

Please God, let him do it, Hawthorne prayed inwardly. He had already betrayed his beliefs by joining the army, and now had taught someone how to kill. The punishment could only be fitting.

The priest smiled at him darkly.

The man spun around, putting the gun barrel against the side of Sadler's head.

"See you in hell!" Sadler roared.

The priest pulled the trigger. Brains and blood splattered against the far wall.

Leaning over, Hawthorne vomited while his tormentors laughed.

The doorway into his cell opened slowly, and a black-bearded warrior stepped into the room. Vincent gazed warily at the man, recognizing him immediately as the warrior who had confronted him on the road.

The priest tossed the gun to Mikhail, who hefted the weapon and smiled. Motioning for the cartridge box, he pulled out a round, tore it open, and poured the powder into the palm of his hand, then started speaking to the priest, who nodded eagerly.

"You show magic of this," the priest snapped, coming up to face Vincent. "Say no . . ." With a shrug he pointed to the snake in the cage.

"Sleep tonight and think."

"How do you know our language?" Hawthorne asked, curious even through the cloud of dread and pain that engulfed him.

The old priest suddenly seemed to shrivel up into the posture of a cripple.

"Yankee, help me," he whined, holding out his hand.

Horrified, Hawthorne realized that he had seen the man before, but as a beggar outside the gate of Fort Lincoln. He had even given the man a copper coin and spoken to him a number of times, feeling sympathy for someone so wretched.

Cackling, the priest stood back up.

"With this," and he gestured to the gun, "we send man to kill your Keane, or maybe his woman too."

The priest then pointed dramatically at the snake, laughed, and stalked out of the room. Two assistants cut the ropes that had held Sadler and dragged the shattered body feet first out of the room, while another picked up the snake basket, grabbed the single torch, and walked out behind them.

Mikhail was the last to leave. Coming up to Vincent, he grinned and then delivered a smashing blow to the boy's stomach, doubling him over. Laughing, Mikhail left the room and the door slammed shut behind him.

Sobbing, Hawthorne collapsed on the floor, dreading the realization that tomorrow morning he would have to try to die, rather than give the knowledge that could threaten his comrades.

Rasnar gestured for Casmar to withdraw now that the tea had been served.

"Go ahead and drink," the prelate said soothingly, "I promise it isn't poison."

Ivor looked across the table and, smiling, pushed the cup aside.

"You insult my honesty," Rasnar replied softly.

"Then be insulted. I'm not so stupid as to drink something you'd serve."

"Come, come. I am far more diabolical than that. If you visit me, then die of some malady shortly thereafter, the blame would rest squarely on my doorstep. More than one man has been falsely accused after the mere bad luck of having an enemy die after the two had shared a perfectly innocent meal. If I kill you, Ivor, I'll do it far more subtly than that, and be sure at the same time of having another of my enemies blamed instead."

"And so what has stopped you so far, if you are so powerful?"

"Ah, my old rival, perhaps I need you, as you need me."

Ivor leaned back and adjusted his glasses.

"Both of us would be better off if the other were dead. This power struggle between the two of us has been brewing for years. My father did what was needed to strip temporal power from your father. Your church has no business in the affairs of state, and you wish to change that."

"But ah, my friend, a reckoning is coming," Rasnar replied smoothly. "The Tugars liked our little arrangement that your father so foolishly upset. The church ruled the nobles, the nobles ruled the peasants. Through our power, all submitted to the Tugar host, and thus lived because of our preaching of submission to their laws of feeding.

"I shall tell you something else as well. Though the church ruled over all cities, we did not interfere when you and your uncouth brethren would fight in the gutter with each other. It was as the Tugars wished, for the cities were divided, and thus there was never a dream of resistance."

"Nor would we resist now," Ivor said gruffly. "It would be madness. There are not twenty thousand warriors among all the Rus, to stand against the hundreds of thousands of the horde. But we are not here to talk of Tugars, but of your plots against me and my holdings."

"But the topic comes back to the Tugars nevertheless," Rasnar replied. "They so ordered the balance of rule, and so it has always been. To tamper with that, without their permission, is folly. You and those of noble birth have the exemption, and the church sells indulgences from the pit to those not of such birth. Together we controlled the peasants, took the taxes, and prevented any trouble that might result in the slaughter of us all."

"And the great grain houses and silver hoards are already half full in anticipation of their arrival three and a half years hence," Ivor replied. "I shall make sure all is in order for their arrival, so why do you worry such about them?"

"I fear you have plans with these Yankees," Rasnar replied sharply. "I saw it the first night after you witnessed their power when they smashed your catapults. I could see that fire in your eyes, Ivor Weak Eyes."

Ivor bristled at the name. He had been Weak Eyes once, but the Yankee gift had solved that. He preferred now the title of Ivor Yankee Owner, and felt Rasnar's taunt an affront. And yes, he had plans, plans to unite all of Rus under his rule. Not since the time of Ivan near twenty generations ago had one man ruled all the Rus. Even the Tugars respected him, taking one of his sons on their endless migration around the entire world. Upon his return Ivan had given the throne to that son, the legendary Ivan the Great.

If he could unite all the Rus, then he could perhaps negotiate that more of the feeding would be leveled against Novrod, thus making his base of power even stronger after the host had left.

But as it had stood before, only the church was totally exempt from even the taxes of the Tugars. The church still had that vast wealth stored away and could use it as bribes to the Tugars and to turn princes one against the other. He needed and wanted that money. His father had not had the nerve to take it, but with the Yankees on his side, he could perhaps even bring down the church and have all its wealth in his coffers.

"But we are not here to talk of Tugars," Ivor said peevishly. "One of your priests led an attack against my Yankees, and thus against me."

Rasnar chuckled.

"It is not funny!" Ivor roared, slamming his fist on the table. "Two of the Yankees were taken prisoners as well. What has happened to them? I must tell Keane something."

"Tell him they're dead. They were killed trying to escape."

"I doubt that. They could show you how the Yankee weapons work."

"We could figure that out on our own," and Rasnar waved his hand as if the topic were of no importance.

"If your priests lead another such attack I'll take several monks from the nearest monastery and hang them from the city wall to rot!"

"You wouldn't dare," Rasnar hissed. "The priests, monks, and nuns are mine to rule, not yours. Touch but one of them and I'll close every church in your land and tell the people that the Tugar feeding will be directed against them alone. I'll tell them as well that I will inform the Tugars that the nobles and merchants were conspiring to resist the horde and must be punished. The merchant class will then ally with me, forgetting the taxes the church once imposed on them."

Ivor fell silent. Rasnar's father had in fact decreed just the same thing when the boyars denounced and removed the priests from all secular power in the Suzdalian realm, and shifted the merchant tax to their own coffers. But at that time it was nineteen years to the next feeding. There had been several riots among the peasants, but the nobles finally restored control and Rasnar was forced to remove the threat when he gained the prelate's chair.

"If you do that, I'll kill you," Ivor said evenly, looking across the table.

"And have a peasant revolt on your hands. Though that scum fear and hate us, they fear their hell even more."

Ivor settled back in his chair with a muffled curse.

"Come, come, my old friend, you and I can reach an arrangement."

"Go on then," Ivor said coldly.

"Help me to kill the Yankees and I'll forget our disagreement."

"Absurd. They are useful allies."

"You are playing with fire. I know they aren't demons, they are men like us. The Primary Chronicle tells how our ancestors fell into the light long ago, and thus came to this world. We know that the Maya to the west and the Roum and Carthas to the east and south came here in the same way.

"But your Yankees are different. How will they react when it comes time to give one of five of their numbers to the Tugar feeding?"

Ivor was silent. He already knew that answer. These men did not understand the larger needs, to sacrifice some so that the rest might live. They had weapons as well, weapons far more powerful than the dreaded war bows of the horde. If but one Tugar was slain by a Yankee, a thousand heads would be taken in retaliation, for thus was the law.

He liked Keane; in some ways he could even call him a friend and as such would spare him and those Keane pointed out for special treatment. But already he knew Keane would not tolerate the taking of any of his men. That was obvious from the anguish the one-armed man had shown over the previous day's losses, and the capture of the one called Hawthorne. Keane had demanded a march at once upon Novrod, and was still threatening it, with or without Ivor's agreement.

"By your silence I know what you are thinking," Rasnar replied softly.

"It is still three years away, and by then they shall be trained in our ways," Ivor stated.

"You're a fool," Rasnar snapped. "I saw the danger of them the moment I observed their power. I know why you wanted them—to use their power against the other princes and thus fulfill your foolish dream of being another Ivan. I know as well that you wish to use them against me. But they will bring you down first, or I will do it myself."

"Priest, if you threaten me again I care not for what injunction is placed upon me, I'll burn this church to the ground tonight."

That was the one predictable fault of Ivor, Rasnar realized. He thought himself to be brilliant, and in some ways he was, but he was also a blustering buffoon, like most nobles. Like foolish children they would rage and fight over a sand castle, only knocking the prize down in the process. Ivor was dangerous when blinded by rage, and he would have to be handled carefully now that his blood was up.

"Let me make you an offer," Rasnar said soothingly.

"My people in Novrod have taken your bastard brother in. They help him even now, and he has gained the alliance of Vlad and Boros."

Ivor growled darkly at the revelation.

"I'll tell you now it was Mikhail that organized the little entertainment of the previous day, with the hope of destroying the Yankees and killing Keane, but unfortunately things didn't quite work," and so saying he extended his hands in a gesture of exasperation.

"Why are you telling me this?" Ivor snarled.

"Oh, just to let you know what I can so easily do against you."

"So what is your offer?"

"I can arrange for a little accident with Mikhail, and for all the world it would appear to be the doing of Vlad or Boros. In turn I'll stir the nobles of Novrod against their boyar, revealing that he had allied with me to destroy you. For even though there is no love lost between Novrod and Suzdal, still nobles will unite against one who uses the church to kill another.

"The rest will be easy. You march on Novrod and take it as your own when the nobles there come to your side. Then when the Tugars come, simply shift a greater portion of the taxes and feeding to that city. The result, your enemy will be crippled and Suzdal will emerge as the most powerful state after the Tugars are gone."

"And in return I kill the Yankees," Ivor whispered.

"But of course. I have some who know a thing or two about poison in water. Weaken them first, then finish them off."

"You are evil incarnate," Ivor hissed.

"I am practical. Of course, for my help you and I will split the spoils of the Yankees. I will even agree that you keep all the great smoke makers that did such damage in that little disagreement yesterday."

Ivor eyed Rasnar closely, unable to speak.

"You know in the end it is the only way," Rasnar said evenly.

Growling with anger, Ivor stood up.

"We made a mistake before when each prevented the other from acting," Rasnar stated. "Both of us feared that the other would get the secret of the Yankee weapons. Thus they lived, and now threaten you more than you think."

"I can control them, and when need be eliminate them."

"Your tea grows cold," Rasnar said soothingly.

With a sweep of his hand, Ivor knocked the cup from the table and started for the door.

"Such a waste. It was a wonderful brew," Rasnar said calmly. "I know in the end you'll come to an agreement on this, for there's no other way out of your predicament. The Yankees are a two-edged sword, Ivor, and you are now balanced on the blade."

As the door slammed shut, Rasnar could not help but laugh, the first time he had done so since the arrival of the Yankees. He knew Ivor all too well. As a boyar he was better than most. But the man thought too much of his own vanity and dream of power, something which could be so easily maneuvered.

In the end he'd agree. If the Rus were to survive the next visit of the horde, he'd have to agree, and in the process the church would once again gain its power back, for Ivor would be beholden to him before it was finished. And besides, with several hundred of the Yankee weapons, much could be done to spread the church's authority over all the boyars of the realm once Ivor was eliminated.

The report had reached him only this morning that two prisoners had been taken, and with the right persuasion would reveal how the magic powder could be made.

Chuckling, Rasnar stood up, threw the contents of his untouched teacup into the fire, and strode from the room.

The feasting had been good. Muzta Qarth rode slowly past the slaughter pits where the scattered bones of humans had been piled up, according to ritual, skulls in one heap, ribs in another, arm and leg bones in the third.

Yet again, though, the disease had been here before them, killing half the population of the village before the first outriders and choosers of the flesh had arrived. Another quarter of the cattle were still weak and disfigured, and thus unfit to eat.

It took over fifteen hundred cattle a day, along with other foodstuffs, to feed the host. When the two out of ten had been consumed they would move on. The only way to feed now was to take every healthy human, good breeding stock or not, young and old, and place the symbolic halter about his neck.

Muzta paused in his thoughts and looked down the hill at the human village, from which the cries of lamentation of the few survivors rent the evening air.

Their anguish moved him not, as the cries of any beast facing the knife moved not those who must eat. But he knew what they would leave behind, when the yurts pushed on in the morning.

The few weakened survivors would most likely perish come the storms of winter, for they would not have even the strength to bring in the harvest. When he returned here again with the next circling the village would be overgrown ruins. A stopping place for the Tugars for a hundred generations gone forever. He had hoped not to feed here at all, and save this place, but Tula and the other chieftains had demanded fresh meat, having gone for a week without a decent feed. Even Muzta had to admit to himself now that the smell of flesh crackling over the fire pits, the kettles of blood soup, the great pies of kidney, and fresh roasted liver had set his mouth to watering.

The final course of the evening, in commemoration of the moon feast, he had eagerly looked forward to. A healthy female cattle of breeding stock had been brought into his yurt. The moon feast usually was the only time that breeding stock were eaten, and thus he felt no regrets. She had been dragged under the special Table of the Moon and her head pushed up and secured in place. Alem himself had done the honors, and with sure deft movements quickly sawed away at her skull.

The cries of the victim were part of the ceremony, the shaman interpreting them for omens regarding the next month. When the sawing was finished, the victim was still alive and conscious, another good omen. With an audible pop the skull was yanked off, revealing the victim's brain, and those around the table reached in with their golden spoons to scoop out the contents, while the cattle struggled weakly and then died.

But then, to everyone's horror, an ugly red knot of evil-looking flesh the size of a small apple was revealed. Nauseated, Muzta spat out the brains he had been chewing on, while Alem cried out that the auguries were too horrible to voice.

The memory haunted him, and he needed no shaman to interpret what it meant. They must race on, he thought grimly, and somehow outdistance this pestilence of running sores, which left the cattle disfigured with ugly pock marks that could turn the stomach of any who even contemplated eating them.

He looked heavenward. The Great Wheel stood at its zenith directly overhead, the sign of late summer. The plan was still good, he realized, even though the horses of the clans were thinning from the constant march without a day to rest, covering in one season the grounds that normally took two years. When they reached the land of the Maya cattle the Wheel would be low, and the first snows falling. Perhaps then there would be rest.

Meditatively he took another bite from the fresh sausage made by his seventh consort and rode on into the night.

Somehow he had slept. Coming up to his knees, Hawthorne looked about the cell, which was bathed by the silvery light of the Wheel and the twin moons that had risen in the eastern sky.

Groaning, he came to his feet and rested his hands against the wall. With a startled cry he pulled his hands back and held them up.

What had once contained the essence of Sadler's mind dribbled off his fingertips and splashed to the floor. Sobbing, he tried to wipe the gore off, the horrid memories washing through his soul.

Could he stand it in the morning? he wondered feverishly. The snake, and the leering grin of the priest while he screamed in terror—could he stand it? And in his heart there was the nagging fear, an inner voice that told him he would break.

The priest knew his craft well, Hawthorne realized. In the mad terror earlier he might have been able to hold out, but now there was only the long night and the contemplation of what was to come.

He tried to form a prayer, to turn inward, as he had once so easily done during the Meeting for Worship. But that seemed endless lifetimes away. He tried to imagine the gray-shingled church at the base of the Oak Grove hill. Snow drifting down silently outside, the peace within, and even the memory of Bonnie Price sitting in the women's section stealing sidelong glances in his direction.

Why had he ever left? he thought self-pityingly. He could be there now. It was still February back home, maybe even Sunday. Longingly he looked at the Wheel, trying to imagine that somewhere up there was his world, where even now they would be praying, perhaps for him.

And in his soul he knew before the priests were finished he would break, condemning more to death by his weakness.

He slid back down to the floor. What could he do? How he wished the priest had killed him instead, ending this nightmare.

The thought started to form. It was a sin, he realized, a horrible sin, that would condemn him to hell. But perhaps the Lord would understand after all. To do it might spare hundreds more from death.

Yet was he not taught that such an equation was fallacy, that it was a logic the world had always used to justify murder? Kill one to save hundreds—the moment that was done and accepted, then killing was accepted.

But suicide? A sacrifice to save hundreds. Even so, that would be better than living out his last moments with the realization of a worst sin—the possible death of his comrades because of his weakness.

Twisting his hands against their bonds, he realized that Mikhail had done a clumsy job with the knot. Bringing the rope to his teeth he worked feverishly, twisting and turning his wrists till they were chafed raw. Gradually the knot loosened and finally the rope fell away.

Steeling himself, Hawthorne came to his feet, looked about the room, and saw at once the instrument of his deliverance. The coils of rope used to bind Sadler still lay upon the floor.

He had to work fast, for he knew fear would stay his hand if he paused to contemplate the enormity of his actions. Quickly he fashioned a noose. Scanning the room again, he was startled to hear a curse come to his lips.

The ceiling was bare; there was nothing to tie the other end to. Desperately he looked about again and then with a chill realized there was only one chance. He'd have to tie the rope to the window bars, then pull his own feet up and thus dangle until strangulation choked out his life.

But when unconsciousness came, would his legs drop and thus save him? There was only one alternative. He looped the noose through the window bars, then pulled the chair that Brian had sat on over to the window. Kneeling on the chair, he then took another coil of rope. With trembling hands he looped two coils around his ankles, hooked the ropes through his belt, and tied his feet securely to his backside.

"God forgive me this sin," he whispered hoarsely. Balanced on the chair, he placed the noose around his neck, cinched it up tightly, then grabbed the chair with his hands.

The memory of snow washed over him, gentle falling snow outside the window of the chapel, and Bonnie's eyes gazing at him.

The chair clattered out from under him and the rope went taut.

"Dammit, he won't do a goddam thing other than send an envoy. He thinks they're already dead," Andrew roared. "I've wasted a day and a half with him. We could have been near Novrod by now. Let them see what a field battery can do to their walls and I'd get Sadler and Hawthorne back damn quick."

"Have a drink, son," Emil said softly, offering his friend a glass of the now precious brandy.

"Those are two of my boys," Andrew snapped between sips. "I lost ten men out there yesterday, counting O'Donald's two. James was the eleventh. I'll be damned if I'll lose two more."

"And what do you propose?" Emil said softly.

"We go back to Fort Lincoln tomorrow morning, put the regiment in marching order, and head for Novrod, and Ivor be damned. The regiment takes care of its own, it always has, and by God it always will. By heaven, man, we've only lost prisoners twice, at Antietam and Gettysburg, and that was to rebs, who at least obeyed the rules of war. You see how Ivor hangs his enemies and criminals from the wall. Good God, man, he took some of their wounded this morning and hung 'em out there to die. It was enough to turn your stomach."

"Damn right," Hans mumbled in the corner of the room. "Damn barbarians they are."

"If Ivor says no?" Emil replied.

"I owe my loyalty to the regiment first," Andrew snapped. "My men come first, and damn anyone who gets in the way of that."

"You might have a full-scale war on your hands. Ivor's the only ally we've got," Emil cautioned.

"Then I'll give him Novrod when I'm finished as a payoff. That ought to make him happy."

"He's in a power game we're not even sure of," Emil

replied. "Attack Novrod and you might upset his cart, and bring everything crashing down on us as well."

"Better that than sinking to their level of justice. I don't want anyone here to think he can take a man from my command to do with as he pleases."

"I think you're wrong," Emil said quietly.

"Then think me wrong. I don't want a word of this until the regiment is formed. You're to load the injured aboard the *Ogunquit* tonight. At dawn we go back to Fort Lincoln and form up."

Hans stood up and smiled, slapping his thigh.

"It'll be a damn good fight," the old sergeant said, looking proudly at Andrew. Draining his glass, he strode from the room.

Andrew turned away. In his heart he knew this was the wrong move; he'd loose a lot more men before it was done. But the strength of the regiment was in the knowledge that every man, if need be, would fight to save a single comrade in distress. None of them could sit idly by at the thought of Sadler, and especially the bright-eyed Hawthorne, facing possible torture.

The world was spinning, his lungs near bursting. This must be a foretaste of hell, and the terror of it made him want to scream, but that luxury could not be had by a man who was hanging.

In spite of himself he started to jerk and squirm on the end of the rope, fighting the wild urge to grab hold of the line and pull himself up.

Suddenly there was a grating noise and the line jerked down several inches, yanking the noose even tighter about his throat. A trickle of stones rained down around him.

The iron bar holding the rope must have moved! Desperate, he reached up and grabbed hold of the rope. He felt his lungs were near exploding. Bright stars started to flash before his eyes; hot streaks of agony coursed to his brain as every nerve seemed to scream for air.

He tried to pull himself up, but his arms were too weak.

There was another grating sound and the rope jerked down another inch. With a final lunge of despair he pulled himself up by the rope, and his right hand shot out and grabbed a bar.

The world was starting to lose focus, as if he were looking

down a long dark tunnel. Hanging now by one hand, he tore frantically at the rope about his neck. For a terrifying moment it wouldn't give.

Suddenly the knot loosened. With a shriek he drew in a lungful of air, and another and another.

Gasping, he worked feebly at the rope, loosening the knot. As he pulled the noose over his head, Vincent let go with his right hand and crashed to the ground.

He wasn't sure if it was a minute or an hour until consciousness returned. His neck felt as if it were wrapped in fiery metal.

With trembling hands he loosened the bonds that held his legs and, weak-kneed, came to his feet. The noose still dangled from the iron bar. Reaching out, he grabbed the barrier and pulled.

The bar didn't move. Sobbing, he pulled again, and still it did not budge. Had he dreamed it in the final moment, and saved himself? Would he now have to face that horror again?

Cursing wildly at his fate, he slammed the bar with his fist, and it gave back easily with a sharp grating noise.

So it had moved! Eagerly the young soldier shook the bar several times. There were several inches of play in it, but a heavy lintel stone prevented it from popping all the way out.

There had to be a way. He'd given up too easily. Had God sent him this sign after all, to use the gift of his mind to find a way out?

Sitting back down, he let his eyes wander about the room looking for some possible way, for he now reasoned his death would not have been stopped if God had not wished him to somehow escape.

An hour later he was ready. It had taken nearly all that time to quietly pry a leg free from the chair Sadler had been bound to. Taking a section of rope he had tied it to the loose bar, and then weaved the rope back and forth several times around a stationary bar and then back to the loose bar again.

Whispering a silent pray he slipped the chair leg in between the ropes and then turn it like a windlass. The ropes started to coil, the slackness going out of them. After a dozen revolutions of the chair leg the ropes were now taut and resistance to his turning motion became harder. Pulling the leg towards his body Hawthorne now needed both hands, and after another revolution he was bracing his feet against the wall, the muscles of his arms knotting and straining.

He felt as if he could not tighten the ropes any further and his prayer changed to a silent curse. A muffled groan escaped his lips, sweat beaded his brow and then ever so slowly he saw the loosened iron bar start to bend in the middle.

"Dear God give me strenth," he whispered.

The bar bent inward, a dusting of mortar drifted down, and then with a grating tear the bar snapped inward, popping out of its mount. With a loud clatter Vincent fell to the floor.

Terrified he snatched up the iron bar and hunched down, staring at the door, waiting for a response from his jailers. For what seemed like an eternity he sat in silence, animal instincts coiling his muscles, ready to spring.

There was no response and gradually he relaxed, stood up and and stuck his head out the window, to see that his cell was a good twenty feet off the ground.

Tucking the bar into his belt, he set to work. A moment later Hawthorne wormed his way through the narrow opening. Grabbing hold of the rope, which was now tied to a well-secured bar, he quickly slid down the line, burning his hands in the process.

Fortunately it was still dark, but in the east there was an ever so faint lightening to the sky. He wouldn't have much time. Looking up and down the narrow alleyway, he realized one direction was as good as another. Pulling the iron bar from his belt, he started out at a run.

For several desperate minutes he feared he was completely lost, and would wander thus until, with the coming of dawn, the alarm would be raised. But turning the next corner, he was confronted by the wooden palisades of the city wall.

For several minutes he peered at it cautiously. It seemed that no one was on the battlement.

He hit the nearest ladder at the run and quickly scaled to the top. Another twenty-foot drop confronted him. Desperate, he looked for some way to get over the side.

"Hey!"

Startled, Hawthorne looked up. A guard was approaching him.

The man shouted something, and Hawthorne, desperate, merely shrugged his shoulders.

The guard came right up alongside and started to speak.

Suddenly his eyes grew wide.

"Yankee!" the guard hissed.

As if driven by animal instinct, Hawthorne slashed out with his iron bar, and with a sickening crunch the man's helmet collapsed inward.

With a shriek, the man staggered backward, fell from the battlement, and was still.

Shouts rose up from a watchtower farther down the wall. An arrow hissed past, missing Vincent by inches.

Closing his eyes, he leaped atop the battlement and jumped.

Hitting hard, he rolled away from the wall, and in an instant was up and running wildly toward the river. Another arrow snapped past. Vincent staggered and fell, and was up again, still running madly, a shaft sticking out of his thigh.

He hit the muddy shore, and grabbing hold of a light skiff, pushed it out into the river. Leaping in, he took hold of the oars and started to pull madly. The shoreline dropped away, the faint outline of the city in the early-morning light drifting from sight as a turn in the river pushed him away from view.

For what seemed like hours he rowed without stopping, unmindful of his bleeding hands and the agony of his throat. Finally as the terror subsided, he looked down at the wound. The shaft was buried in the fleshy part of his leg. Nerving himself, he tried to pull it out, but fell backward weeping from the pain.

He spied a rusty fishing knife in the bottom of the skiff and used it to saw the shaft off near the wound, each cut an agony as the vibration fired every nerve in his leg. Taking off his shirt, he tore out a bandage and bound the wound tight, finally stemming the flow of blood. Then, picking up the oars, he started in again, driven by the fear that the hawk-faced priest would appear at any moment, carrying the snake basket and cackling with delight.

The sun rose to its zenith and crossed the sky. Trembling with exhaustion, Hawthorne finally fell over and lay out to rest. But his rest was disturbed when in the distance he heard a thunder which grew ever louder.

With his last ounce of strength, the boy pulled his head up and looked out over the water. The river was moving faster now, coursing between a series of steep hills. He could see a curtain of spray rising ahead . . . rapids. Looking back up the river, he saw a small vessel like a miniature Viking ship round a bend in the river, its oars rising and dropping rhythmically. So they had caught up after all, he thought numbly.

The skiff started to pitch and roll with the current, but Hawthorne was beyond caring. Swooning, he fell back down, and the blackness washed over him.

It had been a near thing, Andrew thought grimly as he walked across the square of the city. He did not even bother to acknowledge the bows of the residents who stopped to watch him pass. Since the fight by the river, word had spread about how the small detachment had met five times their own number and driven them back with great slaughter, and the mood of the city had changed overnight from wariness to outright displays of affection.

Reaching the cathedral, Andrew pushed open the doors and stormed in.

Two hours ago the regiment had been formed, rations issued, eighty rounds of ammunition per man passed out, the one piece of artillery with a full complement of horses limbered and ready.

When he saw Ivor himself galloping down the road he thought that the confrontation would blow then and there, for surely the boyar had come to threaten retaliation for this action. Their stormy session the night before had not gone well for either, but to his surprise the man had not come straight out and ordered him not to march.

But Ivor reined in before him, smiling broadly, and told him the news. Andrew shouted for the regiment to stand down, and swinging his mount about he galloped back to the city, Kal, Ivor, and Emil following him.

After seeing the results of what had been done, no one could now stop him in his rage.

He strode down the length of the cathedral, his hobnailed boots clicking loudly on the polished limestone floor.

Approaching the altar, he saw Casmar.

"Where is Rasnar?" Andrew shouted.

Startled, Casmar looked back at him.

"I want Rasnar now!" Andrew barked.

"His holiness is in meditation," Casmar said nervously.

"Get him now," Andrew snarled.

"Keane, be careful," Kal, who had followed him, whispered nervously.

"To the devil with caution," Andrew snapped.

"Don't do this," Casmar said, his voice full of concern.

"If you don't find him, I'll look for him myself!" Andrew barked.

"I will go announce you," Casmar replied, shaking his head, and turning, he started for the side door.

Impatiently Andrew stood waiting for only the briefest moments, and then followed Casmar.

"Keane, don't!" Kal cried.

Without comment Andrew kept on his course. Pushing the door open, he stalked down the long corridor. At the far end he could see Casmar turn and look back, an expression of fear on his face. Andrew kept on relentlessly. He came up to the priest, who stood by an ornately carved door. Pushing the priest aside, Andrew slammed the door open and stepped into the room.

For once he saw the prelate completely taken aback. Rising from behind his desk, Rasnar stood motionless, looking nervously to where Andrew's right hand rested lightly on his holster.

"No, I won't kill you," Andrew snapped. "At least not yet."

"And why the act of mercy?" Rasnar replied, quickly regaining his composure and settling back behind his desk.

"Because as I am a liege to Ivor, he would be blamed, so you are protected for the moment."

"Really, Ivor should learn to keep his dogs on a tighter leash."

"I just got one of my boys back," Andrew said coldly, coming forward to rest his hand on Rasnar's desk.

"Yes, how fortunate for you. Perm has been kind to him."

"He told me how one of your priests tortured him, how your animal hiding in his gold robes blew out my man's brains and tried to force Hawthorne to reveal the secret of gunpowder."

"Delirious ravings," Rasnar said smoothly.

"I'll believe my boy before I'd ever listen to your twisted superstitious lies."

Rasnar did not respond. With a steady hand he reached over to a pot and poured himself another cup of tea.

"I'd offer you some," Rasnar said evenly, "but I think it is time for you to leave."

"I just want you to know that as far as I am concerned, the game between you and me is out in the open. You tortured two of my men, your plottings caused me to lose ten others in battle, and I half suspect that fight in the tavern was triggered by your people as well."

"Of that, at least, I am innocent," Rasnar replied.

"I don't care for your explanations. You have a truce with me for right now—I'll grant you that for the sake of Ivor. But if but one of my men disappears, if there is an accident of any kind, if a roof tile should fall on someone or a man gets knifed in a bar fight, I'll be in front of this church at dawn the next day. I'll blow in the doors of this building and bayonet every man inside. Do I make myself clear?"

"Really, you are quite dramatic," Rasnar said, his composure slipping at the open threat that had been laid.

"Now we both know it's in the open between us. I know you for an enemy and you know me. Outside this building I'll acknowledge your position and keep the peace with my men, who God knows would tear this place apart with their bare hands if the truth got out. I'll acknowledge you and respect your customs, but by heaven, man, you'd better respect mine, and from your pulpit there had better not be another word claiming we are devil spawn, or I'll show you just what hell I can create."

Trembling, Kal looked over to Andrew, horrified by what he had just translated. He had been tempted to soften the words, but Andrew had told him beforehand that if he suspected the altering of a single phrase he would drum him out of the camp.

"Yes, we know each other now," Rasnar replied. "Now get out of my church, you infidel!"

Andrew came to attention and smiled sardonically.

"Good day to you, your holiness. I apologize for interrupting your meditations." Snapping a salute, he turned and walked out of the room. Stopping at the door, he winked at Casmar, who stood wide-eyed at the exchange, and then went on out into the hallway.

"That was madness," Kal hissed, nearly running to keep up with Andrew as they stepped back out into the street.

Stopping, Andrew looked at the man and smiled. Exhaling noisily, he pulled out a handkerchief and wiped his brow.

"You people hide your animosities in maneuverings, and plots within plots. We New Englanders are far more direct. We say it directly and up front, and the devil take the hindmost. It'll keep him off balance for a while. He's not used to dealing with that, and I daresay he will back off for the time being."

"I can only hope so, Keane. His holiness is a dangerous enemy."

"Maybe so," Andrew said quietly. "Now let's go back and see that boy."

The tension released, Andrew actually found himself relaxed. Hawthorne would survive, but the boy had been through a nightmare. It was a miracle he had been spotted clinging to the overturned skiff and fished onto shore.

Thank God he was safe, the only good news to happen after the tragic losses of the last three days. It was too bad about Sadler. He had been a good soldier, joining the regiment along with his brother Chris back in the early days of '62. He'd have to talk to Hawthorne about that, for to tell Chris the truth would most likely drive him to murder the first priest he laid eyes on.

For the good of the regiment he'd have to ask Hawthorne's silence about most of the things that had happened, but he knew the boy would understand.

Climbing the steps of the palace, Andrew returned the bows of the guards with a salute and ventured in. Ivor was there to greet him, smiling with eagerness to hear what had happened. The beefy-faced boyar had actually laughed when Andrew had first told him what he planned to say. Of course, it would help him, Andrew realized, to have a vassal who was an outsider and thus not intimidated by the priests.

Smiling at Ivor, he stepped past the boyar and entered a narrow windowless room.

Wild-eyed, Hawthorne tried to sit up as the door opened.

"It's all right, son," Andrew said softly. "You're perfectly safe now."

Feverish, the boy sank back on to the bed.

"How is he?" Andrew asked nervously, looking at Emil.

"He'll pull through all right." He patted Hawthorne on the shoulder. "The neck will heal nicely, but he'll be darn hoarse for a while. His hands are badly torn, and I think he's even cracked his ankle. We'll get that arrow out shortly. But I want this place scrubbed down first and my instruments boiled."

"Hawthorne, you're in the best of hands with old Doc Weiss here. He'll have you up and around in no time. Just settle back and get well. Kal here said he'd be honored if when you're feeling a bit better you'd stay with them so his wife and that lovely daughter of his can look after you. I want you to start practicing your Russian with them, and that's an order."

Tears filling his eyes, Hawthorne looked beseechingly at Andrew.

Gently Andrew sat down on the side of the bed.

"What is it, son?"

"Colonel . . ."

"Go on, you can tell me. I'm proud of you, boy, and I don't blame you for talking to try to save Brian's life. It was a noble act on your part, and braver still that you chose death rather than risk the lives of your comrades. I'm promoting you here and now to corporal for how you handled yourself."

Hawthorne started to shake his head, the tears coursing down his face.

"No, I can't," he whispered.

"Why?"

"Colonel, I—I killed a man."

Andrew was silent. Why did it have to be this way? He had hoped for the sake of this young Quaker that in battle he would never know if a bullet he fired had actually struck a man. But for his first test Vincent had been forced to do it in the worst possible way—up close, looking into the eyes of the man he cut down.

The memories came back. How many had he killed like that up close? Ten at least since coming here. And then there was that reb boy in the Wilderness. He'd shot him so close that the boy's uniform had been scorched, and then for an hour the enemy fire had been so heavy that he had been forced to lie beside the youth, watching the life slowly ebb out.

God, was that all he was good for now, killing, and leading others in killing? He tried to force the thought away.

"I think God would understand why and forgive you," Andrew said gently, holding Hawthorne's hand.

But would God ever understand my own sins and the passion for battle? he wondered sadly.

Chapter 8

Awakening in the hour before dawn, Andrew was surprised to feel the crunch of a light frost on the ground beneath his feet as he stepped out of his cabin.

It was April back home, the fifteenth of the month, he thought as he looked heavenward. As he watched, a fiery meteor crossed the sky, and for a brief moment he thought it must be a portent of some kind, even as he chided himself for such superstition. Was his war still going on back home, or was it over by now, and Lincoln working instead on binding up the wounds of the nation?

Funny, he realized, he was thinking less and less of home in these last two months. They'd been remarkably peaceful, and with that peace the men had turned to their various projects with a will.

The Methodist meeting house across the green was nearly finished; there was even a steeple waiting for the bell, which was the big cause of excitement this morning. The town hall was up as well, and the boys had even concocted a baked-bean-and-ham supper in it the night before, complete with a band, singing, and dancing.

Kathleen had danced the evening away with him, but still there was that wall between them as if both were wary of the possible hurt the other might offer. The Suzdalians had even been drawn into the celebration, and a number of the men had female escorts for the evening.

A sizable community of a hundred or more huts had sprung up outside the earthen walls, housing merchants and twoscore families who had moved down from the city to offer their skills and services to the regiment.

In this quiet time, which Andrew had come to love so much, he walked down Gettysburg Street listening and thinking. The camp was as happy as could be expected. The young single men had seemed to adjust the easiest. Two had already asked for the right to marry, and he now found himself in the uncomfortable role of being something of a father, telling them to wait and let the courtship develop a little longer.

Among the hundred and fifty or so men who were married, some with children back home, it had been far worse. A day did not go by when a grim-faced soldier did not come to him asking if there was any hope of ever seeing Maine again. He had kept up the lie, offering assurances which he doubted would be true, hoping only that in time they would come to accept whatever strange fate it was that had cast them here.

There'd been three suicides, all of them married men, despondent over their fate. Ten others were now confined to the hospital, sitting quietly throughout the day, talking softly to themselves, or to imagined loved ones. Kathleen treated them with loving care, hoping to lure them back, but in his heart Andrew knew there was little hope; they had found a gentle world in their thoughts and would most likely dwell there for the rest of their lives.

He pushed the thoughts aside as reveille echoed in the morning air. From the cabins curses and groans cut through the early-morning chill, and Andrew smiled at the familiar sounds. He'd always found those who could not wake up easily to be a source of amusement, realizing that to such men, a man who could awake instantly, feeling refreshed, was somehow unnatural.

The camp came alive with the morning routines, which he watched and participated in with quiet satisfaction. With morning parade and breakfast soon out of the way, the various companies set off to their appointed tasks. New projects had sprung up almost overnight. A small quarry for limestone, opened by Company B, was now operating on the other side of the river, while H Company was nearly finished with building its first raft for the ferry service to support the operation.

At least Tobias had found a task as well. Two weeks ago he had pulled out and sailed down the river to go explore the freshwater sea and had not been heard from since. Of course, Andrew was worried, but at the same time felt a sense of relief that the quarrelsome captain was out of his hair for a while. Anyhow the showing of the American colors would do no harm.

"Colonel, sir. The men should be ready for you now."

Roused from his thoughts, Andrew looked up to see Captain Mina of E Company standing before him expectantly. He looked especially dapper this morning, his dark thin mustache freshly waxed, his uniform neatly pressed.

"Well then, John, let's go see what you've got."

Together the two strolled out the gate to what was now called the Mill Stream Road and started up the hill. Every time he came up this way Andrew found it amazing how much farther back the forest kept retreating because of the unending harvest of wood. Rounding the first bend in the road they came past a pile of fresh-cut boards, still oozing resin. A loud continual rasping cut the crisp morning air.

Smiling, Andrew paused for a moment to watch the saw-mill in operation. If anything could remind him of Maine it was this. The building had yet to be framed, the rough logs of its skeleton still bare to the weather. There was a good head of water this morning coming down the chute and the ten-foot overshoot wheel turned easily. The driveshaft was an oak beam engaged directly to the wheel. From there a leather drive belt provided power to a five-foot circular sawblade, on the main floor of the building.

Logs were snaked into the back of the mill, straight out of the pond which was still growing and spreading out in the narrow gorge behind the mill. Andrew watched as a team of men guided the log onto the cutting table, strapped it into place, and started to push it forward. A shower of sawdust suddenly kicked up as the blade bit in with a rasping whine.

"How goes it this morning, Houston?"

The captain turned around beaming, and as usual his excitement over this pet project was unlimited.

"It's a-growing, sir," Tracy said, beckoning for Andrew

to come in and have a look around. "We're rigging up a power winch line off the wheel," and leading the way he started down the ladder to the lower floor. The clatter of the wheel and the shrieking of the blade echoed like thunder as Houston pointed about and shouted.

"One of my boys is almost finished cutting the blocks out now. If we had the right tools I'd have it done by now. But Dunlevy says he's too busy on other projects, and we should be happy about getting the blade, and that's that."

Andrew could see Houston wanted his support to shift the blacksmith back under his command, and smiling, he shook his head.

"Dunlevy gave you your blade—now he's under John here for a while," and John smiled with good-natured rivalry at his friend.

"All right. Well, at least I can tell the boys I tried," Tracy said with mock dejection. "Anyhow, we'll rig up a winch here off the main driveshaft, and when we need a new log, we hook the cable on, I push down on this lever here, which engages the gears, and in it comes, saving my boys a lot of sweat. The tough one, which won't be finished for a week yet, is mounting the cutting bed to a sprocket. Once that's in, then the boys won't have to feed the log in by hand. The sprocket will simply push the bed, with the log strapped to it, and a nice even plank will be cut out as easy as pie."

"Good work," Andrew said enthusiastically, clapping Houston on the shoulder.

"Now if only I could get all the water I need. It was bad enough when Fletcher got that dam of his done and started to build up a head of water and wouldn't release any down to me. But now you, John," and he pointed an accusing finger at Captain Mina. "That dam of yours is taking forever to fill."

"Look, do you want my products or not?" John said quickly. "You need me if you want to expand this second-fiddler operation."

"Second fiddler is it!"

"Gentlemen, gentlemen, please," Andrew said, holding up his hand. "We both need each other here, remember. I want John's operation with full water as quickly as possible —we all need what he can produce. Once that's done, you'll have all the water you need. All right?"

"You heard him, John," Tracy replied. "Once that dam

of yours is filled, don't hold back on me. We've all got to use the stream."

"All right, all right, but colonel, sir, my men are waiting for you. Besides, Private Ferguson is just dying to show you his new plans."

Refusing a hand, Andrew made his way back up the ladder and leaving the sawmill continued up the hill. A hundred yards farther up they paused for a moment to watch Fletcher's operation. Even as the mill operated a crew of carpenters of his company were busy putting up siding provided by Houston. This was one place that had to be protected from the rain.

The millstones were small ones, less than three feet across. They were temporary affairs until a couple of boys from B Company could turn out full six-foot stones of granite, which would take at least another month.

But for the Suzdalians it was still a wonder. Every day there was a steady stream of people, most on foot, some driving small wagons laden with bags of freshly harvested wheat, lined up outside the mill waiting for their grain to be ground into flour.

By agreement with Andrew and Ivor the rates were simple enough—one-tenth of all grain ground was kept as payment, and as a result the regiment would soon have fresh bread, for one of O'Donald's boys had been a baker and even now was supervising the construction of several ovens to handle the demands of the regiment.

Passing on up the hill, they came out upon the latest addition to the mill stream's industries. The furnace and attached forge were small, with only a ten-foot wheel for now. But Mina was already talking about expanding it over the winter and building a great twenty-foot wheel by spring.

Smoke was billowing out from a brick chimney, and with each turning of the wheel there was a loud rush of sparks as the bellows driven by the waterwheel pumped in a fresh draft of air.

This project had been the most complex to date, requiring in one way or another the labor of half the regiment to get it ready. Nearly a hundred men had been busy felling wood for weeks, and following the lead of several charcoal makers from the north country of Maine had soon cooked up hundreds of bushels of charcoal of at least passable quality.

The men of B Company had worked across the river,

cutting limestone with the few tools available, crushing it with hammers to serve as a flux which would draw off the nonmetallic parts of the ore to form a brittle glasslike slag.

Finally there'd been the mining of the ore. A site had been located farther up in the hills, and fifty more men had labored intensively using the few picks available to cut the ore into workable chunks and then haul it back down the hill.

Others had worked at building the dam, which now was nearly twelve feet high and would finally rise to twenty-two feet to power the larger wheel already planned to replace the temporary ten-foot one now in place.

Still others had helped to fashion the bellows from two whole cowhides, and the huge earthen ramp to the top of the furnace, where the crushed lime, charcoal, and ore were dumped in for the cooking-down to the final product.

The Suzdalians at least had brick kilns located upriver from the town, and in trade for ten dozen bushels of Fletcher's wheat and several thousand board feet from the sawmill a sufficient quality had been purchased, transported downriver, and packed up to the hill to make the furnace.

Andrew had already noticed a creeping inflation starting to set in as far as prices went with the Suzdalians, and he resolved that a brick kiln would be a major priority, since there was always a need to supply the mills, and the growing town of Fort Lincoln.

"We're ready when you are, sirs," one of Mina's men called as the officers approached.

A regular delegation was waiting for them, including representatives from the Methodist committee, who after intense negotiations had finally won approval for the first casting to be used as a bell for their chapel.

Today's runoff would be modest; Mina had calculated it to be about five hundred pounds of iron, which as soon as it had cooled would be turned over to Dunlevy and his crew of apprentices. A mold for the bell had been fashioned from clay, and when enough iron had been amassed it would be remelted and poured in.

As Andrew looked around he realized that nearly half the regiment was here, since so many had participated in getting this project started. Their pride and excitement was evident in their looks of eager anticipation as Andrew approached.

"Colonel, sir," a grimy private said, stepping forward and saluting, "me and the boys working this here mill would appreciate a couple of words from you."

Andrew looked over at John, who smiled broadly. It was a common joke with the regiment that the professor, whose job before the war had been talking, somehow got tongue-tied when asked to give a speech to the men.

Andrew looked around at the men and smiled good-naturedly.

"I'm proud of all of you," he said. "Proud that you're Union men tested in battle, the finest regiment in the Army of the Potomac," and with that the men cheered at the mention of that most famed army of the war.

"I'm proud as well that you're Mainers, the best from the finest state in all New England," and with that an appreciative growl went up from the ranks, peppered with witticisms about their neighboring states to the south.

"This mill will be the foundation from which other projects will spring that will be the envy of this world."

He looked about and suddenly realized that he had unwittingly slighted the men working on other projects.

"Not to mention the sawyers, miners, and heaven knows what other projects you boys are cooking up," he said hurriedly, and the crowd laughed appreciatively.

"All right, then, enough of the speechifying and let's see what we've got here."

With a ceremonial flourish, John stepped forward and handed Andrew an iron pole and pointed at the clay plug at the base of the kiln. Feeling somewhat clumsy with his one hand, Andrew grasped the pole and thrust it at the plug. After several attempts the clay broke, and as if by magic a hot river of metal poured out into the rough troughs laid out in a bed of sand at the foot of the furnace.

A loud cheer went up as hundreds of pounds of molten metal flowed out, shimmering and sparkling, the heat so intense that Andrew held his hand up to protect his face from the glare.

Beaming with pride, John could not contain his excitement and jumped up and down, until the runoff finally trickled to a stop.

"All right, load her up again!" John shouted. "Let's have a ton of this beautiful stuff by tomorrow!"

John looked about and finally spotted the man he wanted.

"Ferguson, come over here."

From out of the crowd, a slight form appeared, smiling nervously. His glasses made his pale-blue eyes appear owllike, giving the man an almost ridiculous appearance. Andrew had always liked the man, even though more often than not he was in the infirmary, the hard rigors of campaigning simply too much for his body. Several times he had expected to see Jim's name stricken from the roll, but a week later he'd come dragging back, ever eager to try again. He had offered Jim an easier job behind the lines with the quartermaster, but the private had always refused.

Here, however, he had come into his own, his student days studying engineering before the war now making him one of the more valuable men in the regiment.

"Shall we take a look, private?" John asked.

His head bobbing up and down, Jim pointed to a rough cabin next to the mill and led the way, the two officers following.

Stepping into the darkness, Jim lit a couple of pine sticks that were so heavy in resin they burned as brightly as candles. Pointing over to a table, Ferguson rolled out a sheet of paper, which had become available only the week before from the small paper-making operation located back at the fort.

Andrew leaned over the diagrams and could not help but shake his head.

"Are you serious, Jim?" Andrew asked quietly.

"Of course I am, sir. I'm always serious about such things."

"But a railroad? Why would we even need one?" Andrew asked.

"Why not?" Mina replied enthusiastically. "Ferguson here's got it all figured out. It'll be a narrow-gauge line of two and a half feet, saving a lot of effort on grading and tracks. The line would start at Fort Lincoln and come up the Mill Stream Road, then continue on up past here and then to where the ore supply is. Since it would be a light gauge we could use wooden tracks covered with iron straps to get started. I figure we'll only need twenty tons of iron a mile that way.

"The line could haul lime flux, bricks, anything we wanted,

from the river on up. At the top it could haul charcoal and ore down to the mill, and then run lumber and finished iron back to the river again."

"It'll take a lot of work," Andrew said quietly.

"I've got that figured already," John replied quickly. "Actually, not that many of our boys would be tied up. I was talking to Kal only yesterday about it—he claims he's got some relatives that'd make excellent gang bosses. Now that the harvest is coming in there'd be several landholders who'd loan out their peasants as laborers. We could pay for them with the regiment's half of the lumber and some of the Franklin stoves I'm planning to turn out from the foundry."

"Kal, get in here!" Andrew roared.

As if waiting to be called, the peasant showed up in the doorway.

"What is this about you being a gang boss?"

"Colonel, sir," Kal said smiling disarmingly, "it'll be simple enough. I'll subcontract the work out to several of my cousins."

"Subcontract? Just where the hell did you hear that phrase?"

Kal looked around innocently.

"You asked me to learn my English well."

"All right. And I take it you're learning a little capitalism on the side?"

"Well, I am collecting a small payment from the men I'll recruit to help with the grading and cutting of lumber for ties."

"You mean a kickback, don't you?" Andrew asked, struggling to keep control and not burst out laughing.

"I prefer to call it a consideration."

Shaking his head, Andrew looked back at Ferguson.

"What about power? You'll use horses, I take it?"

Ferguson broke into a grin.

"Steam power, sir—a regular locomotive," and as he spoke he rolled out a set of plans for the engine.

"How in heaven's name do you plan to pull that one off?"

"Sir, we have two engineers in the regiment, Kevin Malady and Kurt Bowen, both of I Company, and a couple of firemen as well. I've already been over the *Ogunquit*'s engine from one end to the other, and I must confess to having learned a little something about such things before I joined the army.

"We'll need to expand the foundry, putting in a couple of tilt hammers, an engine lathe and a reheat furnace for steel. I figured it out, and inside of a month they could be operating. In three months the track will be laid, the engine turned out, along with a couple of flat cars and hoppers, and the MFL&S Railroad will be ready to run."

"MFL&S?" Andrew asked, unable to contain his curiosity.

"Maine, Fort Lincoln, and Suzdal Railroad."

"Suzdal?"

"Why, of course, sir—that's the next step, to run a line up the river road straight into downtown Suzdal."

"One thing at a time, Ferguson, one thing at a time."

"Then you approve?" Mina asked excitedly.

"All right, I approve. But no more than sixty men from the regiment working on this—the rest of the labor comes through Kal. The first priority on labor for now goes to the making of more tools. Then comes expanding Dunlevy's smithy shop with your trip-hammers, then the expansion of the foundry here.

"Can you manage that, Mina?"

"Of course, sir."

"All right, then. John, I'm appointing you coordinator of labor for the various operations involving ironworking and the railroad, but you're not to pull men away from Fletcher and Houston, or they'll be raising hell. Is that settled?"

"Of course, sir, and thank you, sir."

"It's a beautiful day, gentlemen, and for right now I plan to take a ride and enjoy it. Good day to you."

Walking out the door, he turned quickly and looked back. Mina, Ferguson, and Kal were all exuberantly slapping each other on the back. Shaking his head, Andrew started back down the trail. They'd most likely been planning this one for weeks, thinking that they'd have a tough sell job.

Frankly, he loved railroads and was already eager for the first ride on the MFL&S.

"You know, you Yankees are really quite amazing," Kal said good-naturedly, looking across the table at Hawthorne, while pouring him another mug of tea.

Vincent had become something of a regular feature in their cabin. He had stayed with them for two weeks while his leg had healed. But since then his visits were a daily occurrence, and it was obvious that his major reason for dropping in was Tanya, who waited eagerly each evening for his arrival. After an hour or two of conversation with the family the young couple would leave for a walk, returning each night just as taps sounded.

The courtship, however, was more than just keeping company with a young lady. Vincent had become part of their family as well, sitting with Kal and pitching in with the chores.

Together they had managed to coax a load of broken and rejected bricks from the foundry, and now Kalencka was perhaps the only peasant in all of Suzdal with a real chimney to his home. Not to mention being the first peasant with an actual clock ticking in the corner, and a Bible, which Hawthorne was using to teach Kal how to read.

That alone had been a source of mystery for the peasant, though he did not say anything about it. For the stories of Kesus, Moos, and Abram were hauntingly similar to what the priest spoke of from the pulpit on seventh days.

"Why are we Yankees so amazing to you?" Hawthorne asked, smiling and looking over at Kal. He stretched back in the chair, and a slight grimace crossed his features.

"Is it your leg?" Tanya asked nervously, rushing over to Vincent's side.

"No, nothing, just a little twinge, that's all."

Kal smiled at the two. The girl had hovered over him day and night, while the burning fever from the wounds racked his body. Even the healer Weiss had appeared nervous for a while, staying long hours at the cabin. The nurse woman Kathleen had visited every day, instructing Tanya carefully in the proper care of a young wounded soldier. But even after the fever had broken, the boy did not seem to recover. At night he would cry aloud, tearing at his sweat-soaked blanket.

Kal would arise, but already Tanya would be by his side, talking soothingly, wiping his brow, till the boy lay back down and drifted off, until another night terror tore into his soul again.

Gradually he recovered, but still there was a sad haunted look to his eyes which had yet to go away.

Since Tanya was his only daughter, Kal worried somewhat more than usual about his little girl who seemingly overnight had become a woman. He had no position, no dowry money, and feared that her life would end in drudgery, killing that vivacious charm that seemed to radiate from her soul. He feared the other thing as well, and since Ivor had not offered exemption to his family, Kal lived in dread of the selections for the moon feast.

He pushed the thought aside and watched the two as they gazed at each other and spoke softly. Already he felt a love for this young man, as if Perm had sent him as a replacement for the boy lost long ago. There was a strength to him, and yet a gentleness as well, so unusual and yet so wished for in someone whom he hoped he might someday call his son.

The cabin was warm and comfortable. A hearty fire crackled in the fireplace, filling the room with a warm cheery glow, and the silence in the room was a gentle blanket of happiness. Loaves of freshly baked bread were on the table, and Ludmilla stood smiling in the corner of the room, watching the couple. Kal looked over at her, and the two nodded with the stirring of old memories that still held after twenty-five years.

The silence lasted only for the briefest of moments before the young couple looked up, and blushing drew apart. Kal chuckled and wagged his finger at the two.

There was a knock on the door, and Ludmilla hurried over to open it.

A wizened old man, with a white beard that tumbled down to his waist, stood in the doorway, leaning on a polished staff of wood. Behind him stood a dozen other men, all dressed alike in simple woolen shirts of white tied off at the waist, their legs protected against the autumn chill by cross-hatched wrappings of cloth.

"Peace and blessings upon this house," the old man said, bowing low.

"And blessing upon you, Nahatkim, and kinsmen, and friends," Kal said, walking over to the door and bowing in return.

As each came into the room, Ludmilla offered him a piece of bread, served on an ornately painted board where a bowl of salt was also set. Each took a sliver of bread, dipped it into the salt, and turning, faced the simply fashioned icon of Kesus that adorned the east wall of the room.

First making the sign of the cross, each man then ate the bread, bowed low to the icon, and then came over to sit by the table.

There was a moment of nervous silence as the men settled in while Tanya and Ludmilla scurried about, pouring tea and laying out platters of bread, pickled greens, and salted meat.

Kal looked over at Hawthorne and smiled. A bit of a trap had been set. Vincent had had no idea that company was coming, nor did he know why these men were invited.

Nahatkim was perhaps one of the oldest in all of Suzdal and thus a man to be treated with respect. Though he was only a leather merchant, even nobles showed some slight deference to him, and in the affairs of the merchants his voice was listened to and obeyed, for age had brought him great insight as well.

The others were all known leaders of the peasants of Suzdal and the surrounding landholdings. Boris, a cousin of Kal's, even knew how to read and was thus held in the highest respect. Tall, strapping Vasilia was a half-caste, born of a peasant woman and a noble. Though ignored by his father, now long dead, he could in some ways travel in both circles, and often intervened for a peasant in trouble, and thus was greatly respected as an adviser and confidant by all of the lower classes.

They were here for a reason, and Kal did not hesitate to start.

"My friend Hawthorne and I were just talking about the mysteries of the Yankees when you good friends arrived," he said innocently, leaning over and patting Vincent on the shoulder.

"Your leg is well?" Nahatkim asked, his wrinkled face filled with concern.

"Yes sir," Vincent replied in Russian. "Thank you."

"You are a brave man," Nahatkim whispered. "Know that you've made enemies, but you have made far more friends by your deeds."

Vincent nodded, unable to reply.

"Vincent, I've told my friends about some of the things you and I have shared," Kal said smoothly. "Would you mind sharing such a conversation with them as well?"

Vincent hesitated for a moment. Keane had cautioned the men on several occasions about being too familiar with the Suzdalians and warned them not to upset the existing order of things. A number of men were already grumbling about that, outraged by the slavery that existed around them. But all realized as well that for the time being, they had to have an accommodation with the ruling class if they were to survive.

Yet was not the truth the truth? His elders had taught him that to witness for the truth might be painful, but could never be denied when called upon. There was no other path that could be taken, and he gave a nod of agreement.

"My friends will ask things," Kal said, "and I'll translate for both you and them."

"My Russian is still very shaky," Vincent replied, smiling.

Kal patted him on the back, and Vincent leaned back in his chair, while Tanya came over and settled in by his side.

"My friends have seen the wonder of your Yankee machines, but I've told them much else as well, especially about how you people live."

"Such as?" Vincent asked.

"Your Union country, and that declaring of how you say?"

"Independence?"

"Yes, that."

Hawthorne smiled and looked about the room. How strange it was here. At home he had always lived by the customs of his people, to observe the words of his elders, to show respect, and to live with the understanding that wisdom came only with years. Now how different it seemed. Gray-bearded men sat about the table ready to listen with rapt attention to his every word.

"In my country, America," Hawthorne began slowly, so that Kal could keep up with the translation, "in the time of my father's grandfathers, we were ruled by nobles, boyars such as here.

"My people, all the people of my land, which we call America, were common men of the soil, and merchants of the towns such as yourselves. We believed that the ruling of nobles was bad. We believed that all men are created by God to be equal. That if a man works, the labor created by the sweat of his brow rightfully belongs to him. That a man should work the soil that belongs to him and him alone, and not be forced to work another man's field unless he agrees to do so and is paid. So the people of America wrote a long speech on parchment. We called it the Declaration of Independence. We sent it to our king and told him that all men were equal and free and that he no longer ruled us."

Gasps of amazement came from the group, and eagerly they waited for more.

"So the king of our land sent soldiers to force us to his will. A terrible war was fought, and the king was cast out of the land. When the war was won, the peasants had driven the king, his nobles, and all their soldiers away."

"So who became boyar?" Nahatkim asked from the back of the room.

"No one."

"How can that be?" Vasilia asked. "For who then makes the laws and rules the people?"

"We rule ourselves. When the war was finished the people met in every town throughout our land. We selected wise men from among ourselves, who were sent to a great council. There at the council these wise men made rules to govern us all. If the wise men made good rules they stayed on the council. If they made bad rules then the people of the town ordered them to come back home, and sent other wise men in their place.

"Throughout the land we also searched for a man who was the wisest of all. He was sent to lead the council. We called that man a president. For four years he would serve us, and then the people would come together in every town and decide if the president was good or not. If he was not a good president we told him to go home and sent another man in his place."

Hawthorne could only hope that his rough explanation of democracy was in the right words. As he finished there was a wild flurry of conversation. Some shook their heads in disbelief, others just looked at him with awe.

A burly peasant with shoulders and arms that rippled beneath his tunic leaned over the table and started shouting at Hawthorne.

"Ilya, my mother's brother," Kal said, "wants to know what happens when a bad man laughs at you, and refuses to go home and instead makes himself a palace to live in."

The room fell silent.

Hawthorne looked about at the assembly.

"If such a man tried to go against the wishes of the people, we would place him in jail."

Ilya laughed, and snapped back a response.

"And if he did not go to jail when you so nicely asked him, and paid soldiers to protect himself, then what?"

"We would kill him," Hawthorne said quietly, with lowered eyes.

"Peasants kill boyars?" Ilya snorted with disgust. "The church would send you to hell."

"The church has no power in our lands. In America a man may pray to God, Perm, Kesus, or whomever he pleases. In America if any priest tries to stop him, or force him to change how he prays, that priest is sent to jail."

"Impossible," Ilya roared.

"Go into our town then," Hawthorne said evenly. "In the center you will see three different churches. One we call Methodist, another Presbyterian, and the third for men who call themselves Catholics. I belong to another church called Quakers. Since I am the only Quaker here, I pray by myself, and no man of another church can force me to do different. If he did so, our leader, Keane, would force him to stop."

The men in the room looked at one another, and shaking his head, Ilya backed down, mumbling darkly. At the mention of Andrew's name, Hawthorne noticed that several of the men touched their left sleeves and spoke excitedly.

"Now tell them about your Lincoln," Kal said quickly, "and the war to free the black peasants."

"Lincoln is the greatest leader of our people we have ever known," Hawthorne started, warming to his subject. "He was a peasant just like myself and like all of you here. The people of my land saw his wisdom and made him their leader.

"Now in my land there were some people who lived far away in the south of the country. They did not believe that all men were equal. So they went to distant lands and captured men of black skin and made them into slaves to work for them."

"Black-skinned men?" Nahatkim asked.

"It is true. They are men the same as you and I; the only difference is that God gave them black skins instead of white.

"The men of the South," Hawthorne continued, "would not end this evil thing, and so a great war came to our land. The men of the South said they no longer belonged to America and wished to keep the black men as slaves. But Lincoln said that was wrong. So the people of the North formed great armies and marched south to free the black-skinned men and to prevent the men of the South from destroying the free land of America."

Hawthorne paused for a moment, knowing that his decidedly abolitionist viewpoint on the war might be debated by some of his comrades, but feeling nevertheless that it was accurate.

"Men such as you would fight to free other men," a young man with a scraggly black beard asked, "even though they were not threatened with being slaves themselves?"

"Slavery is wrong," Hawthorne said quietly. "Lincoln said that if we allow one man to be a slave, then the freedom of all men is threatened."

"And you would kill another to stop such a thing?" Nahatkim asked softly.

Hawthorne looked about the room. Almost imperceptibly he nodded his head.

The room was silent. Perhaps he had said too much. Everyone in the regiment now knew that they were living in the type of land that America had fought two wars to prevent. All the men in the regiment, volunteers and bounty men, were members of an army dedicated to ending slavery forever. Heated debates were waged in the cabins nearly every night over this very issue and their revulsion at the system of boyars, church, and peasants.

No one spoke, and Hawthorne could feel the nervous tension over what he had just revealed.

Kal leaned over toward him and smiled.

"It's such a beautiful evening out," he said softly, "a young man like yourself should not be trapped with old ones like ourselves, especially when there is a young lady who would be delighted to walk with him."

Vincent knew he was being dismissed, and looking over at Tanya he was glad for the opportunity to be alone with her.

Rising, the young couple started for the door. Vincent turned, and in a gesture of respect bowed to the assembly in the Suzdalian manner, an action which caused the men to smile and nod in reply.

The door once closed behind them, the young couple looked at each other and smiled.

"You said many wise things," Tanya whispered.

"I only hope I haven't created a problem," Vincent replied.

Shaking her head, Tanya took his hand in hers, and the couple strolled down toward the riverfront gate, exchanging pleasant greetings to the soldiers that passed by, with more than one of them looking enviously at the beautiful girl by Hawthorne's side.

"Let's walk along the river," Tanya said, and eagerly Vincent agreed.

Leaving the fort behind, the couple walked beside the riverbank, the fields and flowing waters around them shimmering by the light of the Wheel and crescent moon overhead. Reaching a stand of high towering pines, the young couple walked beneath the cathedral-like trees, their feet crunching on the needles, the air about them laden with the crisp pungent perfume of the woods.

It was the first time the two had ever been truly alone like this, and Vincent felt a trembling in his heart. In Maine such a thing was simply unheard-of, and even after the announcement of an engagement a couple walking thus alone at night would cause comment.

Their pace slowed and stopped.

Tanya's arm slipped about Vincent's waist, and ever so gently her other hand ran across his cheek and about his neck.

Her lips sought out his, lightly brushing, then lingering.

Eyes open, they gazed at each other as the kiss did not break away but rather grew in passion. Frightened by what he was feeling, Vincent wanted to pull away, even as his arms went about Tanya's waist, pulling her body against his.

Finally the kiss drifted away, but Tanya continued, kissing him on the cheek and neck, eager to search out more.

"We should go back," Vincent whispered hoarsely.

Again her lips sought out his, and terrified, he felt his resolve weakening, his body reacting, wanting her in a way he had never allowed himself to imagine.

He pushed her away.

"It's a sin," Vincent gasped. "We mustn't."

Tanya laughed softly.

"My love, my love."

"And I love you," Vincent replied, finally saying what had been in his heart for weeks.

"If we love, then it is no sin to my people," the girl whispered.

"Your father," Vincent replied lamely.

"He'll never know, and even if he did he would understand," Tanya said gently. "There might be so little time, Vincent. Perm understands that."

She flung herself back into his arms, and the question that had started to form over what she had just said drifted away, as ever so gently the two slowly sank to the ground, still locked in a lovers' embrace.

"So it is as I told you," Kal said, once the door had closed.

"It can't be true," Ilya retorted sharply. "Whoever heard of such a thing—a world turned backward, peasants defeating nobles, churches with no power, men fighting wars so that other men can be made free?

"No, such a world cannot be. For it has always been that peasants labor, nobles grow fat, and the church grows rich."

"But they made their world different."

"He could be lying," Vasilia interjected.

"I don't think so," Boris replied.

"Go on, Boris, explain why."

"I am in the camp of the Yankees every day, helping to haul firewood. The one-armed ruler, and those who wear swords, I first thought to be nobles. But never have I seen them strike another Yankee. I've seen the other soldiers even argue with them at times, and the sword wearers would listen.

"To even speak a word back to a noble is death for us."

"He is right," Nahatkim said evenly, and all turned respectfully to listen. "These men are different. They all act like nobles, like proud men, but most all of them seem kind as well. Not one has struck one of our people. Many give of their time to help. I saw a Yankee take a bundle of wood from an old woman's shoulder and carry it to her cabin. Would a noble ever do such a thing? Their healer cures children. Our healers of skill only serve the nobles and let the children of peasants die. And priests—not a single priest with them when they came through the tunnel of light."

The others in the room nodded their agreement.

"What do you say, Kalencka?" Nahatkim asked. "You know them the best."

"Old Nahatkim is right about what he has seen. And the boy called Hawthorne is a truth speaker, as is Keane. Keane would say nothing of this Declaration thing when I asked. Perhaps he does not want us to know yet. But from what I have learned of Hawthorne, his priests taught him that being truthful is a great virtue, and strangely, that killing another is the greatest sin."

"So that is why he is so sad," Nahatkim whispered.

"He will heal," Kal said quietly, looking over at Ludmilla, who smiled.

"And to heal him is why you insisted that he stay with you while ill," Petrov, one of Kal's cousins, said, laughing. "Or could it be that you wished to find a son, and to talk with him alone and thus learn more truth about these Yankees?"

"He is a good man. I would be proud to have him in my family," Kal said forcefully and with great emotion.

"As for the information, if the mouse cannot hear through the wall, he cuts a hole to listen."

The men chuckled, shaking their heads. None of them was better than Kal at picking up whatever information might be of help.

"So what is the purpose of hearing this?" Vasilia said evenly. "All of you know I would love nothing better than to get my hands around the throat of a boyar, and wring back the sweat they've taken from my brow, but to do so is madness. Hearing these things will only inflame our dreams, but do nothing in the end. If my lord Uthar but heard a single word of what we knew, we'd all be hanging from the wall of his palace before another sun rose."

"There is nothing yet," Kal said quietly. "But what of tomorrow? Perhaps something will change the mind of these Yankees to help us.

"Perhaps because of them," Kal said softly, "our own people might learn to dream of this Declaration thing as well. Yet the Yankees must be behind us if our secret desires are to come to pass. For now Keane trusts Ivor far too much. As boyars go, he is a good one, far better than his father."

"Or his father's father, the Terrible," Nahatkim mumbled.

"But that will change," Kal stated forcefully, "for sooner or later Rasnar will persuade Ivor, or Ivor will come to fear the machines, growing wealth, and popularity of the Yankees."

"But what of the Yankees and the Tugars?" Nahatkim said darkly, and at the mention of the forbidden word the room fell silent.

The mere mention of the horrid name was punishable by

flogging if a priest or noble heard. Now, to speak of the Tugars before a Yankee was punishable by being flayed alive.

"They will find out sooner or later," Nahatkim whispered. "Since they are not of noble blood, or the church, Ivor cannot exempt them all. Will they allow their two out of ten to be led away for the feasting?"

"I think not," Boris replied. "All know how when the boy Hawthorne was a prisoner, the one-armed man raged, ordering all his men to make ready for war to free him. That of itself stunned me, for whoever heard of a noble that cared if a peasant was taken, unless it was a woman he wished to use at the moment?

"Keane will not stand by as more than a hundred of his are led away to the slaughter pits."

"But to resist is madness," Nahatkim whispered. "A single death to a Tugar and a thousand more are slain. If they fight, all of Suzdal go to the slaughter pits."

"So would you agree that we should stand by in the end, do nothing, and let our dream die?" Kal asked, his voice laden with sarcasm. "We know what the church wants, to surprise them some night and murder the lot, or what I suspect Ivor wants, to use them to destroy the church and his rivals, and then to betray them as well."

"What else is there?" Vasilia retorted.

Kal leaned back in his chair and smiled.

"Is it not obvious, and must we not now start to plan? Until the coming of the Yankees I never imagined that the world could be any different from what it is. Now I have heard of another way, and in my heart I want it to be so for my people."

"And the horde?" Nahatkim whispered.

"They are still three years away, and we could do much before they come, if we and the Yankees were one."

The group looked at Kal in amazement.

"You dream too much," Boris replied nervously. "You dance too close to the flame, moth Kalencka. Watch or your wings will burn and all of us will be turned to ashes with you."

"We shall see," Kal replied, looking craftily about the room.

Kicking his mount into a gallop, Muzta moved forward,

letting out a whoop of triumph, for his goal was at last in sight.

The first snows had started almost half a moon before, and the grumbling in the yurts had been loud. Their marches had always been of an even pace, timed so that the large cities of the cattle would be reached before the coming of winter. Supplies would be waiting then for them, the wood cut, tributes piled, the choosers ready to begin the selection.

He was nearly two weeks' ride ahead of the main host, for in his eagerness he wished to make sure that all was ready for the arrival of his people. Now the city was before him.

They had gained almost a year on their march, but the traveling had been hard. Many had sickened and died, thousands of horses had been lost, and the surviving mounts were gaunt, their ribs showing, their coats mottled and dull.

But they had perhaps outraced the wasting sickness of the cattle at last, and could eat here at their leisure until spring. Replenished, they could again perhaps go at their old pace. Perhaps he would have to wait two seasons for the Rus people after all, instead of forcing the march in one.

Cresting the top of the hill, he looked down upon the city. How strange the cattle were, he thought. The Tugar horde, all the people who wandered the world Valdennia, were as one, with same speech, customs, and dress.

But those who stayed in one place, the cattle, all were different. The Maya cities were one of the more interesting to him. Stepped pyramids rose heavenward, the tallest the greatest structure he had ever seen, reaching the height of thirty or more Tugars into the sky.

From atop the pyramids great fires were burning, and on the breeze he caught the faint wafting of burning flesh. These alone of the cattle ate of themselves. The thought struck him as slightly repulsive.

Tula came galloping up to join the host chieftain.

"It'll be good feasting tonight," he said eagerly.

"Let us hope so," Muzta said evenly, "but where is Qubata? He should be here to meet us."

As if answering the Qar Qarth's question, from out of the gates of the city a band of Tugars emerged and started to gallop back up the hill.

"Smells like something good cooking," Tula said jokingly, pointing to the smoke coming from the pyramids.

Muzta merely grunted a reply.

An eddy of snow swirled about the two leaders, blocking the rest of the world off from view, and then drifted away.

Qubata was galloping hard, and Muzta felt a growing uneasiness.

"Something's wrong," Tula snapped.

"Let us see."

The old general came up, reining his mount in before the Qar Qarth.

"The pestilence, my lord," Qubata gasped.

"How? My announcers were here early this year," Muzta cried, "and said there was nothing. The first choosers arrived here a month back, and they said all the cattle were clean."

"It started only yesterday. By some mystery it has come even as fast as we could fly before it."

Kicking his mount, Muzta turned away.

"What are you going to do?" Tula shouted, pulling up before Muzta's mount.

"We must get ahead of it," Muzta said as if to himself.

"Our people are exhausted," Qubata interjected, "and the snow will soon lie heavy."

"Stay and feast here," Tula replied, "and if need be harvest all the cattle by spring."

Muzta looked back at Qubata, who nodded in agreement.

"My Qarth, stay here at least until the snows start to melt. Our horses, our women and children will be fat again. Then we shall ride hard. We'll cover two seasons' march in one and harvest the Rus before the disease marches yet again."

Muzta looked back down at the city. If the pestilence was here he knew that half the cattle, including many of the fattest, would die, and the horde, hungry as it was, would devour the rest.

There would be trouble in this, he realized. For as long as most of the cattle had hope of life, and their leaders were exempt, there had not been trouble, not in the hundred generations since the first of the cattle had appeared.

Before winter was done, that might change. But there was nothing else to be done, he thought grimly.

"This is my command," Muzta replied sadly. "We stay here for the winter, until the sun starts the snow to melt. Then the host will move hard, covering two seasons in one yet again, to next winter with the Rus."

Tula smiled outwardly, but the thoughts of his heart he did not show. The Qar Qarth's decision had saved his own life, for if he had tried to press on it would then have been possible to depose him.

"And the announcers of our arrival?" Qubata asked.

"Yes, we'd best send them forward at once to the eastern cities of the Maya, telling them we shall be there come early summer, and then on to the Rus, to prepare them for our wintering when the snow falls again."

"They might not be ready for us," Qubata said evenly. "We shall be coming two seasons early."

"Then tell our announcers to make it clear that early or not we expect them to be ready. Have the Namer of Time gather several pets that speak the Rus tongue. Start him riding tonight—he must ride as swift as the wind and get there before the snow stops all from travel."

"Shall we eat, my lord?" Tula said, pointing down to the city.

Muzta looked at the man coldly.

"Not until my people are here," he said evenly, and then, turning back to the west, he disappeared into the storm.

Chapter 9

Rasnar looked across the table at the soldier. Forcing his best smile, he reached into a small box on his desk, pulled out a gold coin, and tossed it across the table.

"I don't want it," the soldier replied, his voice edged with sarcasm.

"And why not? I assume that is why you've come to talk to me."

Searching for the right words in Russian, Private Hinsen spoke slowly.

"I am no fool. I know you or the nobles will kill us all."

Rasnar did not reply, barely able to understand the atrocious accent of the infidel before him.

"I want a promise of my life in return for service."

Rasnar nodded slowly.

"And gold, silver, or women in return as well?" Rasnar asked.

Hinsen's eyes lit up in spite of his desire not to reveal his other motives.

Rasnar laughed softly.

"I can use someone like you, and reward you well," the prelate said, pouring out a fresh cup of tea for the both of them.

"I always reward my friends as they deserve," Rasnar continued, his features lighting with a smile.

Andrew looked up from his desk for a moment, and adjusted the wick of the single lamp that lit his cabin. There was a chill to the cabin, and rising, he opened the Franklin stove and tossed in another log. Winter had settled in over a month and a half ago, but then there had come a long break, which felt almost like Indian summer creeping back again. The weather had held until lowering clouds and cold rains came lashing in during the afternoon.

Tobias had finally returned last week from his explorations, and the camp had been abuzz with stories as the sailors swaggered about, boasting of the things they had seen.

The sea was indeed landlocked, as he had suspected, with the Rus on the northern edge. Rarely was it more than a hundred miles in width, but it had stretched nearly five hundred miles southward, bordered by wide-open steppes to either side. Hardly anyone had been spotted until the southern end of the ocean was reached.

"Carthaginians," Andrew mumbled to himself upon first hearing Tobias's account of what had happened. The architecture and ships Tobias described sounded like accounts of Carthage and their colonies in Spain. Unfortunately there'd been no communication with their city, for at the mere sight of the *Ogunquit* a host of rams had sallied forth. Without artillery, Tobias had fled, pursued eastward to where the sea apparently doglegged into another ocean. Finally turning back northward the captain rounded back up the east coast of what he now called the American Sea. To the amazement of all, a type of freshwater whale was spotted. Boats had been lowered and the chase was on.

Andrew looked up again at the lamp. Whale oil gave a good light, but somehow it bothered him. First of all, the stink from the rough tryworks down by the docks had been horrendous. Second, he felt a strange sympathy for the innocent beast that had been so gleefully slaughtered by Tobias's sailors. He wished somehow that he could order them to cease hunting, but knew that the oil was needed, and thus his personal feelings could not intervene.

Standing, he stretched and went to the door. The rain had eased off, and brief glimpses of the second moon, Cysta, shone dimly through the passing clouds.

Work was going far better than expected. To his amazement, Ferguson seemed to be right on schedule. Kal's work gangs were now almost as good as anything he had seen back in the States. By the hundreds they'd been grading the trail and hauling up tons of crushed limestone as ballast. H Company's ferry service was running full-out from dawn to sunset, carrying the limestone both for the ballast and the foundry, with a second boat coming on line early last week.

The first trip-hammer had finally gone into operation, drawing its power from an undershot wheel hastily constructed in a side channel above the foundry's main wheel. It was barely adequate for the job, but would do till spring when the twin twenty-foot wheels, now being laid out, were put into place. Even with the weak power provided, the iron straps needed for rails were starting to come out, and track had been laid from the dock nearly halfway up to the sawmill.

The boys of E Company had gone into round-the-clock work at the foundry, finally persuading C Company, which had yet to latch on to a project, to throw in with them for a quarter share of the profits. Some of them only came down the hill for morning roll, and the mandatory regimental drill which was still held each afternoon.

There was now even a banking system of sorts. The various companies had elected corporators and a board. It took some rather difficult calculations, but somehow a system had been worked up whereby each company would shift paper credits back and forth for exchanges of goods and services, turning half of all newly created wealth over to the regimental account.

Bill Webster, of Company A, whose father had been a banker back in Portland, was now president of that operation. Andrew had to confess that most all aspects of finance were beyond him and had simply entrusted the bald-headed nineteen-year-old with the task. The boy was obviously delighted with the task normally reserved for someone nearly three times his age, and had set to with a will. Shares for capitalization were being sold to the various companies, and Gates's paper company was turning out a special run of green-dyed currency. They were planning to put the seal of Maine on the back of it and engravings of Andrew, O'Donald, Cromwell, Weiss, and even Ivor on the front.

That had been a source of a rather amusing argument as the four officers bickered over who would get which denomination, since they thought it best that Ivor get the top-valued fifty-dollar bill. Finally they'd drawn straws, and though he hated to admit it, Andrew felt a touch of chagrin at drawing the lowly dollar slot. As luck would have it, Tobias pulled the twenty-dollar slot and had been visibly puffed up as a result.

Turning back to his desk, Andrew looked over the work rosters. A and K Companies were now primarily devoted to lumbering, since most of the boys had been recruited out of the Skowhegan area where the great northern woods was the major source of industry.

C Company was working alongside of E at the foundries and ore mines, while D still held sway at its sawmill, which had finally received its new eight-foot blade that tore through the logs like a banshee gone berserk. H was still taken up with its boats and G with the grain-mill operation, which was running twenty-four hours a day as well. B was over in the limestone quarries, and J had found itself recruited to be dam builders, ready to go in a couple of days with Weiss to start the largest project of all.

O'Donald's men had gravitated to the foundry and the forge of Dunlevy, where the metal was being worked into wrought and cast iron, and just the other day a passable steel had been turned out for the first time.

This didn't even begin to take into account the dozens of smaller projects that had been started by various individuals, including paper-making, and a printing press that was ready to turn out the regiment's first newspaper. Hawthorne was in high demand from the nobles to make more clocks, and Tobias's sailors were turning out oil. Jackson had his bakery—the only problem was that he was still learning how to turn out quality bread, and if it hadn't been for the intervention of Ludmilla and her friends, Andrew believed, they all most likely would have been poisoned by now.

Dr. Weiss was even working on the idea of a small glass works, believing it would trigger a thriving business with the nobles if he could ever master the art of making spectacles.

"Good evening, sir."

Andrew turned in his chair and looked to the door, which he had left open.

"Well, hello, Hawthorne. Out for a walk on a night like this?"

"It's rather nice, actually," Hawthorne said softly, and behind the boy, Andrew could see Tanya.

"That it is, son," Andrew said, looking at the girl, "that it is."

"Well, I saw the door open and thought I'd say hello. We'd best be going now, sir."

Andrew smiled as the couple walked into the darkness, and his thoughts turned back to Kathleen.

What had happened there? he wondered. Since that day over four months back with James she had kept herself removed, spending time with Emil, tending the steady trickle of sick that always came in and the men who had yet to return from insanity, or walking in the evenings by herself.

She had politely refused all his offers for rides, or visits to the city. Was it him after all? Had Mary scarred him so deeply that he could never open up again, and had Kathleen, sensing that, simply backed away? Or was it the blood of the war that had wrapped itself so deeply into his soul that Kathleen could see him only as yet another killing machine, who all too easily could be killed himself? Could he ever find happiness, he wondered, or had that possibility been half killed by Mary and finished forever at Gettysburg? —leaving him now with nothing but the fear of being hurt and the nightmares about his brother that still came to haunt him.

"Your colonel always looks so sad, so distant," Tanya said softly, pressing her warmth up against Hawthorne's side.

"I can understand."

"The same way the sadness is still in your eyes."

Hawthorne was silent. Every night was haunted by the

look that man had given him as the life drained out of him,
or the scream of Sadler, or that moment as he hung drifting
into the darkness. How could he ever explain?

"You are alive, Hawthorne. We have a saying, life is for
all, peasant and noble, love is for the young, with Kesus's
grace contentment and peace for the old."

Trembling, she stepped in front of Hawthorne and looked
into his eyes.

"I love you," she whispered, pulling him close, her lips
brushing against his.

"You're trembling, Tanya," and his arms went about her,
holding her tight, and at that moment the nightmare thoughts
were gone.

"Come away with me. Leave with me tonight," she whispered, between kisses.

"What are you saying?" he whispered back, brushing her
dark flowing hair.

Tears started to flow.

"Just leave with me," she whispered. "We'll run away to
the east. Perhaps there nothing will hurt you."

"Desert?" He started to laugh softly. "Tanya, Tanya,
I'm a soldier. I cannot desert. These are my people and
friends."

"Please, my love," and in her eyes he saw terror.

"What is it?" His hands tightened about her slender arms.
"Why are you so frightened?"

"I can't say," she whispered. "Oh, my love, trust me. We
can leave tonight, long, long before . . ."

Her voice trailed off. She was frightened to tell him that
she knew for certain that a new life was stirring within, a
new life she never wanted to place at risk. The whispered
conversations of her father and his friends terrified her. She
feared he was mad with this wild dream that they were
starting to hatch. For surely it would fail. He would die, as
would her beloved, and even if she was spared, surely the
unborn child would be sent into the pits as punishment
when the Tugars came.

"The colonel has that Rasnar fellow in check. Don't be
afraid of what he might do."

She shook her head.

"It's not that."

"Then what?"

"I can't say. Just leave with me before it's too late. There are people we call the Wanderers who forever travel eastward. We can join them and be safe there."

"Tanya, what is it you aren't telling me?"

She turned her head away, shaking with sobs.

"Is it the Tugars?" Hawthorne said quietly.

Shocked, the girl looked back at him, terror in her eyes.

"It's this thing called Tugars, isn't it?" Hawthorne asked insistently.

"Where did you hear that word?" she gasped.

"Once when I was sick and you thought me asleep, I heard you talking to your father, and that word was spoken. He slapped you lightly as if to warn you. Again I heard it whispered while passing two beggars on the road who were gazing at one of those ghastly statues. Tanya, what are the Tugars?"

"I can't."

Taps started to echo in the background.

"You must go back," she said, trying to pull herself loose from his grip. But he held her tight.

"Tanya, I love you," he whispered. "You must tell me what they are."

"To do so means death for me, my entire family."

"You must tell me, please. I will not run away, I cannot. But if there is something that can hurt my friends I must know."

Sobbing, she looked at her lover beseechingly.

Opening the door, Andrew wiped the sleep from his eyes.

"Hawthorne, it's long past taps. There'd better be a damn good reason for this."

The boy stood before him trembling, his face ashen.

"Sir, it's monstrous."

"What?"

Wide-eyed, the boy looked at him.

"Come on in, sit down."

Andrew went over to his foot locker, pulled out a bottle of brandy, and, pouring a drink, handed it to the trembling soldier. To his shocked amazement the Quaker took the drink and downed it. The lad started to cough, and then as the liquor took effect the trembling eased.

"Sir, I found out about the Tugars."

"Tell me," he said evenly.

Pulling over a chair, he sat across from the private, who started to talk, his voice near to breaking.

There was a knock at the door, and the two looked up. Several drinks were now missing from the bottle, and Andrew wasn't sure if his stomach was churning from the liquor or with the horror of it all.

Before they could respond, the door flew open and Kal came in, dragging Tanya behind him, her eyes puffy from crying.

"Did she tell you?" Kal cried excitedly, looking at Hawthorne.

The boy nodded in reply and, standing, came over to Tanya, who pulled free from her father and flung herself into his arms.

Tanya cradled herself in Vincent's protective embrace. Too much had happened now for her even to dare to tell him of the other news which she had so eagerly wished to speak of. But she could see that now was not the time.

Without asking for permission, Kal poured himself a drink, downed it, and stood before Andrew.

"Kal, this is monstrous, sickening," Andrew said coldly. "Absolutely goddam sickening."

"You mustn't say anything," Kal begged.

"Say anything? Goddammit, man, do you expect me to stand by while twenty percent of my men are dragged out to be slaughtered like cattle? Damn you, I'll fight them to the last before allowing that."

"Colonel Keane, please don't."

"How could you people allow this? Isn't there a man among you to stand up to this? What is wrong with all of you? Better to die weapon in hand than to be driven to the slaughter pits like sheep!"

"Then no one would be here," Kal said dryly. "You have not seen the horde, and I have. They are as numberless as the trees of the forest. They stand near twice our height. Any one of them could lift a man off the ground with a single hand and crush the life from his body. They are as unstoppable as the snow, or the river in spring torrent. Nothing can stay them. Thus it has always been—nobles rule, the church takes, and peasants toil and are chosen to die."

Even as Kal spoke, he kept his inner thoughts hidden, wishing to hear and to see what Andrew would say in response.

"If we do not submit, they slaughter all. Better that two shall die than all ten, for thus we still live. If a peasant dares to say no, the nobleman slays him out of hand, for thus it has always been."

"Such talk sickens me," Andrew snarled. "Better to die as free men than to live as cattle to these fiends."

"Then you will fight them?" Kal asked quietly.

"You're damn right I'll fight them."

Kal slowly started to smile.

"Just what the hell are you smiling about?" Andrew roared.

"I knew you would act like this."

"How else did you expect me to act?"

"Some thought you would give yourselves to Ivor, or even Rasnar, trading your weapons for protection by the nobles, or indulgences by the church."

"Like hell I would. You mean Ivor allows this?"

"His father helped in the choosing the last time, and thus my father went to the pits. It is the nobles' privilege to help select and to spare, and the memory of the wolf is long when it comes to the mice that have annoyed him."

"Why haven't your people fought?" Andrew asked.

"With what, our bare hands?"

Disgusted, Andrew turned away.

"Ivor is coming here tomorrow," Andrew said sharply. "I plan to ask him just what the hell he intends to do when these savages show up again."

"Don't," Kal begged. "It will be death for my daughter and me. Even if you deny we told you, still he'll suspect and kill us out of hand."

"I'll protect you," Andrew said.

"I belong to Ivor. He'd never permit you to harbor a peasant that he can rightfully claim."

"How long till they come?" Andrew asked.

"They are still three snow seasons away from us. Do not jump into the fire before it has even started to burn, my friend."

Andrew sat down and poured another drink for himself,

not bothering to offer one to Kal, or the now slightly inebri-
ated Hawthorne.

"I'll wait," Andrew said coldly. "But by God you'd better
know right now that when the time comes, this regiment will
fight to the last man. If Ivor wants my help, he'll have it.
Otherwise we'll stand against them alone."

"Come, Tanya," Kal said, looking back to his daughter.

Hawthorne pulled her to his side protectively.

"I won't hurt her," Kal said gently, extending his hand,
and led his daughter out into the night.

"Please, Father, I'm sorry," she gasped between racking
sobs.

He didn't know whether to punish or to thank her, but at
least the impasse had been crossed.

"Just keep your foolish mouth closed," and giving her a
chastising swat across the backside, he led the girl home,
and by the time he had reached the cabin the peasant felt
somehow different. Could there truly be another way after
all? Might his dream not be quite so mad as others said?

Somehow he just couldn't get himself to concentrate on
his work. The enormity of what Andrew had confided in
him the night before could not be washed away or simply
turned off.

"Sir, it'll be a hell of an engineering project. We'll need to
build an earthen dam thirty feet high for two hundred yards."
As he spoke, Ferguson pointed to the narrow pass above
the city, through which the Vina River passed, before wending
its way past Suzdal and on into the Neiper.

"What was that?" Emil asked, looking back over to the
private who along with Kal stood beside him.

"There, sir. Partway up the rapids, that's where we should
build it. It'll cause the whole valley farther up to flood, and
there'll be enough of a dropoff here to position a dozen
heavy mills and still have enough water left over to send
down to the city through a covered aqueduct."

Emil tried to focus his attention back to the task at hand.

Ivor, who sat next to him, was obviously confused by
Ferguson, who kept peering through a roughly made survey-
or's transit, and then turned back to scribble on his note and
sketch pads.

Emil looked over at Ivor, wondering how the man could
allow his people to live in such squalid conditions. The

constant threat of pestilence in the city had driven him to
near distraction since their arrival, for if it broke out there,
it would sweep over the regiment in no time. He felt the
answer was simple.

The Suzdalians drew their water from the Neiper and
from the Vina, which flowed past the north wall of the
lower town. The problem was that the damn fools allowed
their raw sewage to go straight back in. Since the city rose
above the two rivers on a series of low-lying hills, bringing
the water up to their dwellings was even harder. Most of
them relied on hand-dug wells, and to his horror their sinks
and cesspools were more often than not positioned sometimes only a dozen feet away.

His prediction had come true regarding the sickness in the
regiment. Nearly thirty boys had come down with typhoid
and other complaints, and two of them rested up on cemetery hill as a result. All of them had sickened after visits to
the town.

So there was only one answer: build a dam farther up the
Vina and trap its fresh waters in the gorge where Hawthorne
had been found after his escape. The dam would be higher
than the tallest hill in Suzdal, and thus the water could be
directed anywhere needed. Of course, the moment Emil had
raised the idea Ferguson had leaped into the project, seeing
in it a tremendous potential for waterpower as well.

Emil turned about and looked back down the valley toward
the city of Suzdal four miles away. How could those people
ever allow such a barbarity to be permitted? Silently he
cursed. Medieval barbarians, all of them. Dammit, Andrew
should load up the *Ogunquit* and get all of them the hell out
of here and leave them to their stink, disease, petty squab-
bles, and the Tugars.

"A beauiful site, sirs," Ferguson said, looking up at the
two men. "It'll take a lot of labor. A dam thirty feet high,
by sixty at the base tapering up, and two hundred yards long
comes to over five hundred thousand cubic yards of fill."

"Now, just how the hell much is that?" Emil asked.

"Well, if we had five thousand men working on it, I figure
it'll be something like nearly a half year to finish it up. But
there'd be one awful lot of power pent up behind it. Tens of
thousands of horsepower."

And water enough to clean that cesspool out good and
proper, Emil thought.

"Many men, way too many men," Ivor growled.

"Perhaps an arrangement could be made," Emil replied, looking over to Kal for a translation. "We'll want the site for new mills, of course, and I'm sure Colonel Keane would be willing to pay with iron or some other such goods to rent your people for the work."

Ivor looked craftily at Emil, ready to start with some hard bargaining. Then in the distance there came the tolling of a bell.

Ivor turned in his saddle and looked. Another bell started in, and then another. Uneasy, Ivor and the guards that accompanied him looked about. Suddenly one of the guards pointed off toward the river road that was visible north of the city.

Antlike creatures appeared to be riding hard. Ivor strained his eyes to see. Reaching around to his saddlebags, Emil pulled out field glasses, raised them to his eyes, and brought the procession into focus.

"In the name of God," Emil whispered.

Nervous, Ivor looked over at the doctor.

"Tugars," Emil said softly.

The boyar blanched as if the word could somehow strike him. For the moment he completely forgot to ask how Emil knew the word.

With a shout, the fat boyar spurred his horse forward, his guards clattering behind them.

"So what got them into an all-fired rush?" Ferguson asked.

Emil looked over at Kal.

"We'd better get down there," Kal whispered.

"Ferguson, get your gear together. Let's go."

And moments later the three were charging down the hill and toward the city, where all the bells were tolling and cries of panic rent the air.

The gates of the city were flung open, and as one the terrified residents lining the street fell prostrate to the ground, none daring to look.

Deep-throated nargas, the thunder trumpets of the Tugars, blasted with a chilling bass peal that sounded like the cries of the damned. A dozen trumpeters rode in, astride their great mounts. Behind them came the rollers of doom, their great kettledrums lashed to either side of their mounts, the warriors of the golden clan swinging their mallets back and forth, setting up a trembling roar like thunder. Six of them entered, and behind them the twenty riders of the guard appeared, their great six-foot war bows drawn, arrows nocked.

And then at last came he who was simply known as the Namer of Time, he who came to let all cattle know that soon they would be honored by the presence of the Tugar horde. For with his arrival the people of Rus must now prepare, to prepare two years early for the choosing, to bring in their harvests, to fill the grain houses, to fatten the beasts they themselves ate and to have all ready—silver, goods, supplies, iron, and finally themselves.

The Namer of Time sat crosslegged on his great platform, which was mounted atop the backs of four horses. Grinning skulls rimmed the platform, bleached rib cages hung from the sides. The pennant snapping above him was the color of blood.

Onward the procession came, behind the Namer came yet twenty more archers, and then finally the pets—Suzdalians who had disappeared with the horde nearly a generation before and now returned home at last. Their eyes were clouded with tears, tears at the horrors they had grown inured to, horror that they were now outcast in their own land, which they had stopped dreaming of long ago.

Eyes wide with terror, Emil stood speechless in the square. What approached was beyond his most fevered dreams. They seemed like some devil-dreamed parody of a man. Eight feet in height some of them seemed; the one atop the platform he judged to be closer to ten. Their faces were sharp, cunning, near devil-like, covered entirely with a matting of hair, as were their bodies. All about him threw themselves face first upon the ground as the procession crossed the great square.

The outriders wore heavy chain mail. Their helmets were red-lacquered, atop each of them a grinning human skull. The nargas and drums thundered and roared, echoing and reechoing across the square.

"Get down, both of you!" Kal hissed, lying on the ground. "You'll be shot if you don't."

He had never knelt to anyone in his life, but this time Emil could fully see the logic of it, and he went down on his belly, pulling Ferguson alongside.

The procession came to the middle of the square. Thundering to a crescendo, the nargas blasted a final chilling roar, and then there was silence.

"Arise, people of the Rus!"

Emil came to his feet, his blood running cold. The Tugar riding upon the platform stood above them, his robes fluttering in the breeze. Looking closer, Emil recoiled in horror. The robes were made of tanned human skin. For the first time in years the doctor struggled to keep from swooning. Beside him Ferguson, wide-eyed with terror, turned and vomited.

"People of Rus," the Tugar roared, his deep grating voice giving a sinister edge to the Suzdalians' tongue. "People of Rus, I come as the Namer of Time!"

A chorus of lamentations rose up from the crowd.

The Tugar extended his great hairy arms, and the cries drifted away with the breeze.

"For it is the wish of Muzta, Qar Qarth of all the northern steppe, to come unto you when the snow flies yet again. Make yourselves ready for his coming, people of Rus.

"Let the boyar of these people, let the holy man of these people, come forward."

Emil stood on his toes to watch as Ivor came down from the steps of his palace, while from across the square the doors of the great cathedral swung open, and Rasnar stepped out, followed by a procession of priests, waving censers of smoke and carrying the great icon of Perm.

The Tugar looked down from the platform at the two.

"Is all as it should be?" the Tugar roared. "Are all the lands ordered for our coming?"

"You are early," Ivor said, his voice cracking with fear.

The Namer raised his head heavenward, his laughter booming in short vicious bursts.

"That is not for you to question, but for me to announce. If not ready now, then ready you must be when the Wheel rises and falls once again with the passing of a year."

"Then we shall be ready," Ivor said nervously, bowing low.

"Two you must choose for me now, for my warriors hunger, then tonight we shall talk of all that must be done."

"Emil, Ferguson," Kal hissed, "start backing out of here quietly."

Emil didn't need any prompting. The menace was becoming all too real.

"Yet all is not ready," came a voice from the square. Emil hesitated and looked back. It was Rasnar!

"Speak to him, Ivor, speak to him of the Yankees."

The Tugar turned and looked down at the priest.

"We shall talk of that tonight. First choose for me our repast!"

"Get out of here now!" Kal hissed.

Feeling a growing sense of terror, Emil followed Kal and Ferguson as they pushed their way out of the square. Emil looked at those about him. They stood numb, as if possessed by a terror so great that their hearts and minds had ceased to function.

Reaching the edge of the crowd, the three broke into a run toward the south gate. Gasping for breath, they reached the guardhouse where their horses were tethered. Looking back up the street, Emil heard a loud cry, and suddenly the sea of faces turned to look in their direction.

Needing no prompting, Emil spurred his horse with such desperation that for a moment he thought the mare would throw him, and then with a splattering of mud the three galloped through the gate and on down the road back to Fort Lincoln.

"They're coming!"

Hans, riding Andrew's mount, came galloping through the gate. Pulling up hard, he looked down at the colonel.

"They're coming, sir. I saw Ivor galloping out front, but not a mile behind them were the rest of those things, with that damned priest riding alongside."

"All right, Hans. Get the men ready."

Nervous, Andrew looked around at his command. Anything that could so badly frighten Emil had to be something truly terrifying.

The regiment was in an ugly mood. He wasn't sure if it was at him, or at what was coming. He had formed them on the parade ground an hour ago and told them all that he knew. His explanation had been greeted with stunned silence.

Hinsen had stepped forward and demanded to know how long Andrew had known of the Tugars. He had to tell them the truth, that he had been keeping the information secret for nearly a week. There was no time for an explanation, but he would have to give one once this crisis had been met.

The orders having been given, the men stood to at their positions along the wall and waited.

"Keep the gate open," Andrew said, and with Hans and the two color bearers behind him he stepped out of the fortress.

Coming straight down the road, Ivor was now plainly in view, his knights strung out behind him. Motioning for Hans and the other three to stay back, Andrew walked down the road to meet him.

Signaling his knights to wait, Ivor continued ahead, reining up in front of Andrew.

"So now you know," Ivor said evenly, looking down at Andrew.

"Now I know," Andrew replied.

"And what do you plan to do?" Ivor asked.

"Submit to that?" Andrew looked up at a man whom he felt he could almost call a friend. "Never!"

"In the square Rasnar named your Weiss and Ferguson as the chosen for tonight. I claimed the right of exemption. It was a difficult moment, and the Namer was not amused."

"Thank you for that, my friend."

"But Rasnar told of you, and he decided to come and see."

"Let him look all he wants," Andrew said coldly.

"My friend, do not resist. Now that the Namer has pronounced his words, he will leave tomorrow and return to the horde. No one of yours will be chosen today."

"Until next year, and then two out of ten of my men will die."

Ivor was silent.

"You knew I'd never submit, didn't you?" Andrew whispered.

Ivor nodded.

"But you will not fight them."

"We all shall die if I do."

"Maybe so," Andrew said coldly. "If you knew that and planned not to fight, then what was your reason for not trying to destroy me at once? Or did you plan to use me first, to overthrow Rasnar completely, subjugate the other cities, and then when we had weakened in your service to finish us off?"

Ivor looked straight at Andrew.

"I had thought of that at first," he said evenly, "but as the months passed I had hoped that maybe there would be another way."

"But time is up, years ahead of when you planned."

"That is true," Ivor said grimly, "and you are my vassal. I order you to submit."

Smiling sadly, Andrew shook his head.

The nargas sounded in the distance, and through the edge of the woods the first of the riders appeared. Stunned, the men of the 35th started to shout excitedly.

"Silence in the ranks," Hans roared. "Show them how men from Maine can stand!"

An eerie silence descended over the fort, punctuated by the growing blare of the nargas and the thundering of drums.

"There is no more time," Ivor roared, and spurring his horse about he galloped back toward the advancing procession.

Andrew returned to stand beneath the shot-torn battle standards. Try as he might he could not still the pounding of his heart as the great platform carrying its terrifying burden drew closer and closer, and finally stopped, the foul breath of the lead horses washing over him.

He looked straight ahead.

"You who are called Yankee, prostrate thyself before the Namer of Time, the voice of Muzta Qar Qarth, and the Tugar horde."

Standing rigid, Andrew did not move.

"Look up at me, Yankee!"

Andrew raised his head. Atop the high platform the Tugar gazed down from a height of nearly twenty feet. His dark fangs revealed by a leering grimace, he gazed down like a hawk examining its prey.

"So you have come through the gate of light as have the other cattle of this world."

The astonishment on Andrew's face showed, and the Tugar roared with delight.

"Yes, we of the horde know of the light, the gate that opens to bring us new races of cattle to feast upon. Some have tried to resist us. Their bones filled our feasting pits. Other, like the Rus you now live among, learned better, as you will learn.

"Learn to live, Yankee, for there is no other way."

The Tugar turned about, surveying the camp before him. His gaze lingered on the *Ogunquit*, and then moved to the railroad track, which ran from the dock and headed on up to the mills.

"The holy man has told me of your mysteries. We will teach you submission."

Andrew remained silent.

The Tugar leaped off the platform, the skull hanging about his waist rattling. He swaggered forward, still grinning. For a moment he paused to look at the flags and then turned to face Andrew.

"Are you the leader of the Yankees?"

"My name is Keane."

"Cattle do not give names unless asked," the Tugar snapped. "But you, cattle named Keane, will learn."

Andrew looked up at the Tugar and fixed him with his gaze. For long seconds the two seemed locked in a struggle. Andrew felt cold, distant, and filled with loathing.

"You are defiant," the Tugar hissed. "I even like that in cattle. You will be my pet. I need one as you to teach me your tongue. Prepare to ride with me back to Muzta Qar Qarth to tell him of your people."

"Like hell," Hans growled, and started to step forward.

"Sergeant! Stand fast!"

"Ah, so the pet has an old one with fangs to protect him. There are cattle on the other side of this world among whom old men and younger ones such as you love each other. Is that it?" The Tugar laughed hoarsely.

Disgusted, Andrew spat on the ground.

With a roar the Tugar's arm swung out. Andrew tried to duck under the blow, but still it caught him on his left shoulder and he tumbled to the ground.

The sharp crack of a carbine echoed out, and the Tugar staggered back. More shocked than hurt, he held up his hand, as blood started to pour out of the wound where a bullet had creased his lower arm.

There was a moment of stunned silence, broken only by Kathleen's scream as she struggled to break from Emil's grasp and rush to Andrew.

Andrew came to his feet, and straightening his uniform fixed the amazed Tugar with his gaze.

His bloodied hand shot out, pointing at Hans.

"Kill me that cattle!" the Namer roared.

"Regiment, take aim!" Andrew shouted, and the five hundred men mounting the wall snapped their rifles down.

Andrew looked out of the corner of his eye at the Tugar

warriors, who, having spread out to either side, stood in their stirrups, bows drawn taut.

"Go ahead," Andrew said evenly. "I'll die, and so will the three out here with me. But I promise you, when my men shoot their weapons at you, they'll be picking up pieces of your body on the other side of the river."

For long seconds the tension held.

"They can do it," Rasnar pleaded, rushing up to the Namer's side. "They can do it, the infidels."

The Namer did not even spare the priest a glance.

Barking a sharp laugh, the Namer slowly lowered his arm, strolled back to the platform, and climbed back up.

"You will be amusement then for Qubata," the Namer growled. "It's been long since that grayhair had sport to chase."

At a bark of command the horses started to turn.

"For you two," and the hatred in his eyes showed, "I will not have your throats slit first.

"No," he said, hissing, "you'll turn on my spit while still alive, and then watch as I draw your livers out and eat them before your eyes."

"Perhaps it will be I who watch your body being shoveled into the ground," Andrew snapped in reply, "for we Yankees would not soil our table with your foul flesh."

The Tugar fixed Andrew with a long hateful gaze. The platform turned and started back toward the city, and the Suzdalians who had been watching fell to their faces at his passing.

Rasnar looked back coldly, and kicking his mount galloped off with the party. Ivor sat for a long moment watching Andrew and then turned and followed the procession as well.

As the procession reached the bridge over the mill stream, the Namer gestured to one of his riders, who reined his mount about and stopped, while the rest of the party disappeared from view.

Andrew watched him for a moment and then, turning, started back into the fort.

"Andrew!"

Hans hit him hard, throwing the colonel to the ground. A four-foot shaft screamed past. There was a startled cry, and the bearer of the Maine flag, who had been standing behind Andrew, tumbled over backward, the colors dropping to the ground.

A rippling volley slashed out from the fort. Tugar and

mount went crashing to the ground. Coming to his feet, Andrew ran over to the soldier who'd been hit and was now covered with the state colors. Already an ugly stain of scarlet was working its way up through the faded silk.

Andrew pulled the flag back. The boy was dead; the arrow had been driven clean through his chest and had buried itself in the earthen wall behind him.

He looked back up to where the dead Tugar lay sprawled on the ground. Several Suzdalians pulled him free from his horse and then dragged the corpse off.

"Most likely wanted to see what our rifles could do," Hans said quietly, "and take you out at the same time."

"A good hundred and fifty yards," Andrew said, judging the range. "That's one hell of a shot."

Kal, Emil, and Kathleen came rushing up to Andrew's side.

"Now they will want a thousand heads for the death of one," Kal said.

Andrew turned and looked back at the body being carried back into the camp.

"The bill's already been paid in full," Andrew snapped in reply.

Chapter 10

"I still can't believe it," Nahatkim whispered. "Three times before in my life I have seen the Tugars come. But never, never have I seen one die."

A mumbled chorus of agreements echoed around the table.

"Did you see his body?" Boris said excitedly. "I got close enough. There must have been half a hundred holes in it. He was torn to pieces—it was a beautiful sight."

"But that was only one Tugar," Ilya retorted. "They are as numberless as fish in the sea."

"Yet there are some among us who will fight," Kal said forcefully "Have we not fought before? When the nobles squabble they drive us out of the fields to march by their sides, and so brothers kill brothers for the sport of the damned boyars.

"It is a time of choosing," Kal continued. "What allowed the Yankees to live was Ivor's hatred of Rasnar, and Rasnar's desire to manipulate Ivor and the Yankees and in the end steal their secrets. But now that the Tugars come early, Ivor is in fear. He will turn against the Yankees."

"Can he beat them?" Boris asked.

"Maybe so," Kal replied. "All they need do is surround the camp and starve them, or find some evil to strike them down first. Perhaps the Yankees, now that they know the full truth, will take their great ship and sail away. If they do, Ivor will fall, and Rasnar will become all-powerful. Then you know that the people of Suzdal will be sent to the pits while Novrod will gain exemption, because Mikhail will gain control of us, and then punish us for revenge."

Nahatkim, leaning on his cane, slowly came to his feet.

"I have seen seventy-seven snows," the old man whispered hoarsely. "Three times I have seen the pits. The first time I watched the girl that I loved dragged in for their moon feast, the second time my father and mother, and the third time—" he paused, his voice choked—"and the third time my only son, with the lame foot, whom I loved more than my life."

The old man looked about the room with rheumy eyes.

"And we allow this," he cried. "We have allowed our names as men to be changed to cattle. They, the cursed church, the fat boyars and nobles, they have used such a thing to rule us, to subjugate us, to rob us, and in the end to take away our pride as men.

"I listened to these Yankees. They know the answer, they know it is better to die now as men than to live as slaves. Better to stand upon a field as men, even if their heads will only be held high for that one day, than to sire children, knowing in our hearts that someday they will be led to the slaughter pits crying in terror.

"What have we become, oh Kesus, for we are no longer men," and with tears streaking his face the old man sat down.

Kal looked about the room. All were silent, their eyes

fixed on Nahatkim, many of them with tears running down their cheeks.

"We fight," Kal said hoarsely. "There are twenty of us to each noble. We will fight the nobles first, and after them the Tugars, and we will make this Declaring thing that Hawthorne spoke of."

There was a nervous tension in the packed room. Kal looked about at the men. Here were representatives from nearly every major farmholding of Suzdal, and the great households of the city. These were the men who could rally the peasants to the cause. Kal knew what had been in the hearts of all of them, the hundreds of thousands of Rus who as the days drew closer lay awake in terror, even as the nobles laughed and the church counted its silver for the selling of indulgences. It was at the breaking point.

He looked about the room, sensing that all of them wanted to believe, but none would dare try.

From the back of the packed room, Tanya pushed her way forward.

She looked at her father and tried to force a smile.

"I have a life in me here," she said softly, placing her hand over her stomach, and turning, she looked back at the assembly. "I'll fight and die rather than let a noble or priest take that from me to be fed into the pit, and if you are men you'll fight with me!"

There was a moment of stunned silence, which changed in an instant to wild shouts of rage that had been pent up all their lives. Daggers came from belts, slamming into the table.

"We fight!"

Dancing and screaming, the men erupted into wild pandemonium.

Kal spun his daughter around, while the group, howling and shouting, let loose a lifetime of frustration and rage.

"How?" he asked, trying to be heard.

"In the usual way," she said, suddenly nervous. "I wanted to tell you, but . . ."

"Hawthorne?" Kal asked disbelievingly.

Smiling weakly, she nodded in reply.

He was tempted to explode with rage, but the look in her eyes and the pride he felt for what she had just helped to create overwhelmed him.

He pulled her close.

"We're going to have find that boy and have a very long talk."

Then, releasing the girl, he climbed atop the table and shouted for attention.

He looked around at the men. When the excitement wore off, he realized, the full terror of what they had just started would sink in. In his heart he feared that before this was done, together or separately, they would all be hung on the wall or led into the pits, but for the moment he did not care.

"We are not pleased with either of you," the Namer growled.

In spite of each other's presence, Rasnar and Ivor could not conceal their terror.

"The Yankees are your responsibility," the Namer continued, pointing straight at Ivor, "and yours," his gaze shifting to Rasnar.

"But we did not bid them to come here," Ivor protested.

"Yet you suffered them to live among you. Their infection of defiance might spread, and it would be a pity to flatten your cities if they should resist us."

His left hand ran over the wound to his arm. Such a thing had never before been done. He had actually been frightened by them, though he dared not show it or admit it to anyone.

The chant singers had told about cattle who had appeared fifteen or more circlings back. Their face hair was pointed, beneath shining caps of armor. A hundred Tugars had died from their smoke makers before they had been stamped out.

Best to let the cattle settle it now, and if any were left of the Yankees, Qubata would finish them. It was not that he feared their numbers—he had counted not half a thousand of them. It was their defiance which could never be tolerated. Breaking them would keep the Rus cattle in line as well. But they must not be allowed to go elsewhere, to hide and breed.

"I leave now with your own problem to settle by my command. But remember this as well. I want their skulls laid out for me, and all of their devices as well when we return. Let them not escape. I want as well for you to save for me the two leaders who showed defiance. I have a promise to keep with them."

He started from the door, and then paused and looked back. "You boyars and churchmen have lived well under our rule, but such things could be changed. It has happened in other lands to those who keep not their lowest ones respectful of our rule."

Lowering his head to clear the door, the Namer strode out into the nave of the cathedral. He looked at the altar, and laughed at the image of the weak gods of cattle who in the afterworlds must offer their own flesh to Bulgatana, father god of the Chosen Race.

Peering anxiously from the window, Ivor and Rasnar watched as the Namer mounted his high platform. The nargas and drums sounded and the procession passed up across the empty square. A knot of peasants stood off to one side, shrieking in sorrow as fifty of their loved ones, hooked to chains, staggered off behind the column, food for the march back westward.

"Now you must be with me," Rasnar said coldly, looking back at Ivor.

The boyar sat down heavily, and adjusting his glasses he looked at his hated foe.

"If all the Rus were united," he said quietly, "peasant, noble, church, we could fight them."

"Are you mad?" Rasnar hissed. "They would smash us into the ground. Do you think I like them, knowing they hold power over us? Remember your station, Ivor. We rule through them."

"We could rule without them," the boyar said coldly.

"You are mad."

"The Yankees could show us how."

"So that was your hope as well, wasn't it? That is why you did nothing for now, and let them build their infernal devices upon your land. You became tempted to defy even the Tugars. But now they come too soon for your mad dream to be possible."

Ivor was silent.

"You know what the Yankees will do. They will fight and they will die. For each death of a Tugar, a thousand must die. If the Yankees can even kill one for one, half the people of all Rus will die in retribution, and I daresay there will be no exemption for nobles this time."

"We could fight alongside them," Ivor said again, coldly.

"If you dare," Rasnar hissed, "then through me all the

cities of Rus will march against you, for there is no love
between you and your brother boyars. They think you fat,
overproud, and desirous of being named Ivor the Great
rather than Ivor Weak Eyes as you really are."

With a snarl, the boyar stood up and started for the door.

"What will it be? Defeat the Yankees and the church will
not object to your becoming the Great. Defy me and it will
be Mikhail instead."

Ivor turned and looked back at Rasnar. Somehow an idea
had started to form over these months, but now he knew it
was dead. Time had played against him. There was no
alternative left, for now that the reality was before him, the
mad dreams had died. He knew after all that the horde was
invincible and he must live.

"I will send messengers tonight," Ivor whispered. "The
nobles will gather from the cities. When the snow falls
heavy again, we will attack them in the middle of the night."

Rasnar smiled.

"But if Keane is taken alive, he is mine. Perhaps I can
still save him, and the same stands for any other Yankee."

"Of course," Rasnar replied.

"As for the Yankee weapons, they are mine as well."

Rasnar did not argue that point. There would be time
enough later to change that agreement.

The boyar stalked from the room, and laughing softly, the
prelate returned to his desk

"All right, gentlemen," Andrew said, settling behind his
desk. "This is an open meeting. I want all opinions."

The room was silent as the various company commanders,
staff, and contingents from O'Donald's and Cromwell's units
looked about, each hoping the other would say something
first.

Finally it was O'Donald who stood up.

"If ever something needed killing," O'Donald said, "it's
those beasties. I volunteered to fight rebs, and I did it
gladly, wanting a good argument to sink my teeth into. But
I didn't hate them. This is different. I'll kill Tugars and
laugh while a-doin' it."

Several of the company commanders nodded grimly.

"I'm an abolitionist man," Houston said sharply. "I joined
to fight slavery. This makes the Johnnies back home look

like rock-solid Republicans. Let's smash this system to the ground, colonel, free the peasants, arm 'em, and fight!"

"I think it's madness," Tobias retorted from the other end of the table.

Normally any comment from the man would draw at best indifference from the infantry and artillerymen, but Andrew noticed that this time there was a difference in the room.

"Go on, Captain Cromwell," Andrew said evenly. "State your views."

"You heard that Kal fellow when we questioned him earlier. These Tugars number in the hundreds of thousands. We can fight and we'll all die. I'm not one for dying in a hopeless cause.

"Now, I've sailed the waters south of here. There's good land to be found, far away from this madhouse. I say we pull out while the pulling's good and hide out till the Tugars have passed."

"And if they hunt us down?" Andrew asked. "For I've got a feeling they can't let people like us live—it would set a precedent that could threaten their entire system."

"Then if they find us, we'll simply load up the *Ogunquit* again, pull out to sea, and move on. I don't think they've got anything to match the steam engines below her deck."

Tobias settled back into his chair and looked around. More than one man was nodding in agreement.

"So we learn to live like hunted dogs, is that it?" O'Donald snapped back. "Always looking over our shoulders, ready to run from our shadows."

"Not always," Tobias retorted. "You heard Kal—they stay for a winter in one area, then move on by spring heading east. Twenty years later they come back out of the west. We need hide only for this one year. When they come back again, we and our sons will be ready for them."

"And leave the people of Suzdal to the sack, is that it?" Mina retorted.

"What good could we do anyhow?" Tobias replied. "They are like cattle, just like the niggers back home who worked like cattle in the fields. If the niggers wanted their freedom so all-fired bad, why didn't they rebel when John Brown started it all? And it's the same with these lazy peasants."

"Last I heard," Andrew said slowly, "those men you call niggers had a hundred and eighty thousand brothers wearing

Union blue. After the battle of the Crater I saw their bodies carpeting the field from one end to the other."

All in the room could see Andrew bristling at Tobias.

"I call those men Americans, damn you," he said.

Tobias backed off.

"Are there any other comments?" Andrew continued, looking around the table, his voice still sharp from the encounter.

"There's the simple logistics of it all," Emil said, leaning forward. "No matter what our pride tells us, six hundred cannot stand before hundreds of thousands. We saw what their bowman did to poor Johnson. Hans went and paced it off later—a hundred and seventy yards that shot carried.

"Even with our rifles they'll close in enough to shoot and simply wear us down."

Andrew found himself nodding in agreement. His initial rage had cooled as the harsh realities of what they faced finally settled in. With only six hundred they'd be surrounded and smothered under a rain of feathered death.

"If we stay, it'll be almost certain death," Andrew said quietly, and the room was silent.

"I have never turned from a fight in my life. You and I have stood together on a score of fields, and never has the 35th run, and the record of the 44th Artillery is as honorable.

"If our deaths here would mean something, then I would order us to stay and fight. But what I wish in this will not be the deciding factor. I cannot order the brave men of this regiment to die, most likely for no purpose at all."

Tobias started to smile, but Andrew's look cut him off.

"If we stay, we'll have to fight Ivor and the nobles first, before we can even take a shot at the Tugars."

"If only the nobles would swing to our side," Houston argued.

"Even if they did, they'd be more hindrance than help. They're nothing but medieval horsemen armed with swords and lances. The horse archers of the horde would sweep them out of their saddles in the first charge."

"The peasants?" O'Donald asked.

"It'd take years to get them ready."

"So you're saying that we pull out," O'Donald said disbelievingly.

"I said I would not order this regiment to stay. Near all of them are volunteers. They volunteered to fight the Confederacy; there was nothing in that agreement about fighting here. This is a different fight, and I feel they have the right to decide this issue for themselves. It is the only fair answer to this question.''

Surprised, the officers looked around the table at one another.

"It's not to be taken lightly, so I'll give them a week. At the end of the week there'll be a vote by secret ballot. The majority will decide in this one, gentlemen, and I will live with that majority. That is all, gentlemen.''

The room emptied, until only Hans was left.

"Well, old friend," Andrew said wearily, "I'd consider it an honor if you'd join me in a drink.''

He filled two tumblers with the last drop of brandy in his possession.

"Did I do the right thing?" he asked, looking at the sergeant. Not since Gettysburg had he asked that question of his old mentor.

Hans's features creased into the slightest of smiles.

"Son, it was the only thing you could do.''

"Dammit, man, I want to stay and fight, maybe even try to persuade Ivor to join me.''

"I doubt if he would.''

"If he were alone, without that bastard Rasnar, I think he'd try.''

"But he's not.''

"I've ruined it all," Andrew said dejectedly.

"Look at me, son.''

Andrew tried to meet Hans' gaze but couldn't.

"I remember when you were nothing but a scared pup. Andrew, boy, you've become the finest soldier I've ever seen. You know how to kill when you have to, and a damn fine killer you are, a regular demon angel of a killer.

"But there's more to being a soldier than that. You love the men of this regiment as if they were your own flesh. It burns a man's soul to be like that—I've seen more than one officer go mad from it—but you've got the strength. You know how to lead these boys, to show them you respect them as men, and, God help you, when the time comes to spend their lives to buy what is needed.

"I thought your decision to fight a war to try and save Hawthorne the most noble act I've ever seen, and the men loved you for it and would have died by the hundreds to see it done. Far too many armies forget that rule, to protect their own no matter what. When soldiers know their comrades will not abandon them, they'll fight the harder.

"But for this fight you can't ask that of them. You said it well before—their knights are useless, their peasants would be slaughtered. I think, son, this fight is beyond us."

"I feel like a coward."

Hans grabbed hold of Andrew's arm from across the table.

"You're the bravest officer it's ever been my privilege to serve. I think this one's a lost fight, Andrew. Maybe in twenty years, as Tobias said, we and our sons will be ready. But you can't throw away your life, or lead the regiment to its doom. Always remember, Andrew, the regiment must survive."

"Do you think the boys will vote to go?" he asked quietly.

"They might surprise you, son."

"You want to stay, don't you?" Andrew asked.

Hans smiled.

"I felt like I wanted to when I saw that evil bastard come riding in, but now . . ." His voice trailed off.

"I'm afraid," Andrew whispered. "I saw that thing and I was afraid, and I'm afraid the men will think me a coward for not ordering us to stay and fight."

"It takes courage sometimes not to fight," Hans retorted. "Dammit, son, I'm so frightened out on the field sometimes I can't stop from shaking, it's just everyone else is frightened too and don't notice it."

"Funny," Andrew said, a strange detachment to his voice, "since Antietam, I haven't been afraid—in fact, I almost love it. That is, till now, and," his voice dropping, "when I sleep."

"Let's see what the boys decide," Hans said softly.

The two fell into silence. Gradually Andrew's head lowered onto the table. Finally Hans stepped around to Andrew's chair, and picking him up, he gently laid the young officer on his cot, removing his spectacles and putting them on the sideboard.

"You've done well," Hans said softly, "but I don't want you dying for a fight you can't win."

Scarlet with embarrassment, Hawthorne stood before Kal, unable to raise his eyes from the floor, while Andrew stood circumspectly to one side.

"I should be angry with you," Kal said in a cold, even voice.

"Yes sir."

"My only daughter," Ludmilla sobbed. "To think a mother should raise her little girl to be like this."

Tanya moved closer to Hawthorne, and protectively his arm went over her shoulder.

Kal looked at the couple. They both looked so young, and his memory went back to a similar meeting long ago. His glance slipped over to Ludmilla, and the common memory was shared in their eyes, and they smiled shyly at each other.

Perhaps it was for the best after all, Kal thought sadly. Tanya had not yet been born when the horde last came, but her older brother, Gregory, had, and it had been Rasnar himself who had chosen him for the moon feast table.

Maybe there were only days left, and no matter what, a year at most, let his little girl have her happiness, to know a brief moment of joy before the end.

His eyes started to cloud with tears. Walking around the rough-hewn table, he extended his arms, embracing both of them.

Hawthorne raised his eyes to look at the peasant.

"You are my son," Kal said hoarsely. "I was proud of you, and the first time I met you I thought in my heart that you would be a fitting son. Now love each other, for it is the gift Kesus gives most abundantly to youth."

Kal stepped back from the two.

"Now sit and eat, my son," Ludmilla said, wiping the tears from her eyes. "Tanya, come help."

Leaning over, Hawthorne kissed Tanya lightly on the forehead. Smiling, she dashed over to Kal, hugged the burly peasant fiercely, and then went into the next room.

Hawthorne looked back at Andrew, who smiled at the young corporal. It still amazed him that the young Quaker, of all the men in his regiment, had been the first to get a girl into trouble. But somehow this was different. The love the two showed for each other was obvious to any who saw them together. He breathed an inner sigh of relief. It could have gone far worse.

"There should be a marriage," Hawthorne said softly, coming to sit next to Kal.

"In the church?" Kal asked.

"If that is your wish and custom."

Kal spat on the floor and shook his head.

"We have no preacher with us," Hawthorne said, and he turned and looked at Andrew, who still stood in the back of the room. "Sir, I was kind of hoping you would say the words."

Flustered, Andrew looked at Kal.

"Sir, we haven't a preacher, and I was thinking you're sort of like the captain of a ship here."

"I think it'd be all right," Andrew replied lamely.

"My house would be honored," Kal interjected, beckoning for Andrew to sit, now that the formalities were over with. "But we can speak of that later.

"I heard your announcement at parade this morning," Kal said, "and I am confused. You are the leader. I thought you decided what was to be done."

"The boys have the right to decide for themselves," Andrew replied. "It is our way for things like this. Back on our world they volunteered to fight for a cause. This cause now is different, and I cannot order them to fight unless they agree to do so first."

"You Yankees," Kal said, shaking his head.

"It is our way, my friend."

"And what do you think will be done?" Kal asked nervously.

"We'll stay," Hawthorne said.

Andrew smiled and patted the boy on the shoulder.

"Let's wait until the votes are in."

"I have three things to say," Kal said, lowering his voice, "and that is why I asked you to come to my cabin with Hawthorne, so it would seem that you were here because of our little family situation."

Hawthorne started to blush again, and good-naturedly Kal patted him on the shoulder.

"Why the need for secrecy?" Andrew asked. "You come to my cabin nearly every day."

"Because I'm advising you to seal your camp off today, to allow no one in or out. I heard your order forbidding your troops to go to Suzdal. But you must not allow anyone to enter."

"Why?"

"Because there will be spies to learn of your decisions."

Andrew nodded in agreement.

"Next, you can expect Ivor and the other boyars to strike you, and strike hard."

Andrew nodded sadly.

"It is what I expected."

"Do you plan to do anything?"

"No."

"But if you moved first against him, you would stop this attack which might destroy you."

"It is not my way," Andrew replied grimly. "I will not fight a war unless it is forced upon me. The men will vote on staying or leaving at the end of the week."

"And how do you think the vote will go?"

Andrew looked at Hawthorne and sadly shook his head. "They'll vote to leave, I'm almost sure of that. If the majority do that, then all of us will go."

There was a look of panic on Hawthorne's face.

"Don't worry," Andrew said, patting him on the arm. "If we leave, those who have helped us, such as Kal and your new family, will be asked to go with us."

"I am still of the house of Ivor," Kal said evenly, "and I cannot leave my people. My daughter and wife I would send with you, but I would stay."

Andrew looked into Kal's eyes, and knew there was no arguing, for if the roles were reversed he would do the same.

"Rasnar will not let you leave," Kal stated softly. "He desires the powers you have—he covets them to make the church stronger than the boyars."

"So they will attack whether we stay or leave," Andrew said, shaking his head.

"Exactly, my friend."

"I must give my men time to make this decision, though. It's their way. Mainers don't make such choices on the spur of the moment, they want time to chew it over."

"I now have a third thing to tell you," Kal said, his voice lowering to a whisper.

"And that is?"

"We will fight the nobles if they move against you."

"No!" Andrew said, coming to his feet.

Stunned by the response, Kal looked at the colonel with confusion.

"You can't," Andrew said quickly. "They're mounted warriors in armor. One of them can kill fifty of you. You'll be facing them with nothing but pitchforks and rusty knives. You might have dreams of some glorious change, Kal, but it's hopeless."

"But Hawthorne told us about your Declaration of Independing and how peasants defeated nobles and became free."

Andrew looking reproachfully at the boy. He had disobeyed orders, and Andrew's anger was visible.

"I spoke what my conscience told me to speak," Hawthorne replied evenly, not showing fear at Andrew's anger.

"It was different for us," Andrew said, looking back at Kal. "We had guns to fight against the boyar's soldiers. We had a big land, hundreds of times bigger than Rus. And we had time—it took us eight years to win. You have no weapons, you have no place to hide when you lose fights, and most of all you have no time. For even if you could hold them for a time, still the Tugars would come and then crush all of you, peasant and noble."

"And you are telling me to watch as again my people are driven to the pits."

Unable to answer, Andrew looked away.

"The only alternative is that you will all die."

"I am willing to face that, Keane."

"I wish I could help," Andrew replied, "but that is in the hands of my men now."

"You do not know what you have perhaps started here," Kal said evenly. "Every time your soldiers went into Suzdal, every time a peasant came to the mill with grain, my people saw how different all of you were. They would go home and whisper about the strange Yankees who did not live under the boyar. And Hawthorne is not to blame for his words. For it has been whispered already throughout all of Suzdal, and even as far as Vazima, and, yes, even to Novrod."

"If my men vote to leave, we will leave," Andrew said quietly. "Do not fight the boyars, and even if we stay I do not wish your blood upon our hands. If we face the Tugars, and the boyars do not, then we will face them alone."

Andrew stood up as if to leave.

"There is one last thing to speak of," Kal said quickly.

"And that is?"

"You will not see me again," he said.

"Why?" And there was a look of concern on Andrew's face.

"A messenger came to me this morning. I am ordered back to the court of Ivor."

"Then you'd best go."

Kal shook his head.

"I will not ask for your protection, for there is too much already between you and him. But I will not go back."

"Then where are you going?"

Kal merely smiled. "I just ask that you take Ludmilla and my darling Tanya behind your walls. Ivor will not trouble you over them."

The two women, who had been standing to one side, came rushing up to Kal, and he held both of them close.

"And there is this final thing. Do not speak a word of what we have said. I trust only two now, you and my son, Hawthorne."

"What are you saying?"

"There is a traitor in your ranks."

Incredulous, Andrew looked at Kal as if he had not heard correctly.

"It is true. One of your men was seen leaving the cathedral several weeks back."

"Who is it?"

"It was storming at the time, and my man could not get close enough to see him. But it was a Yankee. Though he wore a cloak like a peasant, his pants and shoes were seen from behind. The man sensed he was followed and ran into a crowd and was lost.

"You cannot say anything of your intent now, of what was said here, except perhaps to your closest friends, such as the grumbling sergeant or the kindly doctor. For you do not know."

Stunned, Andrew did not react. What could have been offered, to draw a man away from his comrades? How could he have been so naive as not to imagine it? Here a traitor could have wealth or power undreamed of back home.

"It is a sad world we live in," Andrew said softly.

"Goodbye, my friend."

Awkwardly, Andrew followed the custom of the Rus and embraced Kal.

"Could I ask one final favor, though?" the peasant said quickly.

"Anything."

He motioned to Ludmilla, who went to the side table and

returned with the small pocket Bible that Hawthorne had given to them.

"Could you say the words over my daughter and new son now? I wish to see that before I go."

Smiling, Andrew took the Bible, and as he spoke, for the first time since losing John on the fields of Gettysburg, tears came to his eyes to mingle with the tears of the four who stood before him. For though it was a moment of joy, all knew what would most likley come no matter what their dreams and plans.

Chapter 11

"There are over eight thousand men at arms in the city. My warehouses are being emptied by their stomachs," Ivor said, looking down the length of his feasting table. The boyars of all the cities of Rus were there, even Mikhail, and the mere sight of him filled Ivor's soul with anger.

"We still need more," Rasnar replied.

"And strip our lands of all soldiers?" Boros of Novrod retorted. "We are not fools."

Boros stood up and looked accusingly at Ivor.

"You allowed the infection of these Yankees into our land. You plotted to use them against us. Now word of them has spread. You might be deaf, Ivor, but I am not. Many of my landholders refused to come. They fear if they do the peasants might revolt while they are gone. All the spies hear the same thing whispered. No, I am no fool to return and have to slaughter my field workers, especially when the Tugars will want the taxes we must raise for next year."

"You have let things go too far," Ivan of Vazima snarled. "Let the emptying of your warehouses be a lesson."

Ivor looked nervously around. When the fight was won, he thought darkly, these men would turn on him like wolves, kill him, and place Mikhail on the throne instead. He could only hope that the fear of a supporter of the church ruling Suzdal would stay their hands.

"It is understood, though," Ivor said sharply, "that the weapons of the Yankees are divided between us."

"Never," Rasnar replied. "For the Tugars will not allow a device more powerful than their bows to be kept by us. You are all fools to think otherwise. They must go to the church for safekeeping."

Enraged, Ivor turned on Rasnar, who had promised so differently only days before.

"And give you the power?" Ivor retorted.

"The safekeeping. Could any of you trust the other not to hold the smoke sticks back? Then you will all try to conceal them, and the Tugars will slaughter us all as a result."

"Who's to know if we give them some and hide the rest?" Ivan asked.

"I have told them how many Yankees there are," Rasnar replied, "and how many weapons will be given unto them when they come."

"Damn you," Ivor roared.

"It is only to save us all," Rasnar replied sanctimoniously, and smiling inwardly he did not bother to mention that the number he gave was far less than the number the Yankees most likely had. Already he had in his possession four of the weapons captured by Mikhail and had learned how to use them. Now if only that Hinsen would reveal the secret of powder as well, his power would be limitless.

The boyars looked one to the other, and their fear of one another played well into Rasnar's hands. After a long hour of shouting and arguing, all except Ivor finally agreed that the weapons spoil would go to the church. And at that moment Rasnar knew he had truly won what Ivor had blocked for so long. For once the Tugars had gone, he could use the power of the weapons hidden to turn first one, and then another boyar against the others, until finally the church had won back control.

"We do not know, though, what the Yankees plan to do," Mikhail said, returning the debate to the planning of the action.

"They have sealed themselves off well," Ivan agreed. "Our scouts have surrounded their camp. Their walls are manned day and night. We allow no one to get in, but in turn no one comes out."

"Remember what the Namer of Time demanded," Rasnar said. "We must not allow them to escape, for my source of information told me they would decide that issue this very night. If they leave we will have to answer for it next year when the horde arrives."

Rasnar stood up and walked over to the window. Opening it, he looked out, a cold blast of air sweeping in to chill the room.

"Their smoke sticks and the great weapons kill from far away. But if we but get on top of them, our swords and axes will kill them nevertheless. Mikhail in his bravery has already shown us that."

The bearded warrior stuck out his chest and looked about the room haughtily.

"I split the skull of one myself," he said, grinning, and pulling out his ax he held it aloft.

"I believe that Perm has answered my prayer," and dramatically Rasnar pointed out the window.

All day the skies had been darkening from the west, and already the first heavy flakes of snow were starting to fall.

"When darkness falls, we march," Rasnar said, turning back to the assembly. "Perm will cast his cloak over our host, blinding our foe. We will swarm over their walls, coming out of the snow as angels of death to kill the infidels!"

Shaking like a bear to rid himself of the snow, the hooded form came into the back room of the tavern.

Those who looked up at him were silent.

"I could be killed for being here," he said evenly.

"We let you be here," Boris said coldly. "When a priest ventures into tavern after tavern asking for Kalencka, Ivor's man, the word of him spreads even before his feet. We saw you were not followed, so your steps were guided here."

Nervously the man looked about, and his blood went chill. The room was packed with peasants and craftsmen of the city. He realized that there was a fair chance they would slit his throat rather than let him step back out.

"Speak, priest, and be quick about it."

"The army will march in an hour."

"You bring us nothing new," Boris said coldly. "Do you

think us blind? There are eight thousand men of arms in the city. They cannot be roused out without our knowing."

"The Yankees must be warned."

Boris laughed coldly.

"Shall we then slip out of the city to tell them? Ivor has posted guards on the walls, and the gates are closed. If one can even get out of the city he still must slip through the men who surround the Yankee camp as well. We have sent six men to try to get through, and none has returned. We are in this alone now."

Dejected, the priest visibly slumped.

"Kill him," Ilya hissed.

There was an angry growl from the group. A dagger snicked out from under Boris's cloak, and he stepped forward.

"Wait."

Boris stopped and looked to a man sitting in the shadows of the back of the room.

"He's a spy," Boris argued.

"I don't think so," Kal said as he stood up and walked over to the priest.

"What is your name?"

"Casmar."

"That's the secretary of Rasnar," Ilya growled. "Kal, let me kill him myself."

"Wait. Let me ask him why he came to us first," Kal said quietly.

"You are Kalencka?" Casmar asked.

Kal merely shrugged his shoulders and smiled.

"All of Ivor's guards are looking for you. There's thirty gold pieces on your head."

"So much for such a poor head," Kal said, laughing in a self-deprecatory manner. "Answer me, secretary of Rasnar, why would you betray your master?"

"I have stood by his side too long," Casmar said quietly. "He does not serve Perm nor Kesus, but only his own vanity. He and others like him have corrupted the church into something unholy.

"I joined believing," Casmar said sadly. "I still believe, but I do not believe in Rasnar. The church should protect the common people, not hold them in fear, and sell indulgences against the Tugars, for that is an evil thing that makes Rasnar rich."

Casmar stopped and looked about the room.

"Well, that is quite a thing you've said," Kal said quietly, looking into Casmar's eyes. "I wish I could believe you, and then perhaps I would pray again."

"If you wish to kill me," Casmar said quietly, his voice trembling, "then do so now. Just let me pray first to Kesus before you do it."

"A priest who actually prays," Kal said, with no mockery in his voice. He looked around the group and saw the hesitation.

"Let him live," Kal said, "but keep him here."

There was no argument, for many in the room were visibly moved by the genuine piety of the rotund priest.

Kal started for the door and looked back.

"Would you pray for us, priest? For we shall need it very shortly."

Casmar nodded, and Kal went to his knees, and all about him followed suit.

"As He died to make men holy, let us die to make men free," Kal said, looking at the priest.

"What is that?" Casmar asked.

"Oh, a prayer song Hawthorne, my son, taught me," and, grim-faced, Kalencka rose after the blessing and left the room.

"Company A, attention!"

The snow muffled the sound of rifles snapping to position.

"All right, men," Hans said, standing stiffly before the company, "the polls are opened. Line up inside the meeting house, pick up your ballots. Write 'Stay' or 'Leave,' according to your feeling. Once you're done, form up back outside.

"Right face—forward, march!"

Hawthorne pulled up his collar against the windy blast. The snow had started to sweep in just as darkness settled. It felt like home almost, a real nor'easter; already an inch of powdery snow was on the ground.

The camp was on full alert tonight, half the men standing duty on the walls while the other half tried to stay warm inside the cabins. Shifting the men back and forth by companies would mean the voting would take hours, and Hawthorne wondered if he could contain his anxiety much longer.

The politicking had been hard all week. By agreement, the officers had refused to comment one way or the other, since it was not their vote. So the debate had settled fully on the soldiers. He still found it nearly impossible to reconcile his stand with his religious beliefs, for surely to stay would mean fighting and death, while leaving would spare a battle. If he truly believed his Quaker teachings he would have argued for their leaving. But in the face of the monstrosity of the Tugars and the slavery of the nobles and church, his conscience had rebelled.

His heart was torn with the argument even as he had stood up at the town meeting the night before to plead desperately for the regiment to stay and fight, first the nobles and then the hated nightmare from the west.

He found to his surprise that the men listened to him intently, with no catcalls or heated words as when others had spoken. He realized later that they knew his religious convictions and the undoubtable moral arguments he had wrestled with inside himself, and respected him for that.

Only Hinsen had stood up to speak against him, and even those who agreed with Hinsen had shouted for him to sit down.

But in his heart he knew that the vote would go against him. The logic of staying was far too weak. Sergeant Barry had, in a forceful presentation, fully caught the sentiment of many when he expressed his hatred and rage of the system, but then pointed out the tactical impossibility of fighting now. He ended with the proposal that they find another place, build their strength over a period of time, rally the peasants, and then twenty years hence destroy the Tugars when they came again.

"It is senseless to die with no hope of victory, accomplishing nothing," Barry said in the end, "when if we spare ourselves now and prepare, we can one day destroy our enemy forever."

His words were met by a thunderous round of applause.

"Corporal Hawthorne, you're next," came a voice from inside.

Hawthorne looked up at the blowing snow and then stepped into the meeting hall.

The men about the stairs let out a clamorous shout as the boyars descended the steps of Ivor's palace and swung up on their mounts.

The shouts rippled on out across the square to those who

could not see because of the snow, and thundered up the side streets packed with men.

Ivor swung about and looked at his personal guard around him, the only soldiers mounted. All had agreed that the army would advance by foot, since horses would be useless against the walls and also would allow them to advance more quickly as a compact host.

"Let's go, then," Ivor said grimly.

Swallowing hard, Kal looked about. In his heart he knew it was madness, it was an act of desperation he had never truly explained to his companions. There were hundreds waiting in the side alleyways, and thousands more who still wavered, watching to see what would happen. But he had to make this one last gesture, and nerving himself, Kal started to step out of the tavern, but suddenly Boris and Ilya grabbed hold of him.

"I must still try," Kal said, struggling in their grasp. "Perhaps Ivor will listen."

"You will die if you do," Boris hissed. "We'll need you in the hours to come."

Kicking and screaming, he was dragged back into the building. From out of side alleyways hundreds of peasants started to pour out into the street leading down to the south gate. Frightened, they looked at one another. The words of freedom and defiance had inflamed their hearts when it was still only talk, but now the price of it was becoming all too real.

Now as the moment of crisis came, more than one saw the madness and slipped back into the shadows to run and hide.

Nahatkim stood by the tavern and watched, seeing the resolve already start to slip away. Without hesitating, he stepped out into the street.

Ivor, at the head of the host, came looming out of the swirling snow, the other boyars beside him. At the sight of the peasants and craftsmen blocking the way, the boyar let out a throaty growl.

"Disperse, you damned rebels and cowards. Disperse and go back to your hovels, else you will feel my wrath."

The other boyars looked at Ivor with reproach, and whispered to themselves, for surely he must be a poor ruler to have allowed such treason to become more than talk in the taverns, to appear now as armed men in the street.

"I said disperse and go home!" Ivor roared.

The crowd stood silent, nervous, and then in a moment, like snow hitting a fire, the dream melted and the men started to back away.

"You are cattle!" Nahatkim roared, his reedy voice near breaking, and he stepped into the middle of the street facing the peasants.

As one the mob stopped and turned.

"Yes, you are no longer men, you are cattle. Cattle to the Tugars and slaves to the boyars and the church. I am ashamed, for I thought there were men here in Suzdal!"

Nahatkim turned to face Ivor, who sat atop his mount, incredulous as if a dog had suddenly found speech to swear at its master.

"You, Ivor Ivorivich, go back to your palace. Do not march to commit murder."

"What?" His bellowing roar came out almost as a question, so astonished was he by the defiance.

"You have forgotten your people, Ivor. You leave us to the plottings of an evil man who has destroyed the truth of our holy mother church. You go to destroy the very thing that could be our salvation from the Tugars. You have betrayed yourself and us. Lead us, Ivor Ivorivich, against our enemies, the Tugars and the church, and we will follow you gladly. If not we will fight."

There was a moment of stunned silence as both sides stood only feet away from each other, each amazed at what was now unfolding.

In his heart Ivor felt a moment of sickening pain, for part of his mind told him that indeed this mad old fool was right, and that his own pride and fear of Rasnar would destroy this chance to stop the Tugars.

But the other part of his soul, the soul that had been raised a boyar, Ivor son of Ivor, now held sway and drew him into the path of rage.

Unsheathing his sword, he raised the blade high. Nahatkim did not blanch. A serene smile lighted his features.

"I die a man," he shouted triumphantly as the blade came down and set his soul to flight.

A wild explosive roar echoed up from the street. Before Nahatkim's headless corpse had even crumpled to the ground, the peasants surged forward, shouting with rage. Within seconds Ivor found himself fighting for his life, swinging and cutting, and as each body fell another leaped forward.

A wild scream went up as Boros of Novrod's horse slipped on the wet paving stones and came crashing down. Ilya leaped out from the tavern brandishing a club, and before Boros could raise, his helmet was crushed in like brittle parchment, and the boyar went down under the rush.

A boyar had died at the hands of a peasant, and those who could see roared with triumph.

"Kill the boyars, kill the boyars!" the scream echoed and reechoed.

From side alleyways leading into the square, hundreds poured out, and within minutes the sound of battle thundered above the howling of the storm.

Yet clubs, daggers, pitchforks, and wooden spears cannot stand against chain mail and swords, and the weight of soldiers in the square started to be felt.

Grimly the peasants gave ground, while from overhead a torrent of stones, bricks, and furniture rained out of windows onto the heads of the attackers.

Wild shrieks of anguish rent the air. Nobles and warriors, enraged that peasants would dare to strike at them, gave no quarter, smashing down doors, slaying women, spearing children, and the battle started to change into a massacre.

For several minutes he had watched the fighting. The moment the battle had started before the tavern, Casmar's guards had rushed out the door, leaving him alone. He stepped out into the taproom and, spying a back door, opened it and looked out. Several men of arms came charging past him and smashed open the door to a cabin across the street. Casmar was sickened to hear the high piercing shrieks of a woman.

Running into the building, he stood transfixed with horror. A dead child lay upon the floor, its mother screaming in anguish as two of the soldiers, throwing her to the ground, appeared ready to commit rape.

"In the name of Perm, stop!" Casmar roared.

Leering, one of the soldiers looked up at him.

"Let her go!" Casmar demanded.

"It's kill all filthy peasants," the soldier roared back, "kill all these Suzdalian scum, so why waste a little fun first, eh, priest?"

"Leave her be," Casmar replied sharply.

The men hesitated, while the sound of fighting rose up again out in the street.

"Let's go," one of the three said, starting for the door.

The leering soldier looked at Casmar and smiled even as his dagger glided across the woman's throat, ending her cries for mercy.

"You'll have a hell of a parish left by morning, priest," the soldier said, laughing. He wiped the bloody dagger on Casmar's cloak, and then the three, spotting a knot of peasants in the street, charged after them.

"Rasnar," Casmar roared, the word sounding like a curse. "You knew this would happen. It was all part of your plan, you bastard!"

Wildly he ran down the street, dodging past knots of peasants and soldiers. Pulling aside his cloak, he exposed his thin clerical robes. In the confusion it gave him passage, for neither side had yet become so inflamed as to kill a priest.

The south gate was a swirling maelstrom of pushing, shoving bodies. Reaching the wall, he edged his way forward. The mob would surge in upon him till he felt his lungs would burst, and then push out again so he could run another dozen feet.

Reaching the gate at last, he ran on out of the city and down the south road.

Several hundred yards beyond the city he met a knot of Ivor's soldiers who stood in the middle of the road, perplexed by the roar of battle within the city.

"What is it, priest?" an armored warrior asked.

"Ivan's men have betrayed your lord," Casmar gasped. "They're trying to kill him, and the peasants have rallied to his side."

"For Ivor," the guard roared, and the detachment started back for the city.

Turning, he broke into a run. His head started to swim, his lungs were filled with fire. His thin doeskin boots could not block the cold, and with each step through the snow he felt as if he were running on hot coals.

Onward the priest ran, till the pain became all-consuming, filling his entire world with agony. Desperately he begged Kesus for strength to keep him going, and as if in answer the world gradually became numb, till finally there was only the snow, unending snow that swirled and coiled about his staggering form.

"They should be done voting by now," Emil said, standing up to look out of the cabin window.

Andrew merely nodded in reply, lost in thought.

"Looks like home out there," Kathleen said, moving over to join the doctor by the window. "How I loved nights like this when I was a child—the noisy city slowly being muffled by a blanket of whiteness."

Drawing away from Emil, she came over to sit by Andrew's side.

"I think it's for the best, Andrew," she said quietly. "Maybe we'll be able to find a place of peace, where there isn't any war to be fought. I think we've been at war so long we've forgotten what peace might be like."

She reached out and touched him lightly on the hand. Startled, he looked up, and their eyes held. So that was it, he now fully realized. It was my being a soldier, killing men, and possibly being killed myself that so thoroughly sealed her off . . . and myself as well.

He took her hand in his and smiled.

"Sergeant of the guard, sergeant of the guard!" The voice was muffled, distant.

Andrew sprang to his feet and raced for the door. Stepping into the street, he saw a knot of men coming toward him out of the snow, bearing a man between them.

Andrew raced up to the group, and was stunned to see that it was Casmar.

"Get him in my cabin!"

Following Andrew, the group pushed into his cabin and laid the man on the table.

Wildly, Casmar looked around the room.

"The city is in riot," Casmar said hoarsely, struggling to sit up.

"How did you get here?" Andrew asked, noticing the bloodstains on his cloak, and the light boots which seemed to be frozen to the man's feet.

"I ran from the city. I tricked the guards to let me pass. The city is in riot," Casmar cried. "The boyars planned to attack you tonight in the snow while you slept. The peasants revolted, led by Kalencka. The soldiers have gone mad—

they're killing everyone, men, women, children, even those who do not fight. They'll kill everyone, everyone!"

"It could be a trap to lure us out," Hans growled, standing in the doorway.

"Please believe me," Casmar cried. "I saw Kalencka just before the fight—I went to him because I no longer serve Rasnar."

Andrew stared at the man closely, trying to judge.

"As He died to make men holy, let us die to make men free," Casmar said softly, looking into Andrew's eyes.

"Where did you hear that?" Andrew asked, startled by the words, which stabbed into him like an admonishment.

"Kalencka said his new son, Hawthorne, taught him."

"He's telling the truth," Andrew snapped. "It would have been just like Hawthorne to teach Kal that song. That damned fool peasant. I told him not to do this."

"They'll lose without your help," Casmar begged. "Rasnar wants Suzdal destroyed to end the power of Ivor."

"Hans, sound assembly," Andrew shouted. "Which company's at the polls?"

"H, sir."

"Have them man the walls. I want everyone else in the square in five minutes. Now move!"

"You've got to stop them," Ivor roared, storming into the church. "They're killing everyone, everyone, innocent and guilty!"

Rasnar turned from the altar and smiled.

"Good, very good. Let them all die—Perm will know his own."

Ivor, sword in hand, started for the altar. An arrow slashed out from a balcony, dropping Andrei to the ground.

Stunned, Ivor looked at the lifeless body of his son.

Shields raised, Ivor's guards swarmed about their boyar as a shower of death rained down from above.

"My lord, it's Mikhail's men! We'll die in here!"

The men at arms dragged Ivor back, while the boyar bellowed and screamed with grief and rage.

"I know you voted, men, and the ballots have yet to be counted. I've told you what's happening in Suzdal," and he pointed northward, where despite the storm a pulsing glow could be seen on the horizon.

"The city's in flames. Thousands of peasants are dying up there. Dying to overthrow the boyars, with the dream of fighting the Tugars and winning their freedom.

"I joined the Army of the Potomac to end slavery," Andrew roared, "and that same war is being fought here, here and now. I'm going up that road, with or without you men. But if you come with me, we're in this fight till the bitter end. Decide here and now where the 35th and 44th stand!"

A wild angry shout went up from the men, their cheers echoing above the fury of the storm.

"I want the regiment formed in the square in ten minutes, full battle load, eighty rounds per man. O'Donald, limber up your one piece. Company H and Cromwell's command stay here to guard the camp. Now let's move!"

"We're surrounded! The warriors have cut through to the east wall," Boris shouted, staggering into the leather warehouse that had become the third command position of the night.

Kal looked up from the rough map of the city before him and grimly shook his head.

The terror of what he had unleashed, and the guilt of it, had made him feel that in half a night he had aged twenty years.

In his heart he had known that most of the city would not have chosen to fight. He knew as well that Rasnar had hoped for just such a thing, for the soldiers of the other cities, particularly those under Mikhail, would kill without discrimination, and once that started, those who had wavered would fight out of sheer desperation.

But the horror of it he had never imagined. Twice he had been forced to retreat and had seen the streets choked with the dead and dying. Was this all his fault, was his dream madness for ever listening to the Yankess talk?

Oh, how wonderful their words had sounded, words such as freedom, independence, liberty. But never had they told him of the blood, and the killing, the burning and the dying.

He had staked his belief on them, and now he would die.

The roar of battle thundered closer and closer. Kal looked around at his fellow conspirators and smiled grimly.

"When the mouse bites the cat, he should expect to lose more than his tail," and pulling out a dagger, he headed for the door, determined to kill at least one noble before they cut him to pieces.

"All company officers to the front!" Andrew roared, and turning, he raised his field glasses to look back at the city.

God in heaven, he thought, looking in stunned amazement at the panorama of madness before him. As if a curtain had been pulled back, the storm had suddenly lifted, revealing Suzdal, in all its agony, a quarter mile away.

The area about Ivor's palace was in flames, the crackling roar lighting up the sky, while the screams of thousands came down before the wind.

Turning on his horse, Andrew looked back down the road, and his heart swelled with pride. The men had double-timed most of the way, and there had been few stragglers, so determined were they to reach the city in time.

Gasping for breath, the officers came up, gathering around Andrew's horse.

"This is going to be a tough nut to crack, gentlemen," Andrew said coldly, raising his field glasses again for another view.

"All right, the boys aren't trained in city fighting, so here's what we'll do. We can't let the men get separated and cut off into small groups, and once in there it'll be impossible for me to control the fight the way I can in the field.

"We'll attack in column of fours, just as we're lined up now. Companies A through D will follow me straight up the road through the gate and move toward the main square of the city. Companies E, F, and G, you're under Mina. Once you're through the gate I want you to break left, get up on the walls, and work your way around to the main road that runs straight through the city from east to west. Once you've worked your way over, start pushing up the road. Company J and K, you'll hold in reserve at the gate. O'Donald, bring the gun forward. You'll lead off by clearing the gate area, then fall in as support for the attack up to the square.

"Now tell your men to mark their targets. I know peasants will be hit in this—we can't help it. But for God's sake tell your men to try to know what they're shooting at first."

"You're leaving the north and east gates uncovered," Fletcher said.

"Exactly. I want to leave them a way out of there. If we can set up a rout, they'll need a retreat. I'm hoping we'll trigger a panic and they'll run. It's going to be grim work, so be careful. If it gets too hot, pull back to the south gate.

"Understand?"

The men nodded their agreement.

"Artillery to the front!" O'Donald yelled excitedly.

"All right, gentlemen, let's get ready."

Lashing their team, the gun crew galloped down the road, the infantry parting to let them pass.

"Uncase the colors!"

The chilling thrill washed over Andrew as the color bearers stepped to the front of the column. Behind them, five hundred bayonets snapped out of scabbards, rammers were pulled, and cartridges slammed in. Steel-tipped rifles came back up to shoulders, and grimly the men waited.

Dismounting, Andrew turned his mount loose. Drawing his saber, he stepped into the middle of the road, directly behind the limbered gun. Without looking back, he raised the sword high and pointed toward the city.

"35th Maine, at the double time forward!"

Down the slope toward the city they moved, gaining speed. O'Donald, roaring with delight, spurred his mount forward, screaming wildly at the gun crew, who clung desperately to the bouncing, careening limber. Never had he led a charge such as this, racing far ahead of the infantry.

The gates of the city were open before them. Onward they charged, galloping past still forms on the side of the road, and terrified refugees who leaped away at his approach as if he were an apparition.

A wild cry came up from the gate. An arrow snapped past.

"Battle front, unlimber!"

With skill borne from long years of practice, the gun crew turned from the road, the limber and gun skidding in the snow. Even before it had come to a rest the men swarmed off, heaving the gun free from its limber and turning it about to point straight at the gate.

"Spherical case shot, one-second fuse," O'Donald roared, jumping off his mount to join the crew.

The loader rushed up to the gaping maw of the gun, carrying a three-pound charge of powder and a shell that would explode two hundred yards downrange, cutting loose with a deadly hail of fifty musket balls packed inside.

A stream of arrows started to slam into the snow about

the gun. The cartridge pushed in by the loader, he leaped clear as the rammer, leaning in on his staff, shoved the charge and shell home.

O'Donald grabbed a primer and stuck it in at the breech.

"A bit more to the left." The men leaned on the wheels and angled the piece while O'Donald squinted down the barrel.

"Hold it. Stand clear!"

With a thunderous roar the Napoleon leaped back. An instant later the gateway filled with a lightning flash of fire.

Even as the gun fired, Andrew came rushing past, screaming hoarsely, the men now breaking into a charge.

He thought it must be his imagination, a desperate last wish that what was happening would somehow be prevented. Staggering from the sword wound to his arm, Kal backed against a wall, gasping for breath.

There was a pause, so others had heard a thunder as well, but it was only a second before the nobleman, screaming hoarsely, cut in again with his blade.

Near the front of the company, Hawthorne leaped over the mangled bodies that filled the gateway. Ahead, by the glare of the burning palace, he could see the warriors running in panic up the street.

Dear God, he prayed, let them keep running, let them keep running.

He barely spared a glance for the carnage all about him. The streets seemed choked with dead and dying, peasants, warriors, and nobles piled indiscriminately atop one another. Fifty, a hundred yards up the street they pushed, meeting no resistance, while always at the lead were the colors and Colonel Keane, his hat gone, sword raised high, as if he were an avenging angel, with the demon of Sergeant Hans running by his side.

Suddenly the fleeing warriors slowed and stopped, coming up against a crush of men who were heading back down the street to meet the new attack.

Andrew stopped and looked back.

"Spread that company across the street!"

As a corporal it was now his job to help, and following Sergeant Barry, Hawthorne guided the ranks into a double line while behind them Company B drew up in the same formation.

"Front rank, take aim . . . fire!"

"Second rank!" Hawthorne brought his rifle up and pointed toward the still-charging warriors. How can I? his mind screamed at him. Dear God, not again.

"Take aim!" He steadied his hand, drawing a bead on a noble who, screaming and shouting, was driving his foot soldiers forward.

He closed his eyes.

"Fire!"

The gun slammed into his shoulder.

"Company B, six paces forward!"

Hawthorne opened his eyes, and through the tears saw that the noble was gone. Perhaps he had missed the man and he had run away. Hawthorne prayed.

Reloading, he waited.

"Company A, six paces forward!"

He stepped forward, rifle raised.

"Both ranks, take aim, fire!"

"Company B, six paces forward!"

Like a machine, he tore cartridges, his face smeared with powder. He felt as if in a dream, caught up in some devil-made machine, whose gears turned and turned, bringing him forward, and spitting broken bodies out the other side.

Slowly they advanced up the street, stepping over the dead and dying, the snow beneath their feet now churned into a pinkish slush that splattered their uniforms.

Ahead the street suddenly broadened out into the main square.

"C Company forward, A to reserve!" Andrew roared.

Pausing for a moment, Hawthorne looked down at the ground, and recoiled with horror. Nahatkim's face looked up at him, a soft smile on the old man's bloody features.

A bitter hatred coursed through Hawthorne's blood. They had killed that gentle old man, and he screamed with a crazed animal frenzy, his cries mingling in with the wild shouts of the regiment who raged at the carnage about them, and now added to it with every volley.

"A and D companies to the front," Andrew cried. "Form to the right of line!"

Pushing up the street, Hawthorne stepped into the square,

and racing with his command the regiment shook out into a four-company front over fifty yards long.

The enemy had been driven back halfway across the square, stunned by the sudden onslaught, while to the left could be heard the growing rattle of musketry as Mina pushed his men up the flank.

There was a growing sense of desperation from the milling crowd in the middle of the square.

"They're gonna charge," Barry roared. "You can smell it, they're gonna charge!"

"O'Donald, get that gun up here!" Andrew shouted, looking back down the street to where the artillery piece was stalled by the sheer mass of bodies in their way.

"Here they come!"

"Present . . . fire!"

A scathing volley swept the square, but storming over the bodies the warriors pressed forward, screaming hoarse cries of rage.

"Independent fire at will!"

Furiously Hawthorne rammed another charge home. He felt as if all the world were suddenly slowed, his arms made of lead. Ever so slowly he pulled the rammer out and fumbled for a percussion cap.

The wall of shouting, raging men came closer, closer.

He brought his rifle up, pointed, and squeezed.

The face of a man not ten yards away exploded in blood.

"O'Donald, the gun!"

It sounded as if Andrew's shouts came from a million miles away.

Relentlessly they came forward.

A dark shield seemed to fill the world in front of Hawthorne. Bayonet lowered, he met the charge and thrust in.

His blade skidded off the shield. Over the rim he could see the wild eyes of a man intent on killing him.

An ax came down, and he leaped to the right. Gun raised high, he drove in, the bayonet catching his man in the throat.

And then another body filled the world before him, and then another, while all the time he screamed as if one possessed, no longer caring if he lived or died.

"They're running, they're running!"

Incredulous, Kal staggered to his feet. The noble who had

been so intent upon killing him but a moment before seemed to have disappeared into thin air.

All up and down the street, doorways were flung open, people pouring out, armed with whatever they could grab.

Stunned, Kal looked about. Never had he seen his people thus, fire in their eyes, a look of triumph raising them to exultation.

"To the square!" Kal cried. "Death to the nobles!" And his cry was picked up, echoing and reechoing above the nightmare which was now turning to hope.

"You've got to hold," Andrew roared.

They were no longer firing, for the pressure was too great to give his men a chance to reload. He knew that sword and shield against bayonet would win out, but they had to hold, and link up with Mina, who from the sound of battle was pushing in from the west.

Turning, he looked at Hans.

"Bring up the reserve!"

Saluting, the sergeant ran off.

"O'Donald, where the hell are you?" And as if in answer the red-whiskered major came storming up to his side.

Drawing his revolver, he emptied the six chambers in a matter of seconds.

"Best damn fight I've ever seen!" the Irishman shouted, as he pointed to his gun, which was being pushed into line.

"B Company, open up!" Andrew shouted.

Parrying the swarming enemy, the company staggered back past the gun.

A thunderous roar echoed across the square. The Napoleon leaped almost to the vertical and slammed back down.

"Triple canister," O'Donald shouted gleefully. "Two hundred iron balls at point-blank!"

Dumbfounded, Andrew looked in amazement at the bloody swarth that had mowed through the square.

The enemy charge broke and started to stream back northward, while from out of the west side of the square the first bluecoats appeared.

"Let's drive them!" Andrew roared. "Keep them moving!"

Reloading, the four companies fired again, counterpointed by another blast from the artillery.

Volley after volley slashed out, and in silence Andrew watched.

So this was the epitome of what he had become, he thought grimly, feeling a strange horrifying sense of power in the destructiveness unleashed.

Hans came up by his side, while the reserve companies rushed past, forming to the right of the line, their firepower adding to the carnage.

"We're doing murder," Andrew said grimly.

"It's our job," Hans replied, pulling out a plug of precious tobacco and biting off a chew. To his amazement, Andrew reached out and took a bite, handing the plug back.

Breaking in every direction, the nobles and their warriors streamed to the north and east, while from out of the side streets a torrent of peasants poured out, driving the stragglers before them, shouting with wild abandon.

"Cease fire!" Andrew shouted, and the volley line was stilled.

The square was wreathed in smoke, the flames from the palace and buildings about the square illuminating the carnage with a lurid light.

"Hans, get up to Mina and have his command push up to the north. Keep the pressure on them, but show some mercy. If they keep moving, let them go—we've broken them right here. I'll send four companies up the east road the same way, and keep A and B with the artillery here in the square as reserve."

"It had to be done this way," Hans said, looking into Andrew's eyes.

"God help me, I know," Andrew replied. "Now get moving."

Andrew started across the square, but within seconds all semblance of control seemed to break down as a torrent of people, wild with joy, filled the square, laughing, weeping, shouting with joy.

Andrew, leading his men, started across the pavilion to the church, where there was still a knot of fighting between peasants and warriors. At the approach of his men the sound of fighting died away.

At least some were starting to give up, he thought hopefully.

"Surrender!" Andrew shouted. "We offer quarter!"

The peasants backed away, shouting angrily, and as they gave ground, Andrew stood transfixed.

Ivor stood in the doorway of the church.

"Ivor, give up. I'm offering you quarter."

The boyar gazed at Andrew, a look of pain on his features.

Andrew started forward.

"We can work together, Ivor."

The boyar stood before him, a sad smile creasing his features.

"I never wanted this," Ivor said, a distant look on his face.

Andrew could not reply.

"But you were right when you told me the church would destroy me."

"Give, up, Ivor."

Nodding, as if coming from a deep sleep, the boyar motioned to his men, who, letting their weapons drop, started to walk toward the Union line.

Ivor turned to look back into the church.

"No!" And leaping to the middle of the doorway, he rushed into the darkness of the nave.

There was the crack of a rifle shot.

Andrew, sword raised, leaped up the stairs and into the church.

Ivor turned to face him, a look of stunned disbelief on his face. At his feet lay Rasnar, with Ivor's sword driven through his body. A still-smoking rifle rested by Rasnar's side, his fists clenched tightly around the barrel. The priest, who had appeared so powerful in life, now looked pathetic and small, his death grimace a horrible contortion of rage and pain.

"It was meant for you," Ivor said weakly, and drawing back his hands, he revealed a hole in his chest, pouring blood.

Wordlessly the boyar sank to the floor, and Andrew knelt by his side.

"It was meant for both of us," Andrew said sadly.

"Rule my people better than I did," Ivor whispered. "Free them from the Tugars." And then he was still.

Leaning over, Andrew took off Ivor's glasses, and gently closed his eyes.

Coming back out of the church, Andrew beheld a scene of wild jubilation.

He saw Hawthorne leaning against the side of the church, and he went up to the soldier, who stood wide-eyed in shock.

"Are you all right, boy?" he asked.

"I think so, sir."

"It's the same for all of us," Andrew said, patting him lightly on the shoulder. "In there lies a friend of mine. See that his body isn't harmed."

"Keane, Keane!"

Andrew looked up to see Kal pushing through the crowd.

"Keane, I knew you would come," Kal said softly.

"Yes, we came," Andrew said numbly. "We could not let you die."

Kal looked about the square and shook his head.

"Is this the price of freedom?" he asked numbly.

"It usually is," Andrew replied.

"We're free, Keane, we're free," the peasant said as if coming from a dream.

"And there'll be a lot more to pay before you're done," Andrew said, looking at his men, who still stood in ranks, which he could see had been tragically thinned.

"There are still the Tugars."

BOOK II

Chapter 12

As the gates of the city opened, a wild tumultuous shout went up.

Feeling a bit foolish, Andrew spurred his mount, and the regiment stepped forward, drums rolling, the men sounding off with the song "The Battle Cry of Freedom."

He could not help but think of the ancient Romans offering a triumph to a victorious legion commander returning from the field.

Kal and a delegation of city elders stood at the gate. At Andrew's approach they bowed low, turned, and led the way up the street to the town square.

Had it only been two days since he came charging up this street, sword in hand, his soul consumed with the joy of battle? As if in a dream, Andrew looked about. Many of the buildings were scorched, their vacant windows looking like blackened skeletal eyes. It was a miracle, he thought, that the whole city hadn't been lost. Only the shifting of the storm into a heavy rain had ended the conflagration.

All about him were people pressing forward, waving, touching his horse, weeping, laughing. Turning in the saddle, he looked back down the street. His battle-hardened men were grinning broadly at the reception, their song echoing above the roar of the crowd.

> "And we'll fill our vacant ranks,
> With a million freemen more,
> Shouting the Battle Cry of Freedom."

The vacant ranks, Andrew thought sadly. Twenty-five more men are resting now on cemetery hill, and another sixty were still in the hospital with wounds. The toll of Suzdalians would most likely never be known. At least

243

three, possibly four thousand dead, along with a couple of thousand from the other side. Yet still the people celebrated.

Drums rolling, the regiment passed its way up to the city square and made their way toward the great cathedral, where a golden-robed figure stood on the steps of the church.

Drawing up before the cathedral, Andrew reined in, the column coming to a halt. The golden-robed priest raised his hand in a sign of blessing, and all in the square, including many of O'Donald's men, blessed themselves in response.

Reaching out to a young acolyte for support, the priest hobbled down the steps of the church, and as Andrew dismounted the priest shook his hand, which triggered a wild response from the spectators.

"As He died to make men holy, let us die to make men free," Casmar said, grinning, and in spite of all that was troubling his mind, Andrew could not help but smile in return.

"They expect you to say something," Casmar said, beckoning back to the expectant crowd.

He'd been dreading this moment, but knew it would have to be done. Mounting the steps with Casmar, Andrew turned and looked out over the sea of faces.

"Citizens of Suzdal," Andrew started, his tenor voice carrying clearly in the cold winter air. "You have shown yourselves to be men and women determined to be free."

A wild cheer went up, and Andrew had to wait until it finally died down.

"You have fought to win your freedom, and you have paid the first price for that freedom in blood. I wish I could offer you peace, but we all know that is impossible. I wish I could offer you freedom to live your lives as you please, but for now that is impossible as well.

"For we know what is coming to us from out of the west."

All were silent.

"If we are to win, to purchase our freedom from the slaughter pits of the Tugars, it will only be by our being united, by giving heart and soul for the common defense of all. It will be a long road, but a road I pray will lead to final victory and freedom."

"Lead us, Boyar Keane!" a voice shouted from the front of the crowd.

Within seconds the cry went up and soon turned to a chant.

"Boyar Keane, Boyar Keane."

Andrew looked over to where Kal stood and nodded.

The burly peasant, his left arm in a sling, and wearing the rough tunic and cloak of the common people, mounted the steps, and at the sight of him a wild thunderous cheer erupted.

Laughing, he extended his right hand for silence.

"So they have learned that the teeth of the mice are sharp after all," he began, and the crowd roared with delight.

"We need a strong leader," Kal continued. "One who knows war, for there will be war. We need a fox who can show all of us how to be foxes as well. I say that we will have this Yankee thing called a Declaration of Independence when the time comes. However, we must drive away the Tugars first, and for now I want a fox to lead us. I trust Keane. Let us name him our leader and listen to his words. He will not be a boyar—he told me he hates that word. So I say we should call him Colonel Keane, and let him show us how to fight to keep our freedom."

Again a wild shout went up, and before the crowd Andrew and Kal knelt before Casmar, who blessed both of them.

"So now let us celebrate!" Kal roared, the ceremony completed, and the crowd broke into a wild frenzy of laughing, dancing, and cheering.

Andrew looked back down the steps to Hans, who came forward.

"All right, Hans," Andrew shouted above the roar. "Staff meeting inside—the rest have passes till sundown."

"The boys are going to have a day they'll never forget," Hans said, grinning.

"It's going to be the last for a long time, so let them enjoy it."

Turning, Andrew walked into the cathedral, Kal and Casmar by his side. Looking over at the peasant, he couldn't help but grin.

The man was a political master equal to any ward boss back home. The whole thing, the triumph, Casmar blessing them, the speeches, the shout from the audience calling for Keane to lead them, had all been engineered by the wily, simple-looking man.

The morning after the battle it had been Kal who approached him, pointing out some of the political necessities required to bring order back to the city, and Andrew could only wonder if this man had been taking lessons on the side.

Turning past the altar, the three proceeded down the corridor and into Rasnar's old office.

Casmar, grimacing with pain, settled into one of the chairs arranged about the table, and as Andrew's staff and Kal's companions filed in, he beckoned for the rest of the group to be seated.

Casmar looked nervously about, obviously still uncomfortable at the position circumstance had suddenly thrust him into. When Dr. Weiss came in he immediately went up to the new prelate and checked him for fever.

"You should be in bed, dammit," Weiss growled.

"When there is time," Casmar replied good-naturedly, motioning for Weiss to sit by his side.

The last of the staff in the room, Andrew motioned for the doors to be closed.

Andrew looked around the table and felt a chill in his heart.

For some in the room there was still the exultation of what had been accomplished in the last two days. But for others a growing sense of what had been created was finally starting to sink in. For the regiment there was now no chance of backing out, of finding that safe place that Tobias had almost successfully argued for. The regiment was staking its life on Suzdal, and Andrew knew the chance was a slim one.

"All right, then, gentlemen, to business," Andrew said, and the room fell silent.

"First item is order in the city," and Andrew looked over at Kal.

"Yesterday was rough," Kal replied. "I followed your orders and organized a militia to bring control back. Dozens were killed nevertheless as old grudges were settled.

"And," he said quietly, "fifteen were executed this morning for looting."

Andrew looked at Kal and felt satisfied. There was no joy in Kal for the power of life and death. He could only hope it would stay that way.

"Several thousand have left as well, going east to Vazima."

"Glad to be rid of them," Boris interjected. "They're traitors."

"They're not traitors," Andrew snapped back in reply.

"That's another thing about freedom. We've overthrown the old order here in Suzdal, and if reports are to be believed, in Novrod as well. But there'll be many who do not like this. They must be free to leave and go east to live under Mikhail and the other boyars, if that is their wish."

"We've got over a thousand men at arms who've surrendered, and some wish to join us," Kal interjected.

"Good. We'll need experienced soldiers. I'll discuss them shortly. Anything else that needs to be reported now?"

He looked about the room, and all were silent.

"Then, gentlemen, there is one and only one issue that must consume our every waking moment. The Tugars."

The men looked uneasily at each other.

"It'll be impossible," Tobias snapped from the far end of the table. "You never should have destroyed those ballots without counting them. I'm positive the men voted to leave."

Andrew leaned over the table and fixed Tobias with a cold icy stare.

"I am in command of this detachment, Captain Tobias. I gave the men the option to vote when it was necessary. But the real vote was here in this city two days ago. The men marched with me, fully knowing what it would mean, knowing that we were committed to the liberation of these people from the boyars and the Tugars. That vote was taken, sir, and the ballots which I destroyed were no longer valid. For the duration of this campaign I am in command, and you shall follow my orders. Do I make myself clear?"

Tobias was silent but returned Andrew's glare with open hatred.

Andrew turned and looked at Kal, and then swept the room with his gaze.

"I did not want this power, but it is now mine. I am declaring military law for the duration, as we have always maintained with our own detachment. There can only be one person in charge—otherwise there will be chaos, and whatever slim chance we have of beating the Tugars will melt away."

"So you do not believe we can beat them?" Casmar asked.

"The chances aren't very good, your holiness, but by God we'll try nevertheless," Andrew replied.

"Gentlemen, from what little information the people of this city have given us, we can estimate that the Tugars will be able to field well over a hundred and fifty thousand mounted warriors. As of this morning's roll we have less than six hundred men trained to meet them. The citizens of Suzdal and Novrod have no concept of how to fight the Tugars. If they attempt to do so as they are now, it will be a massacre, and Rus will cease to exist.

"If I were the Tugar leader I would not allow a single one of the people here to live, for you have overthrown the leaders they appointed over you. Their only alternative is to annihilate the entire population, or else the infection of what you represent will spread."

"Then why did you fight for us?" Kal asked.

"Because we could not let you die at the hands of the boyars."

"And now you agree to stay nevertheless?" Casmar asked softly.

"We have made our commitment. Our arrival helped to trigger this, and I and my command will not leave you now."

"Then how do we defeat them?"

Andrew fixed Kal and his companions with his gaze.

"In one year I plan to raise a national army. Every citizen will be trained to fight."

"But our bows do not carry like theirs," Casmar said quietly. "We have few horses—we do not have even enough swords."

"If we fight them that way, we'll lose," Andrew replied. "But we will not fight them in the way expected."

"How then?" Kal asked quietly.

"Gentlemen, in one year I plan to create an industrial state out of Suzdal. I intend to place in the field a modern army, armed with muskets and artillery and with all of the logistical support necessary. In that is our only hope."

The men in the room looked at Andrew as if he had proposed an unthinkable madness.

"Sir, may I speak frankly?" John Mina asked.

"Go on, major."

"Sir, do you realize the full import of what you are saying? It is not as if we had the factories waiting for us to churn out all the accoutrements of war. We'll be starting from scratch."

"I know, John, and if you can come up with a better alternative, tell me."

John leaned back in his chair, shaking his head.

"You know it's been done before," Bob Fletcher interjected.

"Where?" John asked.

"The rebs. When the war started they didn't have a single factory for making rifles, artillery, even gunpowder. Their cannon works in Richmond is now one of the biggest, and their powder mill down in Georgia was believed to be the biggest in the world—turns out powder as good as or better than our own."

"But they had four years to do it," John argued.

"And we shall have less than one," Andrew replied. "But I should point out we do have the resources to do it with."

"From where?" Tobias mumbled.

"You've already demonstrated it," Andrew said, looking back at the major.

"So far the boys have built four mills and made a good start on a railroad—Ferguson told me last night he could have a small locomotive ready in another month. Last night I went over the regimental rolls. Most all the boys in the regiment come from Maine, a lot from the factory towns. O'Donald's boys are from the city and quite a few tradesmen in the lot, and Cromwell has a number of men who know steam engines and other things as well.

"Gentlemen, I daresay nearly all the knowledge necessary to build a modern New England factory town is sitting around this table, or outside enjoying the celebrations. We're going to start from scratch, but by heaven we'll do it, because we know the price of failure if we do not."

The men visibly perked up at the passion in Andrew's voice. "I've drawn up a basic plan of organization," he said, and pulling out a roll of note paper from his tunic he put on his glasses.

"We are going to divide our organization into three areas—labor, industrialization, and military training.

"Kal, as of this moment you and your men will be in charge of organizing your people for work. I'm giving you full responsibility and power for this. The various people I appoint for building projects will come to you. You and your people in turn will marshal the necessary forces. We are talking about tens of thousands of men and women who will have to be organized. I'm giving you the full authority of military law under me. Do you understand that?"

The peasant, taken aback, merely nodded in reply.

"Next comes the industrialization. John, I am giving you full authority for that organization. You are to coordinate all projects, give them priority, assign whoever is necessary, and see Kal for the workers."

John leaned back in his chair and smiled.

"I'll be hell to live with for some of you," John said, looking about the table, and the other officers laughed good-naturedly.

"All right, then, John, let's see what has to be done in the following areas.

"The most basic requirement is iron and powder. What would you need for at least ten thousand muskets and a hundred field pieces?"

"One hundred!" O'Donald said excitedly. "Colonel darling, how in the name of the saints do you plan that?"

"They won't be Napoleons," Andrew replied. "I'm thinking of light field pieces, four-pounders at most, that can be moved by a single horse."

"Still, Andrew, that's a lot of metal."

"The artillery will be under your command, O'Donald— let me worry about where it comes from."

"From battery commander to chief of artillery," O'Donald laughed, grinning with delight.

"That's a lot of metal, as he said," John replied.

"What do you need to do it, John? I don't want to hear how much—I want to know what it takes to get the job done," Andrew said looking across the table.

"All right," John said quietly, sitting back and thinking while the room was silent.

"To start, we'll need a foundry, a damn big one, not that little affair back on the mill stream. And that means power, lots of it."

Andrew turned away from John and looked over at Ferguson, the only enlisted man in the room besides Hans.

"Ferguson, what about power?"

"I'd like to say steam engines, sir. Now if we could take the engine out of the *Ogunquit*—"

"Like hell you will," Tobias roared.

"We need the boat for transport," Andrew replied, "and Captain Cromwell, if I do want that engine at a later date, I'll take it whether you like it or not."

"Well then, sir," Ferguson continued, speaking quickly as if to avoid an argument, "I'd still like to say steam engines.

We've got a small one for our locomotive which is half done, but it'll be a weak one at best. To build bigger and stronger ones we'll need precision tools and equipment. That'll take time."

"But I want the power now," Andrew said.

"Sir, Dr. Weiss, Kal, and I went up to survey that site for the dam above the city. I figure it'll take six months with five thousand working on it to get all the earth moved. But once done, it'd deliver a tremendous head of power, enough to handle all we'd possibly need. From that power we can turn out all that the major wants, with plenty to spare for other projects."

"Kal, I want twenty thousand men to start on that dam within two days," Andrew said, and the peasant looked at him wide-eyed.

"But colonel—"

"Do you want to live past next year?" Andrew replied.

Kal nodded, looking somewhat overwhelmed.

"Then all of your people had better learn quickly that this is not working for some boyar and trying to do as little as possible—this means hard work from morning to night."

"But the ground is frozen."

"Then use picks, get below the frost, and start digging."

Andrew looked back to Ferguson and nodded for him to continue.

"Sir, I can have the plans and survey done for the dam in three days' time."

"Good, son. You're now promoted to captain and are hereby assigned all engineering design work. Start with the dam, then with anything that'll create power. You're also in charge of the railroad. I'm authorizing you to form an engineering company. Pick the best men—you can go through the roster book later."

"Thank you, sir," Jim said, beaming with pride.

John looked back at Mina.

"All right, what do you need, if Ferguson can give you the power?"

"Sir, we'll need a major foundry to cook down the ore. Then bigger forges to turn the runoff into wrought iron for the basic needs of metal, and then special furnaces to turn out steel for tools and springs for the gun locks."

"Pick all the men you need, and get started at once. Talk to Ferguson about the best sites, and to Kal about the labor "

"Sir, there'll be a hell of lot going into this," John said.

"Go on, John, I need to know."

"Sir, it's one thing to roll out a musket barrel, but cutting a rifle requires a lot more time and precision."

"What do you suggest?"

"Well, sir, I'd suggest that we turn out flintlock smooth-bore muskets. It'd eliminate the need for percussion caps, which need fulminate of mercury, and I sure as hell don't know where we'd get the mercury for that. I know muskets will only give us a range of a hundred yards instead of the four hundred a good Springfield rifle can deliver. But we can turn out a hell of a lot more muskets than rifles, especially at the start. Maybe later we'll get up to something like flintlock long rifles."

Andrew had been afraid he would hear this. They already knew from experience that the Tugar bows would carry two hundred yards, maybe more, thus outranging flintlocks like the type his grandfather had carried in the Revolution. Tactics would somehow have to be adjusted, but it was better to have muskets than nothing at all.

"What else would you need?" Andrew asked, deciding to worry about tactics when there was more time.

"Sir, we'll need a constant source of iron ore. We've found only that one site. The quality of the ore is good, but we'll need to expand that operation significantly to supply our needs. I've already learned the Suzdalians have another site, but it's way the hell up the river. Next we'll need to cook an awful lot of limestone for flux. Finally, there's fuel, and that's the worst part.

"I can use wood charcoal, though it'll mean thousands of men cutting and cooking the stuff to keep the mills going. We need coal—good hard anthracite would be best. Then we need a retort furnace to cook the stuff into coke, to get rid of the chemicals in coal that would make the metal brittle. Without coal I can't turn out the amount of metal we need."

To Andrew the whole business of metalworking was a mystery. He turned and looked at Kal.

"Have you ever heard of coal?" he asked.

Kal, confused, merely shook his head.

"He means a rock that burns," Emil said. "It's black and shiny and smells when it burns."

"Ah, the gate to the devil," Kal said, and turning to Casmar he talked excitedly with the prelate for several minutes and then turned back to Andrew.

"We call it devil rock. Half a day's walk beyond the hills where you get the iron rock. There's a hole where smoke comes out. There are black rocks there. Casmar says it is dangerous, though, for it is the hole into hell."

This would require some long conversations, Andrew thought. The last thing he needed was to turn another prelate against him who might think that they were digging a tunnel into hell.

Andrew looked through the regimental rolls and found what he wanted.

"O'Donald, your roster indicates that Mike Polawski was a coal miner by trade."

"Came out of Scranton, just before the war. Only Pole in the battery, but a good Catholic boy nevertheless."

"See him at once. Tell him to get together some men, and Father Casmar will locate a guide to check the site out.

"What else will you need?" Andrew said, looking back at John.

"If we've got the fuel, flux, and ore, along with the power from the dam, we'll start work. I think I can figure out how to cast light artillery pieces and some way to roll gun barrels. It'll take some time, though, to put the pieces together."

"I know you can do it, John," Andrew said, forcing a smile.

"There's another problem, though. The mill will be located above Suzdal, since that's where the power is. Our ore is up on the mill stream and the coal maybe six or seven miles beyond that. Hauling it will be hell."

Andrew looked back at Ferguson.

"I want a railroad to be laid out from the dam site, down into Suzdal, along the river road, and then up past the ore pit, and if there's coal to that site as well."

"That's a powerful order, sir. Fifteen, more like eighteen miles of track at least, not counting sidings. Sir, if we use wooden track covered with iron strap, I figure that will mean . . ." He paused for a moment to do a rough calculation. "We'll need something like three hundred tons, and that's making the rail awful light."

Mina whistled, started to shake his head, and then, seeing Andrew's cold gaze, stopped.

"John, the foundry and mill you've going now?"

"A couple of tons a day at best."

"Put everything you have into turning out metal strapping for the tracks.

"Ferguson, once you're done with the dam survey, get your team working on laying out the route for the track. We've got some boys who've worked on the railroads—you're using them already. Get them moving on track layout. See Kal, draw out as many laborers as you'll need to clear, grade, lay ties and stringers."

"The ground's frozen, sir," Ferguson said quietly.

"Build on top of it if need be, we've got the labor to regrade after the thaw."

"I'll see to it immediately, sir," Ferguson replied, grinning at the responsibilities given to him. "Sir, there's another idea."

"Go ahead."

"Mitchell—he's a friend of mine over in E Company—well, Mitchell was a telegrapher before the war. I was talking with him the other day. He said if we could get some copper it would be real easy to set a telegraph up. It'd be a help once the trains are rolling, and really help as well for communication once the war gets started."

It was something Andrew hadn't even thought of, and he smiled approvingly.

Andrew looked over at Mina.

"John, what do you think?"

"Sir, we'd need to find some copper and make a wire works. That's asking an awful lot."

"Assign it to that Mitchell boy. Promote him to sergeant, and get one of your people to start checking on a copper supply around here as well."

John looked over at Ferguson and gave him an ugly stare. Andrew knew that Mina and the former private were already good friends, so he let it pass without comment.

"All right. Gunpowder—any suggestions?"

"Sir, we can get the saltpeter easy enough," Ferguson said. "We'll need to organize teams to dig up every manure pile in the countryside. It's fairly simple then to refine out the nitrates. I'd suggest we dig up all the latrine pits in the city as well—there'll be tons of the stuff in there."

Andrew looked over at Kal.

"It's rotten work. You'll have to get somebody to do it, though."

Confused, Kal could only look at Andrew in amazement.

"Dig up latrine pits to make the smoke powder?"

"Sounds strange, doesn't it?" Andrew replied. "But it's the truth."

"Could it be that when one thunders into the latrine, it stays there till you dig it up and that's what makes the guns roar?"

The room exploded into laughter, and Kal, not taking offense, laughed as well.

Andrew, grateful for the relaxing of tension, let the men trade rude jokes for a moment and then shifted the topic back to the needs at hand.

"What about sulfur?" Andrew asked, looking around the table.

"You know, I heard some of the boyars and nobles here went to a hot spring for baths several miles north of town," Emil said. "I never went up there, but supposedly the water really stinks. Might be a high sulfur content in it, and if so there are bound to be deposits."

"You know what the stuff looks like?" Andrew asked.

"I don't hold with it as a medicine like others, but I've got a good idea what it looks like in a raw state."

"Go up there immediately and check it out."

Andrew looked back at Ferguson.

"Let me ask for a miracle here. Among all your other knowledge, can you make powder as well?"

"Well, sir," Chuck Ferguson began slowly, "I know the ratio of parts, I remember reading about it in *Scientific American*, and how they mix it up and wet the mixture down, then roll it into cakes, and finally grind it to the grade you want. But it'll take some experimenting to get it right.

"It'll be awful tricky, sir. A single spark and the place gets blown apart. This will take some thinking and experimenting."

"If we get the powder we'll still need lead," Mina interjected.

Andrew looked to Kal and his companions, who stared blank-faced.

Ferguson explained the property of the metal to them, and he was met with confused silence.

"We'll need to prospect this one out," Mina finally said dejectedly.

"Start with the people here in town. Search through everything—there's got to be something of lead in this town. Once located we'll track the source down.

"Now, John, what else do we need for armament?"

"If we get everything organized we'll still need cartridge paper for the muskets, bayonets, wheels and carriages for artillery, gun flints, cartridge boxes, shoes, and supplies."

Andrew nodded as John checked off his list.

"Everything you say means an extra job for you, John. Delegate it out as you see fit."

"All right, sir," the major said while furiously scribbling down notes.

"Now the question of supply," Andrew said. "Fletcher, since you showed some skill getting that grain mill started and you're the quartermaster for the regiment, I'm giving you the job of supplying an army and all of Suzdal once the war starts."

"I was afraid of that," Fletcher said, trying to smile.

"I'm expecting that before this is done, we'll have a siege on our hands. You'll have to stockpile enough to see everyone through that, for however long it takes."

"That's pretty damn open-ended, sir," Fletcher said. "I need something more specific to calculate on."

"Bob, I can't give you anything more than that. Now tell me what would have to be done."

"Kal, I understand the boyars were already stockpiling grain for the arrival of the Tugars," Fletcher said hopefully.

"Since the Tugars were thought to be three winters away, we had only laid aside a small portion of what was needed."

Fletcher shook his head sadly.

"I think the first problem will simply be that of labor," Fletcher stated.

"How's that?" Andrew asked, "we've got hundreds of thousands to do that."

"That's not the point," Bob replied. "These people farm the way folks did five hundred years ago. They need seven or eight in the fields to feed ten. You start pulling off tens of thousands to build dams and mills and make an army, and we'll all starve to death next winter, with or without the Tugars."

Andrew felt as if he were caught up in some sort of balancing act.

"So how the hell do we solve it?"

"We'll have to change how they farm, and damn quick."

"How so?"

"If we had one of them McCormick reapers to start with," Fletcher replied, "that'd do the work of twenty-five men come harvest time."

Andrew looked hopefully at Ferguson as if the new captain could work miracles.

"That's a tall one, sir," Jim replied.

"There's got to be a farmer in the ranks who had one," Andrew said hopefully.

"If we were an Illinois or Iowa regiment we'd have dozens of them," Fletcher replied, "but you don't see many of them new-fangled things up in Maine."

"I'll run through the roster later and we'll ask if any of the men knows anything about machine reapers. Now what else would you need to do, Bob?"

"Well sir, besides reapers, we should turn out some good iron plows, tillers, and harrowing machines."

"And I suppose that'll come out of my metal supply," Mina snapped.

"There's no place else," Andrew said quietly. "All right, we won't need those machines till spring planting starts. John, you and Fletcher figure out the allocation of metal and a forge to work on the tools."

"If you could do that, sir, we might have a shot at it," Fletcher replied. "These people have bottles—a good glass works could give us one hell of a lot of bottles for canning food with."

Andrew looked back to Kal.

"There's five or six glassmakers here in the city," Kal replied.

"Good. Send them to Captain Fletcher—they're working for him now.

"What else, Bob?"

"A mill for grinding, and I mean a big one. I'd also want bakeries, and smokehouses for meat. If we can get in plenty of extra salt it'd help for laying up beef and pork, even dried fish. I suggest before the Tugars come we slaughter nearly everything and lay it up. I'd even suggest sending gangs of hunters into the woods to bring in whatever can be found."

"It's all your job, Bob. Again, go to Kal for what you need. I expect a report from you in two weeks' time, with estimates of how many people we'll be able to feed from the Tugar arrival on through the winter, and if need be into next spring."

Glumly Bob nodded.

"Dr. Weiss," and Andrew turned to fix Emil with his gaze, "I have two concerns you have to prepare for. The first is an epidemic breaking out either before the Tugars arrive or once battle has been joined. We can train the best army this world has ever seen, but it'll be wiped out in no time if present conditions continue to exist."

"Just my worry exactly, Andrew," Weiss said excitedly. "This place is a disaster waiting to happen."

Andrew turned to face Casmar.

"Your holiness, we have ways of preventing disease from striking the people. I realize many of the things we have brought with us are strange. But Dr. Weiss could help your people to live more healthily. Dr. Weiss knows many things that will prevent pestilence and plague from striking us and making us so weak that the Tugars will win. I give you my solemn pledge that his arts are good. I'm asking you to work with him on this task. Some things he'll do might seem strange, but please trust him."

Casmar looked at Weiss and smiled.

"His skills made my feet and hands feel better," the prelate said. "And I must say I never did like the bleedings our healers would have given to me."

"Barbarians," Weiss grumbled, and would have said more except for Andrew's gaze.

"I have also heard," Casmar continued, sidestepping Emil's comment, "how he and the woman healer have worked for two days without sleep to help our injured from the battle."

It was the first time since marching out of the camp that Andrew had spared a thought for Kathleen, so engrossed had he been with the affairs of setting up a state and planning for this meeting. He knew Kathleen would rise to the task, but he dreaded the thought of what she must be going through right now. How he wanted to see her! But that would have to wait.

"Your holiness, if anything he says and does troubles you, please see me right away, and I shall be glad to listen to your concerns."

Casmar smiled good-naturedly at Andrew, who again breathed an inner sigh of relief that Rasnar was dead. The last thing he needed was having the church stop Weiss from instituting his practices.

"The next thing, doctor, will be preparing for the siege. We'll need hospitals, medications, and a staff trained by you to meet the needs for this city."

Weiss shook his head.

"Andrew, it'll take years to train these people."

"You have a year," Andrew said forcefully.

Wearily, Emil nodded his head.

"All right, then, the final point of today's meeting. Military preparation. I'm taking personal responsibility for that. We know precious little about how the Tugars fight, and till we do the question of tactics on the field is an open one.

"Sergeant Major Schuder will be assigned the responsibility of training a modern field army of at least ten thousand infantry to fight the same way we do. Sergeant, you are hereby appointed to the rank of brevet major general of the Suzdalian army."

Caught totally off guard, the old sergeant looked at Andrew in amazement.

"Me, a goddam officer?" Hans asked, his look of stunned disbelief causing the gathering to chuckle.

Andrew smiled and nodded at his old teacher.

"Colonel, sir, couldn't we just keep it as sergeant major and forget this officer foolishness?"

"You'll still be a sergeant in the 35th," Andrew said, "but for this job, anything less than general simply won't do."

"Make yourself the general," Hans argued.

"I'm keeping my rank," Andrew replied, "and anyhow, I couldn't hold with giving myself a promotion. But at least I can do it for others. You'll still answer to me, though, if that makes you feel better."

Not at all amused, Hans settled back in his chair.

"Come on, sergeant," Mina said cheerfully, "you'll do a damn sight better than some of those poppinjays like General Pope or Burnside."

"Or Grant," Fletcher mumbled, and there was a chorus of agreements, for the regiment was still bitter about how their old commander had slaughtered tens of thousands of their comrades with futile frontal assaults during the Wilderness and Petersburg campaigns.

Hans mumbled darkly under his breath but offered no further resistance.

"You'll also be responsible for the militia," Andrew continued, "which will be under Kal once the battle starts. Every able-bodied man who is not part of the modern army will be organized and trained nevertheless. Any of the men at arms that come over to our side will be assigned to them as instructors and leaders in battle.

"Tomorrow I'll have the town criers announce the call for volunteers for the modern infantry and artillery regiments. Those men from our command not assigned to various tasks by Mina, Ferguson, or Fletcher will be assigned the task of instruction. When battle is finally joined a fair number of our men will be attached directly to the Suzdalian army, but the core of the regiment will be maintained to serve directly under my command as an independent unit.

"Some of you will find yourselves promoted to field command and staff positions for the Suzdalian divisions, brigades, batteries, and regiments."

The men looked excitedly at each other, the envy some felt for Hans disappearing with this new prospect.

"Just remember Napoleon," Andrew said, smiling at their excitement over such heady positions, "when he said there might be a marshal's baton in a private's knapsack.

"Now, as we prepare a field army, we'll also be working on defense. We have a year to fortify this position, and when it's done I plan to make the rebel works around Petersburg look like a child's sandbox sculpting. The Tugars are going to pay one hell of a price in blood before we're finished.

"Do we all understand what has to be done?" Andrew asked.

The men looked around at each other, still rather stunned by the enormous task before them, but he could see that hope had started to form in the face of the challenge, and as soldiers the prospect of high command would spur them on as well.

"Well, gentlemen, it sounds like there is one hell of a celebration going on out there," and for the first time since the meeting had started the men noticed the distant sound of merrymaking that filled the square.

"Tomorrow the celebrating ends and the work begins. Form back up with your men at sundown, but take the rest of the day for your enjoyment."

Smiles creased careworn faces, and O'Donald stood up, announcing he knew just the tavern for a rousing good time.

The group headed for the door, but Kal lingered behind, joined by Weiss, Hans, and Casmar.

With a look of concern, Andrew patted Weiss on the shoulder.

"Doc, you need some rest. Our friend Casmar must have a place for you to get a little sleep."

"I can't," Weiss said wearily. "When you stop fighting, that's when I begin," and straining, he came to his feet.

"There's thousands of wounded out there," he said sadly. "I've got to do something."

Andrew knew it was impossible to stop him, and with hunched shoulders the doctor left the room.

"We'll beat them," Kal said hopefully. "From all you said I know we will."

Andrew looked at Kal and smiled.

"A lot depends on the Tugars. If we had two years, I'd feel a lot better about it. Every day will be precious. But maybe there's a chance."

Kal and Casmar exchanged glances and looked back at the man who was now their boyar, and each of them could see the unspoken fear in the other's eyes.

Chapter 13

Bringing the rifle barrel up to his nose, Muzta sniffed curiously, then grimaced at the sulfurous smell.

"And how many of these devices do the Yankees have?" he asked grimly, looking back to his Namer of Time.

"I counted several hundred upon the walls of their fortress, and the priest said the number was near correct, my Qarth."

Holding the still-warm rifle, Muzta started to walk across the field, his heavy boots crunching through the thick crust of snow.

"And their big thunder killers?"

"I did not see them," the Namer said evenly.

"Why not?" Muzta snapped, looking back.

"They had them hidden."

"Did you not demand to enter their village to examine these things?" Muzta said quietly.

"No, my Qarth," the Namer responded nervously.

"And why not?"

"Their leader showed defiance," the Namer replied softly. "I struck him to set an example, and his followers pointed hundreds of the thunder makers at me. The priest had already told me of their power, and I knew we would all die if I pursued that path."

"So that's when you left?" Muzta said evenly.

The Namer merely nodded in reply.

Without comment, Muzta continued walking until he reached the human corpse lying in the snow. He looked at the body, which stared up at him wide-eyed, a trickle of blood still oozing out from the wound in its chest. Muzta kicked the body over and then knelt by its side.

He gasped with amazement at the gaping wound in the man's back and stuck his finger into the hole to examine it more closely.

"The metal ball has gone clean through the body," Muzta said, as if to himself.

"As I told you concerning my outrider," the Namer replied. "He was struck over thirty times, and dead before he hit the ground. His body was torn apart."

Muzta stood up and looked back across the field.

"Over a hundred paces, nearly the distance of our war bows," Qubata said evenly.

"These cattle are far too dangerous," Alem, the clan shaman, said sharply, while looking at the Namer with an accusing glance as if he had been responsible for their coming. "You should have stayed until the Rus people had destroyed them for you."

"I felt it important to come back and report, before the heavy snows came. My staying would have taken many more days and would show weakness. When cattle are ordered, they obey. I am sure the Yankees are already dead.

"And besides," the Namer added weakly, "after all, they are only cattle."

"Vulti did his job well as Namer," Tula stated, coming to

the defense of his nephew. "If any are still there upon our arrival, I am sure old Qubata will finish them."

Qubata looked over at Tula and smiled, revealing his dull yellow teeth.

"I am sure you'll be happy to ride with me," Qubata said evenly.

"I am not afraid of cattle," Tula snapped, "as I assumed our war leader would not be."

Qubata growled softly, and reaching over he took the rifle from Muzta's hand.

"This weapon makes cattle into killers. They saw one of ours die from it already, and I say Vulti was a fool to sacrifice an outrider on such an experiment. Now they know they can kill us."

"But there are only a handful of them," Tula replied.

The group was silent for a moment, each lost in his own thoughts.

Finally Muzta looked over at Alem.

"Fetch me the other," Muzta commanded.

The shaman turned from the group and beckoned to one of the attendants, who stood with the mounts while their masters debated.

The attendant came forward bearing a long bundle wrapped in leather and handed it to the shaman. Alem quickly unwrapped the package and handed the device over to Muzta.

The group gathered around for a closer look. It seemed at first glance to be similar in form to the rifle brought back by the Namer, but was clumsier and heavier.

"See here," Qubata said, pointing first to the lock of the rifle and then to the other weapon. "The one from the Yankees strikes the tiny metal cone, which makes a spark. This old one merely had a string which burned. The Yankee thunder maker is lighter and better-made—this old thing is crude."

"How old is this?" Qubata asked, looking back to the shaman.

"It was taken over fifteen circlings ago, according to the secret history," the shaman said, "while our people were encamped near the blue sea. Two great water ships appeared out of the tunnel of light. Aboard them were cattle of dark skin and black beards. We captured one; the other escaped and has not been seen since. They killed many Tugars before we feasted upon them."

"These cattle that come through the gate of the Old Ones seem to arrive with ever better devices for killing," Qubata said quietly.

If only we could close the gates created by the Old Ones, Muzta thought to himself, looking at the arquebus and rifle which he held one in each hand. Each new species of cattle that arrived was more difficult to tame. Perhaps they should look for the secret of the gate and learn to close it, but now was not the time to worry about such a thing.

Muzta looked back at those around him and then let his gaze drift across the open steppe.

The snow was deep, nearly up to the tops of his knee-high boots. To move the hundred thousand yurts of the clan now would be impossible. To send warriors forward would be dangerous, for their mounts would have a difficult time gaining forage. Something in his heart told him that he should try to move now. But such was impossible; the clans were still restless about the breaking of tradition and moving two years in one.

If only the Wheel were higher, he wished. The days were gaining in length. It was nearly two dark moons since the shortest of days; another darkening and they could start.

Muzta looked back to those who stood about him.

"When the snows start to clear, we prepare to move."

"Most likely we'll have to anyhow," Ubata said evenly and pointed back to the Maya city.

"We've eaten near all who are fit to eat back there," Alem said. "In another moon there won't be any cattle left other than those who have had the pox and are now unclean to feast upon. It seems almost a pity."

Muzta nodded in agreement. In his childhood he had once owned a cattle as a pet. He had even come to love it and allowed the pet to ride by his side. When it had died after falling from a horse he had wept openly and refused to see it eaten. That had been the last time he had felt pity for cattle until now.

He knew that when the horde rode eastward again the city of the Maya would be a city of spirits, if indeed cattle did have spirits in the afterworld.

One night he had walked through the city alone, watching as the bodies of the dead were taken out, their calves and mates sobbing with anguish. The sobbing he was inured to, for after all, nearly all cattle sobbed when one was led to the pit.

But this had been different, for it seemed as if an entire species was sobbing, knowing that soon all of them would disappear forever.

What had startled him, though, was when several cattle, cattle who had not been chosen for the pits, came up to him and screamed their rage and hatred at him. To his stunned disbelief, one had drawn a dagger and rushed him. He had slain his attacker and of course all who had witnessed the defiance, but they had died cursing him.

He was used to cattle sometimes struggling as they were led into the pits, but this had been different, almost an act of desperation. The injunction that a thousand extra die for any such attack did not seem to matter to these cattle. Was desperation making the cattle dangerous? he wondered. Could there be a spirit in them worthy of respect after all?

Sadly, he turned away and looked at the city. It was strange how similar yet different the cattle were. They all looked basically the same, and seemed to somehow, in their primitive souls, find an ability to love one another. Yet they could be so strangely different. Each with its own tongue, customs, and curious beliefs. And tastes of flesh as well, he thought dryly.

Some even made things of value, beautiful objects of gold and silver to decorate with, rugs of intricate design, saddles, woven fabrics, even the bows and arrows of the warriors. Thousands of such cattle traveled with the horde, producing objects of great value, and they were cherished as worthy pets. Many had died of the pox, and already Muzta had noticed how certain things could not be replaced without them.

Have we become too dependent on our cattle? Muzta wondered to himself. They had always been docile and learned the truth of submitting to the horde. Many had even prospered under their guidance. Could these Yankees represent some new breed of cattle?

"Their machines that you spoke of," Muzta said, looking back at the Namer.

"I saw little of their devices. The priest said their great water vessel could move without the wind or oars."

Several of the subclan chieftains laughed.

"Impossible," Tula barked. "Besides, we are Tugars. Wa-

ter is for cattle, not for such as we, so why should we care
what they do upon water?"

"I also saw where they had laid strips of metal upon the
ground. The priest could not explain it, and it seemed a
strange waste of good iron."

"That is curious," Qubata replied. "Could they have done
it to show they had more than needed as a trick to us?"

"Or is it a Yankee spell?" Alem asked.

The group looked at one another but none could venture
an answer.

"Can they fashion more of these before our coming?"
Muzta asked, holding up the rifle.

"It must require some great magic or machines," Alem
said, stepping forward and taking the rifle to examine it.
"The powder that was poured into the barrel I have never
seen before, and I believe it must come from the world the
cattle live upon. Cattle have never made such things here on
Valdennia."

"Perhaps until now," Qubata said dryly.

Tula and several of the other clan chieftains started to
laugh.

"Cattle are cattle," Magtu Vu'Qarth roared. "Fit for the
pit, not for warriors. Or is it that since Qubata's teeth grow
dull he will now hide in his yurt when cattle bellow?"

Qubata turned toward Magtu, his hand leaping to the hilt
of his blade.

Smiling, Magtu started to draw his sword.

"Come on, old one," Magtu snarled.

"If blood flows from either of you," Muzta roared, "both
will die by my hand."

Magtu looked toward the Qar Qarth. For the briefest of
moments there was a flicker of defiance in his eyes, and
then, sheathing his blade, he smiled back at Qubata with a
look of disdain, as if saying that the old man had been spared
by the protection of another.

Trembling with anger, Qubata turned and stalked away.

"There is nothing to be done about this now," Muzta said
evenly, pointing to the rifle in Alem's hands.

"We finish the winter feasting here. The Wheel is already
rising high again in the sky. But before the snow is melted
we move. At that time I will send Qubata forward with the
command of a thousand to drive ahead of the horde."

"He could clear out the wandering cattle as well," Alem said.

The others grunted their agreement at that. Every several years they'd send an expedition forward to destroy those cattle who would not submit but rather ran away ahead of the horde. They were a bad example and on a regular basis needed to be cleaned up.

"I haven't hunted running cattle in some time," Magtu laughed. "I will go along for the sport."

Muzta could not refuse a clan chieftain the request, but he could see that there would be problems from this.

"If all is decided, let us return to the city for the new moon feast."

There were loud grunts of agreement, and smiles lit up the features of the group at the mention of the forthcoming festivities and delicacies that awaited, and the group started back to their mounts.

Muzta turned away from the group and strolled over to where Qubata stood alone.

"You should not have interfered," Qubata said, his voice trembling with rage.

"He would have killed you, my friend," Muzta replied.

"Then if I can be killed I should be, for to live otherwise is without honor."

"My friend," Muzta said putting his hand on Qubatat's shoulder, "you must face the fact that your sword arm has weakened with age. It comes to us all."

Qubata looked at his old friend, a pained expression in his eyes.

"There was a time when such as Magtu would never have dreamed to speak to me such. Once I could have cleaved his body in half with a single blow. Now I am nothing to myself or to you, my Qarth."

Muzta laughed, as if his friend had told a foolish joke.

"When I was young I rode behind you at the great battle of Onci and saw your personal strength lay low a dozen Merki. It was not my father, it was you who planned the defeat of the Merki to the south. It was you and your brilliance that saved the Tugar horde from oblivion.

"I can find ten thousand brawling fools like Magtu to swing a sword or draw a bow. But I can only find one mind such as yourself."

"Onci was more than a circling ago," Qubata said.

"The Merki might come again," Muzta replied, "for this pox drives them as well. Hunger might send them north into our grazing grounds. I would turn upon them myself if I thought we had the numbers to defeat them and hold their grounds for our own clans."

"And beyond the Merki are the southern hordes," Qubata said. "We have divided the world after Onci. It would be foolish to start a war yet again, for surely the southern clans would respond."

"But if war does come I need your brilliance. Your sword arm is meaningless to me—it is your mind that I cherish, my old friend."

Muzta placed both hands on the shoulders of the graying warrior and shook him affectionately.

"Let's go back for the feast," Muzta said, both of them now slightly embarrassed by the outward display of love that each held for the other.

"It is not the Merki I worry about now," Qubata said as the two walked over to where their mounts waited.

"The Yankee cattle have you that worried?"

"With their thunder makers they can kill the same as a Merki arrow. Tula's nephew was a fool for sacrificing a warrior just to see how far their weapons can shoot. It might give all the Rus the wrong idea."

"But to stand against all our horde? They would be madmen," Muzta replied.

"We have chosen to forget, my Qarth, that cattle have feelings, perhaps as strong as ours. Our forefathers planned well with the injunction that only two of ten be harvested, since all would cling to the hope that they would not be selected. That we spare breeding stock, and cull out the weak, the deformed, and older ones, taking only the prime cuts for the moon feasts, was a great wisdom.

"But this pox makes them desperate, and these Yankees might upset the time-honored arrangement that has kept order with the Rus, and for that matter with cattle all around the world. One or the other factor could create a great danger.

"The only wise thing Vulti did was to order the rulers of Rus to destroy the Yankees now. Let us hope that has been done, for they sound defiant and could be desperate, and such things make cattle dangerous."

Muzta thought back to what had happened in the city the

night before. Perhaps Qubata was being overly cautious. But there was little that could be done, he thought, before they arrived in Rus. If there was a worry now it was still this strange pox. He could only hope that it would not destroy next winter's feeding.

"My Qarth, we must consider as well the prospect that all the cattle around the entire world might become infected, or that this Yankee way of thinking may spread ahead of us," Qubata said quietly.

Muzta looked over at his friend. So often his thoughts would be voiced by Qubata only a moment later, as if at times their minds had been strangely linked.

"Then we die," Muzta said dejectedly.

"My lord, we must learn to think," Qubata replied sharply. "Before the coming of the cattle we lived by gathering our own food and by hunting. Now we have become dependent on the cattle as our one source of food, never dreaming that it would sicken, or rebel. But the cattle *has* brought us the horse, and if need be we should sweep up its hooved meat, drive it along with us, and breed it so that it can replace the meat of the cattle."

"But there is barely even enough food for the cattle. Only the nobles eat of such things, and we take the rest."

"Then it is time that we learn how to raise this meat," Qubata replied.

"You believe the situation is that bad?" Muzta asked softly.

"I believe it is bad enough," Qubata replied sharply, "that I think we should learn even to eat of our horses."

"Never!" Muzta roared. "There are hardly enough for our own mounts and for the wagons of the families. Would you reduce us again to wandering the world on foot? Better to die! The horse is above cattle, it is wrong to eat of it, even when it is old and can no longer serve us."

"My lord, I think we might be considering even more drastic action before this crisis is past."

Muzta fell silent, unable to respond.

Reaching their horses, the two mounted, taking the reins from their waiting attendants. They started back down the hill. Suddenly Muzta reined in his horse and looked back at the attendants.

"Send somebody back here to pick this cattle up," Muzta shouted, pointing to the human corpse lying in the snow. "We shouldn't waste perfectly good food."

* * *

"All right, Malady, give her the throttle," Ferguson shouted.

Andrew was tempted to stand back, but realized that it would be seen as a lack of faith in Ferguson's engineering ability.

An expectant hush fell over the crowd of Suzdalians, to whom Kal had granted an hour's break so that they could witness the ceremony.

The engine had already been tested the night before, to make sure that everything worked. The worst part had been when Ferguson had the engine raised up on blocks, the firebox stuffed to near overflowing, and then poured on a full head of steam.

Andrew had ordered him to step away—an accident could kill one of the most important men in all of Rus. The youthful engineer, confident of his work, had protested until his commander's stern gaze had forced him to withdraw.

The machine had passed the load test with flying colors, but it still made Andrew nervous when Malady pushed the throttle down.

Puffs of smoke bellowed out from the locomotive, hissing steam escaped, and then, ever so slowly, the drive wheels started to turn.

With a lurch the engine chugged forward, the two hopper cars and single flatbed behind it moving in unison. Andrew and the other dignitaries shifted to maintain balance on the flatcar. Stunned at the sight, the Suzdalians stood with open-mouthed amazement, while the scattering of Yankees, assigned to design and build the railroad, broke into wild cheers.

Malady hauled down on the steam whistle, which shrieked merrily as the engine started to build up speed, and in an instant the hundreds of laborers shouted wildly in triumph.

"You Yankees!" Kal roared, while pumping Andrew's hand.

"It's a start," Andrew said, feeling delighted at this major step.

Pulling out from the dock, the engine chugged past Fort Lincoln, gathering speed. As it reached the first turnoff, the Suzdalian switchman waved that the way was clear. The engine roared past the turnoff to Suzdal and started up the mill-stream hill.

"Fifteen miles an hour at least," Ferguson shouted joyfully, like a schoolboy with a new toy. "Now that we've got better steel for the boilers, and proper lathes and cutting tools to turn out better cylinders, I'll get twice the horsepower out of the next engine!"

"Let's just hope this one holds together," Emil said nervously.

"Why, the *Waterville* is the best damn locomotive on the planet!" Ferguson roared, and Andrew could not help but laugh in appreciation of Ferguson's joke.

The entire contraption looked like nothing more than an oversized toy, with its two-and-a-half gauge and diminutive engine and rolling stock. The engine itself was just an open platform with a boiler bolted on top, powering the small three-foot drive wheels, which were the largest the foundry had been able to turn out to date.

Reaching the base of the mill-stream hill, the engine started up the five percent grade and visibly slowed with the effort. Puffing and steaming, the engine continued on, and Ferguson left the flatcar, leaping onto the wood tender and then to the engine platform.

"I wish that boy wouldn't go near that thing," Kathleen whispered nervously.

Malady and Ferguson appeared to argue for a moment, and finally Jim took the throttle and hauled it all the way down.

Billowing clouds of smoke swirled up, and the engine, picking up steam, roared and strained against the grade and the load behind it. Bouncing over the rough-laid track, the gathering on the flatcar clung to one another, desperately trying to keep their feet.

Cresting the first major grade, Ferguson still held the throttle down as they roared past Captain Houston's sawmill, its Suzdalian operators shouting with delight and fear at the sight of the new Yankee wonder.

The next grade came, and upward the engine pushed, swaying and rocking over the track, and Fletcher's grain mill quickly disappeared from view. Passing Mina's first foundry and forge, which was working full-blast, they continued on up the hill. Another three miles they pressed on, coasting through open fields, where the forest had already been given over to the charcoal works, so that now only the stumps of the once mighty trees remained.

Rounding a bend in the hill, Ferguson laid on the whistle

and lifted the throttle up as a rough-planked station came into view. The engine came to a halt.

Gasping, Emil looked around.

"That boy was nearly the death of us all," the old doctor complained, climbing down off the flatcar.

"He might be the salvation of us all," Andrew replied, leaping down beside Emil and then extending his hand to Kathleen.

"That was certainly exciting!" she said good-naturedly as Ferguson, with youthful exuberance, came bounding up to them.

"I figure near twenty miles an hour on the flat," he announced triumphantly.

"Just take it easy going back down the hill," John Mina cautioned, brushing the soot off his uniform.

"The track on the hill's been graded well," Jim said, a slight defensive tone to his voice.

"Just listen to John," Andrew replied, like a father settling a disagreement between two sons.

Malady, who was now back at the throttle, edged the train forward, pulling under a low bridge from which hung a heavy planked chute that extended up to a large boxlike structure made out of logs. The first hopper coming to rest under the chute, a Suzdalian waved to several men standing atop the large blockhouse structure. Where they pushed open a door above the chute, a torrent of ore came roaring down, filling the first hopper in seconds. Slamming the door shut, they waited until the second car was in place, and the next load was dropped in.

"Nearly twenty tons," Mina said triumphantly.

"And when the *Bangor* gets finished we'll be hauling fifty, maybe a hundred tons a load," Ferguson interjected.

Smiling, Andrew shook their hands, this small sign of praise filling the two with a glow of satisfaction.

"How long before we get the line up to the coal field and the coke ovens?" Andrew inquired.

"Two months," Mina replied.

"But you've laid four miles of track up there already—last week you said it would be done before the next full moon," Andrew stated.

"It's this early thaw," Ferguson replied, coming to Mina's defense. "Sir, we surveyed the route when the ground was snow-covered. There's some marshy ground that'll have to be filled. We found that out last week, after that heavy rain loosened things up a bit."

"And since we laid track in winter, there'll be an awful lot of repair work once this ground softens up," Mina interjected.

Andrew looked over at Kal.

"Once the full thaw hits, I plan to have five thousand working on filling and grading above and beyond the two thousand now working on the line. My cousin Gregory is lining up the work crews now," Kal stated.

Andrew could never stop being amazed at this man. He seemed to have a genius for organization. Though it had been a rough start, it seemed as if all the Suzdalians were imbued with the desire to do anything required.

Andrew looked away from the group as the *Waterville*, disconnected from the rest of the train, pulled off to a siding and turntable.

A gang of workers pushed the engine around, and the engine drifted back down the siding, switching in ahead of the train, and backing it to the cars coupled up for the run back down the hill.

"All aboard!" Malady cried, overjoyed at being back in his old profession.

The party boarded, Weiss looking nervously at the two heavily laden ore carriers now in front of them.

With a toot to the whistle the engine pulled out of the station and quickly gathered speed as they slipped into the first downhill grade.

The diminutive train rocked and pitched over the tracks, and Andrew gulped as he leaned over and saw the long grade back down toward the mills.

The six Suzdalian brakemen stood to their posts and grabbing hold of their heavy oaken levers leaned in with all their weight.

A wild shrieking rent the air, and with sparks flying the train careened down the track. Andrew looked over at Kathleen, who nervously drew closer to him. Her hand slipped out and took his, and he drew her closer. It was the first time they had touched each other in weeks, and he felt a delicious chill run through his body.

There had been no time over the last two months—nearly every moment he had been out on his rounds, while she had jumped into the role of establishing a school to train nurses for the forthcoming battle. Weeks had gone by without their even seeing each other, and he had been surprised when his offer for this day off had been so eagerly accepted.

On down the hill they roared, passing the foundry, grain mill, and sawmill. All the time she stayed close by his side, while even Ferguson showed a look of nervousness at the wild bone-jarring ride.

As they dropped down out of the hills, Fort Lincoln came into view. The switchman leaped to his position and threw the lever over.

The engine roared onward, hitting the turn with such speed that for a second Andrew thought the train would leap the track, but it stayed on its course, rattling over the mill-stream bridge heading north.

Onward they raced, over the rolling countryside, the party relaxing now that the worst part of the ride had been passed, but still Kathleen lingered by Andrew's side.

They came to a gentle downward grade into a towering cathedral of pines. There had been talk of razing them for fuel, but somehow Andrew could not bring himself to do that, war or no war, and he had ordered this stand of forest to be spared.

He was glad now of his decision as the scent of pine washed over him. Looking heavenward, he delighted in the shafts of light breaking down through the towering tops of the forest, and sparing a sidelong glance, he saw that Kathleen was taking pleasure in the view as well.

The train rattled over another bridge and the forest started to broaden out. They charged past the spot where Mikhail had confronted them on the day they had first marched toward Suzdal.

The man was still alive to the east, Andrew thought, uniting the cities of Vazima and Psov, where all who wished to submit to the Tugars had fled, seizing the position of Ivan, who had died, like Boros, during the riots. In many ways Andrew realized it was for the best to have such a place. That way the only ones who stayed were committed. He could only hope, for the sake of the hundreds of thousands who chose not to resist, that the Tugar wrath would not descend upon them out of revenge.

They crested up out of the dale and the city of Suzdal came into view, and at the sight of the train, a distant cheer went up.

Onward the train rushed, the city walls coming closer and

closer. Holding down the whistle, Malady signaled ahead, where the switchman threw the lever over to send the engine northward around the edge of the city rather than to the south heading, still uncompleted, that led down to the docks.

The incongruity of it all filled Andrew with delight. Suzdal still looked for all the world like a vast medieval setting for a fairy tale, its log structures, onion-domed buildings, and church spires standing out sharp and crisp in the chilly morning air. Onward the train rattled, crossing through a gate to pass inside the breastworks, where thousands of laborers now worked to throw up the outer line of defense for the city. It seemed as if the entire city had come to a standstill, as the Suzdalians, filled either with fear or astonishment, watched the *Waterville* chugging past, Malady merrily tooting the whistle and waving.

Kal climbed atop an ore hopper, waving excitedly, and started to dance a jig. Andrew and the others laughed at his antics, all of them knowing that the wily character was showing off to calm the fears many would have over this bizarre contraption.

Running down along the east wall, the track finally reached the northern edge of the city and turned east near the banks of the Vina River and headed toward the great mill. Finally one end of the line came into sight, and the engine slowed and came to a halt.

Breathing a sigh of relief, Emil was the first to jump off, the others quickly following. As the group watched, a team of Suzdalians swarmed up to the ore carriers, attaching ropes to one side. Two burly men stepped up to either side of the car and knocked out wedges under the sides of the hoppers. With a pull on the ropes, the hopper tilted over, while its carriage remained on the track. A torrent of ore spilled out onto the ground, and in an instant a gang of laborers swarmed over the rock and set to shoveling it onto the horse-drawn wagons waiting for the load.

Malady came back to the group, grinning broadly, his face and hands smeared with grease.

"She runs like a honey, she does. Little leaky around the cylinders, and the wheels aren't quite in full round, but not bad for a first try."

Andrew looked at the group and smiled.

"Shall we go up the line and check on the progress?"

"What I was hoping for," Mina said. "A lot's been done in the last week, sir."

"All right, major, lead the way."

Going over to a wagon, the group hopped aboard. Kal jumped up front, grabbed the reins, and snapped the two massive horses into a trot.

Following the track roadbed up the gentle slope, they passed hundreds of men laboring with picks to cut the grade, while others, carrying baskets tied to their backs, struggled with loads of crushed rock.

Kal called good-natured comments to the men. He stopped several times to leap off the wagon, lend a quick hand or trade comments, and then jumped back up and set off again.

"He's like a stump politician splitting a rail or two to show he's of the common folk," Emil said while Kal was off the wagon to help with a group trying to lever a rock free from the frozen ground.

"Another old Abe," Andrew said, and the group laughed.

Rounding a turn in the path, they stopped before a flat open field over a quarter mile across. The field was packed with several thousand men.

Andrew called for the wagon to be stopped, leaped off, and started across the open area.

"Hans!"

The old sergeant turned around, a look of exasperation on his face, and at the sight of Andrew turned back to the group under his control.

"Company, attenshun!"

The hundred-odd men under his control snapped rigidly into place, bringing up the wooden sticks which were still the substitutes for muskets.

"And you call yourselves soldiers," Hans roared, his Suzdalian nearly incomprehensible, and giving up, he turned to a torrent of abuse in English.

The men seemed to understand nevertheless and looked nervously about.

Andrew came up to Hans's side and let the sergeant vent his spleen. Finished at last, Hans looked back at Andrew and snapped off a salute.

"Sir, Company A of the 1st Suzdalian would be honored by your inspection, sir."

"Thank you, sergeant."

"Company, present arms!"

The men snapped their wooden staffs up and nervously looked straight ahead.

With Hans standing respectfully behind his commander, Andrew stepped forward and started down the line.

Could this ever possibly be turned into an army? he thought grimly. The men stood ankle-deep in the slushy snow, most of them with feet wrapped in nothing more than strips of burlap. There was no semblance of uniforms yet; effort could not be wasted in that direction. He had seen the Confederate Army go from the gray that was still around in '62 to the tattered rags of late '64, but even the rebs at their worst could not compare to the wild collection of filthy robes, shirts, and bare knees that stood before him now.

We don't even have guns yet, Andrew thought grimly. It'll be months before they start being turned out in any numbers.

Andrew walked down the line and stopped before a burly man at the end of the ranks.

"You ready to kill Tugars?" Andrew asked, looking the man in the eye.

Nervous, the man nodded back.

"You'll be fine soldiers, just fine. Just remember to listen to the Yankees teaching you. When we're done, we'll see dead Tugars piled up like cordwood."

Andrew slapped the man on the shoulder, knowing that what was said would be shared with the others and spoken in the city by nightfall.

Andrew turned away from the line and looked over at Hans.

"Sir, they're learning the drill—we'll even have them up to regimental drill in a week. But not one of these buggers has any idea what it's all about."

"Just keep at it, Hans, just keep at it."

Andrew walked away from the sergeant, who went back to chewing out the men, and continued to stroll across the field. He stopped to watch several drills, and spotting Hawthorne, he went over to observe what the corporal, who sat on the ground with a knot of several dozen Suzdalians gathered around him, was doing.

Hawthorne did not even notice his approach. On a cleared patch of ground Hawthorne was drawing a line and talking to the men, who eagerly were asking questions back.

Noticing that Andrew was watching them, one of the men snapped to his feet, the others quickly following.

Hawthorne, seeing the colonel, came to attention and saluted.

"Good morning, sir."

"Good morning, son. What are you doing?"

"I was just explaining to the men how by forming two lines we can pour out a continuous sheet of fire to the front, and then I was showing them what a flanking maneuver will do to an enemy line."

"But why not hide when the Tugars shoot?" one of the men asked, unable to contain his curiosity, in spite of Andrew's presence.

Andrew looked at Hawthorne for an answer.

"Because, Dimitri, if we all run off and hide, you behind this bush, me behind another, the Tugars will break our formation up. Once broken up, we cannot shoot together and our officers cannot lead us. No, our line must be a wall, against which the enemy breaks himself—that is our best chance. Also, if we are scattered about they can easily get around our sides, and I showed you how four men on your side can defeat ten without difficulty. If we are together we can prevent the enemy from turning our flank."

"But many of ours will die," Dimitri said, showing his confusion.

"Yes, some of us will die," Hawthorne replied, "but with men like you, many more Tugars will die first."

Satisfied, Dimitri grinned and nodded.

"You're a good teacher, Hawthorne," Andrew said, drawing Vincent aside.

"Thank you, sir."

"Have you ever read Hardee's manual on drill and tactics?"

"No, sir, my reading's never been in that area before."

"Well, son, I think you should study Hardee. It was Hardee's manual and Sergeant Schuder who taught me the business. Come to my headquarters tonight and I'll give you the books."

"Thank you, sir."

"And how is Tanya?"

Hawthorne blushed, and the men, recognizing his wife's name, laughed good-naturedly.

One of them stood up and extended his hand in front of his belly, and the others roared.

"She's not that big yet, sir," Hawthorne said shyly.

"Well, carry on with your work," Andrew replied, and returning Hawthorne's salute he walked back to the wagon where the rest of the group waited.

The party continued on its way up the hill. As the road turned to run along the banks of the Vina they passed the dry river bed which had been stilled for weeks.

The trees lining the bank gave way to reveal the gorge straight ahead. From one end to the other the earthen bank rose above them, covered by an antlike host of tens of thousands of people who, carving away the hills to either side, carried their burdens of rock and soil in a never ending chain.

The group fell silent, as all did when they first saw the great work before them.

"It looks like something out of the Bible or ancient Egypt," Kathleen whispered, seeing for the first time this greatest project for the master plan.

"The walls are up over twenty feet already," Mina said. "We're just over halfway done."

Kal looked back at the group beaming with pride, since, of all the projects, he felt this one to be most his own.

Drawing up to the base of the dam, the group dismounted and in an instant a dozen men were surrounding Kal and demanding answers, each of them clamoring for attention.

With Mina leading the way, the group walked over to the huge brick building that was rapidly going up to house the foundry.

Brick chimneys thirty feet high, and still climbing, lined one wall of the structure. On the other side the first thirty-five-foot wheel was already in place, with three smaller twenty-foot wheels higher up the slope, just waiting for the flow of water to start.

"The water level will be up high enough in another week to start the twenty foot wheels, so we can start cooking the stockpile of ore being brought in," Mina explained. "It'll be another couple of months before the flood backs up enough to get the larger wheels running and eventually there'll be three of them."

Mina pointed out the huge ore cooker which was taking shape.

"We'll start there. The ore flux and coke get loaded in. Once we start running at full power I expect to turn out over eight tons a day. We'll need the heavy power for the tilt hammers and rollers further down the line." He pointed to where a swarm of workers were building the massive frames inside the roofless building.

"Ferguson and I figured that it would be best to go with an older process of making wrought iron and low grade steel for the musket barrels. A British fellow named Cort figured it out about eighty years ago, later on we'll try this new Bessemer process for steel."

Leading the way, Mina pointed out how the molten iron from the furnace would be divided off. The cast iron coming straight out from the hearth would be sent directly into molds for cast iron artillery barrels and shot. The rest would go through to a puddling hearth where Suzdalian labor crews, using heavy steel rods, would stir the incadescent mass, burning out the carbon. The lumps of red hot wrought iron that resulted would then be conveyed to trip hammers and rollers for processing into musket barrels and the wide variety of metal fixtures needed for the army.

The balls of molten metal would then be conveyed to yet another hearth where it would be reheated and poured into the molds for light artillery, while the rest would go through the rollers and hammers to turn out musket barrels.

Finally off to one side Mina pointed out where small quantities of metal would be taken, sealed in crucibles, and cooked to form high grade crucible steel for tools and musket lock springs.

Already that section was hard at work, drawing their power from an ever-laboring gang of dozens of Suzdalians who worked the bellows day and night.

"It's the boring machines that are the hard part," Mina said leading the group out of the massive building that housed the foundry, and to another structure further down the hill.

"We can cast a rough artillery barrel using molds," Mina explained, "but we need to build a heavy boring machine, which will cut out a smooth, and most importantly, straight tube for the gun. I need more high grade steel for the cutting edges on the boring machines.

"The same stands for the musket barrels. We can roll and wield barrels around a form. But we still need to make sure the barrels are true. Heaven knows I'd love to be able to mass produce rifle barrels but that's going to be a hand job, since it'll take months to get the tools made for that.

"Thank God we had half-a-dozen tool and dye makers in the unit or we'd be lost." He directed his glance to where the men were laboring, a gang of Suzdalian apprentices around each Yankee, trying to learn in weeks skills that took years to master.

John pointed out an open window at a rising structure two hundred yards away that stood next to the empty river bed.

"The powder mill should be going into production in another month. But there again we need more supplies, especially nitrates, our operation of harvesting from the city latrines and the barns in the countryside is going way too slow.

"I need more of everything," Mina said sharply, "the old foundry is working full blast to turn out rail and the machinery for Fletcher's farm production but even that isn't enough. Our rail lines could be three miles further ahead if we hadn't diverted the metal for plows, tillers and harrows. I need more power, skilled workers, ore, coke or charcoal, and most of all metal to make the machines."

"Do what you can," Andrew said quietly. He noticed that John was starting to show wear from all the strain, there was a shrill tone to his voice. He knew he was using up his second in command, in fact was using up most of his men who were driving day and night, but there was nothing that could be done about it.

"I know you're doing your best John," Andrew said.

"But I don't think it's good enough," the major said wearily.

Andrew, not able to lie to his second in command, could only fix him with his gaze.

"I know," John whispered, "no discouragement in front of the men."

Andrew nodded in reply.

Trying to force a smile, John turned away from the group and went back up the hill to the main foundry.

"It seems we've lost Kal to his work gangs, and Ferguson to some dispute back in the foundry," Emil said. "I'm heading back to the city, but it's such a splendid day for a walk, you know."

Andrew looked at Kathleen.

"I think Miss O'Reilly and I need to take a walk," Andrew said, and smiling at the two the doctor quietly left.

"How have you been doing?" Andrew asked, suddenly feeling nervous as the two of them strolled away from the work site. Avoiding the crowded road they set out instead over the open fields.

"Andrew, the women are willing enough to learn. I've mastered some of their language, and Tanya has been a tremendous help with translating. But it's like trying to drag these people across a thousand years at the snap of a finger."

Trying to lighten her mood, Andrew raised his hand and snapped his fingers, but she didn't smile.

"You might try to will it Andrew, but customs here die hard. They know there's no escape from what they've done, but I dare say many of them wish they hadn't rebelled."

"But they did, and now they must face the responsibility of it."

"They never would have if we had not arrived," Kathleen said softly.

"Kathleen, I sorely wish that were true. Back home it's early autumn in the year 1865. Maybe the war is over, but for us it isn't. And I dare say that you cannot look at Tanya, or so many others of these people, and wish for them another occupation by the Tugars with their slaughter pits and feasts."

"No, Andrew, I can't," she whispered, drawing close to his side.

"But I do wish for peace for myself," she said sadly.

"And somehow I'm a symbol of the war to you. Another officer who is all so good in the art of killing, and most likely will be killed himself before it's ended."

Wide-eyed, she looked up at him. How could he ever understand, she wondered. How could he know the anguish of losing someone she had once loved. Or the anguish of watching so many die. She'd lost count of the number of times she had held some boy's hand, making believe that she was his mother, or wife, or beloved daughter as he slipped away into darkness.

Each slipping away had tugged a bit of her soul along with it and as she looked at Andrew she knew that if she allowed her feelings to be released by this strange man, the anguish at the end would be too great. This man could be so cold, so full of that terrifying passion in battle, yet in her heart she knew what was beneath that. She could sense the inner horror at what the war had done to him. She still remembered the first time she had seen him asleep aboard the *Ogunquit*. His gentle features showing an almost childlike innocence, which soon changed to a dream-driven torment that had moved her to tears. Had he been too scarred, she wondered, both by the war, and whatever it was that she sensed had happened before the war?

She looked at him closely as they walked across the fields. There was so much she wanted from him, yet never could she allow herself to be hurt as she had been before. To fall in love with this man, only to finally witness the last act as his broken body was brought in before her.

She looked away and they walked in silence for long minutes, passing from open fields into a small grove of towering pines.

Suddenly Andrew's hand was on her shoulder and he turned her around to face him.

"Kathleen, I don't think there's much time," he said quietly, the fear showing in his voice.

"You mean what's coming?"

He nodded his head.

"I can't say it openly to anyone," Andrew whispered. "They all look at me, draw something from me and believe this might just work.

"You know I had a premonition the night we sailed from City Point. A deep fear that maybe this was a trip of the damned. We had killed so many and, God help me, I thought maybe our souls had been used up. Look at what has happened to young Hawthorne. I love that boy for his moral strength, in many ways he's like my own younger brother," and his voice trailed off.

"God help me," Andrew whispered, "he's turned into a killer like the rest of us. You know down deep there was a part of me that wanted to leave here, to run away and hide. But then Kal has to start this revolution and I could not leave them to their fate."

"There was nothing else you could do," Kathleen whispered.

"But all the talk," Andrew said, his voice starting to choke, "all the talk about liberty and freedom. Such a price we have to pay. If there's any chance, which I doubt, maybe Hawthorne's children will know the joy of such things. But you and I, and all these others that I lead, do the paying and the suffering, and at my command, the dying. You don't know what it's like to look into their eager faces, and know that in the end you'll feed them into the furnace. I've been doing that for over three years now. I once loved the power and pageantry of it all, but Kathleen, it's using me up and I don't have much left to give."

In spite of her fear of him, Kathleen reached out and touched his face.

He struggled for control.

"What I'm trying to say, Kathleen, is that I don't think there's much time left. When the Tugars come, we'll fight but . . ." and his voice trailed off.

Her restraint broke, and sobbing she flung herself into his arms.

"I can't find any more strength in me," Andrew whispered hoarsely.

"I'll help you, my love, I'll help you. You must have strength for them."

"I'm afraid of being weak," Andrew said, struggling for control.

"You're strong enough to be weak with me," she whispered through her tears.

She knew at this moment that she was damning herself to yet more anguish, that like all the others he would slip into the shadows without looking back. But this time at least, she would most likely go into the shadows as well.

Their lips touched in the gentlest of kisses, and then again with more passion. For how long they stood kissing neither realized, as each became lost in the other, releasing the feelings both had kept so well hidden since they had first met.

Suddenly Kathleen was aware of a polite cough in the distance.

Startled, the two looked up.

Dr. Weiss was standing at the edge of the grove looking straight up.

"Ah, colonel sir," Weiss said formally, at last lowering his gaze.

Smiling, the two looked back at the old doctor.

"All right Emil, what's so all fired important?"

"Tobias just came back with the *Ogunquit*."

"Damn that man," Andrew said, "he always did know how to interrupt."

"It's good news, Andrew. They've got a load of high quality lead, and by heavens they've even found copper. A courier was coming up here looking for you but I figured I'd bring the news myself."

"Well, let's get going," Andrew said, looking at Kathleen, who stood drying her eyes.

Emil smiled good-naturedly at the two. He had them figured from the start, and by heavens if ever the two needed each other it was now.

The two stepped past him, smiling nervously at each other and then back at Emil as they climbed aboard the wagon he had brought back.

Emil wasn't half so worried about Mina as he had been about Andrew and he congratulated himself on his little plan of suggesting an inspection tour with her along.

"Well, for you two at least it looks like a truly fine day," Emil said, climbing up and grabbing hold of the reins, "a truly fine day," and the three laughed together as the wagon jolted its way back towards the city.

" 'Twas the strangest damn sight I've ever laid eyes on, O'Donald said excitedly. "Like something out of them Roman times. Their ships were driven by oars, with rams on the front, by Jesus. But you should have seen the scallywags turn tail when one of my pieces barked off a shot across their bows."

O'Donald looked around at the group beaming, while pouring another drink.

"Major O'Donald's artillery might have done its part," Tobias sniffed, "but the *Ogunquit* laying off their city finished it."

Andrew held up his hand to fend off any dispute. There was no love lost between the two and the voyage had only heightened it.

It was the glass makers who had started the voyage, when Fletcher had come back one day to report they were using scraps of lead to tint their product and also as a solder to join pieces of stain glassed work together.

The answer had been right in front of them during their meeting after the rebellion, for Rasnar's windows had all been soldered with lead but nobody had thought to look. From the glass makers the investigation had gone to a ship's captain whose family had jealously guarded the secret. Finally bribing the man with a substantial amount of gold it was revealed that the city Tobias had sailed past the last time was the source of the metal.

Tobias had been eager to go alone and was not at all pleased to be accompanied by O'Donald commanding two field pieces and twenty rifle men. Everyone knew it was insurance for Tobias's return but not a word had been spoken about that part of the plan.

"So there we stayed anchored for three days," O'Donald continued, "until finally them scoundrels came out to the ship."

"You was right, colonel darling, them were real tough merchant folk. The haggling went on for days, but finally we traded them a single rifle like you said, some powder and some clocks Hawthorne made. We got all the lead they had, forty tons' worth."

"Not nearly enough," Andrew replied softly. "We need five hundred rounds per man, for up to twenty thousand muskets. That comes to well over three hundred tons of the stuff."

"Oh, but we got a regular trading scheme going. I promised them fifty muskets and one of them four-pound guns, along with five hundred clocks, if they can come up with two hundred and fifty tons more by the end of the summer."

"I don't like this at all," Tobias said coldly. "Arming those heathen could hurt us in the end."

"I know, I know," Andrew said, shaking his head. From what Tobias had already told him the people at the south end of the sea were Phonecians or Carthaginians, the writing samples brought back confirmed that. Chances were they'd take the guns apart, experiment with the powder, and figure things out.

"And the Tugars and them."

"They call theirs the Merki. Claim they're still two years away."

"For their sake I hope so."

"You told them we were fighting?"

"They didn't believe it, said we were crazy."

"So there's no place to run south after all," Andrew said quietly, fixing Tobias with his gaze, but the captain remained silent.

"And the copper?"

O'Donald reached under the table and pulled up a copper urn.

"Got five hundred like this back on the ship, along with a couple of hundred ingots, weighing five pounds or so each."

Andrew beamed with delight. Now it was up to Mitchell to figure out his telegraph system and Ferguson to set up a wire works.

"We promised to return in a month for the next load."

"Let's just hope those people don't figure out how to make a rifle in the meantime," Andrew said evenly, and though the others laughed he was silent. He could only hope that they weren't creating a new problem for their neighbors or if they could survive all this, for themselves as well.

But as he looked across the table and saw Kathleen sitting on the other side, for a moment at least, his fears washed away.

Chapter 14

Again it was the same, Muzta thought grimly, walking down the main street of the city. The streets were empty, the scent of death in the air.

"Can you give me any estimates?" Muzta asked, looking to the chooser for the Maya city of Tultac.

"My lord Qar Qarth, the fever was in full rampage here before we even approached. It is worse than anything we have seen before. With luck perhaps only two in ten will survive, and most of them will be scarred and thus unclean. The cattle claim it started two months back, before the last snows had cleared and we started to move."

"Then we will eat unclean meat," Muzta roared.

His staff was speechless at his outburst. Shouting a wild curse, Muzta pressed on down the street.

Muzta turned and looked back at Alem.

"How, dammit, how? We ride faster—the entire clan is three days' march behind me. They started before the snows even ended. In three months we've made a journey of seven. I thought to rest here till early fall and then push on to Rus before winter. How, tell me?"

"It is a curse," Alem said, looking upward. "Perhaps the everlasting heavens have cursed us."

Muzta looked at Alem with pure hatred. All he needed was for this man to start calling down some heavenly displeasure as the answer to the pestilence on the cattle. In a short breath the horde would turn their wrath somewhere, and Tula, he was sure, would point the finger.

"Our people will stay here," Muzta said grimly. "We eat unclean meat if need be, but we stay here for but two moons and then we push on. We must spare some of the healthy ones here, else when we come this way again the entire Maya people both eastern and western will be gone and there will be no wintering grounds for eight hundred leagues."

"But my lord," Tula said, stepping forward, "that is a circling away. I am more concerned with here and now."

"And I am concerned with the survival of the horde both here and for our next generation as well," Muzta roared.

"If you keep driving us there will not be a next generation," Tula said darkly.

All fell silent at Tula's outburst. There was blood challenge in the air. More than one wanted it settled, even though they knew full well that if Muzta fell to Tula's sword, civil war would most likely be the result.

Muzta stepped toward Tula, who did not back away.

"Are you challenging me openly?" Muzta hissed.

The confrontation held for what seemed like an eternity, until with a growl Tula turned away.

"Send riders back to the horde," Muzta snapped. "Tell them to come forward quickly."

He looked back at Alem.

"And find some religious excuse for eating unclean meat, or you'll be on the end of my sword," Muzta snarled, and turned and walked away.

The group broke away, leaving Muzta to his thoughts. Looking about the empty square, Muzta walked over to the steps of the pyramid and started to climb upward. Reaching the top, he peered into the small sacrificial chamber. The stench drove him out, mumbling darkly about the unclean practices of cattle.

Sitting down on the steps, he gazed eastward. Qubata,

riding hard, should have covered the three hundred leagues to the land of the Rus. He could only hope that his nagging fears about the Yankees were unfounded and that the pox had not reached there as well.

"Just what the hell are they?" Andrew asked, field glasses focused on the strange-looking band making its way down the river road from the northwest.

"The first harbingers of doom," Casmar said. "The Wandering People, we call them."

"Wandering People?"

"They are the ones who choose to flee rather than submit to the horde. They start to appear several months or more before the Tugars arrive. The Tugars have laid down strict laws that if a person flees from their advance he may never return back to his home after they have gone. If they discover that we have harbored such a person, then a thousand extra die. Thus those unfortunate souls are doomed to wander forever, begging and stealing what they can."

"Gypsies," Emil said, borrowing Andrew's field glasses for a look.

"Then if they are here . . ." Andrew said, looking back at the prelate.

"The Tugars are not far behind."

"Get a detachment, Hans. We'll go out to meet them."

Climbing down from the battlements, Andrew mounted his horse while a mixed guard of Union soldiers and a detachment of Suzdalians, bearing the first muskets to come out of the mill, formed up.

Setting an easy pace, Andrew started up the road, his men falling in behind him.

"Never heard mention before of these people," Emil said, bringing his mount up alongside Andrew.

"I guess they just don't like to talk about them. It's the next messenger after the Namer. I only hope we still have six more months, as we originally planned for."

He knew that no matter what happened they could never have enough time. The main problem he'd been wrestling with now was the simple fact that Suzdal could not hold the half million people they now estimated would seek refuge when the war started. A second city was now going up, between the city walls and the outer breastworks a quarter mile farther out. Emil had been fretting constantly about that, and with good reason; maintaining sanitation for so many people, living cheek to jowl, would be darn near impossible. He would have to turn these new people away—there wasn't enough to go around as it was, and the possibility of thousands more would threaten them all.

In the distance he saw the beginning of the approaching column. Reining in his horse, Andrew waited for their approach. There was no reason to expect trouble, but nevertheless the men were shaken out into a line across the path, and with fixed bayonets waited. He wanted them coming no closer to Suzdal, for it was possible that a spy of the Tugars could be among them.

The ragged column approached and finally stopped a dozen yards away.

Andrew felt as if he were looking at some history tale gone mad, with all the pages somehow jumbled up. Several in the group looked like Aztecs or some other such tribe, one of them wearing an ornamental headdress of feathers. Several others wore long pleated skirts frayed and tattered with age; others were in silken robes, one with a samurai sword belted about his waist.

Andrew could not help but point with amazement at a bent-over man wearing the tarnished and battered breastplate of a Roman soldier.

"My God in heaven," Andrew whispered, "are these the other people on this world?"

Weeping, one of the group stepped forward, bowed low in the manner of the Rus, and then, bending over, kissed the ground.

"For seventeen snows I have prayed to come back, to die in the land of my birth," the old man said, "for I have been all about the world and find that indeed my path returns me home."

The man came forward. Overcome with pity, Emil got off his mount and walked up to the man, who embraced him, sobbing.

The others started forward, but Andrew held up his hand, beckoning for them to stop.

"They're just a harmless band of beggars," Emil argued, looking up at Andrew.

"Tell those people to come no closer," Andrew said, looking at the old man. "They can camp out here, and we'll give them food for tonight, but I don't want them coming near the city."

"We won't stay," the old man whispered. "We know we're cursed, but rumor came to us that there were some humans who at last wished to fight, and we wanted to see this with our own eyes."

"How do you know that?" Andrew demanded.

"We are the Wanderers of the World—such word reaches us, and we carry it. But we will not stay, for already not a day's ride behind us comes an advance guard of the Tugar horde."

"What?"

Jumping from his mount, Andrew came up to the old man.

"That is why we came this way to warn you. We could have stayed north of here, but I persuaded my friends to do otherwise."

Andrew looked back at the group, feeling pity.

From out of the fields a knot of Suzdalians came down to the road to look at the forbidden Wanderers. Eagerly the old man scanned their faces.

"Do any of you know Helga Petrovna, from the street of wool merchants?" the old man croaked.

"I know of her," one of the workers cried. "She is married to my cousin!"

"Is she well?" the old man asked, tears streaking his face.

"Yes, alive and well, with three children, one of them near full-grown."

"Then I have lived to know I am a grandfather."

Sobbing, the old man collapsed on the ground, and despite Andrew's attempts to stop them the peasants gathered around the old man.

The rest of the Wanderers came forward, looking curiously at the drama before them.

More and more peasants came out of the fields to join the ever-increasing crowd, and soon there were cries of alarm when word of the old man's warning was passed.

"Goddammit, Emil, there's going to be a panic over this!"

Emil stood up and left the old man while others tended to him. Curious, he wandered through the crowd, amazed at this flotsam that had traveled around the world, sweeping up fragments from a score of civilizations across thousands of years of time.

Several litters were being dragged at the back of the column, tied to an old nag that seemed on its last legs. A number of Suzdalians stood about the litter, gazed upon it, and then drew back.

Coming up to the first litter, Emil saw several children resting upon it, covered with filthy blankets. His heart started to race, and nervously he pulled the blanket back.

A pistol shot cracked, and with a scream, all about Emil scattered.

"Andrew, stop them! Don't let anyone move!"

Andrew could hear the terror in Emil's voice.

Already some of the peasants were running away, looking back at Emil as if he had gone mad.

"Stop them, stop them!" Emil screamed.

Andrew pulled his pistol and pointed toward the fleeing Suzdalians. Most of them stopped, putting up their hands, or dropped to the ground. Panic-stricken, the others continued to run from the Yankees, who had apparently gone insane.

Emil came running up to Andrew's side just as he fired several warning shots, but already the terrified men and women were over the hill and gone.

Frightened, Andrew looked back at Emil.

"It's smallpox," Emil whispered, his eyes wide with terror.

"I tell you, it could kill half the people in this city," Emil said desperately.

"But this thing," Casmar said, obviously confused, "this thing you call innock . . ."

"Inoculation. It'll make people sick for only a little while. I must warn you that maybe some will die from it, maybe even a couple of hundred, but if we don't do it, hundreds of thousands will die and the Tugars will finish off the rest."

"So you are asking me to tell the people that this inoculating is a good thing, even though it might kill them?"

"Yes," Emil said desperately.

"We have lived here for uncounted generations without this inoculating thing," the priest said quietly.

"And you've also lived under the Tugar yoke, and I daresay with regular rounds of plague, typhoid, and God knows what else. If I had more time I could guarantee the inoculation, but we'll have to take it from the dead scabs of those Wanderers who already have it."

"You are telling me that you wish to push these dead scabs into our people, and that will protect them?"

Casmar came to his feet as if the audience were at an end.

"Andrew, show him your arm," Emil said quickly.

Andrew stepped forward and with the doctor's help rolled up his sleeve.

"I had this inoculation," Andrew said. "The doctor gave it to me himself when I joined the army."

"And this made you better?" Casmar asked.

"I was sick for several days, but nothing more than when you get a slight fever. But he is telling the truth, your holiness. The Wanderers we have in quarantine beyond the city are carrying smallpox with them. Apparently they're spreading it ahead of the horde. Several people who were exposed to it ran away, and we don't know who they are.

"I'm telling you, your holiness, if you don't help us, within weeks this city will be a charnel house, I promise you that."

"But this thing—the people might say it is a devilish plot to make them sick."

"He is telling the truth, your holiness," Kathleen said, stepping forward to speak. "I am a healer the same as Dr. Weiss. You know that the two of us worked in the hospitals to save hundreds of your people after the fight to free the city. We could not lie about such a thing."

Casmar shook his head in confusion.

"I believe you," he said, looking straight at Kathleen, "for I have heard the nuns of our order speak of you as a good and holy woman. But the people, they will not believe."

"If you tell them to, they will," Emil said.

"But when some of them die they will claim that the church has misled them once again. I am trying desperately to repair the damage done by Rasnar and the prelates before him. I want our church to help the people in this world, and not just fill them with promises of the next.

"Remember, though, that there is another prelate even now in Vazima, and I have to contend with that. The moment one of our people dies from this thing you wish to do, Igor will thunder from the pulpit against me."

"Let him thunder," Emil cried, "but if he does not let his

people get inoculated as well, the proof will be obvious in a matter of weeks."

"You wish to do this same thing to the people of Vazima?" Casmar asked.

"I'm dedicated to saving lives," Emil said quietly. "I was hoping you could arrange a truce, and I could train some people from that city and save the rest of Rus as well."

Casmar looked at Emil with amazement. Since the great division there had been occasional skirmishes between the border watchers of the two sides, but no contact beyond that, other than the steady trickle of refugees who continued to stream eastward, believing as the months passed that it was better to take their chance with the Tugar pits than to die beneath their arrows and swords.

"I will think upon this," Casmar said quietly.

Frustrated, Emil sat down.

"There's the other problem now as well," Andrew said. "I'm afraid that word has already spread of the advance guard of Tugars, and the city's in a near-panic. What do you think they represent, your holiness?"

"Usually they first send the Namer of Time, a year before the arrival of the horde. About three months before the arrival of the horde the chooser comes. It is he who counts the amount in the warehouses, and under his guidance the selection is begun."

"Then it is not the main body of the horde approaching?" Andrew asked.

"I believe not," Casmar replied cautiously.

"Most likely they're nervous about our being here," Andrew said, looking over at Hans. "If I were their leader I'd send up a reconnaissance in force along with this chooser to check things out."

Andrew settled back in his chair.

"At least five hundred, I'm willing to bet, more likely a thousand," and Hans nodded in agreement.

"Why's that?" Casmar asked.

"Good tactics," Hans said. "That Namer fellow got a good estimate of our size. Figures if we're still here, two-to-one odds should clean us out, and prevent any trouble for the rest of the horde. I'd make it a thousand."

"It's important they don't see anything here," Andrew said. "The farther forward we meet them the better.

"Hans, what've we got ready for action?"

"Precious few, colonel. There's the 35th Regiment, of course, and one regiment of Suzdalians fully equipped, but still only partially trained."

"Artillery?"

"Five guns for the Suzdalian first battery," Hans replied. "That's it so far."

"And O'Donald's away with the *Ogunquit*," Andrew said, as if to himself, "leaving us only two Napoleons."

"That's all we've got, sir."

"All right, Hans. The 35th and 1st Suzdalian to be formed up at dawn, along with both batteries.

"Where do they usually come first?" Andrew said, looking over at Casmar.

"Down the river road."

"There are a couple of passes farther up," Andrew said meditatively. "I've checked the ground over myself. Nice bottlenecks—the perfect place to pen them in.

"Get the men formed, and have Kal come with me. I want our leader to see what this new army can do."

Reining in his mount, Qubata looked suspiciously at the low-lying hills ahead.

Everything felt wrong. They had passed dozens of Rus villages in the last two days, and not a single cattle was in the fields. The few he had seen fled at their approach.

Where were the nobles to keep their people working in the fields? Yet the fields were well tended. In one of the empty villages he had stepped into a barn. There was a strange device within it, a machine that looked like two great wheels set nearly two arm lengths apart. The wheels were tied together by six long blades. Curious, he had pushed the device, and the blades turned, grating against another blade set across the bottom of the device.

It appeared to be some sort of cutting machine, but for what he was not sure, and that made him more nervous as well, and had been troubling his thoughts ever since.

Never had he seen such a machine. Could this be a device of the ones called Yankees?

One of his scouts came galloping back up the road toward where the column waited.

"The road ahead is clear, my commander," the courier shouted, reining in his horse.

Qubata looked back at the long column behind him. He

knew that his warriors were viewing his caution with open disdain. More than once in the last day he had heard a comment from behind his back, saying that he was so old that his brain was becoming that of a frightened child.

"Are you sure you saw nothing?" Qubata asked.

"I have reported all that I've seen," the scout replied, and the warrior looked at him darkly.

"Did the rest of your command fan out to either side of the road?"

"As you commanded."

There was a restive stirring behind him.

He could not hesitate, not here. If he delayed any longer and indeed there was nothing farther ahead, what respect he had left would be finally lost.

With a grunt of disdain he urged his mount into a trot, signaling for the rest of the column to follow.

The host moved down the road, past yet another abandoned village. Again it was the same as before, the crops well laid out, shimmering beneath the summer sun, but not a single cattle in sight. On the road he started to notice footprints of cattle. Could it be they were simply fleeing before his approach?

The tree-clad hills to his left marched downward, narrowing the valley, pushing them in closer and closer to the broad muddy river on the right. He did not like this region; he preferred the open steppes. But the great inland sea, and the river that fed it, required them to swing far northward for several days' march into the edge of the great forest, until a ford could be reached sufficient to cross the great host. The trees closed around them, making him feel tight, uncomfortable.

Going through the first pass, he looked about nervously. A small trail cut away from the main road heading up into the hills. Qubata reined his mount in and beckoned for the scout, while the rest of the column thundered past.

"Did you send someone up that trail?"

"As you told me to," the scout said, his disdain becoming more and more obvious.

Qubata looked at the ground, seeing the hoofmarks of the scout, but the road had recently been churned up by many cattle footprints and several wheel tracks, as if from heavy carts.

"And his report?"

"He has not yet returned," the scout replied coldly.

"What?"

"They are only cattle, my great general," the scout retorted sarcastically.

There was something wrong. He could feel the hairs on the nape of his neck starting to prickle. With every passing second more and more of his Tugars rushed past, some of them shouting jokes, others exclaiming about the pleasure of entering the cool woods. Magtu, with the chooser riding beside him, trotted by, a taunting look lighting his features.

"Old one, are you still looking for demons hiding in the woods?" Magtu barked, and the warriors about him laughed.

Ignoring the taunt, Qubata looked about, hesitating. It most likely is nothing, part of his inner mind kept saying, smarting from the growing lack of respect the warriors showed at his cautiousness.

But there was something wrong, something wrong here. He had to decide.

Standing in his stirrups, he held his hand up.

"Stop the column," he roared.

The warriors before him started to rein in, those behind pulling off the trail to either side to keep from ramming into the ranks in front.

At the same time those who had already passed continued forward, not hearing or not heeding his shout.

Qubata turned his mount, ready to race forward.

And then he heard a distant human shout, clear and defiant, and the world exploded around him.

"Fire!"

A sheet of flame slashed out from the woods. Dozens of Tugars tumbled from their saddles, horses rearing up in pain and panic.

Turning from the volley line, Andrew started to race northward.

Dammit. Another minute or two at most and they would have had nearly all of them caught between the two passes. At best they had a quarter of them in the trap. He had been watching the gray-coated one for the last fifteen minutes, realizing almost at once that this one must be the commander. Somehow the Tugar had sensed a trap. So why did the fool walk into it anyhow, and then stop again?

Another volley slashed out, and the Suzdalians around

him roared with ecstasy to see the hated Tugars fall by the score beneath their guns.

A thundering boom cut out, followed seconds later by three more cracks, the last two the deeper bass of the Napoleons. Two thunderclaps erupted in the road, spilling more Tugars from their mounts, while the four-pound solid shot slashed through the ranks. The artillery position, masked up on the hill near the village where they had fought Mikhail, had been revealed, and now started into a steady pounding toward the village where the rear of the Tugar column milled about in confusion.

But the brunt of the battle would start to tell forward, where the 35th waited, concealed along the first line of hills.

Andrew paused for a moment, watching the developing rout.

"Now, Hans!" he roared. "Charge them!"

"Back!" Qubata roared. "Fall back!"

All about him was madness. Another crashing roar came out of the woods, and in stunned disbelief he saw dozens more of his finest warriors pitch out of their saddles. In the maddening confusion few of them had yet unslung their bows to return fire.

Riderless horses galloped past, Tugars on foot staggered and fell. He saw Magtu being dragged past, his lifeless body bouncing down the road as his fear-crazed horse dashed away.

Another thunderous roar, and still more fell.

Suddenly a wild shrieking cry rose up from the woods. Out of the darkness a horde of cattle erupted, carrying thunder sticks atop which he could see long tapered spears.

But what was even more terrifying was how most of them advanced at a walk, keeping to a line. Coming into the edge of the clearing, they stopped, the first rank kneeling and bringing their thunder sticks up.

There was another roar, smoke and fire filled the air, and the few Tugars who had turned to charge them tumbled to the ground. Transfixed, Qubata hesitated and watched. The line now started to swing about, while from farther down the road another line came up with weapons lowered, their spear points gleaming in the sun. In the middle of the line he saw three carriages with metal tubes mounted between the wheels.

They are fighting with discipline, Qubata thought with amazement.

There was another flash of fire, and he heard a strange buzzing whip past his ears. From behind he heard another roar, and looking back from the direction he had come down only minutes before he saw more of his warriors falling.

Spurring his mount, Qubata galloped down the road. Directly ahead he saw a blue-clad form emerge from the woods raising a weapon toward him. Qubata ducked low in the saddle and another buzzing sound whipped past him. With saber drawn he swept past the man, his arm jarring from the impact of sword on flesh. He did not even turn to look back, but galloped on.

The woods were behind him, his host streaming back toward the village. A thunder roared behind him, and ahead in the village two more blossoms of fire appeared.

All was madness and confusion. Pushing hard, he forced his way through the host trying to restore order.

Some of the warriors were finally fighting back, drawing bows and firing into the woods.

There was another flash and yet more fell.

The scout who had shown defiance only moments before stood in the road before him, his mount lying dead.

"But they're only cattle," the scout cried despairingly as Qubata drew up.

For a moment he was tempted to strike the fool down, but instead he extended his hand and swung the warrior up behind him. Onward he pushed through the village and past a building, now ablaze from the strange burst of fire hurled by the cattle.

At last the village was behind him, and he reined his mount around.

Horrified, he looked at the carpet of dead and dying and back to his warriors who continued to stream away northward.

"How can this be, Qubata?" the scout asked weakly.

"It seems the cattle have learned to fight at last," the old warrior replied grimly.

He watched as from the woods a blue-clad line emerged, while to their left men dressed as Rus peasants came pouring out, shouting ecstatically.

There was nothing he could do now, Qubata realized. To fight now would perhaps kill some of them but to no final purpose. But as he watched and pondered what had been done, he learned. They would have their first victory, but never would it be so cheap again.

From out of the blue-clad lines a single man emerged on horseback. He turned and gestured to his men, and then looked back at Qubata.

So that must be him, Qubata thought grimly. Not as good as a Tugar foe, but at least a foe who knows how to fight.

Qubata stood in his stirrups, and raising his arm, he let out a fierce yell.

From across the field the human held up his hand in reply.

"We go home, my foolish scout," Qubata said grimly, "but when we return we'll know not to think of them merely as cattle any longer."

Andrew watched as the Tugar turned and galloped back up the road, disappearing from view.

Around him was a scene of wild ecstasy. Discipline in the Suzdalian ranks gave way as the men shouted with glee, holding their weapons aloft, taunting the lone rider as he disappeared.

Hans came up, grinning, and looked at Andrew.

"Too easy," Hans said.

"It'll be our last cheap victory," Andrew replied sharply. "That leader had some caution. He made a mistake, but I don't think he'll do it next time, dammit."

So now the secret was out. He would have preferred that the Tugars not understand what they were facing until the main battle was joined. Surprise would be everything, and he had been forced to show his trump card in the opening hand.

"At least it'll boost our morale," Hans said. "Perhaps it's worth it for that alone."

"Let's hope we don't pay for it later, my friend."

Extending his arm with a dramatic flourish Casmar waited while two acolytes rolled up his sleeve. There was an expectant hush as the crowd, packed into the square, stood transfixed.

Emil stepped forward and held up a thin sliver of a needle. Nodding, Casmar first blessed the old doctor and then blessed the hand that held the needle.

Before the prelate even had time to react the needle jabbed him and was withdrawn.

A low cry of amazement came up from the audience.

"It was simple," Casmar shouted, "and thus the pox sickness will not strike all who are treated such. As your leader, my faithful flock, I now order you all to do the same. All churches throughout the realm will be open, and there the doctor and those who are his appointed assistants will help save you all. I also order that at the end of ten days, any who has not such a mark of holiness upon his shoulder be driven out of the city."

Blessing the crowd, Casmar stepped aside for Kal, who now climbed the great platform that had been erected before the church.

"Even mice may slay a dragon if enough of them can spit fire!" Kal roared, and the tension broken, the crowd erupted into wild cheering.

Andrew, standing beside the podium, looked over toward the gutted ruins of the palace. From its high parapets hung dozens of Tugar bodies. It had turned his stomach to allow such a thing, but he knew that it was needed to show the people that the enemy could be killed. What had troubled him the most was the break in Suzdalian discipline. The men had gone completely out of control and slaughtered every wounded Tugar in a mad frenzy of killing. Yet he knew as well what his own reaction would have been if places had been changed.

So now they had finally faced each other, Andrew thought to himself while Kal spoke to the crowd, stirring their morale up. What worried him most was the gray one. If he was no fool, they would be ready for the challenge. The element of surprise was now lost forever.

"I am not ashamed of you," Muzta said quietly, pointing to a cushion next to him.

Wearily Qubata sat down, taking the drink that his chieftain offered.

"You should not have defended me before the council," Qubata replied grimly. "It only weakened your position further."

"I can afford it," Muzta said good-naturedly, "especially for the sake of an old friend. Now tell me what you think."

"As I told the council, they do not behave as cattle any longer. Their machines are deadly. The large weapons that they had hidden on the hill could throw flashing explosions over a thousand paces, and smaller balls of iron just as far.

"But it was the discipline that worries me the most. They did not run about aimlessly as cattle have always done. No, these came forward in lines. They would discharge their weapons, fill them up, march forward, then fire them again. I watched the blue-coated ones, the Yankees—they fought with as much discipline as our own warriors."

"And there was no chance you could have turned the battle?" Muzta asked quietly.

"None, my Qarth. My pride roared within me to somehow rally my warriors and charge. But my old sense told me not to. I had learned much by watching and felt it more important to ponder such things, and come back at another time."

Muzta breathed an inner sigh of relief. The warriors who had returned were loud in their complaints against Qubata, but he could see that his old friend had behaved correctly.

"And what is your plan against them?"

"Use our discipline. We have great numbers, and greater mobility. We must advance in the Cuma, the line formation with waves of arrows covering our advance. We must not rush straight into them, but rather pin them down, and then lap around their sides, where our speed will count.

"Finally—and I know this will hurt the pride of our warriors—those who fight before the lines of men must do so on foot."

"On foot?" Muzta asked, the surprise in his voice evident.

"On foot, my Qarth. Three warriors can stand in the place occupied by one horse warrior. I saw as well that when one is on horse his target is much bigger. Many fell from their mounts when they were shot and others about them became tangled in the confusion and hurt. On foot we might have fared better."

"This will go hard."

"It is as I see it, my Qarth."

"Then it shall be done as you say," Muzta said quietly. "You did not see any of their city or what they had done?"

"I sent the scouts down the west bank of the river after we pulled back. They reported great fortifications going up around the city, and in the hills beyond, buildings that poured smoke. And you might not believe this—I doubt it myself—but one scout claimed to have seen a dragon of metal, snorting smoke. Tied behind it were long boxes, and the dragon was pulling them across the field."

Qubata gave a quizzical look as if somewhat embarrassed for giving such a report, but Muzta listened without comment.

"As you said earlier, many of the Rus cattle carried the weapons like the one brought back by the Namer."

"Yes, my Qarth."

"So they are making them even now," Muzta said quietly.

"That is why we must move hard and fast, Muzta," Qubata said excitedly. "We must leave some of the warriors here to protect the clans, but bring the rest forward quickly. We could send a hundred thousand against them, and still leave another hundred thousand to come up with our women and children. I fear every day that passes will make them stronger."

"And us weaker," Muzta replied, nodding his head in agreement.

Chapter 15

"It's the most amazing damn thing I've ever seen," Andrew gasped, walking around the contraption with open-mouthed amazement.

"We saw a lot of those things during the Peninsula campaign in '62," Hans said, eyeing the balloon with open mistrust.

On the last return of the *Ogunquit* two new cargoes rested below decks. The first had caused wild rejoicing. The Carthaginians had tobacco, and the news was greeted with wild celebration. There was also half a dozen tons of zinc, which Tobias had traded for, not seeing any immediate need for the metal, but bringing it along nevertheless. Almost immediately Hank Petracci, a private from A Company, had come forward with a suggestion for using the zinc which Andrew could not refuse, despite its bizarre nature.

Hank had run away with a circus and traveled with it for
several years before the war. He claimed that he could
make an aerial balloon and inflate it by using zinc and
sulfuric acid. Andrew had not hesitated, seeing the immense
value in having a balloon for reconnaissance, and had given
permission.

Word of the project had spread throughout the city when
Andrew put out an order for all silken gowns to be
commandeered. Avoiding yet another religious controversy,
Casmar opened up the massive nave of the church as a
sewing floor for the balloon, thus dispelling yet another
possible crisis.

Taking the zinc brought back from the Carthaginians,
Hank had the blocks shaved down into a mass of slivers.
Andrew had given him an allocation of the precious sulfur
which Hank cooked and then laid out in the sun, to be
turned into something that Ferguson called sulfur trioxide.

Next the concoction was mixed with water to make sulfuric acid. Early in the day Hank had at last brought the
massive envelope out into the square, and hooked it to a
canvas hose which was connected to a large sealed box. The
box was packed with zinc shavings, over seventy gallons of
concentrated sulfuric acid was poured in, and the box was
sealed shut. Less than two hours later the balloon hovered
above them, ready for its first voyage.

Open-mouthed, O'Donald wandered about the contraption. Reaching into his pocket, he pulled out a cigar of
Carthaginian tobacco and fumbled for a light.

With a wild shout, Hank leaped forward and knocked the
match from O'Donald's hand.

The artilleryman started to bristle at the fiery young private, but Hawthorne immediately stepped between the two.

"Major, there's hydrogen gas in that thing. One spark
and we'll all be flying."

"Most likely straight to hell," Kal said nervously, looking
at the smoking box and the silken envelope which floated
overhead.

"I still can't believe you got all this together," Andrew
said, looking at Hank with open admiration.

"I wish it could be bigger, sir, but silk around here was real
scarce," Hank said. "I figure she'll take two hundred and
twenty, maybe two hundred and forty pounds at most. I
think it just might take Hawthorne and me up together."

Excitedly, Hawthorne turned to Andrew, like a young boy eager for parental permission for a youthful adventure.

"Mr. Hawthorne, you're a brevet captain of Suzdalian infantry—I need you out there more than hanging up in the clouds. And besides, son, why aren't you with your unit drilling them?"

The other officers chuckled. To their amazement the diminutive Hawthorne had turned into one of the best drill masters for the ever-growing Suzdalian army. It seemed that in some strange way his gentle voice, the reputation he had for having escaped Novrod, and his marriage to Kal's daughter made him an object of deep respect among the army.

A number of men from his first command were now serving as sergeants and even as officers among the three divisions that had so far been trained and outfitted.

"Sir, my command is serving guard duty on the wall, not a hundred yards away," Hawthorne said stiffly.

"Well, I daresay it would certainly impress them to see their young officer flying," Andrew said indulgently. "Go ahead and try it out. But take care—we wouldn't want anything to happen to the father of that beautiful little girl!"

The men laughed as Vincent beamed at the mention of his new daughter. Leaping into the basket slung beneath the balloon, he gave his friend Hank a conspiratorial wink.

"All right, cast the support lines free," Hank ordered. The Suzdalian ground crew, going about with great self-importance, followed the orders of this young Yankee whom they half believed was actually a wizard.

Lines freed, the balloon still remained on its launch platform in the middle of the square. With a dramatic flourish, Hank started to untie sandbags strapped around the edge of the basket. With two bags left, the balloon ever so slowly started to rise into the air.

"And now Professor Petracci will show you feats of aerial daredeviltry never before seen or imagined in all of Valdennia," Hank shouted in his best circus-barker voice as the balloon started heavenward.

Startled cries echoed over the city as the swaying basket rose higher and higher, clearing the great cathedral tower.

"Dimitri, Petra!" Hawthorne roared, waving to his men, who stood gape-mouthed on the dockside wall. Seeing their young commander, the men jumped up and down excitedly pointing, and then strutting with obvious pride that they served a Yankee who could even fly.

The rate of climb started to slow, as the weight of the tether rope slowed its ascent.

"Stand clear!" Hank roared, as he cut another bag loose, which crashed into the square below.

Higher and higher the balloon rose, until finally at five hundred feet it reached the end of its tether and slowly bobbed and turned.

"I never thought old Keane would let me come," Hawthorne cried excitedly.

"You've got the flying bug in your eyes, my friend. I could see that the first time you wandered by my laboratory," Hank said expansively, "and so I thought, Here's one that Professor Petracci had better take under his trusting wing," and the two friends laughed.

Thrilled, Hawthorne looked around. To the east the great foundry and mills were working full-blast, billows of smoke swirling from their chimneys. To the north of the foundry stood the powder mill, its great wheel turning to drive the wooden hammers and grinders. Below it stood the long sheds where the powder was taken, there to meet the sheets of cartridge paper and lead shot, to be turned into prepared rounds and packed into boxes holding a thousand rounds. In a separate building dozens of women sewed cloth bags and filled them with powder for the artillery rounds, stacking them up on a waiting flatcar to be hauled back to the magazine within the city.

From the south he heard a whistle and saw an engine, hauling a dozen cars, come rattling through the southside switching yard, passing the old *Waterville* with three empty cars.

Below him, the work on fortifications continued, the outer walls, now twenty feet high, completely surrounding the city.

There was a thundering rattle of musketry punctuated by the boom of a dozen artillery pieces firing in salvo. Looking over to the drill fields, Hawthorne felt a cold chill at the sight of a full brigade of Suzdalian troops, sixteen hundred men, standing in a battle line nearly three hundred yards long. Smoke drifted up from the field, the distant shouts of the participants echoing up at the demonstration of power they had just performed. Thousands more stood to either side, watching the demonstration, their cheers joining in.

He turned to look north and east. The distant hills seemed to rise ever higher, one atop another. The passes seven miles away were clearly visible with the field glasses, and he could see the lines of fortifications that had been laid out. From the hills above the passes he could see the swirling smoke from the boiling fires that were refining down the sulfur for powder.

But the warlike preparations did not hold him as much as the splendid beauty of the rolling countryside showing the first hazy colors of autumn. Stands of oak and maple were already showing the first reds and yellows, the birch shimmering in the warm afternoon light, while in the fields Fletcher's harvesting machines and thousands of workers labored to bring in the harvest.

Looking farther north he could almost make out the clearing that had been cut around the ford, thirty miles away. From the ford he could see the high watchtower that had been built, and even the waving of the semaphore flags, most likely signaling to the line of towers that had been built west and south as watch stations. Swinging his glasses to the west, he saw the distant steppe opening out before him, until sky and land seemingly blended into one. He let his gaze linger for a moment, trying to discern a smudge of either clouds or dust on the horizon.

A muffled groan disturbed him, and turning, he looked back to see Hank sitting hunched over in the bottom of the basket.

"Something wrong?" Hawthorne asked.

"Nothing, nothing at all," Hank said weakly.

"You look a bit peaked, my friend."

"It'll pass," Hank said weakly.

A light gust swirled around them, swaying the basket, and Hank groaned.

"Hank," Hawthorne said quietly, "I've got a question."

Groaning, Hank put his head between his hands.

"You've never flown one of these things before, have you?"

"I just sat on the ground and watched," he moaned as another gust set the basket spinning and twirling.

"Just what the hell is Hawthorne laughing about up there?" Andrew asked.

"Beats me, but I sure am jealous of the boy," Emil said, looking heavenward.

"Well, Emil, maybe when this war's over, Hank there can start a business and give you a ride," and walking over to his mount, Andrew swung into the saddle, his staff rushing to join him.

"Let's get started," Andrew said, spurring his mount, and the group galloped down the east road and out through the main gate.

The outer fortifications rose up several hundred yards beyond the wooden walls of the city. Six months in the trenches of Petersburg had taught Andrew and his men how to dig in, and under their supervision a massive earthen wall had been raised, encompassing the entire city. At each corner, bastions had been built, rising ten feet higher than the walls. If cut off, they could still hold, their bunkers stockpiled with ammunition and rations. Riding down the line, the group passed through the heavily fortified northern gate, crossing the bridge traversing the thirty-foot dry moat. Beyond the gate the open fields beyond were covered with row after row of sharpened stakes, brush entanglements, and trip holes.

Andrew reined in his mount by the edge of the rail line as a train came thundering past. Malady, at the throttle of their newest engine, the *Bangor*, tooted a salute as the train thundered past and turned up toward the mills.

"It's out here where it'll be decided, gentlemen," Andrew said quietly, pointing to the defensive works. "I plan only to try to delay them for a day or two up by the ford and down toward the passes. But it's here that we'll break them."

Andrew paused for a moment and looked about, while wagons bearing the first of the harvest rumbled past on their way into the city.

"How are we doing, Fletcher?"

The rotund captain came up, pausing for a second to look at the piles of apples passing by in a wagon. Snatching two, he came up and offered one to Andrew, who took a bite.

"Some of the wheat harvest is at last hitting the mills, but it'll still be weeks bringing it all in from the outlying districts. I've got several thousand head of cattle and twice as many swine penned in south of the city. First sign of trouble, we'll drive them into the city and start the slaughtering."

"But how much is in so far?" Andrew asked.

"Enough food for sixty days," Fletcher said quietly. "It'll be two months before we've got enough to carry us through the spring and the beginning of the next harvest. You've got a war to fight, sir, I've got to make sure that if we win, there'll still be enough food to feed us through till next summer."

"I understand, Bob," Andrew replied evenly. "Just keep at it.

"Mina?"

The gaunt-eyed major came up to Andrew's side.

"We're up to three hundred muskets a day, sir, a little over ten thousand to date," the officer started, his voice distant, almost mechanical. "We're getting twenty long rifles a day as well, just over five hundred so far. If I had another two months I might be able to turn out more rifles than muskets."

"I can't promise that time, John," Andrew said quietly.

"How about artillery?" O'Donald asked.

"Three four-pounders a day now. The molds have been set for some nine-pounders, but that's more than two weeks away. Ninety pieces to date."

"And the other supplies?" Andrew asked patiently, realizing that his ordnance chief had long since gone over the edge of nervous exhaustion.

"Well, ah, sir, we're casting down that last load of lead right now. I've got near four million musket rounds, one hundred thousand more for our own rifles, and twenty thousand artillery rounds stored up. We're turning out a hundred thousand rounds per day, and five hundred artillery loads. The problem now is the powder mill is at maximum output—that's the weak point. We need over a ton of sulfur a day to meet it, and it's just not coming through. Otherwise I could do more."

"You've done well, John. I'm proud of you—no one else could have done it." The major nodded vaguely in reply.

And it's not enough, Andrew thought grimly, not half enough. In four hours at Gettysburg his men had fired off over a hundred rounds per man. Four pitched battles would use up nearly everything they had. They needed time, desperately needed more time.

Still showing a calm self-assurance, Andrew looked over at his young telegrapher and nodded.

"As fast as the wire works are drawing we're stringing up lines," Mitchell said. "I've run four lines out to the main bastions from your command post in the cathedral. There's a line out to the foundry and powder mill, and back to the Fort Lincoln switch-off as well. I'm also rigging one for the balloon and starting tomorrow will start stringing toward the ford. Beyond the ford we've got signal towers every two miles going straight out to the edge of the steppe. It'll give us plenty of warning. I'm also stockpiling a couple of miles of wire to be strung as needed, once the siege begins. We've got twenty operators trained. A couple of those Suzdalians have really good fists—one can do near twenty words a minute now."

"Good work, son. Keep at it."

Kicking his horse into a canter, Andrew started up the hill, and cresting the low ridge, he looked out at the drill field.

"All right, General Hans, how're they doing?"

Andrew smiled at his old sergeant, who wore the stars of a Suzdalian major general on his uniform, which still carried the old stripes of a sergeant major.

"Never thought I'd be a damned general," Hans growled.

"Well, we've all been giving ourselves promotions of late," Andrew said good-naturedly.

He could well imagine the envy his old comrades back home would have had at the rapid promotions that he had given out. Hans was corps commander, with three divisions of infantry and two battalions of artillery under him. The officers of the 35th, who were now taking orders from Hans, and several other sergeants had not minded too much, but O'Donald had chafed a bit with Hans making the decisions. Andrew half suspected that it had been settled "behind the barn," for both of them showed up one day sporting shiners and suddenly behaving like fast friends.

Houston and Sergeant Kindred of E Company had risen to control of the first and second divisions, while Sergeant Barry now controlled the third. Beneath them others had risen to command the six brigades and twenty-four regiments of four hundred men each in the field. The fourth division was drilled and only waiting for its weapons, while the fifth and sixth had already been formed. Nearly half the regiment was now slotted into command positions, but Andrew wished to retain a core of the old 35th as a rally point of professionals, under his direct command. At Kal's suggestion he had agreed to fill the ranks with veterans from the engagement at the pass, and now there were two hundred Suzdalians proudly wearing Union blue.

The hundred and fifty thousand others that would fight had been organized into militia units, controlled mainly by Suzdalians. Several nobles and many of the old warrior retainers now commanded those formations under Kal.

Andrew settled back in the saddle and watched as the brigade that had fired a volley moments before now practiced shifting brigade front to right.

The right of the line stayed firmly anchored while the double line of sixteen hundred, extending for over three hundred yards, started to pivot like a giant gate, their blue regimental flags and white national colors snapping in the breeze. The left of the line was ragged, the men running at the double, while the distant shouts of the commanders echoed across the field.

"Not bad," Andrew said quietly. "Not bad at all, Hans."

"Could be a damn sight better," the sergeant growled, but Andrew could see the pride his old teacher felt for this new command.

"It's just they've never done it under fire," Hans said meditatively. "That's where we'll find out."

A distant shout disturbed their thoughts, and looking back, Andrew saw a courier galloping out from the city, slashing wildly at his mount and coming straight at them.

"I think," Andrew said quietly, "that we're about to find out."

Muzta reined in his mount and looked up at the wooden tower on the hill. Its lone occupant lay dead on the ground, several arrows in his chest.

Qubata stood over the man, looking meditatively at the corpse.

"What is this?" Muzta asked.

Qubata pointed to the red and green flags that lay on the ground beside the corpse.

"They know we're coming," the general said quietly.

"The man saw us from thousands of paces off, yet still he stayed, signaling, until we dropped him with a volley. Seeing us was not enough—he most likely got a fair count of us as well."

Muzta shaded his eyes and looked northeastward. Scattered clumps of trees gradually started to merge together as the ground rose higher, the distant hills given over completely to a forest whose leaves were streaked with red and gold.

His advance scouts were already lost to view, having galloped on.

"There, do you see it?" Qubata asked, pointing to a flash of red, waving back and forth.

"This tower signaled to that one, and beyond that hill must be another, all the way back to the ford, eighty times a thousand paces beyond. I would be willing to guess the word has already reached the city."

"Two days of hard riding to reach the ford," Muzta said quietly.

"They'll be waiting for us there," Qubata said evenly.

Muzta turned in his saddle as from over the hill came the standards of the Olkta, the ten thousand of the guard, first Umen of the Tugar host. The horsetail pennants fluttered by, commanders galloping past saluting Muzta with raised fists. Spread out behind them, a hundred warriors across, came the first of first, the elite guard of the Tugar horde.

Muzta's heart swelled with pride. For more than a circling such show had been mere ritual. Not since Onci had the Olkta ridden to war. Then it had been their sires; now the sons were in the ranks, and Muzta saw his own three, born to his first-chosen, gallop past, waving gaily. Muzta looked sternly at them for showing such disrespect.

"They are young and excited with the chase," Qubata said, as if apologizing. "Just as you once were."

Muzta turned to Qubata and smiled.

"Was I really that bad?"

"You were an eagle," Qubata said, smiling.

"Then let us climb this eyrie for a look," Muzta replied. Grabbing hold of the ladder, he scaled upward. Reaching the top, he looked back toward the west, and his heart soared at the sight.

A dozen Umen were spread out before him, the serpentine columns stretching back to the far horizon. A hundred and twenty thousand Tugars riding in disciplined formation, their blocks of a hundred riders wide by a hundred deep checkerboarding the vast open steppe.

"Magnificent, simply magnificent!" Muzta cried, looking over at Qubata, who stood with arms crossed, watching the advance.

"As beautiful as Onci," the old general said reflectively, his blood stirred at the sight.

Looking back over his shoulder, he gazed at the gradually rising forest.

"And all of that," he said evenly, pointing toward the host, "we must funnel up into those hills, and finally to a single road across the only ford available. That's where they'll be waiting for us."

"The Olkta will force us a way," Muzta said evenly.

Galloping down the long serried ranks, Andrew looked appraisingly at the division drawn up in the early-morning light.

Ten thousand at his command, he thought to himself. He could remember when Reynolds, his old corps commander, had ridden by in much the same manner, corps battle standards, staff, and couriers riding behind him. He could remember the sense of wonder at such power, and envy as well.

So now he was doing the same, the men in the ranks looking to him as he had once looked to Reynolds.

The three divisions were in full fighting gear—muskets shouldered, a hundred rounds in pockets and cartridge boxes. Blanket rolls were slung over their shoulders, rough haversacks of hide or burlap dangling from their hips holding seven days' rations. They were the most godawful-looking infantry he had ever seen, nearly all the men still wearing the old traditional oversized shirts, cross-hatched leggings, and burlap-wrapped feet of Suzdalian peasants, but they were still soldiers, and their pride showed as they burst into spontaneous cheering at his approach.

Waving a salute, Andrew continued on down the line past the fifty artillery pieces, which would be set up under O'Donald's command, while the rest were held in reserve or on Tobias's ship.

Finally reaching the head of the column, Andrew turned to look back one last time.

Is this how Grant or Bobbie Lee felt? he wondered coldly. There was the cold thrill of it all, that set his heart to pounding, but now there was the terrible responsibility as well. Always before there had been someone above him, to tell him to hold such and such a place, or to march or to retreat. Now it was he alone. A single mistake and in a moment all could be lost. In his old war they had been spurred forward with cries of victory or death. But all knew that even if the battle was lost there was still the prospect of an honorable surrender. Here the old hollow cry was bone-chillingly real. If he made a mistake now, not only his army but all who had entrusted their lives to him would die as well.

He looked over toward the city walls, where thousands stood to watch the departure.

He had not wanted to start the war this way. But the Tugars had forced his hand, coming up far earlier than even his worst fears had imagined.

They had to buy time, to delay the Tugars not just for a day or two but for a week, two weeks if possible. Every day meant more guns, more powder, and most important, the desperately needed food that was still coming in from the fields.

He had to buy time, and the buying would come with his preciously small army.

His staff gathered around him, some grim-faced while others, especially the young division and brigade commanders, bright-eyed and beaming with delight at the prospect of leading such numbers into a fight.

From over by the river the *Ogunquit*'s whistle sounded as the ship started upstream to the ford. Aboard were the men of the 35th as an advance guard, along with the four Napoleons and a dozen four-pounders which would be kept aboard the ship, to serve as a floating battery to cover the ford.

"All right, gentlemen, let's get this army moving," Andrew said quietly. With wild shouts of delight the officers galloped off to their commands, looking somehow ludicrous atop the slow Clydesdales.

Andrew looked down at Mina, Kal, and Fletcher by his side.

"Gentlemen, I'm buying you time with blood. Do you understand that? Time with blood. Now make the most of it," and he spurred his mount forward.

Shouted commands echoed across the field, drums started to roll, colors were uncased.

"Yes, we'll rally round the flag, boys . . ."

The song was started by the first regiment in line, and soon echoed down the ranks.

RALLY CRY   315

It sounded strange in Russian, but the words still brought tears to Andrew's eyes.

> "Shouting the battle cry of Freedom,
> It's the Union forever, hurrah, boys, hurrah,
> Down with the Tugars, and up with our flag,
> Shouting the battle cry of Freedom . . ."

And with Andrew riding alone at the head of the column, the army passed beneath the walls of Suzdal and on up the road to the north.

On through the growing warmth of morning, past the heat of noon, and on into the gentle cool of evening the grim-faced regiments advanced, leaving the two passes behind. Past open fields they streamed, where peasants stood and watched for a moment, then hurriedly returned to their tasks of bringing in the harvest. Laborers stepped aside to let the army pass and then returned to their tasks of digging yet more lines of defense.

Two miles every hour, fifty minutes of march followed by ten minutes of break, and then stiff-legged back up again for yet two miles more.

Stopping at every signal tower, Andrew would hear the latest report. Thirty towers overrun, then thirty-one and thirty-two. He knew that with the fall of each signal position another man was dead, staying to the last to deliver the information so desperately needed.

The Tugars were moving fast and hard. He had thought the eighty-mile warning would give them enough time, but they were pressing in without stop. The *Ogunquit* and the 35th were reported in position, but that would never be enough. Twenty miles were past, and the Wheel now filled the evening sky above them, but still he pushed his men on.

Past village and crossroads the column moved forward. It made him think of Gettysburg again, that strange dreamlike night march when all in the ranks somehow knew that the fate of a nation waited for them on the road just ahead. The night was even the same, cool after a hot day, the steady tramping of feet, the same singsong chant.

"Close up, boys, no lagging now, close up, boys."

The Great Wheel rose higher and higher, and then passed over toward the western sky.

Reaching another signal station, he looked up and called for a report. The man above did not reply, busy with the waving of a torch. Finally, with the message finished, he came down. Following the old form, the Suzdalian forgot to salute and bowed deeply.

"All but the last five signal towers have fallen," the old man said.

Ten miles for them, he thought to himself, and we still have five. They must be as tired as we are. He looked back at the ranks, the men staggering past as if walkers in a dream. He had one regiment of Suzdalians waiting there, and the 35th as well. The men with him needed to rest; worn out, they'd be of no use in what was to come.

"Courier!"

An exhausted boy astride a horse came up and saluted.

"My compliments to General Schuder, and tell him to pass the word for the march to stop. Let the men sleep the rest of the night and bring them up at dawn. I'm pushing on to the ford."

The boy saluted and disappeared back down the road.

Hans, old friend, you'd better bring them up quick if you hear guns, Andrew thought to himself. Groaning from the effort, he got back in the saddle, and with staff trailing behind, galloped northward into the night.

Chapter 16

The lone horseman galloped across the ford, water spraying up at his passage. Standing in his stirrups, he waved his hat excitedly.

"They're coming! They're coming!"

Standing by the bank of the river, Andrew nodded as the man raced across, pushing hard, and drove his horse up the riverbank and into the woods.

It was such a beautiful morning, Andrew thought quietly.

The red sun was cutting the horizon behind him, dark in color, its rays giving the landscape a ruddy tint. He should see that as a portent, but for the moment it was only a source of beauty. The woods were alive with the singing of birds, and the chattering of squirrels disturbed by the presence of men on the ground beneath them.

Andrew looked down the line. The positions were well concealed, the loose dirt from the entrenchments covered with brush, fallen logs, and sod.

He could hear them now, a steady thunder in the distance, like a wave drawing closer and closer. Turning, he went back up the embankment and slid down into the trench, pulled out his field glasses, and waited.

The thunder rose in intensity. Surely they should be in sight by now, he thought. There was a flutter of movement in the woods on the other side. He raised his glasses.

No, nothing.

A movement again, a flight of birds kicking up and taking wing. Then more movement, and now he saw them. A lone Tugar on foot, ducking low, racing to a tree, then another and another, filtering through the woods like an Indian.

So they've already learned, he thought.

Singly, in twos and threes, and now by the dozen, he saw them moving forward toward the opposite bank, two hundred yards away.

"Over there," one of his men whispered, rising up to take a look.

"Stay down," Andrew hissed.

One of the Tugars on the other side stood frozen for a moment looking straight at him, and then turned and disappeared.

The clattering of hooves grew loud, and as if he had suddenly appeared out of the ground a lone Tugar reined in on the opposite side of the ford.

The warrior sat alone, hand over eyes to shade them from the sun. Proud, disdainful of any danger, he sat for long minutes watching.

The tension felt as brittle as glass. Andrew could sense his men and the lone Suzdalian regiment poised, waiting for the command, but he wanted to wait, to let the enemy get close, nearly on top of them, before opening fire.

More and more Tugars were filtering down to the edge of the woods on the opposite shore, advancing no farther. The moment seemed to stretch into an eternity, both sides aware of the other, yet not reacting.

The single crack of a musket tore the silence, like a scream roaring through the peaceful tranquillity of a church.

Andrew stood up, looking for the man who had violated orders. There was another crack and another.

Already the horseman was spinning his mount around, puffs of dust kicking up around him.

"Dammit!" Andrew roared, but it was too late, as the entire Suzdalian regiment cut loose with a ragged volley. The horseman pitched from his saddle; his foot caught in the stirrup, he disappeared down the road.

The range was too far, simply too far for smoothbore muskets, and he wondered that the Tugar had even been hit.

A deep-throated horn sounded from the far side of the river.

And then the sky above the river turned dark as a volley of arrows slashed up from the far bank.

"Get down!" Andrew shouted.

With a clattering rush, hundreds of arrows slammed down around him, and the first casualties dropped into the trench.

"35th! Mark your targets! Independent fire at will!" Andrew shouted.

Singly and then in an ever-increasing staccato, rifle shots rang out. Andrew raced down the entrenchment and reached the position where four guns had been dug in. Sergeant Dunlevy saluted at Andrew's approach.

"Start pouring solid shot into the woods to either side of the ford!" Andrew shouted. "Give them something to think about!"

Seconds later the four pieces kicked off with a salvo, brush and trees splintering an instant later on the opposite side.

From the Suzdalian line north of the ford another volley crashed out, and cursing, Andrew sprinted across the open road and into their lines.

"Colonel Anderson!" Andrew roared, racing down the packed entrenchment. Another shower of arrows slashed into the line, and a man in front of Andrew spun from the firing step like a top, collapsing at his feet. He leaped over the body and pushed on.

"Anderson!"

The young officer, who had been a mere lieutenant only weeks before, turned wide-eyed at the obvious rage of his commander.

"Goddammit, Anderson, you know your smoothbore weapons can't hit the broadside of a barn at this range!"

"The men just started firing!" he shouted back as muskets kept rattling off.

"Stop them, dammit. We're wasting powder. Let them close, let them get closer, dammit!"

Stunned, Andrew watched as Anderson jumped on top of the breastworks.

"Cease fire!" Anderson roared. "Cease . . ." The young officer pitched back into the trench, an arrow through his throat.

Dammit, Andrew cursed silently.

"Major Black!" Andrew pushed down the trench and saw the rotund former sergeant knocking muskets up, shouting, bringing control to the right of the line.

"Anderson's dead!" Andrew shouted, "Steve, you're colonel now. Bring these men under control and stop wasting ammunition!"

Another volley of arrows slashed past, and they ducked against the breastworks.

Black saluted, and without another word to Andrew turned and shouted commands down the line. In another minute the regiment was back under control, hunkered down against the storm, waiting. Andrew pushed back southward, and racing once more across the road, he jumped into the entrenchments of the 35th.

The men were fighting as only seasoned veterans could. Loading their rifles, they'd lean up over the entrenchment, carefully take aim, fire, and then slide back down. The new Suzdalian recruits, obviously rattled, watched and learned. A routine had already been worked out, two or three men loading and passing up rifles to skilled marksmen who snapped off round after round. Through the smoke Andrew could see they were having an effect as Tugar bodies littered the shore.

Leaning against a tree, Muzta watched the action.

"We saw two formations of them, the Yankees to the south of the ford, what must be Rus cattle to the north," Muzta said, looking over at Qubata. "Why are only half firing?"

"Perhaps they wish to wait for our charge, or they might wish to save their fire powder. The third reason could be that like bows that shoot at different ranges, so too with their weapons."

"If that is true, our bows can reach farther than their weapons."

"We are losing dozens to the south," Qubata shouted, above the roar of battle, "north only a handful. It might be skill, or it might be weapons. We haven't seen any others yet, but our scouts on the right are reporting a column of dust coming up the road."

"So they are holding here for reinforcements. We must act quick."

Four sharp cracks snapped out from the enemy side, and an instant later a small tree not a dozen feet from Muzta split in half and came crashing down.

The two looked at each other in surprise.

"A terrible device," Muzta snapped. "What glory is there in fighting against such things?"

"I don't think they are concerned with glory," Qubata replied.

"And their great ship?"

"It is a thousand paces down the river, just around the bend, as if waiting."

"All right," Muzta shouted, "keep bringing more up on their right. I want thousands in there. When the time is right we'll charge!"

The storm of arrows seemed to increase with every passing second. More and more men had slid down to the bottom of the trench, some still, some shrieking, others just sitting quietly, waiting for a clear moment so they could start for the rear.

"Colonel Keane!"

Andrew looked up to see a young Suzdalian boy sitting astride a Clydesdale and looking down at him in the trench.

"You idiot, get under cover!" Andrew shouted.

"Sir, General Schuder reports he'll be up within the hour."

"Well, tell him to hurry," Andrew roared, and the boy, still showing no fear, merely saluted, kicked his mount, and started back to the south.

The artillery kept barking, the woods about him filled with the rotten-egg smell of black powder and burning brush where the gun flashes had triggered an ever-increasing number of fires.

"Keep it up here, boys!" Andrew shouted, and turning, he started back north again. Dunlevy, working like one demented, grinned wildly as Andrew rushed past, his men serving their pieces with skill.

Running behind the low barricade of logs set in the road, he was again inside the Suzdalian trenches. The men looked at him grim-faced.

He knew perhaps the hardest thing on morale was to lie under fire without being able to return the punishment, but it could not be helped.

Black came up to meet him.

"They're taking it hard," Black shouted. "Several have already turned and run. God help me, colonel, I shot one of them. I had to, to stop a panic!"

It was something Andrew had never been forced to do, something almost unheard-of even in the worst heat of battle, but here it was different—they had to keep these men in their positions.

"Here they come!"

Andrew looked up.

Thundering down the road came a lone standard-bearer, holding a horsehair pennant aloft. Behind him it looked as if the very gates of hell had been torn open.

Packed ten across, the Tugars came on at the charge. Standing high in their stirrups, the demonlike images swarmed forward, their wild ululating cries sending a shiver of fear down Andrew's spine.

"God in heaven, help me now," Andrew whispered.

The first rank hit the river, then another and another, sending up showering sprays of foam.

"1st Suzdal," Black roared, "make ready!"

The men came to their feet, some of them crying aloud with fear at the sight. Half the regiment were veterans of the first fight, but then their enemy had been surprised. Now they were facing a charge driving straight at them as the enemy angled northward, the ranks spreading out, coming in relentlessly.

Dunlevy's artillery, with muzzles depressed, sent in a spray of canister, sweeping down dozens, but still the charge drove forward.

"Wait, men, wait!" Black shouted.

A hundred and fifty yards, a hundred, and the forward ranks slowed, letting those behind them move up, gathering strength for the rush. Behind them on the riverbank thousand of Tugars came out of the woods, rushing down to the river's edge, and with raised bows sent sheets of arrows arching over their comrades.

Men started tumbling, screaming.

The charge, gathering up its strength, smashed forward again with ever-increasing speed.

"Take aim!"

Four hundred muskets dropped to the level, the men resting their weapons on the breastworks as they had been taught to.

Seventy-five yards, fifty.

"Fire!"

The first rank of Tugars crashed down.

"Reload, independent fire at will!"

Four hundred steel ramrods pushed rounds home, the men working feverishly. The charge had been stopped for the moment, but over the bodies of the fallen more Tugars swarmed forward, their mounts leaping over the casualties. Scattered groups were rising out of the river, gaining the shore.

Muskets started to snap, first one, and then within seconds dozens upon dozens of shots rang out.

Andrew looked up from the carnage, and to his dismay saw a packed column of Tugars on foot come sweeping down the road, charging into the river.

"Steve, they've sacrificed some cavalry to drive in close—they'll have their infantry up in a minute. You've got to hold!"

More and more horsemen, roaring their defiance, splashed forward and fell, to be replaced by yet more. A knot of warriors gained the shore and rushed right up to the edge of the trenches before falling. Behind the assault, infantry fanned out across the width of the ford, some of them pushing forward in waist-deep water.

Onward they came, while to their front the last of the five hundred cavalry desperately floundered forward. Rifle fire from the 35th, swung now to the right, hit the flank of the advancing host, while Dunlevy's artillery continued to pour in canister with devastating effect.

The enemy line grimly surged forward and at less than

fifty yards came to a halt. Hundreds of bows snapped, the arrows slamming in at a flat trajectory. Though protected to their shoulders by the trenches, dozens of Suzdalians fell backward, the heavy war bows driving arrows clear through their bodies. Though five Tugars fell to every Suzdalian, still they pressed forward, firing as they advanced.

A man leaped out of the trench, throwing his musket away.

Scrambling out of the ditch, Andrew came up and struck him across the shoulders with the flat of his sword.

"Get back in that line!" Andrew roared.

Wide-eyed, the frightened soldier looked up at him.

"Get back or I'll run you through!"

A number of Suzdalians had stopped shooting to watch the drama.

The soldier tried to dodge past Andrew, who leaped in front of him with sword pointed at his chest. Sobbing, the soldier turned back into the trench.

The pressure was building. Standing in full view of both sides, Andrew remained where he was, sword in hand.

Relentlessly the Tugars kept driving ever closer, their showers of arrows covering the advance. The Neiper was red with blood, hundreds of bodies slowly rolling, tumbling downstream, but still more came forward.

And then with a wild shout the shore was gained. Dropping bows, the enemy surged in, drawing swords and battle-axes and raising them high.

Desperately they scrambled up the muddy banks.

"Out of the trenches!" Andrew roared. "Up out of the trenches!"

The Suzdalians surged up, some trying with wild despair to load one final round.

The line started to crack and give way.

"Keane!"

Andrew turned. It was Hans galloping forward, behind him a regiment advancing at the double.

"Form a volley line!" Andrew shouted.

While the 1st Suzdal bled and died, not thirty feet away, Hans formed his regiment, cursing and swearing.

And then, all at once, the 1st gave way, the men streaming to the rear, the Tugars, charging behind them, roaring with delight, spilling into the trench, and coming up the other side.

"1st Suzdal get clear, get clear!" Andrew cried, even as Hans's shout echoed up.

"2nd Novrod, first rank, fire!"

Those of the 1st still in the way dived to the ground, but all too many were caught in the blast. At near point-blank range the Tugar charge came crashing down.

"Second rank, fire!"

Another sheet of flame slashed out.

"First rank, fire!"

Stepping back, Andrew saw yet another regiment and then another rushing up the road, their battle standards snapping in the wind.

And then from down across the river came a staccato burst, the water about the ford churning and splashing as the *Ogunquit*, having rounded the bend of the river to reveal its position, slammed a deadly salvo into the flank of the advancing line.

He looked back to where the 2nd Novrod stood pouring in their deadly volleys, driving back the Tugar toehold. Men in the line were dropping as the fire support from the enemy shore poured in around them.

The 4th Suzdal, forming now to the right of the Novrod position, suddenly added in its weight as well.

Yet still from the far bank, wave after wave of Tugar infantry swarmed forward.

They were smashing them, smashing them hard, but they had over a hundred thousand and he had but ten thousand. He looked over to where Black was reforming the shattered remnants of his regiment.

They can afford to loose soldiers and I can't, Andrew thought grimly.

Andrew turned to look eastward. It had been hours, he thought, but the sun was not more than two handspans above the trees. It was going to be a long hard day, and remembering he was no longer a line officer but commander of an army, he stepped back from the volley line, the staff that had been following him sighing with relief that their battle-maddened commander was still alive.

"It'll be a long day, gentlemen," Andrew said, looking at their nervous faces, "a long day indeed."

"Call them back," Qubata said evenly.

Muzta turned in some surprise to look at his battle commander.

"We're pushing them hard," Muzta said grimly.

"And we're bleeding rivers of blood. Half the Olkta Umen is smashed. Call them back."

"Perhaps you are right," Muzta replied, and nodded to the nargas sounders, who gave voice to their long trumpets.

Ever so gradually the roar of battle on the opposite side of the river dropped away. Muzta could not help but feel a surge of pride in his warriors. Not one broke ranks, not one showed his back as they withdrew across the river and with bows raised continued to pour in sheets of arrows.

The enemy fire slackened, punctuated only by the bellow of artillery, which had rendered the riverbank into a torn confusion of shattered trees and smashed bodies.

A shout of defiance rose up from the other side, and then drifted away.

"We know now that most of their weapons, except for those carried by the blue-clad Yankees, cannot reach beyond sixty paces, to our hundred and twenty. It is senseless to keep feeding our warriors into this bottleneck."

"But we have bled them as well," Muzta said evenly.

"That at least was good. But here our great strength is like a long spear, with only the tip able to fight. We must get around them."

Muzta looked out across the river.

"Here is the only place we know to cross," Muzta said.

"Then we must find another. Tonight I will send the three Umens of Tula and the two of Zan northward. They will stay far back from the river, sending down only scouts to check until a place is found to cross."

Muzta looked to the western sky, where the light of the everlasting heavens hung low on the horizon. It had indeed been a long day.

"My Qarth."

Muzta looked up to see Argun, commander of the Olkta, sitting astride his blood-covered mount.

"We did all that we could," Argun said wearily. "These are not cattle that we face—they seemed possessed by demons from the underworld."

"Yet still we will feast upon them," Muzta said evenly.

He looked at Argun, wanting to ask, yet he could not.

The commander, however, knew, and his face contorted with pain, he shook his head.

"Garth, your youngest," he whispered, and then turned his mount away.

Muzta walked away from his staff, and even Qubata left him alone. Watching the setting of the sun, he could only pray that the most beloved of his sons would cross the sky without fear of demons to rest in the place of light; and the Qar Qarth of the Tugar horde cried alone.

"It's as you feared, Andrew," Hans said, shaking the rain from his poncho and then sitting down at the rough table which besides the cot and two chairs was the sole furniture in the staff tent.

"They've turned our right. About thirty miles upstream. The bastards found that upper ford. Our scouts stayed hidden, and counted at least ten thousand before pulling back."

"I wish we could have covered it," Andrew said grimly, "but if we had, our army would have been split. If they forced us here, the units farther up would have been cut off."

"Well, by the time they get down here it'll have bought us nearly five days' time, and that's what this was for."

"At a price of three hundred dead, and nearly seven hundred wounded. That's ten percent, Hans," Andrew replied grimly. "The 1st Suzdal Regiment is a skeleton."

"And we've got fifteen hundred more muskets and fifteen artillery pieces from the factory," Hans stated evenly. "It's worth the price."

"What time is it?" Andrew asked.

"Nearly midnight."

"If they force the road tonight they might be here on our flank by noon," Andrew said meditatively, looking at the rough map spread out on the table.

"All right, we'll break position here in two hours. We'll pull back five miles to here," and he pointed to a small field that was bordered on the north with open fields, to the west by the river, and to the east by heavy woods.

"Can we chance an open-field fight?" Hans asked cautiously.

"They won't be up to us for hours—we'll dig in through the village and put the artillery hub to hub. Hold them till nightfall, then pull back to the next village"—he looked at the map for a moment—"to Tier. I want a message sent down to Kal to bring up several thousand workers and they'll dig positions there for us."

Hans stood up and then, as if against his better judgment, looked back at Andrew.

"You know that if they flank us down there, we'll lose everything?"

"We need time," Andrew said wearily. "I know the risk, but by heaven we need more time."

"Battalions, fire!"

Fifty guns, resting nearly hub to hub across a front of a hundred yards, fired in unison, sweeping the field, breaking yet another formation of Tugars before they had advanced fifty yards out of the distant woods. Regrouping, the charge swarmed forward, the enemy shrieking and yelling.

"Load canister!"

"Smash 'em up, that's what I say," O'Donald shouted, looking at Andrew. "Smash 'em up. By God I haven't seen anything like this since we broke Pickett's charge!"

Sitting astride his mount, Andrew watched with field glasses raised. This was the fifth charge they'd broken in less than three hours. Only once had the Tugars got close enough to use their bows. From over by the river the *Ogunquit*'s guns added their weight, sweeping the field at an oblique, adding yet more to the carnage.

The woods to the right were heavy with smoke as Tugars kept pushing farther and farther, trying to find his flank. One full division was in there already, a brigade of another moving in to form an angle.

Excitedly O'Donald looked up and down the line as, one after another, gun and battery commanders raised their hands to signal they were ready.

O'Donald put his fist up.

"Battalions, fire!"

A thousand iron balls swept downrange. Sickened, Andrew turned away as the advancing line simply disappeared. The charge faltered, and turning, the Tugars started to stream to the rear.

"Load solid shot!" O'Donald cried.

"Let them run," Andrew said quietly.

"Those man-eating bastards, we can still kill some more!" O'Donald shouted.

"They're brave warriors nevertheless. For heaven's sake, we broke them. Besides," Andrew added hurriedly, "we need to save our ammunition."

Looking to the west, Andrew was relieved to see that in another hour darkness would come. So far the Tugars had shown no desire for night action. He'd wait a couple of hours, disengage, and pull back to Tier to slow them again tomorrow.

Maddened with rage, Qubata rode across the corpse-strewn field. Five days they had been stopped at the ford. For five days more each day had been the same. In the morning the humans would be gone. Formations would be pulled in, scouts sent up, and then yet another village would be in their path, with heavy woods anchoring their right flank, and the river with its damn gunboat the left. At least we've learned what their wheeled weapons can do, he thought grimly. From four hundred paces away he had nearly been killed, the warrior next to him decapitated by a shot from one of their weapons. Charging straight in on them was madness.

Twice Tula had been sent out in the afternoon to flank wide. Waiting through the night, he'd swept in at morning light only to find that the enemy were gone.

Whoever this human was, he was good, Qubata thought grimly. He wished that the man could be taken alive, for surely he would be a pet worth speaking to; perhaps he could even be trained to serve. If not alive, he hoped that at least he could eat of the man's brain and heart.

Qubata turned in his saddle and stared grimly at Alem.

"Shaman, I care not if the night spirits are pleased, displeased, or screaming with rage. I want this army moved tonight."

Alem shook his head grimly.

"Tugars do not ride or fight at night. It causes a curse."

"Then tell your prattle-spouting underlings that you've talked to the sky and they have given a pledge not to curse us."

The priest crossed his long shaggy arms and sat silent.

"Listen, shaman. You know and I know that your powers are a hoax. Old customs work when all observe them, for when Tugar fought Merki, or Uzba, or any of the tribes of the people, he wanted it done in the light, so all could see his prowess of arms.

"But we are fighting men who do not care for glory. I will not waste my warriors again like this," and he pointed to the hundreds of bodies that lay about, ghostlike beneath the pale glow of the twin moons overhead.

"The humans pull back, and are ready. Even now I can promise you that across that field," and he pointed southward, "they are pulling back. Tomorrow morning they will be at the next village, and then beyond that we will have to force our way through the twin passes. If they are allowed to group there we'll pay by the thousands to force our way through."

"He's right," Muzta said riding up to Alem's side. "I will follow Qubata's advice, with or without your agreement, and I should remind you," the Qar Qarth said, drawing closer, "that I prefer my warriors to fight without some superstitious dread that is utter foolishness."

"Must I remind my Qar Qarth that it is unwise to tempt the spirits," Tula said evenly, his shadowy form barely visible in the moonlight.

"I know, Tula," Muzta snapped back, "and if we lose, then you will have yet another excuse to find blame with me. As keeper of the left, you will lead the flank march tonight, but by the spirits of my fathers, you'd better ride hard," Muzta said coldly.

"When last I fought here," Qubata said, looking over at Tula, "there was a road going up into the hills above the first pass that I told you about. It must lead somewhere.

"I'm leading this attack myself, just to make sure," Qubata continued, looking over at Tula with disdain. "I know that terrain. It's just a question of turning their position and perhaps we can still destroy them in the field."

Tula growled darkly and stalked away while Alem looked at the group gathered around him. This final insult he would remember, and if indeed the cattle should somehow stop them, he knew quite clearly now where he could lay the blame.

"I shall tell my people," Alem said coldly.

"We move at once," Qubata roared, "before the sun sets I want the walls of Suzdal in sight!"

Chapter 17

He felt tight, nervous, as if an inner sense were warning him of some lurking danger. Unable to snatch a brief moment of sleep, Hawthorne came to his feet.

Damn, it was starting to rain. So now he had taken to cursing as well. Cursing, killing, even knowing his wife before they had been rightfully married—what had become of him, Hawthorne wondered sadly.

The campfire had simmered down, now hissing as the light cold drizzle drifted down, blanketing the exhausted army in a gradually rising mist. There was a dull brightening to the east. Dawn would be coming soon.

"So my captain cannot sleep?"

Hawthorne went over to the fire and squatted down while Dimitri, who had so obviously lied about his age to join, poured a hot cup of tea into a cup and handed it to his commander.

"Something doesn't feel right, Dimitri," Hawthorne said quietly.

Dimitri looked at Hawthorne, stroking his gray beard, his old weather-creased face breaking into a smile.

"That is why I like you so much and will listen to you, my captain. I hear others talk. Their Yankee captains always say everything will be fine. You do not play such games as if we were children.

"And yes," Dimitri said quietly, "something feels not right. I know Tugars. They are not foolish folk. Five days we have slipped away at night. Tonight is the sixth. I fear tonight they are following close behind."

"Get the rest of the company up. I want all the men on picket line," Hawthorne said quietly. "I'm going back to see our colonel."

Tripping through the underbrush, Hawthorne finally saw

330

the low flickering of a fire and came into the circle of light. Rossignol, who only short months before had been a sergeant, was resting against a tree, sipping a cup of tea. Hawthorne came up and saluted.

"Sir, it might sound funny, but something doesn't feel right. I've ordered my entire company to stand to arms for the rest of the night."

Vince Rossignol nodded wearily and came to his feet.

"Word just came up from Hans. He's feeling the same way. We're letting the men sleep till dawn, then pulling back to the pass at first light."

Rossignol looked up at the sky, which was now covered by dark, lowering clouds.

"Damn rain—if it starts closing in, these flintlocks will be useless. I wish the hell I had—"

"Tugars!"

Hawthorne whirled about. There was the dull report of a musket, another round snapped off, and then the nerve-tearing high ululating roar of the Tugars, so similar to the rebel yell, thundered up around them.

"Jesus Christ!" Rossignol cried, and then staggered backward, a look of disbelief on his face. His hands grasped feebly at the shaft buried in his chest, and then as if his legs had turned to sacks of water, he sank down and was still.

"Captain!"

Instinctively Hawthorne ducked. He heard the slash of steel whisk over his head, and then a thunderous howl of pain.

Looking up, he saw a Tugar towering above him, sword in hand, stepping jerkily, and then crashing down. Dimitri stood over the form, his bayonet still jabbed into the Tugar's back.

Another form came crashing out of the woods. Dimitri stepped low and lunged in hard, catching the creature in the stomach, sending him sprawling.

"Captain, do something!" Dimitri roared.

Dammit, Rossignol wasn't supposed to die! Johnson, the second in command, and May of Company A had both been wounded and sent back. He was the only Yankee left in the entire regiment who could command.

Dimitri stepped back and looked at Hawthorne.

Wild shouts rose up around him, the woods seemingly exploding with struggling forms, the war cries of the Tugars mingling with the steady screams of fear and panic at the surprise.

"Son, do something, anything," Dimitri said quietly, grabbing hold of Hawthorne and looking him straight in the eyes.

As if coming from a dream, Hawthorne nodded. All he could see were Dimitri's eyes.

"Bugler!"

"Here, sir!" A terrified boy came up to his side.

"Blow the rally cry! Blow it for all you're worth! Dimitri, as the men come in, let's start forming a square, and get those colors uncased!"

Coming from his tent, Andrew looked at the woods to the east, where the sound of a growing battle rumbled across the field.

From forward, several scouts came galloping in.

"They're on the other side of the field," a scout shouted. "Thousands of them coming up out of nowhere!"

Dammit! An aide came rushing up, buckling Andrew's sword about his waist, while another led up Mercury, struggling at the same time to saddle the horse.

Hans came galloping up, reining his mount in.

"They've smashed into our flank. It sounds like Houston's division is starting to give way! And this rain, Andrew—if it gets any heavier, the muskets will start misfiring."

"So they've finally hit before dawn," Andrew said, looking across the mist-covered fields. "That general finally learned and broke their usual routine."

Andrew swung up into his saddle. The field pieces forward started to bark out as the first shadow forms came charging out of the mist.

Andrew reined around to watch.

At least this position was a strong one forward, but if they were on the flank he'd be rolled up in an hour.

With every passing second the roar of battle on the right grew louder and louder.

"Hans, if our right's been turned, get up to Houston and pull him out. We'll hold the front here with Barry's division and the artillery. Kindred's division I want in reserve. Position them to cover the passes two miles back. If they've flanked us this bad, they might be trying to spread clear around to our rear. Now move it!"

*   *   *

Grinning with satisfaction, Muzta watched his warriors streaming up to the front. The enemy right was crumbling, and as the light of early morning spread across the mist-covered fields he could sense that Qubata's plan was working. Now all that remained was for the old general to continue his sweep and close the trap.

"Keep moving!" Hawthorne yelled. "Hold this square! You've got to hold!"

They had drilled for this out on an open field, beneath pleasant skies. Now they were doing it for real, through a light stand of forest, the rain coming down, and Tugar archers and charges of ax-wielding warriors pressing in on all sides.

He now had two regiments under his command, the 3rd Suzdalian being swept into the ranks of the 11th as step by step he gave back, holding the right flank from completely collapsing.

Finally the last of the woods gave out into open field. A mile away he could see an endless stream of troops pouring down the road southward.

And then behind him came the sound that struck terror into the heart of any soldier. There was gunfire to the rear, back toward the passes. The enemy was behind them.

"Charge them, charge them!" Qubata roared, standing in his stirrups.

He had not forgotten what he had seen before when crossing into the pass months before. It had taken hours to find it in the dark, but he had reasoned that the side trail that went into the hills must go somewhere. Swinging wide in the darkness, he had driven his warriors forward through the night, until at last they had stumbled upon the narrow road. Pushing hard through the light of early dawn, Qubata knew he was on the right path as they crested up over the hills and then turned westward toward a burned-out village and the flank of the pass beyond.

There would be resistance—he had expected that as the line of fortifications loomed up before him. But by the spirits of his forefathers, if he could drive down out of these hills, the pass would fall and the enemy would be cut off from any hope of retreat.

*   *   *

Andrew could feel a cold terror rising in his heart. Thank God he had sent Kindred's division back, reinforcing the single brigade he had left as a reserve in the pass. But could they hold?

A roaring crescendo came up behind him, and even through the mist and drizzle he could see the dark clouds of musket smoke rising up two miles to his rear.

From out of the woods to his right the last of Houston's division came out of the woods, the darker forms of Tugars pouring out behind them.

So far they'd got most of the units out. For in the confusion the Tugar attack had come not as a hammer blow but rather as a series of ill-timed waves.

"We've lost at least two whole regiments up there!" Hans roared, galloping back from the right, O'Donald at his side.

Andrew nodded grimly.

Hans reined in and looked southward, mouthing a silent curse, and Andrew could see the old sergeant grimly survey the situation.

"If Kindred breaks, we're trapped."

"We're pulling the hell out of here," Andrew said. "Kindred's got to hold the pass. I'm abandoning this position. If we get through, we're pulling straight back to Suzdal. I thought we could hold in the pass for several more days, but it's too late now. Send word to the city that time has run out and to abandon the mills. Now move it."

Hans shouted to his staff, and in seconds couriers went racing off in every direction.

"O'Donald, start leapfrogging the batteries back."

His face lined with fatigue, the artillery commander saluted and, roaring commands, raced down the line. Minutes later half the guns were racing to the rear. The Tugars forward, sensing the breaking of the position, swarmed in, shouting with glee.

Andrew sat motionless, trying to appear outwardly calm. Long experience had told him that a fighting retreat was always far harder than an advance. Now it truly rested upon him. Panic was in the air. Several of the regiments streaming past were more like mobs than fighting units, and he let them pass; there was no hope of rallying them now. The enemy was pressing in from the right not two hundred yards away, and pulling back across the field he could see the last organized formation, a solid square of men moving at the double. Suddenly they would stop, a volley would ring out, and then they would push on. As the last of Houston's division streamed in, the remaining guns of O'Donald's command came off the line.

O'Donald did not pull them out limbered up, but ordered instead that they be pulled back by ropes, while the gunners reloaded on the move. Pausing for a second, the weapons were fired, and then moved back thirty or forty yards to be fired again.

Arrows slashed in around the guns, and with crews wiped out, half a dozen were finally abandoned, but the Tugars, leery of charging straight in on the artillery, were kept at bay.

Moving back with the guns, Andrew nearly cried with relief when from out of the smoke of battle he saw where O'Donald had placed a full battalion of thirty-six guns in the reserve breastworks.

Reaching their protection, the other battalion leapfrogged back to form yet another defensive line across the southernmost pass.

The readied battalion fired a double load of canister, smashing a Tugar charge that was pressing in not a hundred yards away.

The northern pass was less than a half mile away as they pulled back once more. By God, Kindred was holding, Andrew saw, as smoke billowed up from the hill several hundred yards up the slope.

But now they'd have to get him out as well—otherwise when the last of the retreat pulled through it would be Kindred who'd be flanked in turn.

Grimly Andrew looked around, and stopping in the village just north of the pass he knew what would have to be done. For a moment he considered giving it to the 35th as it streamed past. He tried not to let his emotions decide the issue. For several seconds he weighted the two sides and then ordered the regiment on. He would need that core of professionals later; now was not the time to sacrifice them.

"O'Donald, one battery stays here! We need time!" Andrew shouted, pointing to the breastworks, prepared earlier by Kal's work crews.

O'Donald nodded in agreement. They had to buy time now for Kindred to get out.

"I'll take care of it," O'Donald shouted.

"O'Donald, order somebody else—you're pulling back with me."

"But colonel darling, I can't—"

"You can," Andrew said grimly. "I need you. I'd stay myself, but heaven help me I can't either. Now order somebody to stay! They have to hold till we're out of the pass, all of us. We'll signal the *Ogunquit* to lay down support as well. Once the rest of the army's clear, tell the men to spike the guns and make a break for the river. Now do it!"

A battery came clattering past, and O'Donald rode up to it and pointed to the position.

It was Dunlevy's unit, and Andrew struggled not to feel anything. Better that a few die here than that the three thousand in Kindred's command get torn apart.

They'd need infantry support, he realized, and from out of the battle smoke a unit that still held to a square formation came into view. It would have to be them as well.

Andrew galloped over to the shattered unit.

"Who's in command here?" Andrew shouted.

"I guess it's me, sir."

Andrew felt his heart go cold. God, why does it have to be this way? he thought, feeling sick at what he was doing. But he could not change a command because of a personal feeling, no matter how strong.

"You're doing good, son," Andrew said calmly. "I'm promoting you here and now to colonel."

Hawthorne's expression did not change. In Andrew's eyes the boy seemed to have aged twenty years since he last saw him, laughing with childish delight as the balloon went up.

"Hawthorne, fall in by Dunlevy. You are ordered to hold this position until the rest of the army has pulled out of the pass. They have to come down that one narrow road before you. The artillery should force them to keep their distance until they fan out through the woods. Son, if you break before then, Kindred will be lost—for that matter, they'll roll us up completely before we get to the city. Do you understand me?"

"Yes sir. In other words, hold to the last man."

Andrew was silent.

"The *Ogunquit* will support your flank. There's a lot of firepower on that ship. I'm leaving the decision to you

When you feel we're free of pursuit, break for the river. The *Ogunquit* will pick you up.

"I'll see you at sundown, Hawthorne."

The boy saluted.

Andrew started to turn his mount about, then paused. Leaning over, he extended his hand, which Hawthorne grasped.

"God bless you, son. Don't worry about your wife and child. I'll personally look after them."

"God be with you," Hawthorne replied calmly, his voice sounding distant and detached.

Releasing the boy's hand, Andrew galloped off, feeling cold inside, even as he blinked back the tears.

Hawthorne turned back to the line and forced a smile for Dimitri.

"Can you swim, Dimitri?"

"I can learn very fast," the peasant said. "Very fast indeed."

"Let's hope you'll have time to learn."

"Keep moving," Mina shouted. "The tools, for heaven's sake, take the tools!"

Gangs of laborers raced in and out of the building, sweeping up anything that could be moved. A train whistle shrieked, and stepping to the doorway Mina watched as the *Bangor* pulled out from the powder-mill siding, boxcars stacked with barrels, the hopper cars filled with raw charcoal, sulfur, and saltpeter which could still be processed by hand back in the city.

Leaving the building, Mina scaled up the chimney ladder. Gaining the top, he hung on with one hand and looked northward. The rain had died away with a rising breeze from the west, driving before it the pillars of smoke that rose up from the pass. From horizon to horizon he could see hundreds of fires as Fletcher's men pulled in, burning everything that could not be moved. The burning had been going on for days, a pale of smoke rising over Rus from outlying regions all the way up to the border marches of Vazima, forty miles away. Nothing would be left to the enemy. Every barn received the torch, fields not yet harvested were burned, wagons that could not be moved were smashed, the supplies within dumped into the road. Thousands of tons of so desperately needed food went to the torch because time had simply run out. At least the Tugars would find nothing to help them when they came.

The river road was packed with soldiers streaming back toward the city. The gates to the inner wall had already been closed, as the retreating units moved straight from the road to their prearranged positions behind the massive earthen breastworks.

From out of the east gate of the city thousands of militiamen streamed forth, taking their positions. To John Mina it looked as if the world were slipping into total insanity.

Wagons came streaming in from every direction, laden with the harvest from distant fields, their crews lashing wildly at the horses. All seemed madness and confusion. Below him the *Bangor* let loose with a shrieking whistle and started down to the city.

He looked about at all that he had created, a small empire of industry that back home would have been a source of envy. All that he had done was about to disappear, and weeping bitter tears, John started to climb back down, to help with the final loading.

The pass cleared, Andrew sighed with relief. Some semblance of order was finally coming as Kindred's men, extracted from their difficult position, came streaming past, moving at the double back toward the city.

It had been a difficult moment pulling them out of the line. Only O'Donald's skillful use of artillery, which it appeared the Tugars had come to fear, kept them at a distance as the hard-pressed regiments pulled back from their lost position in the passes.

The enemy were mainly on foot, and the artillery, still leapfrogging back, kept them at a distance. Thank God their cavalry, bottled up before the pass, wasn't on his back now.

Cresting the next hill, Andrew saw the city several miles away. Turning in the saddle, he realized that the distant clap of artillery from the pass had suddenly gone quiet. He waited for a moment and then, turning his mount, fell in at the rear of his army.

He'd brought the city eleven days of time. He could only pray that the price had been worth it.

"Now! Now run for it!" Hawthorne screamed.

Throwing down their muskets, the line broke and started to run madly for the river fifty yards away.

He paused for a moment before Dunlevy.

"Don't have a chance, boy," the artilleryman said, holding his side. "I'll give 'em a farewell gift. Now move your ass out of here!"

Hawthorne grabbed the man's hand, and choking back tears, he broke into a mad run. Dimitri, who had been waiting for him, fell in alongside.

The *Ogunquit* let fly with a concentrated broadside, sweeping the Tugar line which was closing in from the north. But those who were now charging up from the south came roaring onward.

He felt as if he were running in mud, his limbs pumping, but maddeningly the ground went by all too slowly.

There was a crack behind him. Hawthorne looked over his shoulder and saw the light gun leap completely over as its triple load of canister slashed into the horde, which overran the position. Dunlevy, waving a gunstaff, disappeared from view.

Men were splashing into the river, the crew aboard the *Ogunquit* screaming wildly, heaving lines in toward shore. A flight of arrows slashed past, churning the water. Dimitri stumbled and fell.

Hawthorne stopped, grabbed the man, and pulled him up.

"Leave me," Dimitri cried, holding his leg. "Leave me!"

"Like hell," Hawthorne roared, and near carrying his friend he crashed into the river.

Still holding Dimitri, he floundered, came up, and leaped forward again. Arrows rained down about him as he held his burden with one hand and, kicking wildly, pushed farther away from shore.

A line shot out from the ship, and grabbing hold, he hung on to Dimitri as a sailor pulled him toward the ship.

Flights of arrows slammed into the *Ogunquit*; it looked like a giant porcupine stuck full of quills.

All about him in the water, more than a hundred men clung desperately to lines.

"Stay in the water!" someone shouted from above. A shudder ran through the ship as the single propeller dug in, swinging the vessel stern first back out toward the middle of the river. Still holding Dimitri, Hawthorne clung to the line, suddenly wondering why he always seemed to get in trouble every time he got near water.

The great boat swung about, pointing its bow downstream, thus acting as a shield for those clinging to the starboard side.

More lines went over the side, and boats were lowered away. Some even jumped over the side, desperate to reach men on the point of drowning. Powerful hands grabbed hold of Hawthorne and yanked him into a lifeboat, along with Dimitri. Sputtering and choking, Hawthorne leaned over the side, gasping for air, as the boat was lifted back up out of the water. Pulled out on deck, he staggered, his legs trembling and weak.

Dimitri looked up at him wanly.

"So I finally learned how to swim," the peasant said, struggling for breath.

Holding back his tears, Hawthorne looked about. There were far fewer than a hundred survivors. Eight hundred from two regiments and a hundred from the battery, and these were all that were left.

He had to keep control, he thought grimly. Turning, he walked astern and gained the quarterdeck.

Tobias looked at him tight-lipped.

Hawthorne saluted.

"Colonel Hawthorne, commander 5th and 11th Suzdal, reporting," he said weakly.

"You were in charge of that?" Tobias asked, pointing back upstream to where thousands of Tugars now swarmed, streaming southward.

The battery along the deck cut loose with another volley, now that the rescue was completed, their shot smashing into the enemy ranks, which pushed on regardless of loss.

"Yes sir, I was," Hawthorne said quietly.

"How old are you, boy?" Tobias asked.

"Eighteen, sir."

"Damn me, that was the stupidest damn thing I've ever seen back there," Tobias growled.

Hawthorne stiffened.

"And also the bravest," he finally added grudgingly.

"Thank you for your support and rescue," Hawthorne stated evenly. "I shall make note of it in my report."

"The hell you say. A report from an eighteen-year-old boy, no less."

"Sir, I am Colonel Hawthorne now. I paid for that title back there, and by God, sir, I expect to be treated with the respect due my rank."

Still shaking his head, Tobias looked appraisingly at the hundred-and-twenty-pound youngster, who stood before him soaked to the bone.

"I think you could use a drink, son."

"I think, sir, maybe I could," Hawthorne replied, fighting vainly to hold back his tears.

"Here they come!"

Malady looked up from the cabin of his engine and gazed to where his fireman pointed.

A dark band of horsemen swung into view along the far bank of the Vina. Urging their mounts forward, they swung out wide from the battlement walls, charging across the dried riverbed, which since the building of the dam had been reduced to a mere trickle of a stream.

"Where the hell's Mina?" Malady roared.

"Still back at the powder mill the last I saw," the fireman cried.

"Damn that man."

Slamming the throttle down, Malady spun the wheels of the *Bangor* until they finally caught with a lurch, and the train, which had been backing down to the protection of the wall, jumped forward. The train started up the hill, gaining speed as Malady held the throttle wide open.

Not easing up an inch, he let the train roar through the curves, the boxcars behind him shaking and rattling.

From out of a side gulley a dozen Tugars came galloping up and reined in their mounts next to the track.

Staring with open-mouthed amazement, they pointed and gestured wildly at the approaching engine.

One of them leveled his bow and fired it straight in at the engine, the steel point striking sparks as it skidded off.

Laughing, Malady hauled down on the whistle, and roaring with fear the Tugars desperately hung on as their mounts kicked and reared.

"Look out, you bastards," Malady screamed as he raced past, giving them a rude gesture. Hitting the next turn, he saw several dozen peasants racing across the field trying to get back to the city. Malady slowed the engine, holding the whistle down. Leaning out of the cab he gestured wildly.

The men and women turned about, and came running back to the track, clambering aboard the boxcars. Holding the throttle wide open, he continued on up the hill, the powder mill at last in sight. Slowing to pick up the switchman for the foundry turnoff, he pressed on.

Still holding the whistle down, he leaned out of the cab. The switchman for the powder-mill turnaround was still at his post. Malady waved in the direction of the mill, and the man pulled his lever over.

"I'll pick you up on the way back!" he roared, as the train headed in on the last stretch.

The switchman for the turnaround waved him through, and the train skidded into the powder-mill siding.

Leaping from the cabin, Malady stormed into the mill.

"Mina, where the hell are you?"

"They can't take this place," Mina cried as he pushed a barrel in under the wooden grinders.

"We've got to get the hell out of here!"

"In a moment," Mina said absently. Reaching into his pocket, the major pulled out a match.

"Goddammit, man!" Malady roared, snatching the match from the man's hand. With a roundhouse punch he knocked John out with a single blow, and picking him up, ran to the door.

"Grab this madman," Malady shouted to his fireman. Turning, he raced back into the mill. Spying a barrel, he kicked the side in, poured it over the half-dozen barrels stacked under the gears and grinding mechanism, and then, stepping backward laid out a trail to the door.

"Throttle her up," Malady shouted.

The train lurched forward, pulling through the sharp narrow curve that pointed it back down the hill. Malady watched the train swing out and start to close in toward the switch.

Striking a match, he let it drop on the powder, which flared into life, the flame streaking back into the building.

Pumping wildly, he raced away. The train drifted through the switch, its operator leaping into a passing boxcar while the fireman looking back anxiously toward his boss.

Running up alongside the cab, Malady leaped in and slammed the throttle full open. The train careened away.

Behind them there was a thunderclap roar. Shouting with fiendish delight, Malady watched as the roof of the building lifted into the air, flame blowing out through the windows.

The hundreds of Tugars who had come in behind the train on its rush up the hill cried out at the sheer size of the explosion and then at the dragon bearing down on them.

Sweeping down from either side, they charged in on the train, a shower of arrows slamming into the puffing, steam-belching giant.

Tying the throttle to full, Malady grabbed hold of Mina's pistol. Leaning out of the cab, he drew careful aim and started to snap off rounds. One after another, Tugars tumbled from the saddle.

One of the warriors, waving a long lance, came alongside the tracks and, leaning over, charged straight at the train.

"Come on, you bastard!" Malady howled, holding the whistle down.

Picking up speed, the *Bangor* bore down, and the Tugar, shouting wildly, continued his mad charge.

A shudder slapped through the train, knocking Malady off his feet.

"Damn idiot," Malady shouted, staggering up to look out of the cab at the mess lying beside the track, "you almost derailed me, dammit!"

Streams of Tugars swarmed in to either side as the train careened through the first curve and down toward the second.

From atop the northeast bastion, several field pieces cut open, their shot screaming in to scatter some of the warriors.

One of the Tugars, swinging his mount in, leaped atop the wood tender.

Malady spun around, with a single shot dropping the warrior.

Another one came alongside, and roaring with delight the engineer grabbed hold of the terrified fireman's iron poker and with a single blow sent the Tugar tumbling off.

Hitting the final curve, the engine came straight toward the breastworks, the gate still left open for this last arrival. Rushing in at over forty miles an hour, the engine roared straight in over the moat bridge.

Malady slammed back on the throttle and grabbed the brake lever, lifting himself off the ground with the effort.

Sparks flying, the engine screamed through the fortification line, the gate swinging down behind them.

"Hang on!" Malady yelled as the train skidded down the track, heading straight into the sharp curve just before the main city wall.

With a shrieking, tearing roar the engine leaped the tracks, dirt flying up in every direction, plowing across the ground, and then with a final gentle nudge it tapped into the log walls of Suzdal and came to a stop.

Thousands had held their breath, watching the drama, and now burst into wild thundering cheers.

Malady alighted from the cab, waving good-naturedly at his admirers. Patting the side of the *Bangor*, he stepped around to the front. Climbing up on the cow catcher, he pulled out the spear point that was imbedded in the front plate and then stepped back to look at his wreck.

"Best damn train ride I ever had," he whispered in awe.

"Here they come."

Sick with exhaustion, Andrew stood atop the northeast bastion, watching as the Tugar host, several thousand strong, came forward on foot.

Artillery started to snap out rounds, cutting bloody furrows in the charging ranks, which slammed into the first row of entanglements. Cutting aside the brush and stakes with their powerful two-handed axes, individuals continued to push in, all semblance of order in the charge broken.

Andrew turned and nodded to Hans.

Shouted orders raced down the line from division to brigade and finally to regiment. A thousand muskets roared. Still the enemy pressed in, weaving their way through the trap holes, stakes, and barriers. From two hundred yards out, several thousand more Tugars in support stood in massive formations. Their volleys of arrows darkened the sky, to rain down with little effect onto the protective logs, covered with earth, that formed a canopy over the heads of the defenders.

The leading edge of the host reached the edge of the dry moat. Some leaped in, but most simply stood gape-mouthed at the barrier still to be traversed before coming to blows.

From out of the ranks an arrow soared heavenward, a red streamer fluttering behind it. Deep-throated horns rang out, and as one the Tugars turned and retreated, leaving the field covered with hundreds of casualties. The fire on the walls died away.

"So what was that all about?" Kal asked.

"Testing our lines," Hans replied. "Professionals—damn good professionals out there."

Sighing, Andrew turned away and looked at his staff.

"Too close," he whispered. "We almost lost it all back up there," and he nodded vaguely toward the north.

"All right, Hans, what's the bill?"

Hans pulled out a scrap of paper and started down the list.

"In twelve days, over four thousand dead and wounded, eleven field pieces lost, over a thousand muskets and other assorted equipment. Over half of all artillery and a third of infantry ammunition expended. Three regiments wiped out, all of them this morning, a third of the rest, especially in Houston's division, losing more than fifty percent.

"Houston's dead, Kindred's wounded, and in the 35th and 44th we took thirty percent casualties."

Hans stopped and looked over at Andrew, who stared at him exhausted and hollow-eyed.

"A hell of a performance for my first command, wouldn't you say, Sergeant Hans?"

"You stopped over ten times our numbers for nearly twelve days. That too was a hell of a performance, sir," Hans said sharply. "We got enough muskets to form another division and enough artillery for another battalion, and we made up near half the ammunition fired off. Fletcher reports we got enough now for full rations to last five months. That, sir, to me was a victory."

Andrew tried to force a smile.

"And forty percent casualties under my command," he said weakly.

"You did what had to be done," Hans replied, a slight edge of reproof in his voice.

"Of course, as I've always done," Andrew replied distantly.

"Well, look what the cat dragged back," O'Donald interrupted, looking over his shoulder.

The group parted as Hawthorne, with Dimitri limping at his side, came through the edge of the group and, wearily coming to attention, snapped off a salute.

"Colonel Hawthorne reporting, sir. The remains of the 5th and 11th Suzdalian and third battery are back in the city. It's sundown, sir, and you said that's when you'd see me."

It had been too much today, all of it too much, Andrew thought, looking at what he had turned the young private into—yet another killer. Just like John, he thought sadly, just like Johnnie. I took this boy and plugged him into a hole and left him to die.

"Colonel now, is it?" O'Donald roared. "Soaking wet like a drowned kitten and yet 'e's a colonel."

Grim-faced, Hans looked sharply at O'Donald who became quiet at the look of reproach.

"Dunlevy?" O'Donald asked, suddenly turning serious.

Hawthorne looked away and shook his head.

O'Donald turned from the group and walked off.

Andrew stepped forward, and taking the boy's hand, he tried to force a smile.

"You did well, son. I'm proud of you."

Proud of making him a killer, he thought, looking into Hawthorne's eyes, eyes that had seen far too much.

Andrew tried to force a smile, and finally exhaustion, shock, and all that had happened overwhelmed him.

"Thank God you're safe, at least you're safe," and dissolving into tears, he embraced the trembling boy who was now so like himself.

"We face something unlike anything dreamed of before," Qubata said, looking back at Muzta.

The strange chase had held him breathless, and to his amazement he had actually found himself secretly cheering for the man who with such bravery controlled the smoking, breathing dragon.

What manner of men were these to have changed the Rus cattle into such warriors? There were six thousand dead Tugars lying back across thirty miles, another twenty thousand injured. Three Umens were completely shattered.

"We shall not be fools," Muzta said grimly, his attention again focused on the massive walls and entanglements that surrounded the city. Thousands upon thousands of his warriors were streaming past, galloping across the fields to encompass the city.

"We learned on that final attack that this will not be easy," Muzta continued. "If they had not met us and fought us I might have been a fool and ordered you to send in all the Umens to charge and lost five times as many, to no purpose.

"No, we will do this slowly and carefully. Though I prefer my cattle fattened, we will let these grow thin for a while before finishing them off.

"Come, my friend, we have harvested more than a thousand bodies today. At least we shall eat well tonight."

"I'll come shortly," Qubata said quietly.

The old Tugar watched as darkness drifted down over the field, blanketing the waiting city in night.

Somehow, he thought quietly, I shall never quite enjoy my food ever again.

Chapter 18

"Sir, message from northeast bastion."

Andrew walked over to Mitchell and sat down by his side, listening to the clicking of the key. The young soldier sat hunched over, writing with a stub of pencil. Finished, he tore the sheet off and handed it up to Andrew.

"Well, I'll be damned," Andrew mumbled. "All right, Mitchell, tell them I'm coming up.

"Orderly, get out my dress uniform and be quick about it, and send for Kalencka and his holiness."

Leaving the headquarters room, Andrew crossed the hallway into his private room. The orderly was already pulling out his one good uniform, and with the young Suzdalian's help Andrew quickly dressed.

There was a knock on the door.

"Come on in."

Kal came through, his heavy tunic covered in dirt, with Casmar stepping in behind him.

"The Tugars are asking for a parley," Andrew said evenly.

"What does it mean?"

The two Suzdalians looked at each other in surprise.

"It is a trap, Andrew," Kal blurted out. "Turn it down."

Andrew looked over at Casmar.

"You must remember, Keane, they view us as nothing but cattle to feed upon. If a bull had gored you, would you then go speak to it under rules of war? No, you would trick it any way you could and then slay it. They want our leader, and will do what is needed to get him."

"I'm willing to take the chance," Andrew said quietly, buckling on his sword, "if the terms are right. It's been over a month, my friends. Perhaps they grow weary of this siege."

"It is we who will run out of food first," Kal said quietly.

"But they don't know that," Andrew replied, "and perhaps, my friend, you are wrong on that account."

The two were silent.

Dressed, Andrew stepped out of the room and back into his headquarters.

"Mitchell, send a message up to Hans at the northeast bastion. I want the 35th to report to the east gate, along with the 5th Suzdal. Tell Hans I'll meet him at number three bastion."

The telegrapher bent over his key, and calling for his staff and couriers, Andrew strolled out of the room, down the main corridor of the cathedral, and out into the square.

All about him was quiet, grim. The sixteen hundred men of the reserve brigade sat in small clusters about the square, huddled over open fires to ward off the chill in the late-autumn air. Overhead, Petracci's balloon hovered on the end of its tether. Andrew could almost feel some small pity for Hank. The man had never mastered the contraption he had designed, and had learned to take up a bucket after his first day aloft, to spare those who were unfortunate enough to be directly below.

With pale, drawn face, he stayed at his task day after day, ascending each morning to observe any changes in the deployment of the Tugar lines.

Mounting his horse, Andrew cantered out onto the east road and started down the hill.

The front was strangely silent. At least the parley had brought that respite, Andrew thought. Nearing the eastern gate, he started to pass the first signs of damage. Work crews were still sifting through the smoking ruins of what had once been an entire block of warehouses. The Tugars had knowledge of siegecraft, and the shelling from their heavy catapults was becoming more serious with each passing day. Thousands of men now worked around the clock on fire watch to drown the hundreds of flaming bolts that rained into the city every day. And nearly every day some fires got out of control.

Andrew reined in for a moment and looked over the ruins. At least fifty tons of food lost in this one. If they keep this up, Suzdal will gradually burn down around us, he thought sadly.

He nodded to the soot-blackened workers who had stopped to look up at him and then pushed on. Passing out the east gate, he saw the blue uniforms of the 35th marching in column out of the hard-pressed northeast bastion, coming down the military road to meet him.

They still looked good, he thought with a smile. Over a third of them who had come here a year ago were gone now, but then, hadn't it always been that way? At Gettysburg he'd lost half of them in a single day, and again at Cold Harbor. Yet the regiment still endured. The battle-torn standards came past, snapping in the brisk chilled breeze. Emblazed upon the national colors, two new names had been stitched in, the Ford and River Road, the names added to the list which had started with Antietam.

Men looked up to him, nodding in recognition with that old familiarity that veterans kept for their leader, while the new faces looked up at the now legendary Keane with simple awe.

Hans, riding beside his old regiment, came up to Andrew and saluted.

"They have an envoy out there. Speaks pretty good Suzdalian. He asked for you directly by name and requests a parley."

"What guarantees will they give?"

"None at first, and so I told him to go to hell."

Andrew chuckled softly.

"Still expect us to come crawling to them, I guess."

"Well, he came back fifteen minutes later. The offer was ten warriors as hostage, and I told him you weren't worth anything less than a hundred of their finest and that still wouldn't be enough.

"Now, that started the beast to growling, but damn me if he didn't agree at once."

"They must want a look at me real bad," Andrew said quietly. "He also said that they are giving blood bond for you, whatever that means."

Andrew looked back to Casmar, who showed open amazement.

"Blood bond is a Tugar pledge of fair play. But I've never

heard of its being given to a human before. This is truly unique."

"Well done, Hans," Andrew said, smiling.

"Bring their hostages into this area. I want additional troops around, and bring up some rations. Offer some beef to them as well, just to set them thinking."

Hans tried to force a smile.

"Take care, will you?"

"It should be an interesting change of pace," Andrew replied, and nodding for the gate to be opened, he trotted out beyond the breastworks, the 35th falling in to either side of the road and presenting arms.

He felt somehow naked as alone he crossed the moat bridge and reined in his mount.

The envoy sat alone on the other side, towering above Andrew, a cold dispassionate look on his face.

"You are the one-limb human who leads these cattle," the envoy said coldly.

"I am Colonel Keane, commander of the Suzdalian army of men," Keane snapped back. "If I hear the term 'cattle' but once more, this parley is finished."

The Tugar gave a snort of disdain and raised his hand in the air.

From out of the Tugar siege lines a column of warriors stepped out and trotted down the road.

Andrew felt a moment of fear watching them draw closer. If this was indeed a plan to kill him, here would be the chance.

"Steady men, steady," he said, looking back at his escort, who stood nervously, hands clenched tight around their weapons.

Andrew eased his mount to the side of the road, and in a display of bravado, which he hoped did not look like playacting, he simply looked straight ahead, not sparing a glance for the Tugars as they trotted past, their heavy footfalls echoing in rhythm as they crossed the bridge.

"Lead the way, envoy," Andrew said haughtily, and touching spurs to his mount, he followed as the Tugar started back toward his own lines.

The stench of death hung heavy in the air as they passed the area of pitfalls and entanglements where bodies still lay from the first day of the siege. Clearing the region at last, the two galloped another hundred yards and crossed into the Tugar lines.

Their position was a strong one, and in many ways an imitation of his own fortifications, Andrew saw at once. Earthen ramparts had been piled up, with positions for the rock- and spear-throwing catapults covered by heavy logs, to absorb artillery fire.

Weaving through a sally port, Andrew felt a moment of cold fear.

The path ahead was lined on either side by hundreds of Tugars in full fighting armor. Though he was mounted on his horse, most of the warriors, who stood stiffly to either side, still towered above him.

Their sharp angular helmets covered all but their eyes, which gazed out at him with hatred and contempt. War bows were strung, and double quivers filled with four-foot bolts hung from their shoulders. From shoulders to knees hung a heavy curtain of chain mail, and at their belts dangled great axes or swords.

He had not seen such as these at the battles on the river road—they must be the heavy shock troops for a task like the one he had presented. The helmets he had seen before, watching them through field glasses while the steady sniping went on day after day, killing many without much result other than misery for both sides.

As he reached the end of the line, Andrew was stunned to see a separate contingent of Tugars bearing muskets. Booty from the last battle, he realized. They probably had only a handful of rounds per gun, but it was unnerving nevertheless.

Onward they rode, and Andrew felt that most likely the main purpose of this parley was to do nothing more than awe him with the Tugar strength. Unit after unit lined the road—foot archers, horse archers, heavy lancers, and then a row of double-torsion catapults with stacks of ten-foot spears piled up like cordwood.

Then finally there was something he could not ignore.

Turning a bend in the road, he saw a long line of human warriors, standing grim-faced. Approaching the unit, Andrew reined in his horse to face Mikhail, who looked at Andrew with open hatred.

The man's face was deeply pit-marked. So he had caught smallpox, Andrew realized. The tales that had filtered out of Vazima before the battle had started horrified him. Nearly a third of the population had died, another third sickened and horribly disfigured. Of course, the prelate, Igor, had blamed it on the church of Suzdal.

Emil had repeatedly sent envoys, begging to let him stem the pestilence, but Igor had refused, a refusal that had finally resulted in his being shoveled into a mass burial pit.

At Andrew's approach, Mikhail leaned over and spat on the ground. Several Tugars who had been riding escort behind Andrew came up and positioned themselves between the two.

"Let's finish it here and now," Mikhail growled. "Sword against sword."

Andrew looked at the pox-scarred man without comment.

"It was you who brought this down upon us!"

"You could have fought with us against the common foe," Andrew said evenly.

"And die as all of you fools will die."

"If need be, die like men," Andrew snapped. "I'd rather that than crawl as a slave for the Tugars."

Mikhail's hand leaped to his sword hilt. The Tugar closest to the boyar barked a warning as his own blade snapped from its scabbard.

Mikhail sat motionless for a long moment and then gradually let his hand fall. Andrew almost felt a sense of pity for the man, now shamed as he was before his warriors. Spurring his mount, he continued down the road.

Out of range of the city's field pieces, the great tent city of the Tugar warriors was spread out before him. Each tent was like an overturned bowl twenty feet across and half as high.

The week before, the first of the tents mounted on wheels had appeared down the river road. The strange procession had continued day after day, to encamp in the fields above the dam, the city of women and children stretching to the far horizon. Along with them had come yet more warriors numbering in the tens of thousands to move in around the siege lines.

Moving farther up the hill, Andrew rode past several felt tents which were nearly a hundred feet across, but even these were dwarfed by the great center structure. He had gazed upon it many times through his binoculars, but drawing close to it Andrew was stunned by the magnificence of the shelter. Rather than the simple felt of the warriors' shelters, this one appeared to be covered with gold cloth that gave it the appearance of a great dome that shined dull red in the sunlight.

The entrance was hung with great curtains of silver-threaded velvet, the awnings held up by ornately carved poles embedded with rare and precious gems.

The envoy reined in and dismounted, beckoning for Andrew to do likewise. As he climbed off Mercury, he caught a faint sniff of something on the wind, and looking to the side of the great tent, he saw a thin curl of smoke rising from a pit. It appeared as if the ground about the pit had been freshly raked over and cleaned, but that could not hide what it was.

The envoy followed his gaze and then looked back at Andrew, his mouth curled in the slightest of grins.

With cold hatred in his eyes, Andrew stared at the envoy with contempt.

"We cleaned away last night's feast before your arrival," the envoy said, smiling. "We didn't want to frighten you away."

"And when this war is done with," Andrew said slowly, "I'll personally see to the task of shoveling your body into the ground."

The envoy said nothing, but for the briefest of moments his control seemed ready to slip. Then, turning away, he beckoned for Andrew to enter the great tent.

Alone, he walked into the shelter, its soft darkness a relief after the glare of the sun. Pausing to let his eyes adjust, Andrew looked about, trying not to let his inner fear show. If they wished to kill me, he reasoned, they would have done so by now; or could they be saving me for something far worse? His heart suddenly started to race at the thought.

"You who are named Keane, come forward to my presence."

His eyes adjusting, he could see several shadowy forms sitting before a softly glowing brazier in the center of the tent. Taking a deep breath, Andrew strode forward. There were only three in the vast cavernous shelter, the entire effect of the large empty space making him feel even smaller and more vulnerable.

I would try to create the same effect, he reasoned inwardly. This is all part of the game within the game, to deceive, to intimidate, and to learn. The realization calmed his fears, and when he came to a stop a dozen feet away from the three Tugars, his heart was calm again.

The one standing to the right he felt he had seen before, and then the realization came that he was the Namer of Time. The one to the left appeared old, his long shaggy hair nearly all gray with broad streaks of white.

Andrew immediately recognized him as the Tugar warrior he had seen before the pass, and riding almost every day on inspection around the siege lines.

Andrew nodded slightly in recognition, and to his surprise the Tugar returned the nod.

The old one's eyes looked at him with open curiosity, which were a contrast to the sense of caution he felt from the powerful, towering Tugar who sat between the two.

"He is the one," the Namer said to Muzta, who sat quiet, without any outward show of emotion.

"It is traditional," the Namer said in Russian, looking back at Andrew, "for cattle to abase themselves before Muzta Qar Qarth, and before all of the Tugar race when summoned to appear."

"I remember you," Andrew said quietly, "and you will recall I did not abase myself then, nor shall I now, nor will I be addressed with the word 'cattle.' "

The Namer started to speak, but Qubata extended his hand for silence and spoke quickly to Muzta.

"I know some of your tongue," Qubata said evenly, motioning for the Namer to withdraw. Without comment, the Namer strode from the tent.

"As a child I had a Rus pet, and I have decided to learn it again," Qubata said, sitting down beside Muzta. "You call yourself Keane and are a Yankee?"

Andrew nodded in reply.

"You are the one who created the army of Rus?"

"I and the other Yankees who came here with me merely guided them. The rest they did themselves."

"I am impressed by what you have created, Keane."

Somewhat surprised, Andrew nodded a thanks.

"Ask him why he and those with him did not bow down to my rule," Muzta asked, and Qubata delivered the question.

"Because we will not submit to your slaughter pits," Andrew said evenly.

"Our rule has been fair and just," Muzta said. "We

take but two in ten, even though it is in our power to slaughter all."

"It is not justice," Andrew replied, "it is keeping men as herds, to be culled and harvested at your wish. That to us is worse than slavery."

"Yet the vast majority still live," Qubata replied. "Yet the vast majority could still live, if you submit."

"Is the purpose of this meeting, then, to offer terms?" Andrew asked.

"That is the wish of my Qar Qarth," Qubata replied. "Submit now, and we will take but the traditional two in ten. Your machines must be turned over and you will be forbidden to make more. Do that and you will be boyar, and granted the right of giving exemption to any you choose, within reason."

"No."

Muzta bristled at the simple, curt response, not needing a translation to explain, but Andrew could sense that his answer had been expected.

"You know you will all die if you resist. Some may die, or all will die. I see no sense in that."

"I am surprised at this offer," Andrew said evenly. "Would you submit to us, if it were we who owned the slaughter pits? You are a proud race, and I think you would fight to the death as well."

Qubata translated to Muzta, who looked at Qubata as if he had not heard correctly.

"But these are cattle," Muzta said. "Such a thing is unheard-of."

"The cattle we know have always been trained, already subjugated by our forefathers. These Yankees are different. We see how they fight and have trained the Rus. When we thought we had them trapped, I was stunned at how many sacrificed their lives so their companions could escape. That is something a Tugar would do to save his clan, and now we see it in them as well."

"I am almost glad he did not take our offer," Muzta said evenly, still looking at Andrew. "They are too dangerous. We must annihilate them all."

"That is what we have been trying to do," Qubata said dryly.

"See if you can find out the other things I wish to know."

Qubata looked back at Andrew, who had stood patiently during their hushed conversation.

356 William R. Forstchen

"When did you come through the tunnel of light?"

The new subject caught Andrew off guard.

"When I met your Namer he spoke of that as well," Andrew said. "Then you know of the tunnel?"

"It is how all men arrive here," Qubata replied.

"Have any men ever gone back?" Andrew asked, unable to contain his curiosity.

So this one would like to leave, Qubata realized. The answer to the question he did not know, and feeling some desire to be honest, he shook his head.

"Would you like to go back?"

"Some would," Andrew replied. "Some might wish to stay."

It could be an answer to these troublesome creatures, Qubata thought, and then he turned his direction back to Andrew.

"My Namer reported that it was early in the summer of the previous year that you arrived."

"That is correct."

"Then you did all of this, built your machines, made your army, and overthrew the rightful rulers all in that time?"

"Yes to the first two," Andrew replied, "but it was the people of Suzdal themselves who rebelled and asked us to lead them."

Qubata looked back at Muzta and translated.

"The boyar Mikhail is lying then, as I suspected," Muzta replied. "This is another first—cattle rebelling against the lords we appoint over them."

"The presence of these Yankees tipped the scales. It is as the few prisoners we took have said."

"What is the tunnel?" Andrew asked, when the two had paused for a moment and were looking back in his direction.

"You do not know?"

Andrew felt there was no sense in playing a game of lies and simply shook his head.

"Perhaps someday we will tell you, for a price," Qubata said evenly, gaining satisfaction from seeing the frustration in the man's eyes.

"Is there any further purpose, then, to this interview?" Andrew retorted. "I have told you we will not submit. I will offer you these terms, though. If you withdraw from our city we will not hinder nor attack you. That is the only agreement I will offer. I suspect that rather than we, it is you who are growing short of food. You could find more elsewhere, but your pride or perhaps your desperation prevents you from leaving us unpunished. Do not let your pride destroy you."

The audacity of this one, Qubata thought, feeling a sense of admiration for the man.

"You know that we shall defeat you," Qubata replied softly, without any threat in his voice.

"And when you are done, where will be your victory?" Andrew replied. "We will leave no bodies for you to feast upon, for as we die we will burn or bury our corpses. You will have nothing in the end.

"I know this," Andrew continued, venturing a stab. "You have come here two years early, something unheard-of before. This was not at first because of us, though your arrival with just your warriors was obviously a response. You were driven here by something else. I have heard of your rivals the Merki."

"How do you know that?" Qubata asked in surprise.

"Our great ship sailed to southern waters and there met people who do not expect their enemies for yet two more years. But I do not think it is the Merki that brought you here early."

"Then please tell me," Qubata replied coldly, not wishing to show interest but unable to contain himself.

"Starvation," Andrew replied. "You have allowed yourselves to become dependent on us alone for everything you need. When was it last that Tugars found or raised their own food? No, you have lived off our backs and our sweat. And then your cattle," and as he said the word his expression flared with anger, "started to die."

Andrew paused for a moment to let Qubata translate.

"A disease always seemed to be just ahead of you, and that is why you rushed onward, desperate to outrace it. As fast as you marched, still the disease spread before you. If you know of the Wandering People who flee before you, you should know as well that the disease travels with them. If you slow, the disease slows. Go quicker and the disease spreads faster. I think, Qubata, that you and your people are at the end of your rope. It is you who are starting to starve, not we.

"And I might add," Andrew said dryly, "we Yankees know the way to prevent the disease, for you should know by now that only those of Suzdal have been spared its ravages. We offered it to the rulers of Vazima, and they spurned us. A third of them died, and few are left healthy, enough for your pits or to bring in the vast amounts of food your people need."

Stunned, Qubata turned away and spoke to Muzta.

"Can it be true?" Muzta asked in surprise.

"There is most likely no other explanation," Qubata replied. "It was all so simple—we should have seen it. We could try to hunt down the Wanderers, but you and I know there are always more of them."

"Then we are truly doomed, even if we win here," Muzta said softly. "Send him away. We need to speak of this, and I wish him not to know of our concern."

"I think he senses that already," Qubata replied.

"Send him away."

Qubata nodded and looked back at Andrew.

"We shall speak again," Qubata said softly. "You are free to go, one named Keane."

"And your name?" Andrew asked.

"I am Qubata, sword master of the Tugar horde," he replied, not feeling any insult at such a question.

"It was you whom I saw in the first battle, and have faced on the field."

Qubata nodded.

"A masterful move before the passes," Andrew said ungrudgingly.

"I should have had you all, except for the courage and sacrifice of your men," Qubata replied, surprised that he was speaking so to a human, but unable to respond in any other way.

"You are free to go," Qubata said, "though we might speak again."

Andrew nodded and to his own surprise came to attention and saluted before turning to leave.

"Keane."

Andrew turned to look back.

"You know you will lose in the end."

Andrew did not reply.

"If need be we'll sacrifice fifty thousand to gain your walls, for there is no alternative for us but victory," Qubata said softly.

"As is the same for us," Andrew replied grimly.

* * *

"They are a pestilence and must be destroyed," Tula roared, and his cry was picked up through the gathering of clan leaders.

"If we let them live," Zan said, coming to his feet, "then what they are will be ten times worse than the pox that ravages our cattle. Surely you are mad to think of terms with the likes of them."

Muzta sat quiet, while all about him was chaos.

"We can take their city now!" Tula shouted.

Qubata came to his feet.

"Yes, we can take their city," Qubata said softly, "and there are two ways. We can wait to starve them out, and that can take months and we shall starve, or we can assault them, and thousands, tens of thousands, of ours will die."

"We are dying anyhow," Tula roared.

"Or we can come to terms," Qubata said quietly.

There was a moment of stunned silence, and then bellows of rage. Muzta, who sat to one side, looked straight ahead, and as Qubata looked in the direction of his Qarth, Muzta's eyes lowered. The old general stared at his friend and then looked away and stepped to the middle of the tent.

"As sword holder of the horde, I demand to be heard, in the circle of speech," Qubata said evenly.

But still the shouting continued, until at last Muzta came to his feet and the gathering fell silent.

"As sword holder of the horde for a circling and a half, he shall be heard," Muzta said evenly.

"To hear his outrage!" Tula shouted. "To hear what you yourself might believe!"

Muzta turned to face Tula, hand on sword.

"As Qar Qarth I say he is to be heard," Muzta said, a dark menace in his voice.

Tula with open contempt turned away and stalked to the back of the tent.

Qubata, as if rousing from deep contemplation, looked back up.

"I have served as master of swords to the Tugar horde for one and a half circlings," he began quietly. "I commanded at Onci and at Ag, and at Isgar. Before that I served as commander of the Olkta, and before that down through the ranks to my birth from a family of the common folk. Always I have placed the survival of the horde and the honor of my

Qar Qarth above myself. And thus is the reason that I say we must come to terms with the Yankee and Rus people."

An angry murmur started again and then died away as Qubata remained standing in the circle of speech, which when once granted to a Tugar could be held unless directly withdrawn by the Qar Qarth.

"And with that experience I believe I speak what is best for the horde.

"I have grown and lived and turned to my age with the customs of our people. There was a time when our sacred ancestors, if legends are to be believed, traveled even as far as the stars of the Wheel, and built strange and wondrous devices. Devices that we still see vestiges of today, such as the gateways, the tunnels of light which on occasion bring to us beings from other worlds. It is said, in the books of the shamans, that such devices could once be opened and closed at will, and thus our fathers traveled far, having placed these things on many distant worlds.

"It is said as well that when one traveled through the gate, time as great as many circlings passed, yet to him who traveled it was but as a moment. But that understanding is lost, and the gates only open at such and such a time by chance into our own Valdennia. In the land of the Merki it is said that their cattle are different, coming from yet other worlds, though I have not seen that.

"But be that as it may, our fathers were once powerful beings."

"And why do we need to hear this recitation?" Tula snapped. "It is not our concern. Our fathers were gods, but we are Tugars of the horde, masters of the world that we forever circle in our endless ride."

"It is precisely why you need to hear it now," Qubata said evenly. "Why have we lost these arts, this knowledge? What has become of the Tugar people?"

"As I said, we are masters of the world," Tula growled.

"Perhaps eons ago, but are we truly the masters now?" Qubata replied.

The assembly grew uneasy and looked one to the other.

"What have we become?" Qubata said softly. "Are we truly the masters? I am starting to think not."

"Because some foul cattle have fought us?" Zan snapped. "We shall flatten them, and plow their bones into the earth."

"It is deeper, far deeper than that," Qubata replied.

"However it was ordered, it came to pass that a hundred or more circlings ago, our ancestors did not slaughter the strangers that came to our world but saw a use for them. We spared them. We set rulers over them to control them when we were not present. We took from them their horses and bred them to our size and use. We spaced them about the world, giving unto them rich lands where they prospered and grew. We came as well to eat their flesh.

"And we have become slaves to them."

His words were met with stunned silence and looks of confusion.

"Look about us," Qubata said quickly, before outrage could overwhelm him. "What do we produce? Nothing! Each year we ride to yet the next country of what we call cattle and slaughter them and take from them, and then in the spring ride on to our next year's pasturage.

"Finally we have taken them by the thousands to ride with us as well. We call them pets, but what are they truly? If a thing is to be finely wrought, it is done by a pet. If anything of importance, even our bows and arrows, is to be made, it is done by those whom we winter among, or again by our pets. Thus we have come to know only how to fight, to beget children, and to take from what we call cattle. For what Tugar would dare to lower his dignity to create with his own hands what can be made by cattle or pets instead?

"And now we are slaves to them. With the coming of the pox, look at us now. Already certain things cannot be replaced—even our supply of arrows starts to grow short. We have forgotten everything our fathers knew and live only off the flesh and labor of others."

"As is our right as Tugars!" Tula roared, and the assembly, coming to their feet, shouted their rage at Qubata, while the few who had listened closely remained silent.

"I knew you would not listen," Qubata said, repeating his words several times before the assembly had finally quieted down.

"So why do you waste our time then?" Zan shouted.

"As a warning," Qubata replied coldly, "and as a final appeal.

"These men are changing. Those who came to us a thousand years ago we were still superior to in weapons and in strength. I have heard Alem speak of the dark-bearded ones who came in a great boat, not unlike the ship of the Yan-

362 *William R. Forstchen*

kees, and how they slew more than a hundred before dying. I have seen their thunder weapon. Now come the Yankees, and their thunder weapons are yet more advanced.

"Do you not see? The race of men is progressing while we stand still."

"So we kill them as soon as they appear from the tunnel," Zan said evenly. "It is that simple."

"Perhaps we can, and that would be an answer. But should we not realize what can be seen? We are slowly slipping backward from a race that could once step to the stars and now cannot even make the weapons our enemies use against us.

"I walked through the great buildings the Yankees used to make their war machines in. Not a Tugar of the entire horde could create such a thing with his own hands, yet these people did it in less than a single year," Qubata roared.

"We still see the fragments of the great cities our fathers once built, and we stand before them as children. We do not build, but the humans do."

"Is there a finish to this?" Tula said coldly. "We need not the ramblings of one who has grown too old to lead and is now afraid."

Qubata looked back at Muzta imploringly, and the Qar Qarth did not move, but Qubata could see in eyes that his time to speak was near an end.

"Then listen to these final words. In parley with the Yankee leader a moon ago, he told us they know the secret of the pox, that it is we ourselves who drive it before us."

"We have all heard that. It is a cattle lie," an Umen leader from the back shouted.

"Then why has the pox not struck them, but has laid waste Vazima and all other places we have been too?"

"They have been lucky, that is all," the leader replied.

And as he looked about the assembly, Qubata could see that even the simple logic regarding the disease would not be accepted.

"I say this, and then shall hear your decision, already knowing what it will be.

"Make terms with these people. Offer to them an end to the slaughter pits and this war in return for food to see us through till the next season."

"Food of cattle, we tolerate," Tula snapped, "but it is the

right of the people to eat the flesh that only Tugars may enjoy. Thus it has always been. Without human flesh we will starve."

"Then we must find another way, for before the humans, did not our fathers eat the food they themselves created? Make terms. In exchange for the peace, they will show us how to stop the pox racing before us.

"I do not say we shall be defenseless. We shall continue our ride about the world, take our tribute, but no longer in human flesh, and then learn from these creatures their secrets. In that is our only hope of final salvation."

Wearily, Qubata looked about the assembly.

"For surely if our fathers once walked the stars, perhaps someday we can learn from these humans how again to make machines, and thus return to what was our true heritage before we fell.

"For what are we now but a race that has slipped into decadence, slaves to the very race we thought we had enslaved?"

Sad-eyed Qubata looked back to his old friend, who, rising, fixed him with his gaze.

"I know this is where we have come to a path that parts, my friend," Qubata said evenly, and then looked back at the assembly.

"My words are my own, and not of my Qar Qarth."

"The cattle must be destroyed," Muzta said evenly, looking past Qubata.

"My friend is an old one who has led us well. But if we leave these Yankees to live, surely when we return they will be too strong to destroy. They must die now."

"Even though we shall starve if we stay," Qubata replied, "for if we advance, the pestilence will still be before us. The Yankees hold the key to that. They can show us how to stop it."

"They must all die and be thrown into the pits," Muzta said sharply. "We will attack until they are dead. You have tried to spare the lives of our warriors with this siege," Muzta continued. "For that you have done well, but each day now we grow weaker. Snow is already in the air. There are half a million undiseased cattle in that city, and I will have them!"

Nodding sadly, Qubata reached to his waist and unbuckled his sword belt, letting the weapon drop to the ground, and then looked back at the assembly.

"My words were my own," the old warrior said sadly. "My Qar Qarth needs one to lead who has the flame of youth in his blood. I retire now to contemplate my final days."

The assembly was silent as Qubata strode from the tent, his head held high. Many of the older clan leaders and warriors lowered their heads in respect as he passed, but among most gathered at the meeting there was an air of excitement and expectation.

Muzta watched his old friend leave and silently cursed. Something in his heart told him that perhaps there was truth in his words, but to change course now was to roar at the wind and expect it to turn away. His own position was far too precarious now, for the bloody losses in the first attacks and the tediousness of the siege were making tempers short. He could fall as well if the situation was not soon changed. For weeks he had tried to argue that point with Qubata, who grew more and more distant. When the clan leaders had called for this meeting he knew that there would be this final parting of ways.

Muzta looked about the assembly, which waited expectantly.

Finally his gaze rested on Tula, and he nodded. The clan leader stepped forward and eagerly swept up the sword, to the roars of approval of the gathering. Muzta looked at his rival without expression. At least now if there was a failure the blame could be shifted. If there was victory, he, Muzta, could still take credit.

"It is time for feasting," Muzta announced, and growling with delight the assembly streamed out of the tent. Two clean ones had been selected for tonight. They were of prime breeding stock, young and full-fleshed, a meal that would divert his quarrelsome nobles for at least a little while.

Tomorrow they could plan, and with good fortune this war would be finished soon, no matter what the loss, which of course would be Tula's responsibility as well.

"It doesn't look good, does it," Andrew asked quietly, still sweeping the enemy position with his field glasses.

"There's something big brewing out there," Hans replied. "All day long there's been riding back and forth. Petracci reports that they've pulled back a lot of them wheeled tents with their women and children—there's not a single warrior now in the upper camps.

"Down!"

The two ducked as a heavy bolt skidded off the roof of their shelter and went careening behind the lines.

"Couriers seem to be doing a lot of galloping up and down the line," Hans continued, cautiously peering back over the rampart.

"I was hoping they'd just continue this damn siege."

"Even though we'll get starved out before spring?"

"Postponing the inevitable, but still postponing," Andrew said quietly. "God knows if they attack it'll cost them."

"Apparently they've changed their minds."

"When do you think they'll hit?" Andrew asked.

"Too late today. First light tomorrow."

"If I were they, I'd push it along the entire line, all six miles of it. We'd have to crack somewhere sooner or later."

Hans merely nodded in agreement.

"All right, then," Andrew said, his voice slow and deliberate. "All units to stand to, two hours before dawn. We'll follow the plan as written. Houston along with the 35th and a battalion of artillery in reserve. The other three divisions on the outside wall, headquarters linked to each division by telegraph. If they force a breech, we'll fight to contain it, but if it starts to spread, we pull everything back to the inner wall."

Andrew looked over at Kal and Casmar.

"I want all noncombatants evacuated from the outer circle starting at dark."

"We'll lose nearly half of all quarters," Kal said softly. "The city will be packed to overflowing."

"We knew that all along," Andrew said sadly. "They've got to stay out of the way of the troops, and they've got to stay calm no matter what. Your holiness, I hope you've got one powerful set of prayers to offer?"

Casmar forced a smile in reply.

"If it is the will of Perm, it is His will," the prelate said evenly.

Without trying to wake her, Hawthorne leaned over and gently kissed Tanya on the cheek. She stirred ever so slightly and then curled back up. Stepping to the cradle, he looked down lovingly at Andrea, straightened her blanket, and then left the room.

Is this what I fight for? Hawthorne thought quietly. Is this what it finally all comes down to in the end? Could I ever stand by and watch my family disappear into the pits and not fight?

Reaching over to the corner, he took his sword and buckled it on.

Or is there more to it now? his other voice whispered. Have I become like the wild beast after all and tasted blood? It was becoming all so easy now, all so easy with the thrill, the cold-blooded thrill of facing death and dealing back to it.

Could he ever forget the moment when he had formed the square, the terrified men looking to him and taking something from him? Taking that something and turning, fighting back. He had never felt so alive as at that moment, every nerve tingling, exalting in life and the power it could give.

He tried to still the voice, but it would not go back to sleep as he wished it would, for even now that feeling was stirring again.

Opening the door, he stepped out into the night and returned Dimitri's salute.

"Your regiment is formed and ready, sir," Dimitri said, smiling broadly.

He loves this as well, Hawthorne thought to himself.

"All right, major, now all we have to do is wait."

"I wish you'd go back into the inner city," Andrew said, a slight note of pleading in his voice.

Brushing the hair from her eyes, Kathleen looked up at Andrew and smiled.

"You know I can't do that," she said softly. "My place is here at the forward hospital. Don't worry—if anything happens I'll have plenty of time to get inside."

Both knew the lie in what she said, but neither could admit it.

Awkwardly they looked at each other, both afraid to admit their fears.

He reached out to hold her, but at his touch she felt herself go rigid.

"Go," she whispered, her voice choking. "Just go. I can't stand the thought this might be goodbye."

"I'll see you at the end of the day," Andrew replied, trying to keep the trembling of his own fears contained.

Kissing her lightly on the forehead, he turned and left.

I can't look at him, she thought, fearful that to do so would somehow be a portent of doom. But as he stepped out of the hospital hut her gaze came up to linger on his form receding into the dark.

"Please God," she whispered, "not again, please not again."

Looking to the hills north of town, he saw their tops bathed in the first red glow of dawn, the light streaking the bare trees, turning the snow the color of blood.

Without comment, Muzta Qar Qarth nodded to Tula, who with a triumphant shout turned from his leader and galloped away. A single narga was given voice, followed by another and another until from one end of the lines to the other a thousand horns thundered and boomed with the call of death.

Chapter 19

"As terrible as an army with banners," Andrew said, looking over at Emil.

The two stood atop the cathedral tower, spellbound by the pageantry of war spread out before them.

From one end of the city to the other the enemy host was drawn up, nearly two hundred thousand warriors, battle standards raised, weapons drawn, the deep rumbling boom of the horns reaching a bone-numbing crescendo.

A dark cloud seemed to rise heavenward, a hundred thousand arrows mingling with flaming bolts, catapult spears, and boulders. In response, a rolling thunder of artillery sounded as over a hundred guns let fly with their deadly loads, followed seconds later by another cloud of arrows and then another.

A wild roar rose up, and as one the horde rushed forward, swarming up out of the trenches and into the deadly killing field separating the two lines.

Onward they came, impervious to losses, waving their swords and axes on high, while behind them yet more clouds of arrows arched overhead.

In seconds the range closed, as the advance swept through the entanglements, leaping over the pitfalls, smashing aside the rows of sharpened stakes.

From the north end of the line a billowing cloud of smoke snapped out, and then like a quick fuse raced down the entire length of fortifications. Hundreds of Tugars tumbled to the ground, yet still they pressed forward, shrieking their terrifying cry.

"Better than reb infantry," Andrew said evenly.

"And more terrifying as well," Emil replied. The old doctor looked at Andrew and patted him on the shoulder.

"I'd best get to my post," Emil said evenly. "Looks like I'll have a lot of business today."

The two, sensing that somehow a parting was coming, looked at each other nervously, and then without comment Emil stepped onto the ladder and went below.

Volley after volley tore across the fields, and as quickly as a Tugar line went down, more rushed forward, driving ever closer to the breastworks. The supporting archers, in block formations, started to weave their way through the entanglements, lowering their trajectories until finally they were shooting straight into the defensive lines. Already Andrew could see casualties tumbling from the firing line, militia units helping to drag the wounded off into the protection of the sheltered ways that led back into the city.

The ground between the outer breastworks and inner wall was rapidly turning into a deadly killing ground, for anyone outside the sheltered paths was forced to run a gauntlet of indirect fire raining out of the skies.

Fires started to break out in the new city between the two walls, those struggling to contain it falling victim to the deadly suppressive fire.

The thundering roar of battle seemed to wash over the city in waves, the horrible screams of the casualties, the unceasing cries of the enemy, and the now continual rattle of musketry and artillery blending into one inferno of sound unlike anything Andrew had ever experienced before.

Just north of the east bastion, dark forms appeared atop the breastworks, leaping into the fire-pit lines. A wild melee of hand-to-hand fighting broke out, reserves of spear-armed militia rushing up the side of the breastworks and pushing and shoving to close the sudden breach.

The telegraph key next to Andrew started to clatter, and Mitchell bent over and furiously started to take down notes.

"Barry, sir," Mitchell called out, "asking for another regiment of musketmen."

"Not yet, dammit," Andrew snapped. "It's only minutes old. Tell him he's got to hold with what he has."

The breach on the wall started to widen. Nervously, Andrew focused his field glasses on the endangered line. He could see Kal's command unit surging forward with thousands of men and prayed silently that they could somehow plug the line. Before he had always stood in the line, caught up in the terrible thrill, losing himself in the strife. Now he had to stand here alone, waiting to move his pieces, to hold as long as possible against the inexorable wave.

"The first breach, my Qarth," Tula roared triumphantly. "The sun not two handspans above the horizon and already we are winning."

Excited, Muzta fought to keep his mount in check, focusing his attention on the gradually expanding hole.

"Push more archers up on the flank to support them," Muzta shouted. "We must stop them from closing it. Keep the pressure up all along the line!"

Grim-faced, Kal stood in the open field, oblivious to the men who circled their leader, holding their shields aloft to protect him from the deadly rain which lashed down around them.

Militia by the thousands swarmed forward, shouting their defiance, and by the hundreds died before even reaching the breach.

The Tugars continued to swarm through the hole now fifty yards wide, some of them now completely off the wall and wading in on the level ground, swinging their swords with deadly ease, slaying two, even three with a single blow.

All was a wild mad press of confusion. From the high bastion to the right, field pieces were swung around, pouring their deadly load down into the swarming sea of confusion below, taking friend and foe alike with each blast.

Yet still the Tugars pushed forward. The militia started to break, looking over their shoulders nervously to the eastern gate, which was aswarm with men coming out to close the gap.

"All right, my mice," Kal shouted, clumsily holding a sword up, "let's see what we can gnaw from them," and despite the protests of his staff, he started forward into the insanity.

"Let's go!" O'Donald shouted, racing out from the northeast bastion. Leaping onto the cab of the *Bangor*, he roared with delight as Malady set the throttle down. The engine strained with the load, its wheels spinning, and then with a lurch the train pushed forward and started clicking down the tracks. Its whistle shrieking, the engine picked up speed, the militiamen swarming down toward the breach leaping to either side as the train, bearing its two metal-shrouded cars ahead and behind the engine, tore down the track.

The press of men around the track grew thicker by the minute, shouting and screaming as waves of arrows slashed into their ranks, while buildings to either side roared into flames. Coming around a bend between two infernos, consuming now-empty warehouses, O'Donald saw their goal a quarter mile away.

"Christ in heaven, Malady, get us there," O'Donald cried.

Crawling out of the cab, O'Donald climbed along the side of the engine, hanging on to the railing as the engine jostled and swayed. Steel-tipped shafts slammed against the engine, striking sparks. Reaching the front coupling, he leaped onto the car ahead of the train and clambered on top.

The track ahead was aswarm with men, who struggled to clear a way, the engine now going ahead at a crawl, its whistle shrieking incessantly.

"Clear it, goddammit!" O'Donald screamed. "Clear a way!"

Gradually they pushed forward, yet at the same time it seemed as if the battle was rushing outward to them as well.

Militia units started to break, struggling vainly to get out of the way of the dark horde. Hundreds of Tugars were now leaping over the battlement, oblivious to loss.

The train hit a low trestle that spanned a broad shallow gully and started to pick up speed again. When it reached the other side, the press of bodies started to give way as militiamen now pushed to the edge of panic started streaming by in the opposite direction.

A lone Tugar stood on the track, staring wide-eyed at the train. Raising his spear, he hurled it at O'Donald, who, ducking low, fired off a shot, sending the warrior staggering to one side.

The train hit the edge of the breach, so that ahead and to the left there was only a thin line of militia giving way, under the inexorable weight of the charge.

"Stop it here, Malady!"

There were still militiamen forward, fighting desperately, but he couldn't wait.

"Get down!" O'Donald screamed. "Get down!"

Those who could see or hear what was about to occur dived to the ground, covering their heads, but not all were aware of what was happening behind them.

"God forgive me," O'Donald whispered, crossing himself, and then, reaching down, he pulled open the hatch between his feet.

"Open up and let the bastards have it!"

The sides of the car dropped open, revealing the muzzles of four Napoleons.

A deafening roar snapped out, the guns firing in sequence, the recoil knocking O'Donald off his feet, and for an instant he feared that the entire car would tumble clear off the track. The other car followed suit with its six four-pounders. Over a thousand iron balls, along with hunks of chain, glass, and scrap metal, slammed into the breach.

The enemy attack was staggered by the blow.

Racing down the length of the car, O'Donald leaped back to the engine, burning his hands when they hit the hot metal. An arrow slashed by, tearing open his sleeve, and his arm suddenly felt like ice. A sheet of arrows came in as he leaped into the cab and ducked down beside Malady.

"Keep inching her forward," O'Donald shouted.

The train rocked again as one after another the four heavy guns forward and the six to the rear repeated their performance.

Behind the train, the militia, taking heart, started to swarm back into the breach. Climbing over the wood tender, O'Donald crawled through the hatchway into the aft car.

The Suzdalian crew were wild with excitement, loading

their pieces, pushing them up through the hatches, and firing into the enemy at near point-blank range.

Arrows skidded in through the firing ports, finding their marks, yet as quickly as a man fell another leaped in to finish the task and fire once again.

"Raise your sights for the walls!" O'Donald cried. "Sweep them damn archers off!"

Moving to the first gun, he sighted down the barrel, spinning the elevation gear down so that the barrel slowly climbed. Satisfied, he stepped back, grabbed hold of the lanyard, and gave a sharp yank. The flintlock trigger set into the breach snapped down. The gun exploded, punching out a whirling hunk of chain and nails that swept the wall clear for half a dozen paces.

Gradually the train inched forward, sewing up the breach as it passed, until finally, as they pushed their way to the edge of the parapet protecting the eastern gate, the Tugars started to break, falling back before the death-dealing dragon.

Heartened, the militia swarmed forward, oblivious to the losses caused by the arrows still raining down. From out of the gatehouse bastion a fresh regiment of musketmen swarmed, pushing up the wall to plug the hole. Within seconds their fire started to sweep outward, driving the last of the attackers back into the moat.

Covered in sweat, his face blackened with powder smoke, O'Donald crawled out of the armored car and forward to Malady, who looked at him, grinning broadly.

"Not the best ride I've had, but pretty damn close," Malady shouted, his voice pitched high like that of a man who was near deaf after the thunder of fire.

"Hold it here!" O'Donald shouted, and leaping from the train he ran toward the covered entryway into the gatehouse. A minute later he came back out, pointing southward.

"Another breach down by the Fort Lincoln road! Let's go!"

As the train pulled out, O'Donald looked back on the carnage they had wrought. For a hundred yards of line, barely a place could be found where the ground was visible. The buildings between the track and the wall were ablaze, casting their lurid light on the carnage.

So thick were the dead and wounded that O'Donald did not even notice a lone peasant who lay spread-eagled on the ground, the standard bearing the image of a mouse by his side.

* * *

"Keep pressing!" Tula shouted, his voice near to breaking. "We cannot stop now—we cannot stop, do you hear me?"

The staff gazed at him, some with fear in their eyes.

Tula looked back at Muzta, who sat expressionless on his mount.

"It is a question of who will break first, my Qarth. They cannot take this pounding much longer!"

Muzta did not even bother to spare his war leader a glance. The sun had shifted to the western sky, yet still the outer works of the cattle held. Half a dozen times they had slashed a way in only to be driven out, by the concentrated blasts of the dragon, or thunder weapons and gun men lined up behind the wall. This has got to end, it's got to end, Muzta thought grimly.

"Prepare the Olkta," Muzta said, looking at Tula, "and send them in there," and as he spoke he pointed to the northeast bastion, wreathed in smoke. "Bring up as many catapults as possible to that position. We move in late afternoon before the sun disappears."

Tula nodded his agreement and gave the orders, sending his couriers galloping out.

Now they will see our surprise, Muzta thought grimly. Though he hated to pollute his people with the instruments of the cattle, which took away all heroism, there was nothing else to be done.

"Bring him over here!" Kathleen cried, horrified at what she was seeing.

An attendant threw a bucket of water across the rough-hewn table, and the casualty was laid down.

Weakly Kal opened his eyes to look at her.

"This mouse forgot to duck. I must talk to O'Donald about his aim," the peasant said, trying vainly to smile.

"Oh Kal, Kal," she whispered, trying to force back her tears.

She had studied with Emil for months preparing for this day. Why the hell wasn't he here? Arrow wounds, cuts, and stabs she could patch, but this? She had helped Emil after the first round of battles, but now for the first time she would have to do it on her own.

A young Suzdalian girl came up to Kal's side and gently

tried to cut his tunic off. He tried to stifle his screams as the blood-caked garment was peeled off the wounds. Working quickly, the girl wiped the blood off the mangled arm.

Turning away, Kathleen stuck her hands into a fresh bowl of tincture of lime, rushing to scrub.

What was this, the fiftieth, the hundredth casualty today?

A thunderclap roar echoed through the room, the wounded inside stirring nervously and looking about with fear. From outside the door she could see a building collapsing in flames.

Don't think about it, she kept trying to tell herself. Don't be afraid.

She motioned to the boiling kettle. An attendant pulled a hot pincer out of the fire, and using it to reach into the kettle, fished out the instruments, laying them on a freshly boiled rag.

Nerving herself, she came up to Kal's side.

"It'll hurt," she whispered soothingly.

Kal grimaced and closed his eyes. She already knew what would have to be done, looking at the mangled limb, but hoping against hope, she slipped her finger into the wound. Arching his back, Kal let out a muffled scream as her finger, probing inward, felt nothing but jagged splinters of bone.

Gently she pulled her hand back.

"You know what I have to do?" Kathleen whispered.

Wide-eyed, the peasant merely nodded.

"We still have something to put you to sleep while I work," Kathleen said, motioning to her assistant.

"Do you have enough for everyone?" he asked.

"Of course," she said, lying.

"I think for once I'll take advantage of my rank and take the special treatment," the peasant whispered.

"Go to sleep now," Kathleen replied, her voice husky.

The attendant stepped forward with the paper cone and started to place it over Kal's face.

"Now your colonel and I can buy our gloves together," Kal whispered, trying to force a laugh even as he drifted off into blessed oblivion.

"Dear God, please let me save this man," she said, openly making the sign of the cross for the first time in years.

Bending over, she started to cut.

Wearily Andrew leaned against the parapet, trying to

force down a cup of scalding tea brought to him by a young acolyte. The entire outer ring of the city seemed wreathed in flames, covered with a roiling blanket of smoke, punctuated by unceasing explosions, and roaring fires now consuming most of what was left of the new city.

"Can we stop them?" Casmar asked nervously, looking out at the madness.

"We at least are making them pay for their dinner," Andrew said grimly.

Mitchell, sweat streaking his face in spite of the cold, tore off another sheet of paper and handed it to Andrew.

Andrew turned and looked up at the balloon hanging several hundred feet above him. Picking up his field glasses, he tried to see through the smoke in the direction Petracci had indicated to him.

A gust of wind came out of the west, and for a moment, as if a curtain were being drawn back, the smoke parted.

Andrew put down his glasses and looked over at Mitchell.

"Send word down to Houston to prepare to move the rest of the reserves to the northeast bastion on my command. Contact the south bastion and tell them to move the armor train northward and be quick about it. Tell Hans we're bringing up everything we've got."

Andrew handed the field glasses over to Casmar, who gasped in disbelief.

"This is the test," Andrew said coldly, taking the glasses back.

Since dawn the attack had been raging all along the line. Half a dozen breaches had been cut, the latest and worst down by the south wall, where he had finally been forced to commit half his reserves, which were just now sealing the breach.

And now, as the sun hung low in the western sky, the enemy were throwing their major blow, the block of fifty thousand warriors who had stood motionless throughout the day coming now like an arrow point straight at the northeast bastion.

Muzta Qar Qarth pulled his mount over to the side, letting the first lines of the advancing host march past. A hundred nargas were about him, sounding their deep-throated call, a hundred drummers of doom swung their mallets, setting up a thundering roar that put one's hair on edge.

"Muzta, Muzta, Muzta!" the Olkta roared, as they climbed up over the entrenchments and started forward at the double, Tula in the lead. Thousands of mounted archers swung out to either side, bending their bows, aiming heavenward, launching their deadly flights, and then yet another and another.

"May I still ride with you, my Qarth?"

Muzta turned to see Qubata come up by his side, wearing the simple armor of an ordinary warrior, a battered scabbard hanging at his side.

Muzta was silent for a moment.

"You should be with the old ones," he said quietly.

Qubata tried to force a smile.

"You would not heed my warning," Qubata said evenly, "and thus Tula has given you this," and he pointed out across the bloody field of action.

"But you are still my Qar Qarth, the horde are still my people, a place of battle still my choice for where I wish to die. Besides, I heard my little experiment was about to be used, and I wished to see it."

"Go back," Muzta said evenly.

Qubata shook his head.

The briefest of smiles crossed Muzta's features.

"Let us go see what these creatures you now call men are made of," the Qar Qarth said quietly, and bringing his mount around, he fell in alongside the advancing ranks.

"Hold your fire!" Hans shouted, leaping up onto the battlement walls, oblivious to the rain of arrows slashing past.

Their reserves were nearly depleted. Nearly ten hours of continual fighting had consumed ammunition at a fearful rate.

The first ranks were coming in at the charge. Crouched low, Hans held his carbine up high, and then pointed it straight down.

A thousand muskets and a dozen artillery pieces snapped out.

Instantly the view disappeared in clouds of billowing smoke. From out of the shadows he saw the enemy swarming forward, leaping into the moat, scrambling up the sides.

Jumping back into the protection of the bastion, Hans looked around at his battle-weary men. They were stretched to the limit. They had to break this attack quickly or break themselves.

Along a front of four hundred yards, the concentrated wave hit, pushing relentlessly forward. Within minutes he could see shadowy forms gaining the top of the breastworks, tumbling over as the defenders fired wildly, and then yet more would leap to fill the gaps.

Never in all his years had he seen such fury in attack. Not even at Antietam when six times the rebs had charged across the cornfield, their casualties stretched out in rows from the devastating volleys that greeted them.

"Ammunition is almost out!" an aide shouted, pointing back to the magazine, where men were hurriedly pulling out boxes laden with cartridges and packed artillery rounds.

Looking back over the wall, he saw something that left him speechless.

From out of the Tugar formation a double line came running forward, their long legs bounding in ten-foot strides. Leaping into the moat, they scrambled up the wall, just south of the bastion, shouldering aside the warriors in front of them. In their hands they carried muskets.

They've figured out how to use them, Hans thought, feeling sick with the shock of what was unfolding.

As one the enemy gained the top of the wall. Hundreds of muskets were lowered, pointing straight down at the defenders, who were still in double line, grimly holding on.

A sheet of fire washed out from the Tugar line. A hundred or more casualties tumbled back from the breastworks. In an instant the regiment holding the line broke and started to run at the sight of the Tugars who now bore weapons like their own.

A storm of ax-wielding warriors came over the wall, charging through the Tugar musketmen, who clumsily reloaded their pieces.

Several artillery pieces in the bastion swept them with canister, knocking down dozens, but still they held. Another volley slashed out, ripping over the heads of the ax warriors sliding down inside the breastworks, tearing gaping holes in the Novrodian regiment which was attempting to regroup. The line broke apart from the blow, and, panic-stricken, headed for the rear.

The militia who had surged up to plug the hole stood dumbfounded at the sight before them, and with wild cries of consternation started to flee.

Hans watched grim-faced as within seconds a hole two hundred yards wide was cleaved into his position.

"The other side too," someone shouted, and racing down the bastion line, Hans came up to the northwest corner. Down by the river road he saw another hole, even bigger than the first, with Tugar musketmen swinging outward, their fire punching the defenders back.

From over by the river the *Ogunquit* was pouring out broadside after broadside into the flank of the charge, but still the enemy pushed in regardless of loss.

Hans walked over to the telegrapher.

"Signal back to headquarters," he said quietly. "Low on ammunition, am abandoning the northeast bastion, suggest entire outer line be evacuated."

Hans turned away from the wide-eyed signaler and looked around at his staff.

"Spike the guns, and let's get the hell out of here before it's too late."

Horrified, O'Donald leaped atop the armored car for a better view as the train, backing up the track, came to a halt.

From the outer breastworks to the inner wall, the Tugars were swarming in by the thousands. There was no hope of going forward, as thousands of panic-stricken men streamed past, pushing in a giant seething mass through the eastern gate by his side to reach the supposed safety of the inner city.

O'Donald ripped open the hatch and stuck his head into the car.

"Tear open the sides and get the guns out of here," he screamed.

Jumping down, O'Donald ran down the length of the car, yanking off the bolts that held the collapsible side in place. The men inside pushed outward, and the side of the car dropped out.

Grabbing hold of ropes, the gun crew swarmed out, pulling on the Napoleons. The pieces were edged out and clattered down the car side, which was now a ramp.

The men struggled to control the one-ton monsters which crashed into the mob streaming past, crushing a number of refugees. No one stopped to help the fallen in the mad flight.

Racing past the *Bangor*, O'Donald prepared to climb atop the other armored car. But he saw it was useless to try—the mob was pressing in too tight around the train.

"Spike the guns and get the hell out!" O'Donald shouted to the Suzdalian crew, who abandoned their weapons and, falling in with the Napoleon crews, started to maneuver the weapons to safety on the other side of the eastern gate.

"Malady, let's get the hell out of here!" O'Donald shouted, climbing back into the cab.

"Just let me shut her down," Malady shouted. "I'll be along in a minute."

O'Donald grabbed hold of his hand.

"Don't do anything stupid," the artilleryman said, staring straight into the burly engineer's eyes.

"Who, me? Get the hell out of here, you dumb Irishman."

Sensing something, O'Donald pulled the revolver out of his holster, tossed it over, and disappeared into the swirling retreat.

Grabbing a heavy wrench, Malady jumped from the cab and rushed to the front of the train. Climbing onto the coupling he disconnected the engine from the forward car, which had held the heavy Napoleons. Then he climbed atop the engine and swung the wrench down, smashing the steam safety valve into a mass of twisted metal.

Climbing back aboard the cab, he grabbed hold of his Suzdalian fireman by the scruff of the neck and heaved him bodily off the train.

"Can't take this ride, son," Malady shouted.

Opening the steam valve wide open, he let the pressure build, waiting as the panic-stricken mob stormed past. Finally the first Tugar came charging by, mingled in with the crowd, and then another and finally a surging mass.

He released the brakes and opened the throttle a notch. The *Bangor* lurched backward, gaining speed, while with each passing second the pressure in the boilers continued to build.

Malady leaned out of the cabin, looking past the wood tender and armored car.

A solid line of Tugars, in discipline ranks, were coming forward at the double.

"I'm going with you, *Bangor!*" Malady roared as the train smashed into the enemy line like a hot razor cutting through ice.

With a revolver in either hand the engineer fired away, roaring with delight.

"Come on, you bastards!"

The engine careened up the track, slamming into a body of mounted warriors, the armored car derailing from the impact.

Hundreds of Tugars swarmed over the crippled dragon, slashing at it with swords and axes, clambering into the cab of the engine as pistol shots still rang out.

In an instant all disappeared in a swirling mass of steam, fire, and exploding metal.

At the gallop, Muzta, with Qubata at his side, angled his mount up the side of the parapet, the horses dancing skittishly over the bodies. Gaining the top, he reined in for a moment, exulting at the view.

For hundreds of yards to either side, his army was sweeping forward.

A deep hollow roar washed over him, and looking to his left he saw an outward-rolling cloud of steam and fire. Grim-faced, Muzta watched as the white shadow of death swept away, revealing a massive hole in the line. The battle paused for a moment, and then his host pushed on toward the eastern gate.

"Magnificent!" Muzta screamed, watching as hundreds of archers now turned their fire away from the enemy and, kindling burning brands, started to launch an unending stream of fire against the wooden walls of the inner city.

"Make sure the catapults are dragged forward," Muzta cried. "Position them all along these battlements and on that corner fort," and as he spoke he pointed to the northeast bastion, where a horsetail standard now fluttered in the evening breeze.

"It's magnificent, Qubata, magnificent."

But the old warrior was silent, looking grimly at the thousands who lay upon the field, the price for this madness.

"Let us go forward and draw some blood," Muzta cried, pointing to a swarm of militia fighting desperately to get through the narrow northeastern gate.

"Get him out of here now!" Kathleen cried to her assistant, standing next to the litter held by four stretcher bearers. "Take him to Dr. Weiss—he's in the main cathedral."

"Come with us now," the girl pleaded.

"In a minute," Kathleen said, trying to be heard above the unbelievable uproar outside the hospital. "I can't leave this man here till I'm finished," she said, pointing back to a young Suzdalian clutching his shot-torn leg. "He won't make it if I don't stop the bleeding. Get Kal back to safety!"

Kal tried to say something, raising his head from the litter. Quickly Kathleen knelt down and kissed him on the forehead.

"Tell Andrew I'll always love him," she whispered.

Turning away, she returned to the table, and talking softly, she eased the wounded soldier into his sleep and started to work.

"Clear a way," Andrew cried, trying to force through the terrified mob.

At the head of the column he felt helpless, unable to move forward as thousands streamed past him. The 35th had formed a rough line before him, sorting out the broken regiments rushing in, sending them up to the wooden walls of the inner city, which were already engulfed in flames.

"Andrew!"

Through the gate Hans came into view, blood streaming down his face.

Andrew dismounted and pushed up to his old friend.

"You can't stop it out there," Hans said, leaning over his horse and gasping for breath.

"I thought maybe we could save those men still outside."

"If you send what's left of our reserve, they'll get swallowed up. We're going to need them in here."

Andrew looked at Hans, realizing the final difference between the two of them. He would still risk whatever he had to try to save his men. What he had done to Hawthorne still haunted him. Hans, however, could stand by when need be and make the sacrifice.

"You can't do anything for them. Those that can make the gate will have to do it on their own."

"Let's take a look, then," Andrew said, trying to still his inner anguish.

Gaining a ladder to the wall, the two climbed up and stepped out onto the wooden battlement, even as an unending stream of fire arrows whistled down about them.

The area about the gate for a hundred yards across was a

horrifying knot of soldiers and militia desperately seeking
safety, the Tugars pushing in from all sides.

"Get the 35th up here," Andrew cried. Moments later the
blue-clad men came scrambling up onto the wooden battlement and started to pour in a scathing fire on the ring of
warriors pushing in on the terrified circle of men.

Casualties started to tumble from the battlement as, unmindful of their losses, the regiment fought to keep the
pressure off their retreating comrades.

The knot about the gate grew smaller and smaller, the
Tugars pressing in hesitating at last beneath the deadly rain
of rifle fire, delivered by seasoned veterans who could not
miss, so compacted were the lines of their enemies below.

Toward the back of the mob Andrew saw a litter and
instantly recognized who was being carried. With the litter
barely through the gate, the portal was finally slammed
shut. The walls were now roaring with flames, the aged
wooden logs igniting under the incessant sheets of fire arrows poured into them. Already some of the men were
giving back from the heat and smoke that engulfed them.

Horrified, Andrew watched while knots of survivors who
had not gained safety fought with a final desperation as the
Tugars closed in for the kill.

Rushing from the battlement, Andrew reached the street
and saw the litter being carried forward with the crowd.

Pushing his way through, he stopped the litter and leaned
over.

"Kal, my friend," Andrew cried, looking at the gaunt-
eyed man before him. Andrew looked over the blanket and
saw the emptiness where Kal's right arm should have been.

"Kal," and kneeling down he touched his friend gently.

Stirring, Kal looked up and tried to force a smile.

"This wound will do wonders for my career as a Yankee
politician," Kal said wanly. "Now our people will have two
one-armed candidates for president."

Andrew could not help but force a smile, realizing that
Kal could still somehow joke, even as the world came crashing down about them.

"Your Kathleen saved my life," Kal whispered. "She is a
good doctor."

"Kathleen? Did she get out of there?" Andrew asked, his
voice choked with fear.

"Surely," Kal whispered, his voice growing hazy as he started to drift off. "She said she'd be right behind me."

The peasant tried to say something more, but blessed unconsciousness swept over him.

"Get him to Doc Weiss at the cathedral," Andrew said.

The party continued on their way. Numbly he stood up and looked at the now closed gate.

"You've got to get back to your post, son," Hans said softly, his hand resting on Andrew's shoulder.

"Damn them all," Andrew whispered hoarsely.

Terrified, she looked up at the towering presence coming through the door.

Feebly a, wounded Suzdalian came to his feet, raising a musket.

With a backhanded blow the man's head was swept away, the Tugar roaring with delight.

More and more poured in, laughing, shouting, their swords rising and falling mechanically in a frenzy of killing.

She looked down at her patient, his leg half off, arteries still spilling blood which she had been racing to stem.

At least he'll never know, she thought, releasing her hand from where she had been tying off a knot.

In silence she waited for the end, the Tugars seeing her, but paying no heed yet as they joyfully continued with the butchery.

A roaring bellow filled the room, even as a Tugar, grinning wickedly, started to advance toward her. Startled, she jumped at the sound. A Tugar dressed in armor of gold stood in the doorway. As one the warriors in the room bowed low, fear in their eyes.

The golden-armored warrior advanced down the length of the hospital room, looking at the carnage and the still-living men lying in their cots, waiting stoically for the end.

The Tugar came up to Kathleen and stopped, looking down at her, his teeth glinting in the firelight. Looking back over his shoulder, he spoke rapidly, and a bent-over warrior with graying arms and mane came up to his side.

"Are you a healer?" Qubata asked.

Startled that a Tugar could speak Russian, Kathleen merely nodded in reply.

Qubata pointed to the man lying on the table.

"You are attempting to heal him?" he asked softly.

"For you people to slaughter?" Kathleen said coldly. "I'll let him bleed to death first. It's more merciful."

"I promise him his life," Qubata replied. "I give him my exemption. Now heal him."

Kathleen, trying to still the shaking of her hands, went back to her task, hooking loops of thread over arteries, tying them off quickly, cutting back more, tying off again.

Finally most of the leg was cut away. Grabbing hold of the saw, she cut through the bone, and picking the scapel back up, she sliced away the last of the flesh.

Pushing the limb aside, she bent over, grabbed hold of the extended flaps of flesh, folded them in, and stitched the wound shut.

Finished, she looked back up and started to tremble.

"You are a Yankee woman," Qubata announced evenly. "I know no one of this world who could do what you have done, not even among our own people."

"Because you're too busy with butchering instead," Kathleen snapped back angrily.

"I have heard many reports from the people of Vazima who fled from your Yankee commander, Keane. They say he had a Yankee woman. Are you she?"

Kathleen remained silent.

Qubata slowly nodded his head, then spoke to Muzta.

Muzta, looking about the room, said something to Qubata in reply and started to leave. Stopping at the door, he pointed at Kathleen, spoke a short command, and then stepped back out into the battle.

"What did he say?" she asked nervously.

"Just that there is much good meat here," Qubata replied evenly.

"And myself?"

"You as well," Qubata replied softly.

The sound of battle gradually ebbed with the setting of the sun, so that Andrew, sitting in the jam-packed square with his staff, thought for a moment that he was going deaf, for how else could it now be so quiet.

Drained with exhaustion, he stood up and looked around. An expectant hush had fallen over the men as they looked at each other uneasily.

Mitchell came out of the cathedral, a note in his hand.

Taking the paper, Andrew scanned the contents, then handed it over to Hans.

"Let's go hear what they have to say. Hans, your holiness, would you please come with me as well. Tell Emil to join us too," he said evenly, going over to his mount.

The three started down the jam-packed street, lit by the soaring fires consuming the outer wall. At their passage, all fell silent, looking up numbly at their leaders. The streets were now clogged with women, children, the old and infirm. Many of them were weeping, searching through the confused ranks. Others, finding a loved one still alive, clung desperately to his side.

"What do we have left?" Andrew asked.

"The three forward divisions are just about shattered. Many units lost sixty, even seventy percent," Hans replied. "Most of the artillery on the outer wall is lost. We have the one division in reserve and a battalion of guns. That's about it."

"Militia?"

"Broken, Andrew. Most of them are searching now for their families. They'll fight when the time comes, but not with any organization. It'll be street-by-street with them, nothing more."

"So we have three thousand men in one intact division and maybe another four thousand disorganized men lining the walls."

"That's about it. As near as I can figure, we broke at least ten of their large block formations, but they have at least five, maybe ten, in reserve."

"Well, we gave them a hell of a fight at least," Andrew said dryly. "But it's not enough, just not enough."

Coming to the edge of the wall, Andrew was stunned by the massive inferno consuming their final line of protection along the northern half of the city. Already some sections were caving in amid showers of sparks that rose upward on the westerly breeze.

Sections of the city down in the lower northern half were ablaze as well, driving yet hundreds of thousands more to the protection of the upper city.

A small section of wall not yet consumed stood out darkly, the eastern stone gate beneath the wall still shut.

A knot of men from O'Donald's command stood about the gate, their four-pounders deployed across the road, and at Andrew's approach O'Donald came limping up.

"They drew back off and then we saw this knot of Tugars come up waving a white banner," O'Donald said. "Shot a couple of them, but they simply stood there. Finally we realized they wanted to talk, so I called for a cease-fire and sent a message up to you."

"All right, then," Andrew said wearily, "let's go up and find out."

Climbing up atop the gate, Andrew looked out over the flame-lit field. To the north he could see all of the new city given over to flames, which even now were starting to subside, the wooden walls to the old city shrouded from end to end with fire. Long sections had already collapsed in, leaving large gaping holes in the line. Beyond the new city, shadowy blocks of Tugars numbering in the tens of thousands stood poised for the final assault.

Calling for a torch, Andrew held it aloft as Hans and Casmar came up by his side, followed a moment later by Emil, who climbed up the ladder, his uniform soaked nearly to the shoulders with blood.

"The one called Keane—is he now present, with the holy leader of Suzdal, and the healer of the Yankees?" the Namer of Time shouted, coming forward.

"We are here."

"I am the Namer of Time. Once I rode to your city and was insulted by you. Now I have come as I promised under the rule of my lord Muzta Qar Qarth, master of all Tugars and cattle."

"What is it that you want?" Andrew said coldly.

"The submission of all the cattle of Suzdal and of the Yankees. Behold, your armies have been driven from the field, their corpses filling the bellies of our warriors. Your flimsy walls of wood to the north burn down to mere kindling. Your defiance is at an end, and in our mercy we now offer you terms."

"Go on then," Andrew replied, wishing somehow that perhaps there was still hope, even though he knew such dreams were vain.

"I speak now to the holy one, and not to the Yankee who has created this tragedy. The people of Suzdal are to surrender immediately to the horde. Your city will be destroyed for your act of defiance, but we will spare you, exacting tribute of five in ten for punishment. But the rest of your people will be taken to new places and there allowed to build again.

"For your Yankees we offer life as well. But you will become the pets of the horde. Those with skills we will give tasks to according to their abilities. But we demand, as is our right, the knowledge to stop the pox sickness.

"If you refuse, none shall be spared, all shall go into the feasting pits. Know as well that your defiance will cause the death of yet millions more from the pox. These are our terms. If you refuse, know that the city shall be ours. Be not fools, for surely you know that you have lost."

Sick at heart, Andrew looked at his companions.

"It has come to what I always feared it would," he said softly. "We tried as best we could, but their numbers were just too many."

Casmar looked at Andrew, putting his hand on the young officer's shoulder.

"Yet you showed us how to be men," the prelate replied, a gentle smile lighting his features.

"If you wish to surrender, your holiness, I will accept it."

The priest stood silent for several minutes as if lost in prayer.

"No," he said softly, finally breaking the silence. "No, I think not."

"There are hundreds of thousands who could live," Andrew said weakly.

"Live to be cattle again. Live so again boyar and church will grow in its corruption, squabbling, feeding their own people into the pit. I'd rather that for this final night we showed those creatures outside that men were not meant to be slaves. Let our people be consumed in the fire together, pure at the end, men and women no longer beasts. That will be something the Tugars will never forget. Perhaps word of what we have done will spread with the Wanderers and give hope to others. We have hurt them sorely here. In their hearts they must know that we represent a change in the order of this world, and to submit would only show that in the end we were weak, the cattle they expect us to be.

"No, I will not order my people to go into the pits without a fight. God bless you now, my son," the prelate said, making the sign of the cross over Andrew. "If you wish to take your people with you and leave aboard your ship, I shall understand. Perhaps then you can carry on your struggle somewhere else."

God help me, Andrew thought. So this is the ending of it, that cold premonition of long ago now at hand. How he had fought to delay it, and in his soul he feared that with this vain hope of freedom he had led not only his regiment to final doom, but all the people of Suzdal as well.

"We stand by you to the end," Andrew said softly.

"If we gave them the secret of vaccination, they'd use it just to breed more cattle," Emil said, trying to come to some accommodation with his code of saving life.

Casmar nodded for Andrew to give a reply, and feeling numb with remorse and yet fired with a rising hatred, he stepped back to the battlement.

"You'll have us when we're dead," Andrew roared. "We'll pile our corpses into the fire to keep them from you. If you want the city, come take it over the bodies of your warriors."

The Namer shook his head, stunned with the response.

"Then what is written in the soul of the sky must be," the Namer replied, "and I shall search for your liver when this is done.

"And to the one called Keane, my lord wishes you to know that the Yankee cattle named Kathleen shall be brought before his table when the battle is done!"

"God damn you to hell!" Andrew screamed, reaching for his revolver. Pulling the weapon, he shouted with incoherent rage as the Namer galloped off before Andrew could fire.

His companions stood silent, horrified. Finally Andrew turned back to face them, his features wooden, lifeless.

"Prepare the men," Andrew said coldly. "Form the 35th and our artillery in the square. That's where we'll make our final stand."

"I told you they would answer such," Qubata said evenly, looking over at Muzta, who sat grim-faced as the Namer galloped back up to his side.

"I want the city leveled by morning. Take prisoners when possible to fill our pots later—too much meat has gone to waste already," Muzta said coldly. "Let us finish with them, for they are a damnation to this world."

"In your inner heart you know I am right," Qubata said gently. "This never should have happened."

"Yet it has," Muzta roared. "I have lost three times ten

thousand dead, and twice as many wounded. I want them to pay."

"And bleed ourselves to the edge of extinction?" Qubata replied.

"It is nearly done, my Qarth," Tula cried. "Now let me finish it!"

Wearily Muzta nodded his head, and as Tula galloped off to the north, the nargas signaled for the storm to be unleashed.

"In your inner heart you know I am right," Qubata again whispered.

His features drained, Muzta merely looked to his old companion and forced a smile.

"Perhaps too much has happened here today to go back to what I wish might have been. Your time has passed, my friend. Now stay with me through this night."

"And the woman?" Qubata asked, as if in an afterthought.

"What of her? I shall at least gain some pleasure when I feast upon her brain."

"To take a bitter vengeance on a worthy foe who fought merely to save the lives of his people? Venting your rage on someone who is innocent—will that change this?"

"Yes!"

"She could teach us much about healing, perhaps even revealing how to stop the pox, But more than that, she is worthy of our respect, as is Keane. My Qarth, if that is what you truly wish, then I am sad for you. I will serve by you tonight, but Muzta, I can no longer even call you my friend."

Muzta turned and started to say something, but his words were drowned out by the rising thunder of battle.

The northern half of the host started to sweep forward, and within minutes were crashing over the charred walls. The screams of hundreds of thousands rose up from the city as the Tugars, roaring with triumph, pushed inward.

"Keep a ring to the south," Muzta commanded, "I want everything else poured in through the breach. I want no more lives wasted against any walls that still stand.

"Now let's go in there and finish this slaughter," Muzta said, his voice edged with what Qubata knew to be a deep sadness.

Chapter 20

Horrified, Hawthorne turned to look back into the pit of hell. The entire northern sky roared with the conflagration, and still they came on and on, till Tugars, fire, and the endless stream of refugees blended into one sustained nightmare that drove him to the edge of reason.

He had given up all hope of keeping his command together in the fear-choked rampage. All order was breaking away as the terrified masses filled the streets southward so that it was impossible to move. The Tugars, unrelenting in their fury, pushed them ever back, slaying as they advanced.

Reaching the square, he looked around, dazed. Drawn across the great square stood the last remaining formations, in the center the men of the 35th and O'Donald with his four Napoleons.

Staggering, he was swept along with the surging mass of humanity. Perhaps he could still get to Tanya and the baby. At least Andrew had allowed them to be moved into the cathedral for the end. Weaving through the crowd, he reached the lines of the 35th, collapsing with exhaustion, Dimitri, clutching the flame-scorched standard of the regiment, the only one left to his command.

"Your regiment, boy?" Hans said, coming up and pulling him to his feet.

"Gone. I lost contact with them down by the docks."

"You did what you could, son," Hans said evenly. "Find a rifle and get in the line."

"Is this it, then?" Hawthorne said numbly.

Hans merely nodded in reply and pushed his way through the press, roaring for the people before him to clear the square.

Leaving Dimitri with a knot of Suzdalians from a dozen different regiments, Hawthorne pushed his way into the cathedral, looking desperately about. A service was going on, Casmar at the altar, but his words could not be heard above the wild shrieks.

Pushing his way forward, he kept screaming for Tanya. A young acolyte came up to him. Grabbing hold of Vincent's sleeve, he pulled the boy down a packed corridor, opened a door, and guided him in.

In the narrow room he saw Kal look up at him, Tanya, the baby, and Ludmilla by his side.

Kal's eyes were questioning. Hawthorne shook his head sadly and sat down by the old peasant's cot.

"We gave them a fight they'll never forget," Kal said weakly, reaching out and taking Hawthorne's hand. Tanya, kneeling down beside him, said nothing, trying to hide her fear.

"It's just this damn fire I fear," Kal said weakly. "I've always been afraid of fire. Must have been from seeing their roasting pits when I was a boy."

"The entire lower city's in flames," Hawthorne said softly.

"I always told Ivor he should make ways to stop fires. Seemed like every twenty years most of the city would burn. The stupid fat man never could see the sense of building cisterns. Ah well, so now it'll burn once and for all."

"The wind out of the west is stirring it up," Hawthorne said, as if by talking the fear of the moment could go away. "At least the flames aren't coming this way—they're blowing straight over the Tugar camp. I heard some of their tents have caught."

"Let 'em get water from the dam," Kal mumbled. "Hell, at least something I built will be left."

Suddenly Hawthorne stood up and looked about the room. Grabbing hold of Tanya, he kissed her for a long lingering moment.

Nothing was said, but both understood what the parting meant.

"God keep all of you," he whispered and then pushed out the door.

Going through the door, he made his way down the corridor, and finding a narrow doorway, he pulled it open and raced up the stairs two at a time, till reaching the top he stepped out breathless.

"Colonel Keane?" he cried, looking about.

The few staff members there shook their heads and pointed back down into the square.

Hawthorne went to the eastern side of the tower and looked out. Flames from the city were racing straight eastward, lighting the sky. Across the entire lower half of the city, down to the dry banks of the Vina, Tugars by the tens of thousands were pushing forward, pouring in through the gaping holes in the defensive line.

Turning, Hawthorne looked straight up. Petracci's balloon still dangled overhead, its lone occupant leaning over, his terrified cries lost in the uproar.

Hawthorne leaped to the steps and raced back down. Pushing his way through the crowd, he forced his way back out into the square. Seeing several of Andrew's staff, he called to them, asking for the colonel, and like their comrades above they simply pointed out to the square.

"Find him!" Hawthorne shouted. "Have him meet me where the balloon is launched!" The men looked at him as if he were mad, but several started off in search.

Shoving his way through the crowd, Hawthorne made for the center of the square. A walk that before would not have taken more than a couple of minutes now seemed to take hours. At last he reached the platform, the men of the 35th anchored around it, the Napoleons flanked to either side.

"Help me get Hank down," Hawthorne shouted, pointing heavenward.

"Jesus, we forgot all about that fool," one of the men said. Grabbing hold of the windlass, several men started to wind in the cable. Twirling and spinning, the balloon came back to earth, straining out on the breeze so that it almost hit the highest spire of the church. Downward it came, largely ignored by the multitude in the square, so intent were they on the doom sweeping up from the north.

At last the balloon dangled directly overhead. Hank climbed over the side and leaped out, collapsing on the platform.

"I've been up there sixteen hours," he gasped. "You bastards forgot about me. I thought for sure that some burning brand would hit it and blow me apart!"

"Have you ever seen one of these things flown in free flight?" Hawthorne demanded.

"Are you mad?" Hank said faintly. "I'm never going up in that thing again. It could kill you."

"Then, dammit, get out of my way," Hawthorne shouted.

Looking around, Hawthorne could not see Andrew or Hans. Then the hell with it—he'd do it with or without orders.

Leaping off the platform, he saw O'Donald and pushed his way up.

"O'Donald, do you have any barrels of powder with your guns?"

"A couple of hundred pounds tied to one of the limbers."

"I need a hundred pounds now!"

"What the hell for? I'm going to pack the guns with it and blow them apart when we run out of shot."

"Just give me the powder," Hawthorne shouted desperately. "I'll tell you about it while we're loading."

"Captain, we can't leave them," Bullfinch, the young first officer, pleaded.

"It's lost, dammit," Tobias shouted. "It's all lost. So what the hell good is there in staying? I told that Keane a year ago he was a fool for staying here. With this ship we could have carved out our own empire without fear of these Tugars. But no, the damn fool wants to go and free these Suzdalians, like another Lincoln freeing the niggers.

"The hell with him. Now cast off the line. We're pulling out while we still can."

Bullfinch looked about at the men on deck. Tobias had shrewdly allowed his Suzdalian gun crews to bring their families aboard the night before, and he could sense that all of them, now seeing a way out, would follow the captain.

"With this ship we'll go back to those bastards down south and make ourselves kings. Now let's go."

"You can go to hell," Bullfinch snapped, heading for the gangplank. "I'm staying here. I'd rather die now than live with the shame you'll bear."

Bullfinch stepped down the gangplank. A young private from the 35th came out of the crowds lining the dock and raced for the gangplank.

"I'm going with him," the private cried.

"Who the hell is that?" Tobias roared, standing alongside the field gun trained down the gangplank, which he had used to keep the mob back.

"Private Hinsen, sir!"

Tobias smiled.

"Come aboard, private. I need men like you!"

Grinning sardonically at Bullfinch, Hinsen shoved his way past and leaped aboard the ship.

The lines were cast off, and the lone officer stood in silence as the *Ogunquit*, making steam, turned out into midchannel. With the river foaming under its stern the *Ogunquit* turned southward and disappeared from view, pushing its way past the dozens of ships, packed with refugees, that were making for the inland sea.

"You're a madman, God bless you," O'Donald shouted, passing up a pick and shovel.

"Just tell Keane if you can find him."

"I'll try, but not much luck on that now. It's your decision and mine, and I say do it!"

"You have any matches?"

"What a damned question at a time like this," O'Donald roared, pointing to the conflagration. Fumbling in his pockets, he pulled out a container of lucifers.

"Just a moment," and reaching into another pocket he pulled out a cigar, bit off the end, and started to strike a light.

"Don't!" Hawthorne cried.

"Already done, laddie," as the flame snapped to light. Puffing cheerily, O'Donald looked back to the north.

"Might as well enjoy it while I can," he said grimly. "Goodbye, laddie, and good luck. Blow 'em to hell."

Pulling out a knife, he cut the tether line and passed the blade up to the young pilot. As the balloon started up, O'Donald unholstered his revolver and tossed it into Hawthorne's outstretched hands.

The balloon, burdened to its limit, hung motionless. A single sandbag remained on the side, and Hawthorne cut it away.

With a bounce the balloon started to climb away. As it cleared the ruins of the palace to the west, the wind grabbed hold of the gas-filled bag, pushing it straight at the cathedral. There was nothing to do but hang on. The main steeple filled the sky, and with a jarring thud the balloon slammed into it, skidding up the side.

Terrified, Hawthorne hung on, praying the balloon wouldn't snag on the top of the steeple. Ever so lazily the balloon rolled across the side of the tower and then pulled free, swinging the basket beneath it in wild crazy arcs.

The entire panorama of the battle was spread out before him. To the north in the silvery moonlight he could see a tightly packed double line of Tugars around the northern end of the city, no longer advancing. The streets were packed from end to end with the fleeing populace, who were so tightly jammed that no more space could be found. Directly beneath him the last line of defense was formed against the final massacre—the shattered remnants of the army drawn up across the square and on down the main east road all the way to the stone gate.

Northward the entire lower quarter of the city was engulfed in flames, the streets and broad avenues packed with advancing Tugars who even now were reaching toward the central square. Behind them he could see formation after formation pouring into the city, their cheers for blood and loot rising darkly in the night air.

Straight eastward the balloon soared, gaining height, rising into the darkness, its bottom still lit by the flames below.

And then straight ahead he could see his goal standing out clear.

"What was that?" Qubata asked, looking off toward the east and pointing.

"Just some burning embers," one of Muzta's staff said disdainfully, feeling he had lowered himself by talking to someone who had shown such weakness before his Qar Qarth.

"No, I think it was their floating bubble," Qubata said quickly.

"And so what if it was?" Muzta replied.

"Send someone after it," Qubata said. "There could be some purpose to it."

"Go after it yourself, old one," Muzta said, his voice now distant. "I think what is in the city is not for you."

There was no tone of dismissal in his voice, only a deep sadness.

"Then by your leave, my Qar Qarth," and bowing from the saddle, Qubata turned his mount around and galloped back off to the east.

Several of the staff started to laugh, but Muzta whirled about, his gaze silencing them.

"Take care, my friend," he whispered. "Perhaps you were right after all."

Pointing forward, Muzta spurred his horse into a canter and started into the city.

This is where it is best to finish it all, Andrew thought, coming back from the line formed down on the eastern road. Reining in his mount, he leaped off, then slapped Mercury across the rump and sent him free.

Stepping up to the national and state flags, he looked up at them lovingly, as if they were some final link to back home.

Home, he thought, letting his memories drift to golden autumn days, hazing with smoke and warmth, and to the dark clouds of winter, surf pounding on the rocks, snow swirling down, deadening the world in its muffled blanket.

If only he could see Maine but one more time. To have Kathleen by his side, to walk through the woods, his old border collie leaping through the high grass before him.

Stirred from the memories, he looked back up to the flags, which snapped in the breeze. He could not pick a better symbol to die beneath. Like many who had fought in countless wars before, he almost believed that the spirits of all those who had fought beneath these standards might somehow still linger within them, watching their comrades on this final field of strife.

Antietam was when he had first followed them, new flags glinting in the sun. And then through Fredricksburg and Chancellorsville to those four hours at Gettysburg where he had first led. Then on into the Wilderness, Cold Harbor, to Petersburg, and then at last to here.

Johnnie was most likely here somehow. At least, no more would there be the dreams. Perhaps now Johnnie would rest easy, his brother at his side to tell him no longer to be afraid.

The last of the fleeing populace streamed past, and in the distance the horde came forward at the charge.

Andrew unsheathed his sword.

"All right, let us show them how men from Maine can die!

"First rank, present, fire!"

Grabbing hold of the dangling lanyard, Hawthorne pulled, the rope giving easily in his hand.

The basket seemed to drop out from under him. Instantly

he realized he was releasing too much gas, but there was no way to push the opening closed. As more and more gas spilled out, the basket fell with ever-increasing speed.

He'd fall short of his goal, he could see that now. The balloon, still spinning in the wind, came rushing down. Climbing up into the ropes, Hawthorne hung on and closed his eyes.

With a bone-numbing crunch the basket hit, the still partially inflated balloon streaming out, dragging him over rocks and tree stumps until finally all was still.

Staggering out of the wreck, he looked about.

There was no one around. But they must have seen him pass.

Reaching into the basket, he pulled out a fifty-pound barrel and raced past the collapsing envelope. Hitting the side of the hill, he scrambled three-quarters of the way up and briefly looked around. This was as good a spot as any, he reasoned.

Turning back, he scrambled down the slope, pulled out the other barrel, along with the pick and shovel, and staggered across the field and back up the slope again, gasping for breath.

Throwing the barrel down, he raised the pick and started to slash at the ground wildly. Within minutes he was soaked through from the effort. He ripped off his jacket and tossed it to the ground. Pausing, he looked back westward, and the sight of the city in flames spurred him on. Angling the hole in, he continued to work, cutting the ground, spading the soil and rocks out, till finally he had to crawl in on hands and knees, wrenching rocks out with his bare hands till blood poured from them.

Hoping that he had cut the hole far enough in, Vincent grabbed the first barrel and punched a hole in its side. Bending over, he jammed the barrel in, scooping out a handful of powder and sprinkling it about the sides of the hole. Taking the next barrel, he punched another hole, this time shoveling several handfuls of powder into his jacket. Next he started grabbing rocks, some weighing half as much as himself, and shoved them in around the barrels.

Taking the scoops of powder from his jacket, he worked a trail out from the hole and then for several feet beyond. There wasn't enough, he realized suddenly. Dammit, he thought, I should have pulled out more. But it was too late now for that.

Going over to his jacket, he reached in and pulled out the container of matches.

He heard a rock tumbling down the slope behind him.

Whirling about, Vincent saw a Tugar not a dozen feet away, caught in the open as he tried to sneak up from behind.

Hawthorne grabbed for his pistol, dropping the matches.

The Tugar did not move.

"I know what it is you are doing," the gray warrior said evenly.

"Then watch me do it," Hawthorne shouted. Whirling about, he pushed his revolver straight into the powder and fired.

With a flash the open powder ignited. Shouting, the Tugar leaped forward, even as Hawthorne scrambled away. Reaching the trail of fire, Qubata threw his body on it, trying to smother the flames. An instant later the ground seemed to lift straight up, hurling the old warrior aside like a broken doll. Knocked down by the concussion, Hawthorne curled up, covering his head as a column of dirt and boulders soared more than a hundred feet into the sky and came raining down. Deafened, he staggered to his feet.

Nothing, dammit. Nothing had happened!

There was a low groan from farther down the slope. Staggering, bleeding from burns and slivers of jagged rock, the boy half walked, half crawled to the torn body of his enemy and rolled him over.

"I would not have killed you," Qubata whispered. "Once I could kill, but no longer. I just wanted to stop you, to hold you and stop you from killing my people."

Stunned, Hawthorne sat down heavily and looked into the old Tugar's eyes.

"It should have never been this way," Qubata whispered. "We were wrong. Perhaps we could have changed things together.

"I'm sorry, young man, sorry that . . ." His voice slurred away and was still.

A rumble cut through the ground.

Hawthorne looked up to where the charge had been set on the face of the dam. A section of wall more than thirty feet across suddenly gave way. The water exploded out.

Like a torn sheet of rotten canvas, the rupture grew with every passing second, spreading wider and wider, as thousands of tons of water ripped through the rock-and-earth barrier like a razor-sharp knife. Downward it cut as well, and seemingly within seconds it had slashed clear down to the bedrock. A thirty-five-foot wall of water, pushed by the billions of gallons behind it, exploded straight outward. Struggling, Hawthorne came to his feet and tried to pull the Tugar's body clear.

But the torrent cut closer and closer.

"I'm sorry," Hawthorne said numbly, and turning, he staggered across the face of the dam, heading upward to the hill that anchored the north side, even as the earthen wall collapsed behind him. Reaching the protection of the hill, he threw himself down on the ground.

Water always did bring me trouble, he thought, trying to push the other thoughts away, but they would not leave.

So they might have become like me, and in the end I've become like them, Hawthorne thought, his mind filled with torment.

Gathering speed on the downward slope, the wall of water, now two hundred yards wide and piling up to fifty feet or more in height, rushed forward, slamming against the side of the hills, exploding with fury, driving a howling wind before it.

The torrent turned in its channel, smashing due west, spreading out and heading straight for the lower city.

God will never forgive me now, Hawthorne thought numbly. I've just killed tens of thousands by my hand.

"We're down to five rounds a man, colonel!"

The last rounds fired from the Napoleons, O'Donald and his men fell in with the shrinking ranks of the 35th. Volley after volley of arrows slashed toward them, men seeming to collapse with each passing second, so that it appeared as if they would soon be carved away to nothing. The Tugars had learned not to charge guns, at least, their serried ranks holding on the far side of the square, archers packed three and four deep. The volley line which had held so long was now falling silent beneath the deadly hail.

As the fire slackened, a lone voice lifted up from the ranks.

"Yes, we'll rally round the flag, boys,
We'll rally once again,
Shouting the battle cry of freedom . . ."

In an instant the song rippled down the line, the men raising their voices, shouting their defiance at the enemy as they clustered about the flag.

A cold shudder ran through Andrew at the sound of it. Once before, at Fredricksburg, he had heard them sing as they fought, but not since then.

The sound of their voices sent a cold chill running down his back, filling his eyes with tears, filling him with a final pride in this last moment for the regiment.

Never had he seen troops hold so well, not giving an inch, as the shrinking ranks slowly pulled in around the colors. The line had held like a rock, the men determined to die where they stood.

Andrew looked behind the lines. There was no more room for the masses of people to flee. Most of them were now on their knees praying, waiting for the end.

Hans came up to Andrew's side.

"Not much more we can do," Hans said grimly. Reaching into his pocket, he took out a stub of chewing tobacco, and bit off half, and held out the last tiny piece. Andrew took it, and Hans smiled with affection.

"Remember Joshua Chamberlain?" Andrew asked.

"Who from Maine wouldn't?"

"I taught with him at Bowdoin. He was in a fix like this once at Gettysburg when the men ran out of ammunition. I guess I'll do the same as he did. Can't do any worse."

Hans, raising his carbine up, chambered a round, then looked over at Andrew and smiled.

"Son, you're the best damn officer I ever served with," Hans cried.

Andrew stepped ahead of the ranks and pointed his sword forward.

The men looked at each other wide-eyed.

"35th Maine! Charge, boys, charge!"

A wild fevered shout came up from the line, a sharp final angry release to die fighting.

The young flag bearer holding the Maine colors leaped forward, waving it wildly, and started to race madly toward the Tugar lines.

An arrow caught him in the chest, knocking him to the ground. At the sight of his fall the line simply exploded forward, Webster, the bespectacled banker, snatching up the colors and holding them high, leading the way. Down the line the Suzdalians, seeing what was happening, gave voice to an exuberant shout, not knowing if they were rushing to some still-dreamed-for victory or to death.

And so on across the square the charge of the 35th Maine and 44th New York surged ahead, still singing, heedless of losses. The Tugars who had been firing on them so confidently paused, confused by this final act of defiance, and then from behind they heard a growing thunder.

Not believing what he saw, Muzta, who had climbed to the roof of a building on the north side of the square to witness the final battle, stood in gape-mouthed awe.

Beneath the twin light of the moons he saw the dark wall surge up over the outer breastworks, which gave way beneath the rushing wave. His treasured Umens, which moments before had been pouring into the city, shouting with triumph, fled panic-stricken in every direction. But they could not outrace the power and weight bearing down the length of the valley, and screaming in terror, the host disappeared.

Like the hand of a giant, the wall of water smashed into the city with a thunder that shook as if the world were coming to an end, so that the building beneath his feet tossed and swayed.

The wave swept over and through the shattered walls, and as if a curtain were being drawn over the battle, the lights from a thousand fires simply disappeared, covering the entire lower city in a mantel of fog and hissing steam, so that within seconds the world was plunged into darkness.

"You were right after all, my friend," he said, awestruck, "as I knew in my heart you would be."

Climbing down off the roof, Muzta leaped to the street, and turning eastward, he started out of the city, his terrified staff streaming behind him.

The charging line paused and was still, as before them the fires that had raged but seconds ago disappeared, like the flame from a lamp suddenly sniffed out.

A thunder echoed through the air, a wave of dank hot air

blowing up from the side streets whisking about the men, smelling of charred wood, wreckage, and death.

"Merciful heaven, what is it?" Andrew whispered, standing in stunned disbelief.

"The boy did it!" O'Donald shrieked, leaping in front of the now stilled line.

Whooping with ecstasy, O'Donald raced up to Andrew's side.

"He blew the dam! Hawthorne blew the dam! I plumb forgot to tell you he was going to try!"

Wide-eyed Andrew looked across the square now silhouetted by clouds of steam racing straight up, the ground still shaking beneath his feet as the pent-up fury of the river continued to roar through the lower city, destroying all in its path.

Turning, he looked back at his men, who stood struck dumb.

"Now, men now, let's finish it! Charge!"

Cheering wildly, the line surged forward again, their cry echoing down across the square all the way to the eastern gate. Behind them the terrified populace stood up, pointing and shouting. First one, then another, and in an instant by the thousands they surged forward, waving clubs, spears, their bare hands, crying that Perm had answered their prayers and a miracle had been delivered to them.

Racing at the fore, the Maine and national colors at his side, Andrew bore down on the Tugar line.

A bow was dropped, then by the hundreds the weapons clattered to the pavement, and they fled, piling back down the streets, pushing to go north, east, anywhere to escape the avenging fury.

Tugars who but moments before had believed victory and pillage were at hand staggered in stunned disbelief as the one-armed Yankee waded into their ranks, his men shouting hoarsely, slashing with their bayonets, driving the now terror-stricken mob into the darkness.

But there was no place to flee.

Rushing down darkened streets, the Tugars plunged into the roaring current, and with wild cries were swept away into the night.

Pushing forward, Andrew cut and thrust, totally lost in the pure shock of battle madness. And then there was nothing before him but a swirling night of storm-tossed waters foaming past.

Horrible cries echoed from the torrent, and in the stygian shadows he saw desperate forms drifting past, clinging to logs, broken boards, each other, howling like the damned that they were.

To the side of the road Andrew saw a knot of Tugars, wide-eyed, looking in equal terror at Andrew and at the dark death sweeping by.

All around him the sounds of battle were drifting away, church bells were ringing out, and wild cries of joy were soaring up from the city.

He looked back to the terrified enemy.

"There's been enough for one night," Andrew said. "Take them prisoner."

The knot of men still with him surrounded the Tugars and led them away.

Panting with exhaustion, Webster stood at his side, the Maine flag fluttering in the damp breeze. Through the press, Hans and O'Donald came up to his side. From out of the darkness the cries of thousands continued to rise.

Turning, he looked at Hans, who stood impassive, still chewing. Surprised, Andrew realized that somewhere back on the square he had swallowed his tobacco, but somehow his body had not rebelled.

Together they stood watching as the Tugar army disappeared in the night.

"I hope, gentlemen," he said softly, "that I've fought my last battle."

Chapter 21

"They're leaving, sir."

Rousing from his cot, Andrew looked numbly about the room.

"How long have I been asleep?" he asked.

"The doctor told me to let you sleep the night," the young orderly said. "It's almost dawn."

Rubbing his neck, he sat up, letting the young man put his boots on for him.

Emil appeared in the doorway.

"It's true—their tent wagons are pulling off to the south and east. We started to hear them move in the middle of the night."

Blinking, Andrew looked about.

What happened yesterday? he wondered, and gradually the memories filtered back.

There had been nothing but the waiting for the next assault. The Tugars to the south of the city had disappeared back up into the hills. He had stood and watched throughout the day. It always seemed to rain after a battle, he thought. At dawn the heavens had opened up with a cold chilling downpour, adding to the dark gloom.

As the sky had grown lighter, the dark floodwaters had gradually started to recede, revealing a horror beyond imagining.

Thousands upon thousands of Tugar bodies lay tangled in the charred wreckage, torn and contorted, pinned high in branchless trees, scattered in among blackened logs, by the hundreds dotting the river, floating downstream on the swollen Neiper.

Right up to the ugly gash of the blown dam the entire valley had been torn apart, the encampments of the enemy host, the great tent of the leader, all of it simply gone, as if swept away by the hand of an angry child who had become enraged with his toys.

Destitute bands of Tugars staggered about. In spite of his rage at all that had been done, he could not help but be moved by the thousands of Tugar women and children who wandered across the muddied field, turning over bodies, looking and looking, their high keening wail reaching up even to the city walls.

All day he had waited, marshaling his lines, but in his heart he knew it was over. At some point he must have collapsed, for he had no memory of leaving his post or of coming to rest in this room.

The orderly done with his task, Andrew came to his feet.

"How's Kal?" Andrew asked.

"Doing smartly, no sign of infection. I taught that girl well," and even as he spoke the words he regretted them.

Andrew looked at the doctor vacantly, unable to reply.

"Form up a guard and let's go out and have a look," Andrew said quietly.

Rousing from his bunk, he stepped out into the hallway where Casmar stood as if waiting.

"I know you have a heavy burden," the priest said softly. "Not just for her, but for everything. Do not blame yourself, Andrew Keane. Remember that in the end you have saved our people."

Andrew knew the sincerity with which the priest spoke, but how could he explain what he felt now? There could never be a healing for him, not now. In his heart he realized fully what it had been that held Kathleen back from him for so long, and what had warned him as well.

Nodding his thanks, he stepped down the hall and into Kal's room.

The peasant was sitting up in his cot, eating a broth that Tanya was feeding to him.

"They're pulling out," Andrew said, and Kal's features lit up in a grin.

"So they've had enough of the mice after all."

Andrew, trying to force a smile, nodded in reply.

"We share your sorrow, my friend," Kal said quietly. "My life came back to me through her hands."

"Hawthorne?" he asked silently, mouthing the name.

Kal shook his head.

Emil came into the room and looked at his patient.

"Would you care to go out and have a look? I think the air might do you good," he asked.

Excitedly, Kal tried to swing his legs out of bed.

"No you don't. I've got a litter waiting outside the room."

Four men from the 35th came in, gently lifted Kal off the bed, and put him on the fur-covered stretcher.

"Let's go see," Andrew said. Tanya, her eyes red-rimmed, stood up and went out to join her father.

With Casmar falling in beside them the group walked down the great nave of the cathedral, still packed with wounded, and stepped through the great doors into the sunlight.

A thundering ovation went up. The square was packed from end to end with people.

Andrew looked over at Casmar, who simply shrugged his shoulders.

"A little celebration I planned to honor you," the prelate said, breaking into a grin.

Embarrassed by the wild demonstration, Andrew walked down the steps of the church. To his delight, someone had found Mercury, who snorted and pranced as Andrew approached. Affectionately, he patted the horse's side, then swung up into the saddle.

As the stretcher bearing Kal came down the steps, he struggled to sit up, and holding up his left hand, he waved to the crowd, which roared with approval, calling his name.

The men of the 35th and 44th were drawn up in column of fours. Andrew quickly scanned the line. How thin it now was. Over half of them gone, the remaining veterans looking battle-worn but proud.

Andrew drew up alongside the regiment, his pride in them near overflowing. Turning to the two flags, he snapped a salute, and then, looking back to the regiment, he saluted them as well, and their cheers joined in with the crowd.

Coming to the front of the column, he saw Hans mounted off to one side, his corps flag and the four division standards of the Suzdalian army snapping behind him.

"Well, Hans, do you wish to ride in this one as a general or as a sergeant major?"

"I think, son, I'll take the sergeant major position for today."

He brought his mount over to Andrew's side, and they waited until Emil came up on horseback to join them, with Kal's litter and Casmar on foot leading the way.

The column started off toward the eastern gate. The road to either side was lined with thinned regiments of the Suzdalian and Novrodian troops.

"God, how many we lost," Andrew said quietly, scanning their ranks.

As he passed each regiment he saluted their colors, and the men stood rigid and proud.

Coming past the 5th Suzdal, he saw Dimitri standing beneath a flame-scorched regimental standard, a knot of less than a hundred men gathered about the flag. The flag snapped in the breeze, and emblazoned in English across its side he saw two words:

"Hawthorne's Guards."

Andrew reined in and saluted the flag, the Suzdalian major looking up at him proudly, with tears in his eyes.

"We've molded an army here," Andrew said evenly, continuing down the road.

"As good as the Army of the Potomac," Hans replied sharply.

On down to the gate they rode, passing O'Donald's batteries. The major was waiting for them and swung his mount out to join the line.

Behind them the men of the 35th started to sing, the regiments of Rus picking up the words and singing in their language.

"Yes, we'll rally round the flag, boys . . ."

The detachment rode out through the eastern gate.

Before him the harsh reality of war came rushing back. Wreckage was everywhere. Thousands of bodies still carpeted the field. Looking north, he saw where the flood had reached its maximum height, a wall of flotsam piled ten feet high in some places, the shattered remnants of the *Bangor* slammed up vertical against the wall.

O'Donald had told him about that. If he could give Congressional medals he knew where he would pin one of the first.

"The only thing as terrible as a battle lost," Andrew said softly, "is a battle won."

Across the far hills he could see the tent wagons moving away, as if the ground were covered with thousands of humpbacked creatures moving toward the edge of the world.

"You released the prisoners?" Andrew asked, looking over at Hans.

"A lot of people wanted to kill 'em. It was a little touchy last night, but we got them out of the city."

Then at least there was still some civility left. The war was over as far as he was concerned; there was no sense in holding three thousand Tugars that would have to be fed from the tight supplies still left. Some had argued for keeping them as slave labor, but the force of his argument, and, to his pride, the shouted outcries from his regiment, had ended that argument in a hurry.

Pushing forward, the group reached the edge of the battlements, and making their way over the sally-port bridge, they stopped at last. For long minutes they lingered, looking toward the vanishing host, while on the city walls thousands stood cheering.

From out of a stretch of woods above the Tugar line a lone warrior appeared.

Taking up his field glasses, Andrew brought him into focus.

"Muzta," he said quietly.

Without comment, he spurred his mount forward into a canter.

Hans, Emil, and O'Donald galloped up to join him.

"Could be a final shot to get you," Hans said cautiously.

"I think not," Andrew replied.

Reaching the Tugar siege lines, he weaved his way through a sally port as alone Muzta cantered down to meet him, a man trotting by his side.

"Wait for me," Andrew said, and despite their protest he moved ahead to where Muzta had reined in his mount.

The Tugar looked down at him appraisingly and then nodded to the lone man he had brought along.

"My lord Muzta Qar Qarth wishes to speak to you," the man said in Suzdalian.

"And who are you?" Andrew asked quietly.

"I was taken from here a circling ago. I have been the pet of Muzta as a fashioner of gold."

Andrew looked up at Muzta and waited. Slowly the Tugar began to speak.

"My lord wishes to thank you for the release of the prisoners, though you most likely did not realize that among them was his only surviving son."

Andrew looked questioningly at the interpreter.

"The other two died fighting against you," the interpreter added.

"We have both lost ones that we loved," Andrew replied evenly.

"He wishes to inform you that the Tugar horde leaves to go east and south. Though his people and yours are still enemies."

"There was no need for this war," Andrew replied.

"For my people it was as unstoppable as the wind and the rain," Muzta replied. "Perhaps now we shall starve, but that is my concern and no longer yours."

Andrew merely nodded in reply.

Muzta lowered his head and spoke softly.

"Some of my people now claim that all humans must die. Perhaps for the sake of my race they are right. Perhaps we may still rule you, perhaps not, and maybe it will be different, as a friend of mine once wished. I need tribute from those whom we ride to. And yes, we might take of their flesh as well."

"I think that might no longer be true," Andrew replied. "The Wanderers undoubtedly have spread the word before you. Your warriors are gone—you can no longer rule as you once did."

Muzta paused for a long moment and then nodded in reply.

"But perhaps we can barter something as we circle once again."

"And that is?"

"An end to the pox," Muzta replied. "You have a healer with you. If I left a number of my healers here for several days, would he teach them his magic? Then I would send them before the horde and offer this thing in exchange for food."

"Emil, come up here."

The doctor came up to Andrew's side, and Andrew quickly explained what had been asked.

Smiling, the old doctor nodded his agreement.

"Give me a couple of weeks and I'll teach them asepsis surgery, and how to make anesthesia as well. God knows with all their wounded they're going to need it. If that's all right with you, Andrew?"

Andrew nodded in reply, watching as the doctor explained what he would do to help out, the translator speaking in turn to Muzta.

With a look of surprise, Muzta contemplated the two before him.

"What manner of men are you?" he whispered.

"Merely men who wish to be free and are willing to pay the price for it."

Muzta nodded gravely.

"I leave now. Perhaps we shall meet again when twenty seasons have passed. Perhaps I shall hold my rule, and maybe remember and use the words of an old friend who perished here. Perhaps I shall come armed, perhaps not. As I leave, I will give you two gifts, in memory of that friend, who I know would wish it such, and for the gift of my son you returned to me so freely, when it was your right to slay him out of hand.

"Goodbye, human called Keane."

Muzta turned his mount about and then paused. He spoke quickly to the translator and then galloped off, leaving the man, who stood in silence, stunned by his freedom.

The Tugar commander paused at the top of the hill and beckoned. Two of his warriors came out, and leaping from their mounts, untied the ropes around the arms of two humans. Looking back, Muzta stood in his stirrups, and raising his head back, he gave a long ululating cry that spoke of pain and sorrow. Rearing his mount up, he disappeared over the hill, the two guards galloping off behind him.

Tears clouding his eyes, Andrew watched as she came running down the hill.

He jumped from his mount and dashed forward, shouting with joy as Kathleen leaped into his arms. Oblivious to the thousands who watched, the two sobbed in each other's arms, whispering, laughing, and again crying.

"I never thought I'd see you again," Andrew said, wiping away his tears.

"I never thought I'd see you again," she said, holding him close.

"I want Father Casmar to marry us right now," Andrew said, his heart bursting with joy. "I never want to be separated from you ever again."

Nodding, she kissed him again. There was another shout of joy beside them as Tanya dashed forward, flinging herself into Hawthorne's outstretched arms.

Andrew looked over at the young man whose eyes now looked so terribly old.

Andrew stepped over to him and extended his hand.

"How are you, son?"

"I think I'll be all right, sir," Hawthorne whispered.

"You saved us all," Andrew said.

"But at what price, sir?"

"There's always a price," Andrew replied. "I wish the world, any world, were different. But here and now there was a price for what we are, and you paid it. Remember that as you watch your children grow—let us hope in peace. Someone has to bear the nightmare so others may gently sleep."

"After they took me prisoner, it was Muzta who ordered me saved," Vincent whispered. "It was a strange thing, sir. Last night he told me a good many things about the Tugars, their ancestors, even about the tunnel of light that brought us here from earth. When we've got time, sir, I'd like to tell you."

"First we need a long rest, and time with our loved ones," Andrew said quietly. "Then there'll be plenty of time to talk."

Andrew looked again at Kathleen and smiled. Now with her love perhaps the nightmares would finally go away.

Together the two couples started back across the field, their friends circling in around them.

Eagerly Kal reached out, taking Hawthorne's hand, while all about them the regiment gathered, shouting with joy.

"So when do we get our constitution?" Kal asked, looking up shrewdly at Andrew.

"I said I'd only run things till the war was finished," Andrew replied.

"Excellent. Tell me, Andrew Keane, were you thinking of running for president?"

The men of the regiment started to howl with delight.

"Honest Keane!" they shouted. "Republicans for Keane!"

Andrew looked about, shaking his head.

"Well, one way or another there's going to be a one-armed war hero as president," Kal replied, his features aglow. "As of today I'm forming a Democratic Party and running for president of the Republic of Rus."

Leaning back, Andrew roared with delight, not even realizing that he was laughing for the first time in months.

Reaching out with his right hand, he grabbed Kal's left.

"I knew you were a politician the first time I set eyes on you," Andrew said happily.

"And this manifest destiny thing," Kal said. "Why, I was thinking with that steam train we could sweep democracy and freedom out around the world, following a transcontinental railroad."

Stunned, Andrew looked over at Hawthorne, who shrugged his shoulders, trying to feign innocence over the leaking of that bit of information.

"First I think we have a new republic to build right here," Andrew said, pointing back to the city. "And it's time we began."

And together the group started back up the hill, where eagerly the people of Rus, and those who had come to join them, joyfully greeted their first day of peace and newfound freedom.

WILLIAM FORSTCHEN

William Forstchen, born in 1950, was raised in New Jersey but has spent most of his life in Maine. Having worked for more than a decade as a history teacher, an education consultant on creative writing, and a Living History reenactor of the Civil War period, Bill is now a graduate student in military history at Purdue University in Indiana.

When not writing or studying, he devotes his time to the promotion of the peaceful exploration of space or to one of his numerous hobbies which include iceboating (a challenge in Indiana), scuba diving (an even greater challenge in Indiana), and pinball machines.